Found in Bliss

Other Books by Lexi Blake

ROMANTIC SUSPENSE

Masters and Mercenaries
The Dom Who Loved Me
The Men With The Golden Cuffs
A Dom is Forever
On Her Master's Secret Service
Sanctum: A Masters and Mercenaries Novella
Love and Let Die
Unconditional: A Masters and Mercenaries Novella
Dungeon Royale
Dungeon Games: A Masters and Mercenaries Novella
A View to a Thrill
Cherished: A Masters and Mercenaries Novella
You Only Love Twice
Luscious: Masters and Mercenaries~Topped
Adored: A Masters and Mercenaries Novella
Master No
Just One Taste: Masters and Mercenaries~Topped 2
From Sanctum with Love
Devoted: A Masters and Mercenaries Novella
Dominance Never Dies
Submission is Not Enough
Master Bits and Mercenary Bites~The Secret Recipes of Topped
Perfectly Paired: Masters and Mercenaries~Topped 3
For His Eyes Only
Arranged: A Masters and Mercenaries Novella
Love Another Day
At Your Service: Masters and Mercenaries~Topped 4
Master Bits and Mercenary Bites~Girls Night
Nobody Does It Better
Close Cover
Protected: A Masters and Mercenaries Novella
Enchanted: A Masters and Mercenaries Novella
Charmed: A Masters and Mercenaries Novella
Treasured: A Masters and Mercenaries Novella, Coming June 29, 2021

Smoke and Sin
At the Pleasure of the President

URBAN FANTASY

Thieves
Steal the Light
Steal the Day
Steal the Moon
Steal the Sun
Steal the Night
Ripper
Addict
Sleeper
Outcast
Stealing Summer

LEXI BLAKE WRITING AS SOPHIE OAK

Texas Sirens
Small Town Siren
Siren in the City
Siren Enslaved
Siren Beloved
Siren in Waiting
Siren in Bloom
Siren Unleashed
Siren Reborn

Nights in Bliss, Colorado
Three to Ride
Two to Love
One to Keep
Lost in Bliss
Found in Bliss
Pure Bliss
Chasing Bliss
Once Upon a Time in Bliss
Back in Bliss
Sirens in Bliss
Happily Ever After in Bliss
Far From Bliss, Coming 2021

A Faery Story
Bound
Beast
Beauty

Standalone
Away From Me
Snowed In

Found in Bliss

Nights in Bliss, Colorado Book 5

Lexi Blake
writing as
Sophie Oak

Found in Bliss
Nights in Bliss, Colorado Book 5

Published by DLZ Entertainment LLC

Copyright 2018 DLZ Entertainment LLC
Edited by Chloe Vale
ISBN: 978-1-942297-03-1

Dedication

To everyone who needs to know the way to Bliss...

Dedication 2018

It's years later and I hadn't realized how much I missed Bliss. I knew when I started the Lexi pen name and made the difficult decision to step away from Sophie that I would miss the town I'd come to love so much. I created a new family—McKay-Taggart—and sadly moved on. But working on these books again reminded me why I started writing Bliss in the first place. Bliss is a place where everyone gets a second chance. It's a place where people get along—even when they don't agree. It's a place where people believe, not merely in their dreams or religions, but they believe in each other. Bliss is not utopia. Pain and struggle occur there. These characters don't ask for an easy life and they know they have to work hard to build something great. But they also know that they must do it together. In the world we live in today, I need Bliss. So this is dedicated to the people out there striving every day to build a better world—whether you're doing it in a high-powered job or raising good kids, whether you're doing it from the right or the left, whether you're giving away millions or engaging in simple acts of kindness—this book is for you.

Prologue:
The Road to Bliss

Denver, Colorado
Eight years ago

Holly Lang stared at the papers. "What is this supposed to mean?"

Scott Lang sighed, barely glancing up from the desk in his beautifully designed Congressional office. "It means what it says, dear. My father was right. You're a liability. I'm never going to move out of state politics with you at my side. I'm going to make a run at Washington in two years. I can't do that as long as I'm married to you. Don't get me wrong. You're a gorgeous woman. You're fun, and the sex is amazing. Was at first. I was caught up in it. I should have done exactly what my father told me to do. I should have screwed you until my eyes popped out and then married a proper political wife."

Rage threatened to choke her. "Well, I think you can tell your father that I feel pretty damn screwed."

Nearly ten years of marriage down the drain. She'd done everything the bastards had asked her to do. She'd worn the right clothes, gone to all the proper parties, kept her mouth shut when she wanted to scream. More than that, she'd done everything he'd needed her to do. She'd dropped out of college to support him. She'd had their baby.

She looked through the papers, catching on one particular clause.

"Well, I understand you mean to enforce the prenup."

He sat back, cold blue eyes assessing her. His perfectly coiffed hair had a hint of silver at the temples. His stylist put that in once a month. Scott's hair didn't have a hint of silver. Those strands were dyed to give him a regal air of maturity. Like everything with her husband— soon to be ex—it was an illusion created to play to his voters. "That is what a prenup is for, dear."

"Your timing is impeccable." According to the prenup, if she'd stayed married for another six months, she would be paid a sizable sum if they divorced. At the time when she'd signed the damn thing, she'd hated that clause, hated the whole idea of a prenuptial agreement. It had seemed so unromantic. But she'd been madly in love. She'd signed it because she'd known they wouldn't need it.

Two years in, she'd realized that Scott was a vacuous idiot who cheated on her at every given opportunity. But she'd had Micky to think about. Her son was everything to her.

Scott's fingers drummed along the top of his desk as though he was bored by the whole scene and ready to move on. "I've had this on my calendar for years. I was never going to give you that money. I would have divorced you last year, but I was up for reelection, and it doesn't look good to the voters."

Bastard. So cold blooded. What had she ever seen in this man? "How is it going to look now? You're kicking your wife and child to the curb. I'm sure your constituents are going to love that."

The reptilian smile that crossed his face chilled her to the bone. In that moment, she knew she was screwed. He opened a manila folder. "Oh, I think they'll understand when they see these."

Five photos were laid out in front of her, each more damning than the next. Her stomach churned as she looked at those pictures. Whoever he'd paid had done a damn fine job with Photoshop. The woman in the photos was a dead ringer for her. It looked like she was standing outside a seedy motel with her husband's bodyguard, Rick. Her hand was on his chest, his on her hip. The next picture featured a deep kiss as Rick's hands delved into her blouse. She turned her eyes away from the other two pictures. They were taken through the window and showed her riding the bodyguard, her head thrown back.

"Dare I ask who played the part of me?" Tears threatened to squeeze out of her eyes. Rick had always been nice to her, but she supposed her husband's money and influence bought anything he wanted.

"It doesn't matter. Rick is ready to go on record to the press. The motel manager has proof that you've been going there every week for several months. It's all lies, but that's irrelevant. The press will see what I want them to see." He pulled the photos back in and neatly stacked them. "I don't particularly want to use these. I think it would be hard on Micky, don't you?"

Micky was only nine, the light of her life. He went to a private school, and they would eat him alive if his mother was involved in a sex scandal. Of course, she wouldn't be able to afford that school now. She would have to find the best public school she could and do whatever it took to move into the district. "Yes, it would be hard on him. We'll go. I won't give you any trouble."

"You'll go, Holly. And you won't give me a bit of trouble or I can make you look like the world's most unfit mother. If you walk away now, I'll give you that cabin of my grandfather's, ten thousand dollars, and monthly visits with our son. If I hear a hint of trouble from you, I'll make sure you never see him again."

Holly felt her world fall away, tipping over and rearranging itself into something she didn't recognize. Micky? Her baby? "You can't take my son away."

His face softened marginally. "I can give him far more than you can. You have to see that. He's an amazing kid. The best thing we ever managed to do together."

"Then why are you holding him hostage?" The cold, flat line of his mouth told her everything she needed to know. Micky would be the carrot he dangled in front of her to keep her in line.

"He's a Lang. He's not going to be raised outside of the family. I'm going against my father by offering you that ratty old cabin. He would prefer you left Colorado, but this way you can see Micky once a month."

Yes, she could see her father-in-law's fingerprints all over this scheme. Malcolm Lang hated the fact that his precious son had married

15

a woman with no connections. Her father-in-law made no attempts to hide the fact that he couldn't stand her. He'd called her a cheap floozy and a gold-digging whore on a regular basis. At the beginning of their marriage, Scott had defended her, but as his career had taken off, he'd simply ignored her.

"Do we have a deal? If you refuse, it's going to be war, Holly. Do you really want to take me on?"

Oh, hell yeah, she wanted to take him on. She wanted to smash in his cosmetically perfect face. She wanted to torch his car. She wanted to cry because everything she loved was being taken away. She didn't have anyone. Her parents were gone. She had no siblings. She had her son, and if she fought for him, he could be grown before she saw him again.

If she fought for him, he might end up thinking she was everything Scott would call her. There was no doubt in her mind Scott would go to the press and Micky would get caught up in it.

Any way she looked, her son lost. She had to find a way to mitigate the damage.

"Where is this cabin? We've never gone there before." Defeat began to settle in.

He sat back. The smug look on his face proclaimed his victory. "We don't go because that town is a bit of an embarrassment. Why my grandfather loved it, I have no idea. It's a town called Bliss."

Bliss. There was nothing even vaguely blissful about her life now, but it looked like this town was going to be her home for a while.

"I want to see my son before I go."

"Of course," Scott said. "I'm not a monster."

Holly waited while Scott called her son in. She held her boy and explained that she was leaving. That she had a new home. She hoped Bliss would treat her better than Denver.

* * * *

Sierra Leone
Six years ago

Caleb Burke held himself as still as possible. Night had fallen. He knew it. The crack under the door of his tiny cage had gone pitch black

16

long ago. Cage? It was a fucking reinforced closet, and it was the only place he felt halfway safe. He could feel the wall against his back. All he had to worry about was his front, and he could hear the closet door if it opened.

How long had it been? Weeks? Months? It seemed like forever since that moment the rebels had taken over his clinic, killed everyone in sight, and forced him to march through the jungle to this place.

If only one of the fuckers hadn't recognized him, he would be dead, his body left behind in the jungle alongside Caroline's.

It would have been a fitting end to their marriage.

His throat threatened to close up every time he thought about Caroline's face when she'd arrived at his clinic. She'd sauntered in like she was walking into one of the shops on Michigan Avenue where she spent most of her time. She'd said she had something to talk to him about, something serious that couldn't wait until he deigned to come home. He'd felt a bit frozen because he'd had something to talk about too. Divorce. He'd had the papers drawn up. They gave her everything he had, all the money, the houses in California, New York, and the Hamptons, the stock. He'd been willing to sign it all away with the singular exception of his charity.

He was glad he'd been gentlemanly and let her speak first.

He hadn't needed to give her everything he had. She'd taken enough all on her own. She'd told him boldly that she was pregnant. He'd felt his world twist into something ugly. He didn't love Caroline, but the fact that she'd cheated on him kicked him in the gut.

Especially since he knew damn well who she spent all of her time with.

And then she'd been gone, her eyes dulling before his ears had even registered the shot that had taken her life.

Caroline was dead. His nurses were dead. They'd been raped before they were slaughtered. Two sweet, vivacious girls from the Midwest who had come to Africa because he'd convinced them they could save the fucking world. Africa had eaten them alive. He'd had to hear their screams as they'd been used. He'd been almost relieved when they'd stopped.

And the final insult had been the fact that he'd been left alive for one reason and one reason alone. Money. His family would pay for his return. His privilege, a thing he'd spent his whole life trying to deny, had been the only thing that spared him.

His stomach gnawed with hunger. His family wouldn't even recognize him anymore. He'd become more animal than man. He survived day to day, but it no longer meant anything.

Still, his breath caught in his chest as he heard a tiny creak that let him know someone was moving in the room outside his cage. He shrank back, the hard feel of the wood behind him a comfort.

What fresh hell awaited him this time? In the early days, he'd been somewhat useful. They'd forced him to play doctor. He'd stitched up their soldiers, some who couldn't be more than nine or ten. He'd dug bullets out and performed surgeries that turned his gut when he thought about the horrific circumstances surrounding them. He'd put the boy soldiers back together and sent them out to kill some more.

Things had changed in the last few weeks. His hands shook too much. He was too weak. He was starving and losing his will to fight.

Was this the moment when they got rid of him?

"I'm in. No sign of the target."

The voice was quiet, almost silent. Caleb had to strain to hear, but what he heard was English. Unaccented English.

"Two Tangoes down."

Tangoes. Military, and not the ragtag group that had taken him. American military.

The door jiggled quietly, the lock holding. And then an amazing sound. A little snick that let him know the man on the other side of the door would make a halfway decent thief.

"Dr. Caleb Sommerville?"

Burke. He'd gone by his mother's maiden name for years, not wanting to trade on the Sommerville influence. Now it didn't matter. He nodded his head. No one would have sent in a special ops team to save Caleb *Burke*. Caleb Sommerville was another story. His brother, the senator, could perform miracles. It was surprising that Eli would bother. He had to know that Caroline was dead.

Caroline, who had been carrying Eli's child.

"Is there anyone else being held?" The question was quiet coming out of the soldier's mouth.

In the deep gloom, a single ray of moonlight cut into the small shack, illuminating his savior's chiseled features. Dark hair, dark eyes, and a square-cut jaw marked the man who reached down to untie him.

This was the way he spent most of his time now, bound in a box, only taken out a few times a day to eat and use the latrine.

"Only me. Everyone else is long dead." His voice sounded raspy. His throat felt like he'd gargled sand. He'd given up talking long ago.

"Can you walk?"

He nodded and fought back a groan as the blood started circulating into his hands again.

"Excellent. My name is Lieutenant Meyer. I'll be your rescuer today. This rescue of your person is brought to you by the United States Navy and SEAL Team 8. We hope you have a nice rescue, and please feel free to fill out the questionnaire at the end of the trip. Tips are welcome."

Lieutenant Meyer had a strong sense of snark.

"Sorry, my CO says my sarcasm will get me killed one day. Let's get you out of here while they're too drunk to notice we're leaving. And you can call me Wolf."

Lieutenant Wolf Meyer put a hand out and hauled him up. It was the first human contact he'd had in months that didn't cause him to shrink away.

Twelve hours later, he was on a plane back to the States, the knowledge deep in his heart that he would never feel at home again. They could take him to the States, but he'd left his soul behind.

* * * *

Moscow, Russia
Eight months ago

Alexei Markov stared at his partner, Ivan, his mind not quite processing the news.

"We leave for America tomorrow." Ivan slapped at the small table they sat at, nearly disrupting the vodka shots in front of them.

"America?" He said the word, tasting it on his tongue. It was bittersweet. Even all these years later, he could still remember his brother, Mikhail, talking about how their lives would be when they made it to America. Back then, Alexei had dreams of becoming a professional hockey player. Those dreams died when Dimitri Pushkin had his brother killed. A new dream had been born that day. A dark dream.

"Don't you see? This means we're moving up. If Pushkin trusts us to handle his American business, it won't be long before we're his right-hand men." Ivan was grinning, though no amount of mirth could make the man look happy. Ivan looked like what he was—a stone-cold killer.

Is that what he would look like years from now, after he'd had his revenge? The longer he pursued this path, the more he questioned himself.

No. He was too close to his goal. He would not give it up because he'd suddenly developed a conscience. Ivan was right. It was good that they had been selected to go to America. It meant he was one step closer to standing in a room with Pushkin and delivering his brother's revenge.

"What are we supposed to do?" Pushkin had many business interests in the United States. He had dealings with mobsters, drug lords, politicians. All of the disgusting bottom-feeders.

Ivan snorted. "We have to pick up a painting and bring it back. We're supposed to meet with someone in Dallas. How funny is that? We can go and be cowboys."

Pick up a painting? That sounded far too simple. "Something sounds wrong."

"You worry too much, Alexei. Nothing is wrong. The boss likes paintings. He's always trying to impress people. I don't understand it. I wouldn't pay for a painting a child could do. Have you seen the man who puts paints on his pig's feet? He has the pig run across the canvas and then sells it as art. Most of the pig's work is better than the stuff the boss collects."

Alexei had to force himself not to roll his eyes. Ivan wasn't the most cultured of men. "Is this painting by someone famous?"

"How am I supposed to know? All that matters is that Pushkin wants the painting. We're to get it and deliver it to him ourselves." He slapped at the table again. "I'm telling you, Alexei. This is our time. We will meet with the man himself. A private interview. You're good with people. I'll handle the killing. You can handle Pushkin."

Alexei leaned forward. So far he had managed to work his way up in the organization with fairly clean hands. He'd killed mobsters, of course. Many. Each one had been a killer in his own right. He worried that to move into the inner circle, he would have to spill innocent blood. The thought brought bile to his throat. "Why would there be killing when all we have to do is pick up a painting?"

"There is always killing, my friend." Ivan hoisted his glass. "Drink with me, Alexei. To America, where our dreams come true."

His dreams had died long ago. The need for revenge was the only thing that pushed Alexei Markov forward now. He picked up his glass. Long ago, he and his brother had talked about the women they would marry in America. He'd been young, but he'd dreamed of a lovely American bride, with a sweet smile and soft, feminine ways. Silly dreams. He wouldn't have that woman.

Chapter One

The lights of the party seemed to flare and focus like a spotlight on the man who had just walked into the room. Like Caleb Burke needed anything to highlight the disaster happening right in front of his face. He felt his heart seize, a cardiac episode waiting to happen. Acute myocardial infarction. Yep. That was what was happening. He was about to have a fucking heart attack, and he knew exactly who to blame.

"No." He said the word. He said it a lot, but this time he really, really meant it. Caleb watched as that big Russian stood over sweet Holly, his dark eyes promising all manner of comfort, and he knew he wasn't ready to let her go.

Of course, he also wasn't ready to take her.

Fuck.

"No?" Alexei turned to him, seeming to notice for the first time that he wasn't alone with Holly. Moments before, the Russian had walked into the reception hall where Stefan Talbot and his new wife, Jennifer, were hosting their wedding party. He'd marched in like he owned the place and zeroed in on Holly.

Alexei looked the same as he had months before, but it was easy to tell he'd changed. There was a relaxed set to his shoulders he hadn't had the last time he was in Bliss. But then the last time Alexei Markov had been in Bliss, it had been as a member of the Russian mob.

"Get your hands off her."

"My hands are entirely to myself." And Alexei still had trouble with English.

"Caleb, what's wrong?" Holly asked, her face turning to him. Wide green eyes stared up at him in confusion. She was so gorgeous. Every time she looked at him, he felt it straight in his gut. And his cock. *Damn it.* He had to turn away from her.

"You shouldn't be here." Caleb couldn't take his eyes off the Russian. It was nothing less than the truth, though he had selfish reasons for pointing it out. "You're supposed to be in witness protection."

Alexei shrugged, his eyes going back to Holly as though her presence was a magnet he couldn't avoid. "I told you. The trials are over. All the men who worked with Pushkin have been put in proper jails. I finish my testimony last week. I am here today. I am free man."

Free? After everything he'd done? Alexei Markov had blown into town eight months before as a mobster. Just because he'd turned state's witness and saved Jennifer Waters and Callie Hollister-Wright didn't give him a free pass. He tried not to think about the fact that the Russian had saved Holly, too. Alexei had thrown his own body over hers, taking the bullet that would have ended her life. It didn't erase the crimes he'd committed before. "You killed a bunch of people, and they let you go free?"

"He only killed them to save me, Caleb. And Stef got a couple, too. No one's talking about putting him in jail." Holly was already reaching for the Russian's hands, her face turning upward in greeting. "I'm so happy for you, Alexei. I'm happy they let you come back to Bliss."

A cloud crossed Alexei's face telling Caleb everything he needed to know.

"They didn't let you come back, did they?" Caleb asked. "You're on the run."

"No running. I take taxi and then train and then bus. Bus drop off at The Trading Post. It was closed, but Ms. Teeny was kind enough to leave note on door telling me about the wedding." After his quick explanation, Alexei turned back to Holly. "You look like beautiful doll."

Caleb grabbed at his tie, loosening it. The damn thing was a noose around his neck. Why had he come to this thing? He should have done what he always did. He should have stayed at home until someone needed him. He should have barricaded himself in his office and stared at medical books until his eyes wouldn't stay open one second more and he was forced to fall into that hell he called sleep. Yeah, that would have made for a great night. But no, he'd gotten on this monkey suit and headed to the Feed Store Church to attend a wedding, all because he'd wanted to watch Holly walk down the aisle. He'd wanted to see her in a beautiful dress and imagine for one second that she was walking toward him and he was normal. That he was twenty-five again, marrying the right woman this time with his whole life ahead of him.

Not once in that daydream had he included a second man in the scenario, though given where he lived, he should have known that would happen whether he liked it or not.

"Thanks," Holly said to Alexei, her face lighting up.

Caleb flushed. He hadn't told her she was beautiful. He'd nodded at her. Why couldn't he talk to her? He'd been good at this once. He'd gone to parties and balls. Why couldn't he talk to one small-town waitress?

Because she was the *one*, but he was too fucked up to deal with it.

"You do look really pretty." He forced the words out of his mouth. He didn't say the ones that were locked inside. She didn't look pretty. She was beautiful. Inside and out. Holly Lang practically glowed in his mind. With auburn hair that curled and caressed her porcelain shoulders, Holly was a vision of everything feminine. She stirred his cock and his mind. He thought about her all the time.

Yeah. He wasn't going to say any of that.

Holly turned toward him, a vibrant smile on her lips. When she smiled that sunshine-goddess, center-of-his-whole-fucking-world smile, he always thought he would turn into a puddle of goo at her feet. *Yeah. That would be really sexy, Burke.*

"Tell her more, Caleb. You do well." Alexei was smiling at him like he was a toddler who'd finally managed to walk.

What the hell was that about?

"Alexei!" Stefan Talbot strode forward looking resplendent in his

24

tux. He wore a broad smile on his face.

Alexei turned and smiled back, his face opening in a way that belied his years. Alexei was twenty-eight years old, but when he smiled, he looked barely twenty.

"I'm so glad to see you, my friend. Did the paperwork get pushed through?" Stef pumped Alexei's hand in greeting.

"The papers are all pushed. I soon will be as American as the pie with many apples. I will pass my test. I know all of American history. Ask me anything. I love the Constitution and Bill of Rights. I can sing whole preamble to Constitution."

"I sent him a copy of *Schoolhouse Rock* to help out," Jen Talbot said, sliding her hand into her husband's. "I bet he can sing all about lonely bills, too."

"Indeed, I can." Alexei bowed slightly to the bride.

"Stef, you helped Alexei get his citizenship?" Holly asked.

"You must have paid through the nose for that, Talbot," Caleb said, well aware bitterness was dripping from every word. "There's a nice long wait usually."

"The government was happy with all the help Alexei gave them with organized crime," Stef explained. "I only had to grease the wheels a little."

"Well, hell," a new voice said. "Alexei. Did the aliens finally let you go? They kept you for an awfully long time."

Mel Hughes stood in the middle of the dance floor looking utterly incongruous in a white polyester tux that had to have been handed down from the Bee Gees. Of course, he couldn't be without his lucky trucker hat and the tinfoil that kept the aliens from attacking his brain. Mel was a kook, but a lovable one. He only went slightly insane a couple of times a year, and Caleb had tranquilizer darts perfectly dosed for Mel's height and weight. He kept them in his truck. He'd thought about using them on Max Harper from time to time, but he worried it would take more than horse tranquilizer to change Max's attitude.

"No aliens, sir. Only federal marshals." Alexei moved closer to Holly, stepping in like he was her date. "They were very kind to me."

Mel's face crinkled, but he shook his head and patted Alexei on the back. "I'm real glad to hear that, son. Now, can I talk to you, Doc? We got an emergency."

Caleb felt a part of him relax. Thank god. Someone was dying, so he didn't have to deal with his suddenly out-of-control love life. He looked over at Holly.

"Go," she urged him. "I'll be fine."

He nodded and started to walk away with Mel. He grabbed his bag from the table he'd been assigned to. He never went anywhere without the small leather bag his father had given him when he'd graduated from Johns Hopkins University.

He glanced back to where Holly stood, surrounded by friends. Of course Holly would be fine. What did she really need from him? For the last week, she'd needed him. Bliss had played host to a serial killer, and no woman in town had been left alone. He'd spent several sleepless nights on Holly's sofa thinking about the fact that he could have been in her bed if he wasn't such a complete freak. He had seen it in her eyes when she'd told him good night. She would have accepted him. Hell, she'd been hurt that he didn't make a move on her. That had made his heart ache.

How would Holly have taken it if she'd made love with him only to discover he couldn't sleep in a bed? The list of things he couldn't do had driven him out of Chicago. It would cost him Holly, too.

"Poor bastard," Mel said, shaking his head as he looked back at Alexei. "He doesn't even know he got taken. It happens that way sometimes. You should check him out, Doc. I got a distressing memo about some new experiments the Reticulan Grays are performing concerning male pregnancy. We wouldn't want that poor Russian fellow to find himself incubating an alien."

He wondered if Holly would reject Alexei if he became the first of a crop of male mothers. Probably not. She was an awfully tolerant woman. "What's the emergency?"

Mel frowned. "It's Cassidy."

Nope. No one was dying. Cassidy Meyer was a classic hypochondriac with a bit of Chicken Little syndrome. And she believed in aliens. Cassidy was a one-stop mental disorder shop. And she was a very nice lady.

"Hemorrhagic fever or bird flu?" Cassidy had gotten over the plague several weeks before. It shouldn't come up again so soon.

"Oh, it's the Ebola again. It's the third time she's had it, Doc." Mel shook his head. "Those alien experiments ruined her immune system, I guess."

Caleb knew that if his colleagues were in his position, Cassidy Meyer would find herself on a seventy-two-hour mental health hold, but he'd long ago learned that sometimes tolerance best served his patients. Cassidy wasn't a risk to herself, and the sweet lady wouldn't hurt a fly. She simply believed she'd had a couple of alien babies and routinely got some of the world's worst infectious diseases. As the CDC had stopped coming out when she called, he was the last line of defense between Cassidy Meyer and the brutally cold world.

Besides, he owed her son his life. In more ways than one.

Wolf sat next to his mother, his large hand holding hers. He patted her back with his free hand, an amused look on his face. "Doc, we're glad you're here. Ma's organs are liquefying as we speak."

Cassidy looked up at him, her hands shaking a bit. "My hands are numb, Doc. I'm afraid my son is right. It's going to get me this time. I think my liver went. I feel it."

He took her pulse. It was strong. "Let me get something ready for you, sweetheart. I can fix you right up."

"You can stop the Ebola?"

Caleb smiled. "I can stop the Ebola, no trouble. And what I'm going to give you has the added effect of keeping aliens away for a while, but you need to come in once a week. Can you do that for me?"

Cassidy's eyes lit up, a sure sign that no hemorrhagic fever had invaded Bliss. "I sure can, Doc."

Caleb stepped away, allowing Mel to lean down and hold her hand while Caleb gestured to Wolf to join him.

Wolf Meyer was a big, bad Navy SEAL, or he had been until a few months before when he'd been forcibly discharged after injuries taken in battle. He was a rough son of a bitch, but he was also a loving son.

"Has she been taking the B-12 I gave her?"

"Not unless she took it with her into the bomb shelter she and Mel have been holed up in. On the plus side, she managed to knit caps for everyone in town and a baby blanket for Paige Harper. Oh, and she perfected her Crock-Pot stew. Expect to get a big batch next week," Wolf said.

Cassidy Meyer tried to take care of the people around her. It was only right that someone looked out for her, too.

"Her blood work showed she's anemic. The numbness in her hands is a function of her vitamin deficiency. Injections will be easy for her to absorb. Once a week should do it. If she forgets, I'll find her. Don't worry about it, Wolf. She's really quite healthy."

He'd reached into his bag. He'd known this was probably coming. Bliss had been up in arms for a week over the Marquis de Sade case. It had been a good bet Cassidy had been ignoring her health. He kept a supply of B-12 on hand.

Wolf shook his head. "You're the most frustrating man I know."

He measured out the proper dose of B-12 in a hypodermic needle. "I'm not known for my bedside manner."

He was actually. He was known for having a perfectly horrific bedside manner. He couldn't even blame it on the PTSD. He'd been a gruff bastard before his world had turned upside down.

Wolf groaned. "That wasn't what I was talking about, Doc. I was talking about how you're handling the train wreck occurring right in front of our eyes. Are you really going to let that man waltz away with your woman?"

Caleb pulled the needle back out, squirting up to make sure all the air was out. "I don't know what you're talking about. Holly isn't mine."

"But she could be. You can't tell me you don't want her."

What he wanted didn't matter. Did it? Could he do it? He closed his eyes for a moment. He didn't want to have this conversation, but it was hard to ignore Wolf. "I think it's for the best. I can't have a normal relationship with her."

When Caleb opened his eyes, Wolf was staring at him in that "dumbass said what?" way of his.

"Normal doesn't mean a damn thing here," Wolf pointed out. "No one is going to ask you to leave here, Doc. Bliss is your home. The people here love you for everything you do for them. And they don't give a crap about your bedside manner. Do you know how many doctors have tried to get me to put my mother in a mental facility?"

He glanced back where Mel was hugging Cassidy's small body to his, his lips kissing her forehead. "She doesn't need to be in a facility. All she needs is a little understanding."

"Yes, and you're the only doctor who is willing to give it to her. Those two are happy because Bliss lets them be. Why can't you be the same?"

Frustration welled up. "Damn it, Wolf. I can't even sleep in a fucking bed. How is Holly going to handle it when I fuck her and then go sleep in her closet because I can't stand to sleep in the open?"

Wolf's dark eyes turned soft. His hand came out with a brotherly pat. "You'll tell her why, and she'll snuggle with you after finding another home for her shoes. It's not Holly's reaction you're afraid of. It's yours. You can't go on like this forever."

"Sure, I can." He could foresee many years of misery. Unchecked and unbroken. Yep. He could be lonely forever.

"Like I said, frustrating." Wolf took a step back. "If you ever want to talk…"

"Since when do I talk?" Caleb replied sarcastically.

One perfect day on the ice was the last time he'd sat and talked about anything beyond medicine and forensic reports. He'd had to talk about autopsies way too much lately. But that one day had been nice. He'd played hockey with the Farley brothers and gotten to know a guy from Russia. They had talked about their families, mostly their brothers. He'd really talked to that man. Of course, his newfound friend hadn't bothered to mention that he was a member of the mob in town to cause trouble. For some reason, Caleb had relaxed around that guy. The same guy who was literally waltzing off with his woman. Alexei had moved Holly to the dance floor where he was putting his enormously oversized paws all over her.

"All right, then," Wolf said, concession obvious in the slump of his shoulders. "Well, thanks for helping out with my mom. I promise to bring her by once a week. Hey, maybe if you convince her I'm taking the shots, too, she'll stop trying to feed me beets."

Caleb grinned. He only owed Wolf so much. "Nope. I'm afraid this doesn't work on your alien DNA. And I'm the one who gave her the recipe for tofu and beets. And the beet smoothie."

Wolf's frown made his whole face turn to granite. "You son of a bitch. Do you know how horrible that was? And I had purple teeth for days from that smoothie. Asshole. This is how you treat the man who saved your life?"

"I'm looking out for your alien DNA, man." And he liked fucking with Wolf. It made him feel almost normal.

He walked back to Cassidy, gave her a shot in her left butt cheek because that was what he did at a wedding, and packed his bag up. He looked out at the dance floor.

Holly swayed in Alexei's arms, her gorgeous body moving with grace as he led her around. Caleb's hands tightened into fists at his sides. Why the hell did Alexei deserve her? And what was he going to do about it? He strode out of the room before he did something he would regret, like attack a man at Stefan Talbot's wedding. He'd given an oath to do no harm, but he really wanted to harm that asshole. He stalked down the hall. He needed to think. His brain was running a hundred different directions, every single one of them leading to a path of rejection and humiliation.

The halls were deserted, thankfully. Everyone was in the ballroom having a great time. He could hear the music, the chatter, the clinking of glasses. It was all at a distance, but then everything was. At a distance. He was on the outside, staring in at the life that happened to everyone but him. He couldn't blame anyone but himself. He'd wrapped himself in a hundred different walls, building them so fast and so high that he would never break them down.

But suddenly he wanted to. Because he wanted Holly. He'd wanted her the moment he'd seen her. He'd spent the last year of his life watching her at Stella's. It had almost been a relief when a serial killer had come to town. He'd had a reason to get close to her that he couldn't deny. He'd been able to stay near her for days.

And he'd talked to her. Or rather, he'd listened. He'd taken her with him on his rounds. He was a country doctor now, and that meant driving from place to place, practicing in unorthodox ways. Holly had been a sympathetic helper. She hadn't flinched when he'd lanced a boil or vaccinated screaming babies. She'd held the man's hand and sang to the babies to get them to calm down. She'd been curious and quick to learn. She was a natural nurse, and he'd been a better doctor for having her around. It had felt so good to have her next to him in the cab of his truck.

Why the fuck was he walking away?

He needed to think. He needed someplace small where he could think. He hated it, but when he needed to clear his head, he needed a closet, someplace tight where he didn't have to worry about his back. He spied the supply closet.

He was about to open it when he heard the moans.

"I wouldn't do that if I were you, Doc. Not unless you want a spectacular view of Rafe and Cam's junk in use."

Caleb turned and saw Rye Harper leaning against the wall with a teasing smile on his face. The cowboy had a tux on, but he'd ditched his tie, and there was a Stetson on his head. "Why are Rafe and Cam showing each other their junk in a…oh. Laura's in there with them."

Laura Niles, Rafe Kincaid, and Cameron Briggs were Bliss's latest trio. They'd only been together for a short time, but they seemed to be getting into the groove.

"And Max, Rach, and me have dibs on that closet. We talked Stella into watching Paige. Do you have any idea how hard it is to doubly penetrate a woman with a baby monitor that goes off every ten minutes? Seriously. It's not as easy as it sounds. We've been looking forward to this." Rye leaned in and pounded on the door. "Hey, you've been at it forever. Give a fellow a chance!"

There was a muffled shriek, and then a masculine voice shouted back. "Screw you, Harper! Find your own closet."

Rye frowned. "Fine. Dibs on the coat closet."

Rye turned and ran toward the closet down the hall.

Caleb sighed. Maybe a walk would do him good. He forced himself to go for a run outside every day. In the beginning, he'd barely been able to walk from the car to the house, but now he did it all the time. He even fished regularly. It was only on occasion that the panic hit him. Yes. He needed a walk.

Maybe then he could figure out how to deal with his heartache.

* * * *

Alexei Markov settled his hand on Holly's waist with a deep sense of satisfaction. She was here. He was here. No one was going to arrest him. He knew it was an odd thing to consider, but he'd had to worry about being arrested for so long that being able to not worry about it was freeing. No cops would come between them. Just one cranky doctor, but he had a plan for dealing with him. Yes, Alexei Markov was a damn lucky man. He'd come through hell with only a few scars.

Bliss had given him back his life.

"Have you healed up? The last time I saw you, you were still in pretty bad shape." Holly looked down at his torso where a bullet had torn through his gut.

"I find life is perfectly fine without spleen."

Caleb had been forced to remove it and resection a part of his

31

bowel. Caleb Burke had stayed with him through the first terrible moments all the way through the operating room. It had been Caleb's hands that held him together. It had been Caleb's cranky voice that had told him he better live.

Alexei pulled her close. Dancing was an excellent way to get a woman close to a man. He was grateful for whoever decided to have a band and dancing at this wedding. It gave him a brilliant excuse to do what he'd always wanted to do—rub himself all over her.

"How was witness protection?" Holly's feet moved in time to the music. "I read your letters, but you didn't talk a lot about what it was like."

Terrifying. Lonely. He'd been shot at multiple times. It was to be expected when mobsters were involved and prison time was on the line. Alexei had gotten used to the feeling of a Kevlar vest around his chest. He'd become close to the two US marshals assigned to protect him. Michael and Jessie. Michael was the badass former Marine, and Jessie matched him. Only she did it with a feminine flare. He'd been sad to say good-bye to them.

Except he hadn't exactly said good-bye. He'd done exactly what Caleb Burke had accused him of. He'd run. The marshals had wanted him to stay in Florida where he would have become someone named Howard Solev. But he'd always known he would come back to Bliss. He'd always believed he would come back for Holly.

And he owed Caleb Burke. It was a debt he intended to repay.

"It was fine. The motels were roaches, but I watch a lot of television. I learn much of the language. I watch all of your shows. *Gilligan's Island* is my favorite."

A laugh escaped her lips. God, he'd dreamed about those lips. "Tell me you haven't been learning the language from old sitcoms."

"What be you talking about, Holly?" He'd liked *Different Strokes*, too.

She leaned in, her laughter so much more musical to him than the song playing. "Well, this should be interesting."

"I also watch much reality TV. I don't like modern shows. Too many murders. I do not need to watch so many shows about blood splatter and the trajectories of bullets. But I like the ones about the housewives. Except for New Jersey. It is too close to mafia. The womens there could be bosses. But Atlanta is fun. How are your heifers?"

Holly's eyes went wide. "I don't have any cows, Alexei."

Holly apparently wasn't up on the lingo. "Your friends. Laura and Nell and Rachel and Callie and Jennifer."

She shook her head and looked around as though afraid someone had heard them. "Oh. Yeah. That's strictly a Southern thing, Alexei. Seriously. If you call them heifers, the Real Housewives of Bliss might cut off your balls."

So many nuances. "Well, please to keep balls on body."

He had plans for his balls. And his cock. He wasn't about to lose them now.

She flushed, a bright pink color staining her cheeks. She would look like that when she was aroused. Her face would flush, and a fine sheen of sweat would cover her when he worked over her, his cock so deep inside. "Yes. I think that's best."

How soon could he get her under him? Was five minutes too soon? He'd dreamed of having her for months. Every time he closed his eyes, he saw her face and her smile and her soft body. Holly Lang was the embodiment of everything he wanted out of life. She was funny and sweet. Her letters to him kept him going. He'd risked a lot to stay in touch with her. Every new city he'd been to he'd managed to find a way to mail her letters or send her texts from phones he wasn't supposed to own.

He wondered if Caleb had even bothered to read the letters he'd mailed to him.

He twirled Holly, loving how her body moved and her eyes twinkled as she took joy in the dance. He pulled her close again and began to maneuver her toward the hallway. He was happy to see familiar faces, but he wanted to get her alone. He wanted there to be no doubt in her mind that he'd come back for her.

"Walk with me." He couldn't screw that phrase up.

"All right." She put her hand in his. She was a voluptuous woman, but her hand was small in his. Trusting. He wasn't going to let her down.

"Are you in town for a while?" Holly asked as she walked beside him. The hallway that led to the yard outside was deserted. Everyone was inside enjoying the party.

"I am here to stay. Stefan has been kind enough to help me with my citizenship. I would like to make Bliss my home."

Her hand squeezed his. "Really?"

They passed a closet. It shook and a low wail came from behind the door. Someone was having a good time in that closet. Damn, but he was happy to be back in Bliss. Had she thought he would only come for a visit? "Really. I talk to Gene at Movie Motel. He agree to let me stay until I find a place to call my own. Gene is very forgiving man. I do have to promise to not murder anyone while I am in motel. Apparently after Ivan killed the girl in one of his rooms, his motel gets called The Murder Motel for a while."

The Movie Motel had been where he and his former partner had holed up while tracking Jennifer Waters and the painting that held twenty million dollars in bearer bonds. Of course, Alexei hadn't known that at the time. Ivan had murdered a young woman he'd thought was Jennifer. It was a death that made Alexei's heart ache every time he thought about it. If only he'd been back to the room sooner, he might have saved her. He'd only saved Jennifer herself by killing his partner. It had been one of his last acts of violence.

"Oh, don't let him make you feel bad about that. You didn't kill that girl. And the Movie Motel was booked solid for months. Every ghost hunter in the country came out. It was a huge deal. He upgraded the drive-in screen off that money."

"Really? He had the ghost hunting crews come out? Which ones?" He'd watched those shows as well. Though he did not understand why men would wish to spend time hunting ghosts.

"Oh, yes. A bunch of those shows turned up. I don't remember which ones. I kind of tried to avoid them all. And Nell had a shaman from one town over come in and bless the place to rid it of evil. Of course, when they found out there was a real ghost, they all ran. I've never seen grown men in coveralls run quite so fast."

"I am glad all worked out. I like the Movie Motel. It is nice place." Way nicer than anything he'd stayed in lately.

He opened the door, and the night air hit him. He loved the way the mountains smelled and how dark it was. The sky was lit with a million candles. Each one seemed like a possibility. He'd spent so many years in smoggy, clogged cities plotting revenge. Now he was in a tiny nothing town and everything was open to him.

And there was nothing he wanted more than the woman beside

34

him.

"Come here." He tugged on her hand, pulling her toward a picnic bench. He could still hear the sounds of music coming from the reception hall, but they seemed to be alone here. It was a cozy nest surrounded by the beauty of the night. "Tell me how you've been. Tell the stories about your friends—who are not cows."

She hopped up on the tabletop, her peach-colored dress crinkling slightly. "I've told you all the stories. I wrote to you."

"Yes, and now I want to hear them from your voice." He'd forgotten her soft, Western accent.

Her head shook, and he could tell she was slightly embarrassed. She probably wasn't used to the attention. As far as he could tell, she hadn't dated for a long time. He intended to make her very used to affection. He intended to lavish her with it. "Well, Laura's in love. She's getting married next. They haven't made it official, but Rafe and Cam are living with her. I think they were the ones in the closet."

Laura was the pretty, blonde former FBI agent. He'd spent a lot of time learning about the people of this town. He'd managed to find out an enormous amount of information on many of the citizens of Bliss. Except for the man named Mel. There were many classified documents concerning him.

"Callie is coming up on her due date. It's a boy. She's ready to not be pregnant anymore."

"How is your friend Nell?" Holly often talked about Nell.

Her face lit up. "She's trying to talk Callie into burying her placenta under a tree after she gives birth. She wants us all to have a ceremony to reaffirm our ties to the earth. You can imagine how that went over with Nate and Zane. Oh, and her husband finally reached a breaking point, and he hauled her into a bomb shelter, so now she's claiming that Henry is a caveman because he won't let her protest with her breasts."

"Why does she protest her breasts?" Breasts were nothing to protest in Alexei's mind. His eyes drifted down. Holly's breasts were beautiful. How long should he wait before he took her in his arms?

A smile curved her lips up, and Alexei realized she knew what he was looking at.

"I am sorry." Now he was the one who was blushing. She made him feel like a kid again. The things he'd seen and done during that dark time when he'd pursued revenge should have assured that he would never blush again, but Holly made him feel different, more innocent.

"For what?"

He put his hands in his lap, a reminder to keep them to himself for now. Holly deserved to be wooed. Holly deserved flowers and nice dinners. Holly deserved a man with a job. He had to find a job. "I should be careful. I am to be gentleman around you."

Her whole face fell.

"Oh, god, not you, too." She hopped off the table. Her hands went straight to her curvy hips, and those gloriously green eyes narrowed.

"I say wrong thing?" He said the wrong thing all the time. He tried to figure out how he'd insulted Holly. He'd wanted so much for this to go easily with her.

"What is wrong with me? You write me all these letters. You come back here and ask me to dance. I really want to know what it is about me that puts men off. I have nice boobs. They aren't the perkiest things in the world, but they're big and soft. And these are childbearing hips, damn it. It isn't fair. Everyone in this town gets a little something something. Even Stella. Hell, Mel gets laid." She leaned in, her voice going to a mere whisper. "You told me you thought about me during private times. I guess I thought that meant something dirty."

Alexei smiled slowly. She thought he didn't find her attractive. He knew what it meant to get laid. He wanted to get laid with her very, very much. "There is no problem. The private times were very dirty. I think about you in the shower often. Well, I'm in the shower when the thinkings come. And then I come. I thought you would want something different than a man pawing you."

"Do you have any idea how long it's been since a man pawed me? A woman needs a good pawing every now and then."

Tears had formed in her eyes. Alexei wasn't going to have that. What had Caleb been doing? He'd assumed that Caleb would date Holly. It had been obvious to him that Caleb had a thing for her. When he'd walked in the door and seen them standing close, he'd wondered if he'd missed his chance. Then Holly had been amenable to dancing with him. He got off the table and ran a hand along her hair.

"You do not belong to Caleb?" He had to know. If Caleb had already claimed her, he would have to honor it.

"I don't think he wants me," she admitted with a long sigh. "He's nice to me, but he doesn't want me that way."

That wasn't true. If there was one thing he knew, it was that Caleb was crazy about Holly. Even as he'd lain dying on the floor of the sheriff's department, he'd been able to see Caleb's love for Holly. But the fact that Caleb hadn't made a move gave him the door he needed to make his dream come true.

He stood over Holly. "Then I still have a shooting at you?"

Her face went blank, and then a smile crossed her lips. "A shot at me. Yes, you have a shot at me."

"You don't care for Caleb?" His plan wouldn't work if she didn't care for Caleb. How would he handle that? He owed Caleb his life, but he wasn't sure he could walk away from her.

She bit into her bottom lip. "I care about him, but it hasn't worked out for us. I don't want to jump into bed with you, Alexei. Well, that might be a lie, but I don't want to do it tonight. That doesn't mean I wouldn't welcome a kiss. Russians kiss when they greet someone, right?"

"*Da, MIlaya moyA*," he said, dipping his head. *My sweet.* And he was about to find out how sweet she was. He lowered his mouth to hers, reveling in the way her breath caught. Her arms came up to his elbows as though she needed to balance herself. He placed his hands on those curvy hips and brought her close. "*Ti takAya krasivaya.*"

Her mouth was so close, her breath mingling with his. "I don't know what you said, but I liked the way you said it."

He closed the distance between them. *Beautiful.* He'd told her she was beautiful. He'd said it in his own language because he didn't want to screw up.

Her lips were so soft, and he pulled her into his arms, finally where he'd wanted to be for the better part of a year. And he still had a shot. He had a shot at her. And he had a shot to pay back Dr. Caleb Sommerville. He'd researched his savior. He knew Caleb's secrets. No one knew it yet, but Alexei had plans to save them all.

Chapter Two

Holly's heart rate tripled in the amount of time it took for Alexei's lips to finally touch hers. Forever. She'd waited forever. She'd dreamed about him ever since that day when he'd taken a bullet for her. He'd covered her with his body and begged her to stay still. What should have been a nightmare had turned into an act that revitalized her will to live. Up until that moment, she'd been merely existing, surviving for the moments when she could see her son. Alexei had been willing to die to protect her, and he hadn't even known her. When he'd been taken from the hospital by the feds, she'd known that something lovely and amazing had walked out of her life.

His heat seeped into her bones, making her wonder why she hadn't noticed the cold before. His hands found her waist, and she was pulled deliciously close. There it was. The hard ridge of his cock pressed against her stomach, making her ache in the sweetest possible way. His mouth was soft on hers. His lips cajoled, opening her and playing teasingly with his tongue. Even in heels she felt small compared to the big, gorgeous Russian bear.

His tongue finally touched hers, and her hormones began singing a

Hallelujah chorus. So long. She'd been so long without this feeling, the radical pounding of her heart, the racing of her blood. She'd been dull inside, and now everything sprang back to life.

She kissed him with everything she had, pressing her body close to his. He was so tall, so big compared to her. She ran her hands up his biceps. Even through the material of the suit he wore, she could feel how muscular he was. He was sex on a stick. Tall and broad and gorgeous, his dark good looks would make the most spectacular contrast to Caleb's gold and red hair and brooding handsomeness.

Caleb.

Why did she have to think about Caleb? Alexei took over the kiss, his mouth dominating hers as thoughts of Caleb intruded.

He'd been her shadow for almost a year. Not in a creepy way. She almost always felt his presence, like a guardian who only stepped into the light when she absolutely needed him. When her roof had been damaged and she thought she might lose her cabin, a contractor had shown up with a paid-in-full work order in hand. When her car had broken down and she told the shop to take their time with it because she didn't have the money to fix it, he'd left her a ridiculously overblown tip in the exact amount. She'd tried to pay him back, and his favorite word had popped from his mouth.

No.

Caleb said no, but she could see so plainly he wanted to say yes. Was she ready to give up on him?

"I scare you, no?" Alexei asked, pulling away.

She looked up at him, really looked at him. She looked past his killer face and his body that would send any woman into heat. What was she doing? He was a god of a man, and she had sagging boobs. Oh, sure the girls looked good in a structured bra, but when she took it off, she worried they might hit the floor one day. She'd been so dazzled by his sudden reappearance that she hadn't thought about the difference in their ages. Alexei was totally out of her league. It was one thing to write flirty letters with him. Another thing entirely to start a real relationship. She should ask a couple of questions. "How old are you, Alexei?"

God. She was forty. Alexei looked so young. Just a kid. What was she doing?

"Age is number, nothing more." His growl was low and

suspicious.

"Oh. I disagree. Please tell me."

"I am almost twenty-nine." His mouth twisted as though he knew he was saying something that would upset her.

She tried to push away from him. "Seriously? Alexei, let me go. I'm too old for you."

"No. If I let go, you run and not come back to me. I wait too long. And I've done things that age me. Holly, this is a number. It means nothing."

"No, it's almost a teenager." Twelve years. She was twelve years older than he was. She was older than Caleb, too. Oh, what was she thinking?

"You will calm down, or I will to spank ass." Alexei's face went hard, the charming man fleeing in an instant, and in his place was a predator.

Yeah, that got her juices flowing, too. Wow. When had she gotten to be such a freak?

She stiffened in his arms. "You let me go this instant."

His hand came up, snaking into her hair. "You think you can dismiss me like small child. I am not child, and I know what I want. I will walk away if you can tell me you do not want me. I will not walk away because you think people will laugh at you. Do you know the things I have done? If you want reason to not give me chance, then tell me I am too dirty, too bad. Tell me my soul is too filthy for you, and I don't deserve you. You tell me these things, and I will let go. Not that I am too young. I haven't been young in years."

She stilled in his arms, his words penetrating her embarrassment. He'd been through so much. He'd lost his brother and then his revenge because he'd made the choice to save lives rather than take them. He was good. She brought her hands up to frame his face. "Everyone deserves a second chance."

His eyes pinned her. "Then give me one."

He would want more one day. He would need someone younger, someone his own age. It would break her heart. "I don't think this is a good idea. Alexei, have you thought about the fact that you might want a family someday?"

"I want you more."

And she wanted him, but there were so many barricades in the way. There was their age difference and her son. God, what would her son think? And Caleb. Why couldn't she get Caleb out of her head?

And why did she have to think about tomorrow? Why couldn't she have an affair? Why did everything have to be forever? Her marriage hadn't been forever, after all. Maybe it was time to have a wild fling.

"Give me chance. Let me woo you. Go on date with me. Let me prove this can work."

He was so earnest, so sweet, she couldn't walk away. And she wanted to know what it felt like to wrap herself around him, to know he was surrounding her. "I want you, Alexei."

His smile threatened to light up the night.

"But we have to talk about that spanking thing," she said as primly as she could. She wasn't going to try that. No. Maybe just a little.

His smile turned distinctly wolfish. The hand in her hair tightened, lighting up her nerves. "I think you like idea. And I very good with spanking. You will like what I do. But for now, I think gentleness is required."

He pulled her close again, not attempting to hide his arousal. He rubbed against her as his tongue surged into her mouth. This time was different. He'd claimed he was going for gentleness, but she could feel his will. He was gently dominating her, and she loved it. She softened against him, wrapping her arms around his neck. She was on the tiptoes of her cream-colored heels.

And then she was fully in his arms. He lifted her off the ground, his easy strength taking her breath away. He lifted her up, her shoes falling off, but it didn't matter. All that mattered was his mouth on hers. The silky slide of his tongue caressing hers made her womb flutter. She was softening, getting wet and ready for him.

The hard wood of the picnic table was suddenly at her back. She cursed the tight fit of her dress. Hadn't Brooke Harper ever heard of bridesmaids getting lucky at weddings? The slim pencil skirt made it difficult to get her legs open, and suddenly spreading her legs seemed like a really, really good idea. Alexei loomed over her, staring down. She could feel the approval rolling off him in waves. It was a balm to her ego. Maybe she wasn't so old if she could put that look on a man's face.

"No one will mind if we are necking?" He smiled as though he didn't really care if she said no.

"Sweetie, no one says necking anymore. We're going to have to get you up to date on the lingo. We're making out."

His body came down on top of hers, crushing her against the top of the table. She was caught between a rock and a big hard place. Yep. She wished she could spread those legs wide.

"I like this making the out with you."

She didn't have time to correct him. His mouth came down again, this time against her neck. He pressed kisses along her neckline, all the while murmuring in Russian. She let her hands drift to his hair. It was slightly long, curling at the ends. It was silky to the touch.

She gasped as his hand caressed her thigh, pulling at the silk of her skirt. And his lips were getting dangerously close to the bodice of her dress. Her nipples strained against her bra. Her heart raced. She wanted his mouth everywhere.

The sound of footsteps brought her out of her haze.

"Alexei," she said, pushing at him. "Someone's coming."

Even here in Bliss, discretion was called for. And Nate Wright was known to ticket people for public sex. He was always looking to upgrade the appliances in the sheriff's department break room. Alexei's head came up, his eyes a bit glazed.

"Don't let me interrupt you," a familiar voice said.

Holly closed her eyes in horror. Caleb. Of all the people to find her in flagrante almostus, it had to be Caleb.

Alexei smiled as if he was happy to see the man. "Hello, Caleb."

With easy grace, he lifted himself off her and held out a hand. She was wobbly on her feet as they touched the grass.

"Do you even have a condom?" Caleb asked, a harsh rasp to his voice.

"Caleb!" Holly felt her cheeks flare with embarrassment. She suddenly felt like a teenager caught with her boyfriend.

Alexei simply laughed. "I shall have to be buying the condoms."

Caleb's face was drawn in rough lines, his eyes narrowing close together. "And you should have a blood test. You shouldn't start having sex without making sure you're clean. Be in my office tomorrow at nine. I'll make sure you're safe."

"Caleb," she started, but Alexei held out a hand.

"It's all right," Alexei said, his voice a well of patience. "He's only looking out for you."

Caleb's arms folded over his chest. Somewhere along the way, he'd chucked both his tie and his suit coat. She preferred him this way. He'd looked stiff in the suit. His natural, lean grace was on display now. And his temper. "Someone has to. Someone has to make sure jerks don't take advantage of her."

"He wasn't trying to take advantage of me," Holly explained. Though she didn't want to, she continued. She had been the one to push the situation. She didn't want Caleb to be mad at Alexei. "He wanted to be a gentleman. I asked him to kiss me."

"He was doing more than kissing." Caleb didn't seem interested in letting his anger go. He held it tight, like a child with a prized toy.

"Not that it's any of your business, but we weren't going any further." Why was she explaining this to him?

"Of course not," Alexei said with a smooth smile. "No further. Just the out making."

"What?" Caleb asked.

"Making out. We were making out. And when do you expect me in your office?" She crossed her hands over her breasts. Caleb didn't need to know that her nipples were still hard.

"What? Why? Are you sick?" Caleb took a step forward, his hand coming out and laying over her forehead. "What are your symptoms?"

She forced herself not to roll her eyes. The minute she coughed, Caleb was all over her. It had occurred to her on occasion that the way to get the man in bed was to fake a horrible disease. He might slip inside her during his examination. "I don't have symptoms."

Nothing beyond being all kinds of hot and bothered and frustrated out of her mind.

"You guys okay?" Laura Niles asked, walking up with her two men. Cameron Briggs was a huge hunk of all-American male, while Rafael Kincaid was all Latin lover.

Holly looked up while Caleb took her pulse. Laura was one of her closest friends, but damn sometimes she envied the tall blonde with killer shoes. Laura looked happy, her face slightly pink from her closet exertions. Laura hadn't had to pick between Rafe and Cam. They had come to a happy agreement between the three of them.

"Your pulse is fast," Caleb said with a frown. "And you do feel a little hot. Maybe I should take your temperature. There's something going around."

"I do not have anything. My pulse is fast because of the make-out session, and that's precisely why my skin is warm, too." Having a two-hundred-twenty-pound Russian on top of her had done nothing to cool Holly off.

Laura's eyes widened. "Okay. We'll leave you three to work this out." Laura started to walk away. She turned around and mouthed "call me."

Holly pulled away from Caleb. "I was asking about my blood test."

His gorgeous features crinkled in confusion. "Why do you need a blood test?"

She ground her teeth together. "Because it's the right thing to do before starting a relationship."

His face went blank, his jaw slack. "Oh. I think you're fine."

Alexei was at her side, his hand reaching for hers. "She is fine. She is beautiful and perfect."

"I don't see why he needs a blood test and I don't." It seemed a bit like a double standard.

"Hookers," they managed to say at exactly the same time and with exactly the same blank expression on their faces, like it should have been a foregone conclusion.

She felt her face go up in flames.

Alexei brought her hand to his lips. "*Dushka*, I didn't have relationships. I had the intercourse. It means I paid women for my pleasure. It was the lifestyle."

Caleb shrugged. This was the part of Alexei that didn't bother him? "He's trying to say he viewed sex as transactional before he met you. He wasn't looking for a relationship, so it was better to pay someone. Women view sex differently than men. If there's money on the table, no one gets hurt. But they can get the clap."

"There was clapping a couple of times, I will admit. I am very good, but Caleb is right. I will take all of the tests. I do not wish to hurt you."

"He means he doesn't want to give you crabs." Caleb frowned ferociously.

Alexei sighed. "I would know about the crabs. I'm healthy. I always use the rubber."

Caleb shrugged, one shoulder arching aristocratically. "We'll see about that."

"Please stop." She wanted the utter humiliation to end. She'd only wanted a few stolen kisses. Now everyone was going to know that her pseudo boyfriend had accused her halfway make-out date of spending too much time with hookers because the worst gossip in Bliss was coming their way.

Callie was waddling up. Holly couldn't help it. There was no other way to describe it. Callie Hollister-Wright waddled, her enormous belly stretching the dress she wore. She smiled gamely, a hand on her pregnant belly.

"Alexei! It's so good to see you!" She opened her arms, and Alexei hugged her. "I can't believe you came back."

"I can," Zane said. Zane Hollister was one of Callie's hubbies. "I think everyone knows why he came back."

Callie elbowed her husband. Nate Wright, her other husband and the sheriff of Bliss, held out a hand to Alexei.

"It's good to see you. Are you all free and clear with the feds?" Nate asked. Though he'd once been a fed, she knew Nate hated to see them roll into town.

Alexei shook Nate's hand. "Mostly."

Nate groaned. "I'll let Logan and Cam know to be on the lookout. Caleb, it was good to see you. We're going to get this sweet lady home. Any day now, you know."

Caleb's whole expression changed. She loved that about him. He could be a hard-ass most of the time, but when someone needed a bit of kindness, Caleb was there. "Any day now. You call me, Callie. Even if you're worried. Call me. Not Nell. I've told her you aren't giving birth in a kiddie pool."

Zane groaned. Callie merely smiled. "I know, Doc. I was mainly in it for all the free ice cream. Nell always brought me ice cream. And honestly, now that I've had a couple of Braxton-Hicks contractions, I'm pretty sure I want to be drugged up."

"Me, too," Nate said, his face slightly green.

"I'll see what I can do. You call me. Any time and I'll be there," Caleb promised.

And he would. She'd never met anyone as devoted to the people around him as Caleb. He could be dreadfully gruff at times, his bedside manner terrible, but there was no question in her mind that the man cared. Caleb didn't see himself that way. She knew if she asked him, he would say he was merely doing a job, but it was so much more than a job to him. Caleb saw a person in trouble and he helped.

Why couldn't he see her?

Callie walked away with her men, and a heaviness settled around Holly's heart. Callie hadn't been forced to choose. Laura had gotten everything she needed. Rachel was probably somewhere kissing her men.

But Holly would have to choose. She would have to decide if she wanted the hot, sweet Russian who was years younger and would only want a fling, or Caleb, who couldn't seem to make up his mind but who might be good in a long-term way.

Being forced to choose sucked.

And it was getting late. The night was moving on. She needed space. She stepped away from both men. "I should be going."

They stood side by side, each beautiful in their own way. Neither stopped her. They both simply watched her as she walked away.

Story of her life. By the time she found Nell and Henry, she'd wished she'd never left her cabin.

* * * *

Vincent Cavilli looked around his small motel room. It certainly wasn't the worst place he'd been forced to hole up in.

He'd chosen Creede as his home base because it was close to his target but not so close he would be forced to deal with the locals. Though he was well aware that his appearance was bland and forgettable, it was always best to hedge his bets by staying outside his mark's area.

He walked to the window and opened the curtains. He liked the mountains. This part of the country was gorgeous and clean. So unlike the city. And it made for a much harder kill.

No one noticed him in a major metropolitan area. He'd worked in all of the world's great cities. New York, London, Paris, Tokyo, Sydney. He'd killed in them all. It wasn't hard to work in urban areas. Everyone kept their heads down and paid attention to their own shit. People actively ignored others in cities.

Not so here. He'd already been forced to converse with both the motel owner and a father of four on vacation with the most obnoxious children he'd ever had the displeasure of sharing a lobby with. Seriously. He'd considered taking the kids out. It would be his way of giving back. His version of pro bono work. He'd considered playing the asshole, but people tended to remember assholes, so he'd smiled and laughed and talked about the hiking he would do.

Luckily, the US Army had trained him well. It had been a while, but he could hike and track and build a shelter if he needed to. He wasn't planning on it. He planned on getting some advice on the best trails from the locals and then spending his days working. If he did the job right, it wouldn't take more than a day or two. He mentally went through his list. *Get a lay of the land. Identify the target. Figure out the best method of taking out the target and enacting the plan.*

An accident would be best. Again, because he wasn't in a city, he needed to cover his tracks. Murders in small towns got a lot of attention. Car accidents, heart attacks, even animal attacks were more common here. As he didn't work with animals, and poisoning someone was harder than television made it out to be, he was thinking about fucking with the mark's car.

God, he hoped the mark had a car.

The cell phone he'd bought specifically for this job trilled. He sighed. He had all the relevant information. Why did he need regular phone calls? Fucking micromanagers. He'd tried to explain to his current employer that it was better they didn't communicate, but it was obvious the asshole wasn't listening. Mobsters. He hated working for them, but they paid well. Unfortunately, they also believed they knew his business better than he did.

With a deep sigh, he answered the phone. "Yes?"

"Are you in place? Did you receive the package?"

Ah, and his employer had more than one employee. This one didn't sound like she came from Jersey. Fuck. He hoped the asshole hadn't put this duty off on some freaking law student. Real smart. *Here's your checklist for the day. Call about the appeal. Make sure the argument papers are formatted. Oh, and call to check in with the assassin we hired.* Idiot.

"I received the package. It should take me a few days. I have to see a friend."

"Ah, so you found the house of your friend."

"Yes, the directions were impeccable, thank you." At least the idiot wasn't coming right out and asking him how long it would take to complete the kill.

"We thank you. I'll be watching for your progress. Please contact this number when the job is done." The connection closed suddenly.

Amateurs. If he didn't need the money so badly, he would have avoided this job altogether. He preferred to work outside the US, but the serious money was here.

Two hundred thousand dollars and all he had to do was kill one simple target. He would attempt to make it look like an accident. If he couldn't do that in the time allotted, he would shoot the fucker. A car accident would be more elegant, but a bullet would do the job, too.

He took a deep breath of mountain air, trying to banish his wariness. He couldn't turn this job down. He simply had to watch his back and try to fit in. It shouldn't be too hard. It was late summer, and there were tourists everywhere. He would be one more tourist among the throng. A city dweller looking to get back in touch with nature.

His mark would never know that death was coming.

Vince sat down at the crappy desk and pulled out his file. He went over all the particulars of the person he was being paid handsomely to kill.

The kids next door screamed and turned the television up far too loud.

It would be a miracle if he got out of Colorado with only the one job under his belt.

Chapter Three

Alexei walked from the recreational center to the Movie Motel, his heart light in ways it hadn't been for years. Holly had responded to him. She'd softened like butter the minute he'd touched her.

The gravel crunched under his feet and the air was brisk on his skin. How long had it been since he'd simply enjoyed the world? Since he'd even acknowledged there was beauty and goodness in the world? He stopped, letting the night flow around him, grateful he'd made it. He breathed in, letting the air fill his lungs. This was the right place to be, the right thing to do. He could feel his brother's approval. This was what he owed Mikhail—to lead a good life, to bring joy into the world.

He laughed as he opened his eyes. If he kept it up, he would get emotional. It happened a lot since the day he'd made the choice to let revenge go. He started walking toward the motel again, his head filled with happy plans. He was going to have to find a car. He was going to have to find a job. All of that would have been taken care of for him if he'd chosen to stay in witness protection, but Holly was more important than such minor matters.

"'Night, Alexei." Gene waved at him from behind the counter. The door was open, and Gene had a bag of popcorn in his hand. "How was the wedding shindig?"

Alexei followed his line of sight. From where he was standing, Gene could watch the screen. It was playing a Doris Day film. The Technicolor of the movie lit up the night.

"I miss wedding, but I enjoy the dancing very much." He'd loved the feel of Holly's body pressed against his. He'd loved it even more when he'd covered her with his own. He'd meant what he'd said to Caleb. He'd only been kissing her and touching her. He had no intention of their first time together happening on a picnic table. There would be time for freaky sex in odd places later. The first time would be in a bed with flowers and wine. And maybe a cranky doctor.

Gene nodded. "I bet you did. You Russian fellas are real good dancers."

"You were not invited?" It seemed like almost everyone in Bliss had been invited to the wedding. The hall had been filled to the brim with guests.

"I don't like to leave this place much," Gene explained with a sigh. "Besides, if I had left, I would have missed a couple of new guests. Real nice folks. You know, I offered Stef and Jen a room for their honeymoon. They wanted to go to Hawaii." Gene's head shook like he couldn't understand why anyone would willingly leave Bliss.

If Alexei had his way, he would take Holly on a great honeymoon. Someplace nice and tropical, where he could enjoy the sight of her in a bikini and he and Caleb could go fishing.

Because he intended to be in a happy threesome, though he wished the man who was to be his partner was less of a stubborn ass. He'd met donkeys with heads less thick than Caleb's. Doris Day continued on her quest for love on the big screen behind him while Alexei changed the subject.

"Tell me something, Gene. I am needing to find work. Do you know of anyone who needs good employee?"

"What kind of work are you looking for?"

Well, he'd spent the last several years working for the mob. He was excellent at interrogating criminals, laundering money, and covering up crimes. He doubted anyone was looking to hire a thug. "I am good with cars."

Gene's eyes lit up. "I heard Long-Haired Roger was looking for a mechanic. Now, you want to make sure you find Long-Haired Roger and not Roger. They're different, but lots of people get them mixed up. Roger is kind of mean, and folks around here are pretty sure he's planning on attempting to secede from the US. I don't think Uncle Sam is going to let Roger form his own country and name it Rogerville, but he gets touchy about it, so I would avoid him. Now, both Long-Haired Roger and Roger are married to women named Liz, so you can't tell them apart that way. And their wives are sisters. And they don't much like each other. I think their dad should have come up with different names, but he just called them Liz One and Liz Two."

Gene, he'd discovered, could talk for long periods of time. He knew everyone in the area and had a story about each person. Unfortunately, Alexei didn't have time this evening to listen. He needed to shower and sleep. In the morning, he had to meet with Caleb and then find a job. "I will find the Roger with long hair."

"Oh, he doesn't have long hair anymore. He went bald a couple of years back."

And Gene could be very confusing. "Perhaps you give me address."

"Now that's a real good plan. I can do that." Gene wrote down the address, and Alexei bid him farewell.

Perhaps by tomorrow he would be gainfully employed. Maybe between the blood tests and a real job, Caleb would relax a bit.

Maybe when Caleb realized he wasn't alone in caring for Holly, he would discover that he could handle a relationship. After what had happened to his wife, he couldn't blame Caleb for being scared of commitment. Watching his wife murdered in front of his eyes would have had an effect. But Alexei meant to draw Caleb back into life. He was too good a man to let himself wither and die. He'd given Alexei his life back. Alexei meant to return the favor.

He was about to open his door when he noticed someone had beaten him to it. He wasn't a fool. There were still people who wanted him dead. He'd left a small thread hanging in the door. It was on the concrete of the sidewalk now. Gene's staff didn't clean at night.

Someone was in his room.

He calmly pulled the Glock from the holster at the small of his back and flicked off the safety. Luckily Holly hadn't noticed it. He would more than likely have to explain why he walked around armed all the time. But for now he was thankful for the feel of it in his hands. He thought briefly about leaving. He could head for town and talk to whoever was manning the sheriff's office, but this was his problem. The last thing he needed was to run into Logan Green and ask him to watch his back. The last time he'd talked to Logan Green, the man had been tortured and nearly killed by Alexei's mob boss, buying Alexei time to save Holly. If Stefan Talbot hadn't come along, he wasn't sure Logan would have made it. No. He wouldn't ask anyone to risk his life. If he really had people trying to take him out, he would have to consider leaving Bliss. He couldn't risk Holly.

In one smooth move, he opened the door and got into a firing stance, his legs strong beneath him, both hands on the gun.

And sighed because his past had caught up to him in the form of a couple of law enforcement professionals. And they were kissing on his bed. He now knew who had checked in while he was gone. "You could not make love on own bed?"

Michael Novack rolled off his partner and looked up at Alexei with a grin on his face. "We're lucky that was you and not someone else. One of these days they're going to fire us."

Jessie buttoned up her shirt. Unlike Holly, Jessie didn't blush. She simply winked at Alexei and smoothed her straight dark brown hair. She was dressed in her normal uniform of slacks and a button down. Jessie dressed like she was one of the boys. It suited her slender, athletic build, but Alexei greatly preferred Holly's curves. "Surprised to see us? We were surprised you left."

Was he surprised to see the US marshals in Bliss? Not really. But he'd hoped they would let him go. "The job was over. The trials are done."

Michael was a former linebacker. He often told Alexei about his college days. He flexed his arms over his head, displaying a body built on broad lines. He was dressed in dark slacks and a button down, though it fit him differently than his partner/girlfriend. "Two of those cases are still on appeal. I explained that to you."

Appeals. Yes. There was nothing appealing about the prospect. The appeals process could take even longer than the trials. It was a criminal's last legal way out. "I don't wish to stay in Florida motel room for years waiting to see if criminals' lawyers will get them out. I wish to get on with life."

"So you traded a motel room in Florida for one in Colorado?" Jessie asked, a smirk on her face. "That doesn't make a lick of sense. And this place is boring. Even the movies are super old. I don't get it. Unless, of course, there's a girl involved."

He'd never mentioned her name to either of his handlers. He'd kept that to himself. He'd erased her texts and burned her letters. He wanted no mention of her to come to anyone who might leak it. Now that the trials were done, he'd felt safe enough to come back to her. No one would care that Alexei Markov had disappeared into the west and found his wife. He would even insist that Caleb be the one to legally marry her so there was no record of his name linked with hers.

"Her name wouldn't happen to be Holly Lang?" Michael asked.

"How did you know?" Shit. He'd fucked up. He'd known he couldn't keep it a secret, had never meant to from the locals, but he didn't want anyone outside of Bliss to know about her.

Jessie looked at him sympathetically. "No one broods the way you did over anything but a woman."

"I don't know. I think I brood over many things. Dead brother. Many crimes committed in name of revenge. Lots of peoples wishing to eviscerate me." He had a long list of worries.

"Yeah, you're a walking mental health issue," Michael replied, his dark head shaking. "But we always knew it was about a girl. We had your file, man. Holly Lang is a local waitress. You saved her life."

"She is nice lady." He downplayed it. Let them believe he would have done the same for anyone.

"And you're in love with her." Jessie wasn't going to let up. Alexei had often compared the slender brunette to a badger. She could be mean and stubborn when she got an idea in her head. "You're here for her. And don't think I didn't know about the cell phone. I'm just a great believer in forbidden love."

Michael sent a leer her way. "She is. Now marriage is another story. She doesn't believe in that at all."

Dark eyes rolled. "Dude, seriously? You bring that up now? We would both be fired."

Michael wouldn't let up. "Or one of us could move to a different department, maybe something less life threatening."

Jessie's lips pursed. Alexei got the feeling this was a well-worn argument. "Sure you can. Enjoy the paperwork, buddy, because I'm not moving."

Alexei reholstered his gun. He wouldn't be using it this evening. "Please to be having relationship discussion later. Tell me if you're taking me back into custody."

He would have to find a way to talk to Holly. He couldn't disappear again. He couldn't walk into her life, kiss her for all he was worth, and then step back out. It would crush her, and he didn't trust Caleb to pick up the pieces. Not yet. Caleb was like the nursery rhyme Humpty-Dumpty. He required piecing back together after a long fall. But Alexei couldn't put him back together again if he was holed up in a motel in some nondescript city in Middle America.

"Technically, if you don't want witness protection, we can't force you into it. You've proven valuable to the government, but not in an eyewitness fashion. If you choose to leave the program, we can't stop you," Michael explained.

"I choose to leave." He breathed a deep sigh of relief. He'd done his duty by putting the criminals away. He'd saved lives by cutting their careers short. Now it was time to do his duty to Caleb and Holly.

"I told you we shouldn't have called him Howard." Jessie smiled at him. "We knew that would be your answer, but we're here anyway. Look, we've grown to give a shit about you. I think the judge is going to throw these suck-ass claims out, but if I'm wrong, we should know in a week or so. We don't have to tell our boss you're opting out yet. We'll explain we've moved you to another location, and if these dirtbags get another trial, we go deep and take this Holly person along for the ride."

"No. I do not wish this for Holly." Holly would wither being forced to change her name and stay in cheap motel rooms, always hiding. And she wouldn't go. She couldn't live with never seeing her son again. "If I must go, I will go alone."

"I hope it doesn't come to that," Michael said seriously. "We should know soon. In the meantime, neither one of us has mentioned your new home to anyone. Not even our director. You should be safe here. I take it you traveled under an assumed name?"

"Of course. I take bus. Not much securities there." Just very smelly people on his particular bus. But when a person wanted to be anonymous, there was no better transportation.

"He'll be fine, babe," Jessie assured him. "And we'll have a mountain vacay. We're in the room next to you. We can be here in two seconds flat. Well, unless Mr. Horny here has his way, and then it's more like fifteen, twenty seconds."

"Bitch." But Michael said it with deep affection.

It hadn't taken Alexei long to discover that the partners were more than mere friends. He'd spoken with Michael about it. They had only been lovers for a few months, but Michael loved her deeply, and Jessie seemed to feel the same way. They acted professionally while working, but Alexei could see that they were going to take advantage of their impromptu vacation.

And he would take advantage of his.

* * * *

Caleb cleared off his desk. He checked and rechecked his exam room. It was small and really the only neat room in his office beside the teeny tiny waiting room that almost no one used. No one waited in Bliss. In Chicago, he'd had a huge waiting room with perfectly designed furnishings. Every inch of that space had been modeled to give the patient a calm, peaceful place to wait while the doctor took his time. He'd paid a decorator a fortune to ensure that his office was the best. Well, his wife had paid a portion of his fortune. He'd never given a crap about any of it. He'd only wanted to work, but his wife and family had insisted that Dr. Caleb Sommerville have the most prestigious-looking office they could afford. Two years later, he was in a mobile hospital in Africa. Yeah. Caroline had loved that.

He now had two folding chairs and a whiteboard where people could sign up for appointments. More often than not, all that was on his board were snarky notes.

He hated bringing Holly to his office. He avoided it when he could. When he'd needed to be with her twenty-four-seven, he'd taken her on his rural rounds and then back to her place. If she spent too much time here, she would probably wander into his living quarters, and he definitely didn't want that. The apartment over the clinic was a stark glimpse into his soul. *Yeah. 'Cause you've fooled her with your charming banter. She'll be shocked to find out you don't give a crap about decorating. Because she thought you were fucking Martha Stewart before.*

55

What the hell was he doing? Why was he worried about this? It wasn't like it mattered. He wasn't starting a relationship with Holly. He was protecting her. Protection was all he could give her. He'd proven he couldn't handle a real relationship. He'd put his work in front of his marriage. He'd started out with feelings for Caroline, but he'd cared so little for her in the end that he'd left for months at a time. She'd had to travel halfway around the world to tell him she was leaving, and then he'd gotten her murdered.

He didn't deserve Holly. He couldn't give her the life she needed. He was too dark for her. How could he tell her all the things he thought about, dreamed of? He couldn't.

But then did Alexei really deserve her?

"Knock, knock." A soft feminine voice floated in from the outer office.

Caleb stopped. He didn't think he had any appointments. Only Alexei's extremely thorough checkup and Holly's intensely awkward one. How was he going to put impersonal hands on her? Even checking her pulse gave him a hard-on.

He certainly hadn't been expecting Nell Flanders.

"There you are!" Nell didn't walk. She sort of floated, as though her dainty feet didn't quite touch the earth she claimed she was so connected to. Nell was a healthy thirty-year-old with shiny brown hair and a penchant for public protests. "I'm glad I caught you before you opened up."

God, he hoped she wasn't going to ask to go on rounds with him. Nell had a reputation for attempting to experience what she called life lessons. She'd tried working with almost everyone in Bliss in order to connect with the people around her. Her experiments had ranged from the successful—she was quite good at selling baked goods at The Trading Post—to the utterly disastrous—she'd nearly given Max Harper a heart attack when she had tried to set all of his horses free. Luckily Max was a damn fine horse trainer and on a short leash from his far more patient wife. Otherwise, Nell Flanders might have been in trouble.

Caleb didn't need trouble today. He had all he could take. He would run these tests for Holly, and then he would leave town for a few days because he wasn't going to watch her date Alexei. No way. No how.

Except he had to. Callie was having a baby. Fuck. He couldn't leave. First he had to deliver the baby, and then he had to stay around because newborns required checking. Maybe he could call someone else in? Who was he kidding? There wasn't anyone else.

"Uhm, am I interrupting something?" Nell stood, staring at him, a basket of green in her hand. Some sort of plant.

"No."

She looked around the office, her eyes studying the surroundings. "Oh, well, you seemed to be concentrating. I thought you might have been doing some serious meditation."

More like some serious freaking out. "I don't meditate. What do you need?"

Yep, his bedside manner was in full swing.

"I wanted to talk to you."

He stared at her, suspicion tickling at him. No one wanted to talk to him. He'd cultivated a reputation as a taciturn bastard. If it wasn't about a physical malady, no one attempted to engage him in conversation. He could sit for hours in Trio or Stella's beside someone and never utter a word until it was time to go. "Hello" and "good-bye" was about what he'd trained people to expect from him. That and "take a deep breath" or "this is going to sting."

Except Alexei. He'd talked a lot that day. And he'd taught the Farley brothers. He'd felt bad for those kids from the moment he'd heard they were getting bullied, but until Alexei had talked to him about it, he hadn't done anything. That day by the pond, he'd really talked to Bobby and Will. He'd given them advice his own father had given him. It had been easy because he'd known if he fucked up or said the wrong thing or had a panic attack, Alexei would take care of them.

"Have I lost you again?" Nell asked.

"All right. I'll hear you out," he said slowly. This was Holly's friend. He could listen.

"I want to talk to you about Holly."

Or not. He turned back to his equipment, dismissing her entirely. How large bore of a needle could he convincingly use on Alexei without breaking his Hippocratic oath?

He could hear her foot tapping an impatient rhythm against the linoleum. "I'm not going to go away because you ignore me."

"Most people do." And he liked it that way.

A confident huff came out of her mouth. "Most people haven't handcuffed themselves to giant trees for days at a time. You know, you learn a lot when you protest. I know how to talk when being screamed at and threatened with bodily harm and various lawsuits. I've been called every name in the book. I've been shot at and played chicken with a bulldozer. I won. You can ignore me all you like, and I'll keep talking until you listen to me. That can be now or five days from now. I've cleared my calendar."

Crap. He believed her. He turned back to Nell, who set down the potted plant and smiled. He gave her his best scowl, but she simply brightened her smile. She wasn't going away no matter how much he tried to intimidate her.

He knew when to retreat. "All right. I'm listening."

"You know I like you, Caleb."

He wasn't sure how he was supposed to respond to that. He hadn't thought about whether Nell liked him or not, but she seemed to require a response. "Thanks."

Her smile widened. "Oh, thank you. I really do like you. You're a healer. You have a healer's aura. It's beautiful. You're lucky. Some people get auras that don't blend well with their natural coloring, but yours is lovely. Unfortunately, you also have a black cloud that follows you around."

Again, he had no idea what she wanted, but she stood there, her doe eyes wide, forcing Caleb to respond. "Sorry."

She waved him off. "Oh, you can't help it. Something happened to you, something traumatic to damage your aura, but it's fixable. I don't suppose you have any interest in seeing a shaman? She makes awesome Blizzards, too. I can get you in for half price."

No way was he going to Crazy Irene unless he needed some steak fingers. "No. I'll keep my dark cloud."

She continued on as though that had merely been the opening volley in her attack. "It's not a literal cloud, of course. Just a dark lining around your naturally sunny aura."

Now he was sure she was insane. He'd never been sunny. Not one day in his life.

Nell continued, her voice filled with earnest pleading. "But you let that dark cloud affect everything. I can see plainly that you have feelings for Holly."

Now it was time to lie. "No, I don't."

"Yes, you do. Everyone knows it. You're not exactly hiding it."

He thought he had been. "What gave me away?"

She stared at him like he was speaking a foreign language and then replied slowly. "Uhm, you go into the diner three times a day. You turn around and walk out when Holly isn't working. I happen to know that Stella has taken to giving you Holly's schedule so you don't scare her customers by walking into the middle of the diner, staring everyone down, and then walking back out without saying a word. Seriously, Caleb, people think you're a terrorist or something."

"I accept that." As long as no one shot at him, he really didn't care what they thought. And a shot of adrenaline never hurt anyone. It was good for the heart to have a shock every now and then.

Nell crossed her arms over her chest, frustration evident in her squared shoulders and down-turned mouth. "You scare the tourists. Strangely though, you don't scare Holly. She doesn't seem bothered by the fact that you stare at her like a tiger waiting to pounce. I think what makes her sad is that you haven't pounced at all, and now Alexei is going to pounce, because let me tell you, that tiger isn't sitting on his hill waiting for gosh knows what to happen. That tiger knows he's hungry, and he's going to eat your pie, Caleb."

He was having trouble with her line of logic. First he had a cloud following him around, and now he was a starving tiger on a hill and he had an odd diet. "Tigers eat pie?"

"In my version of life, they do. In my perfect world, tigers are vegans, too."

And in Nell's perfect world, he would crap rainbows. "Are you asking me to pounce on your best friend?"

Her hands came up, fists pumping in victory. "Yes. I am so glad you understand. I don't get it, but sometimes people don't think I communicate well."

It said something about him that he sort of understood her. "I don't think pouncing on Holly is a good idea. I don't think I would be a good boyfriend."

Nell stepped forward, stopping shy of putting a hand on his shoulder. "I think you're underestimating yourself. You can do anything you want to. Are you willing to try?"

He wanted to. It was right there on the tip of his tongue to say yes.

Maybe he could pretend to be the same man he'd been twenty years before. He could pretend he still believed in things like happiness. "It's not a good idea."

She frowned but held her ground. "All right then. You were my front-runner, but since you're getting out of the game, I have to ask you to step aside. I mean really step aside. No more longing looks. No more charging in when trouble happens. Yes, we all know you're the one who paid for her roof and her car, and you're the one who forced the mayor to okay the new stop sign in front of Stella's because you're worried she could get hit crossing the street. And the next time there's a killer in Bliss, let someone else take care of Holly. And there will be a next time. We all know that."

His entire body tensed at the very idea. He wouldn't be able to breathe not knowing that she was okay. When she'd been in danger before, he'd needed her right there or he'd have been utterly worthless.

Nell's finger wagged his way. "You don't like the idea, do you? Well, I don't like my best friend crying over you. It's time to decide if you're in or you're out. And if you're out, you need to leave her alone. What you've done isn't fair."

"I never even asked her out." He could hear the sullenness in his voice. He sounded like a fucking five-year-old. Why did that asshole have to come back? Why couldn't he have stayed in Florida? He was forcing Caleb to make decisions he didn't want to make. Holly had been crying over him? God, he hated the thought.

"No, but you made her think you liked her," Nell replied. "And I think she might hold back from Alexei if she hopes there's a chance for the two of you. Let her go. Let her be happy with Alexei. Unless, of course, you want to join them."

"Fuck no." He didn't share. He wasn't going to get involved in one of the crazy threesomes this town seemed to thrive on. Even if they did work out and everyone was happy and secure. Nope. Not going there. "Do you think he genuinely cares about her?"

Nell's eyes softened. "I think he was willing to die for her, and he barely knew her name. He's been reliable in communicating with her, and that can't have been easy given what he's been through. I think she'll be safe with Alexei."

Confusion was riding him hard. He didn't want to think about the long letters Alexei had sent to him. They had been full of confessions and gratitude at first, and then he'd simply started telling Caleb about his life. As if he wanted to know. He'd only read them because he'd had nothing better to do. "Then why the hell would you want me to be with her if you think Alexei is so damn good for her?"

Nell didn't react at all to his huffiness. She merely smiled, though it struck him as a sad thing. "I thought Holly would be good for you. In some ways, I think you need her more than Alexei does. But you don't see it, and I can't make you. You're going to follow this path. I can see it plainly now."

He felt his chest tighten. Holly was going to be with Alexei. Holly was going to choose the Russian.

Choose? You never gave her a choice, and now it's too late to force her into one. She would be miserable and possibly resent the hell out of whoever made her choose. Face it. You fucked up. It's what you do.

Nell sighed. "No moving you, is there? I suppose the world needs its mountains like it needs the air. Well, since you've made your decision, you should know that if you screw up Holly's new relationship and her happiness, then I will do very terrible things to you."

It was like Snow White threatening to kill him. "Terrible things?"

She nodded primly. "Yes. I don't know what those things are yet, but I have an excellent imagination. And I have years of pent-up rage. Oh, I lock it away because I believe anger is useless, but I swear on the god of your choosing and whom I honor because I honor all religions, that I will find a use for all that rage. I will direct it at you, and it won't be pleasant. You like to be alone, don't you?"

He was pretty much always alone. Even in a crowd of people. "Yep. So don't think that turning the town against me will hurt too much."

Nell's brown hair shook. "Oh, I would never do that. Bad, bad karma. It does strike me, though, that a man of your persuasion needs a friend. You know, someone who would be around you all the time, talking to you, keeping you company. Yes, someone who talks as little as you do probably wants to listen to someone like me talk a lot. I can talk for hours. I never let up. I can talk about everything. Ask Henry."

It put a chill through him. She would do it, too. Nell Flanders, twenty-four-seven. "Well played, Nell. I'll consider it."

Her chin came up, and she nodded shortly. "See that you do. I'll make a list of the topics of our conversations so you'll have a better idea of how terrible this could be. In the meantime, I brought you a plant. Your office needs a softer touch. Even if no one ever sits in this waiting room, it would be better for you if you had something lovely and lively to call your own. I don't even want to see your apartment, do I?"

His apartment had a leather recliner, a television, and a card table. It had a bed, but only because it came with the building. He'd never slept on it. There was nothing on the walls. No pictures of his family or knickknacks. Nothing at all that celebrated a life. Everything was utilitarian. And a bit messy.

"I'll find some more plants. You'll see. The oxygen the plant gives off will make you feel better. You have to water it once a day." She stopped and stared at him. "I'll take care of that. And maybe I'll upgrade the waiting room a bit. You won't mind. I know you won't."

He got the feeling that if he did mind, she would start talking. "Nope. Feel free to decorate to your heart's content."

She turned on her Birkenstocks as the door opened again. "Hello, Alexei."

And, of course, Alexei smiled and reached for her hand. Charm seeped from the asshole's pores. "Ms. Nell, it is good to see you. You look lovely this morning."

Nell blushed. "Thank you. That is kind of you to say."

"I only to speak the truths." The bastard smiled widely, taking both of Nell's hands in his. "I am going to be dating Holly. I would love to do the double with you and Henry."

Nell's eyes went wide. "Oh, no. Despite his very open mind, Henry isn't into sharing or swapping or any of that stuff."

Alexei's confused face turned toward him. It was blatantly obvious that he had no idea what Nell thought he'd said. He thought briefly about letting the fucker hang, but the words came out before he could stop them. "He was talking about a double date, not a foursome. But I find it interesting that your mind goes there."

He was satisfied by her flushed face and completely silent mouth. Oh, it opened, but nothing came out for a moment. He'd finally found a way to silence Nell Flanders. Maybe this minor war she'd started wasn't over yet.

Alexei, ever the gentleman, stepped in. "So sorry. Many, many apologies. I am not interested in the swappings of wives, merely in sharing of meal."

"Of course. Henry and I would love that. Thank you, Alexei." Nell hurried out.

Unfortunately, Caleb had the feeling she'd be back.

Alexei turned to him, bowing slightly. "Thank you for the translation, my friend. My words are still muddled in brain. I do not always understand English sayings. And they change so quickly. Now that I am back here, I think I will watch more of the MTVs so I can speak more like an American."

Dear god, he would sound like he was straight off the Jersey shore. "All I know is that if you're reliant on me as a translator, you're in serious trouble. I almost let Nell believe you wanted an orgy."

"No orgies. Just a very happy relationship. One where Holly gets everything she needs. If that comes from me, then good, but I think she is so much womans, she might require more." He said it with a serious expression on his face.

He wasn't sure how to take that. Yep. If Alexei needed him to translate, they were all in trouble. He didn't understand the guy.

Good thing he understood his job and his duty to his patients. A deep sense of joy lodged in his heart. Alexei might waltz away with the girl, but not until he'd been thoroughly examined. Thoroughly. After all, that was a doctor's job.

He felt a smile cross his face. He was pretty sure it wasn't reassuring. He pulled on his latex gloves. "So, do you want to start with the blood work or the prostate exam?"

Alexei went a little pale. "I am being sure I do not know what this prostate is. Well, I have suspicion."

Now Caleb grinned widely and held up a tube of lube. "Don't worry about it, buddy. It's all a part of the service. You need a prostate check every year."

"But I promise not to use prostate in making the love with Holly. I will keep her far away from prostate." Alexei backed up, his eyes going to the lube.

Nope. He wasn't getting out of this so easily. "Sorry, buddy. It's this or a full colonoscopy. Welcome to America. Now please bend over."

Chapter Four

Holly pulled her car into the parking lot in front of Caleb's office. It was located at the end of Main Street, close to Stella's, but she'd only made it past the front door once, and that was when Caleb had been guarding her. In the year Caleb had been in town, she'd never been sick enough to come into the tiny clinic. The one cold she'd come down with had been dealt with in Caleb's ruthlessly precise fashion. She'd sniffled at the café one morning and found herself at home in bed with a neti pot, chicken soup, and a ton of orange juice. She hadn't even felt that bad.

And yet it was a sweet memory.

She got out and closed the door to her tiny piece-of-crap vehicle. She was lucky she'd been able to afford the sucker, but sometimes it made her depressed. The same way Caleb did.

What was she doing? She was about to walk into Caleb's office and take a blood test to prove she was a healthy sex partner to a twenty-eight-year-old god of a man.

She opened the door to his small clinic. It didn't even have a nameplate, just a simple red cross and stenciled black letters proclaiming it to be Bliss County Clinic.

Caleb had done a lot for her. She hadn't even thought to get him a nameplate. He wouldn't think to buy one. He never thought about things like that, but he did think to make sure she was safe. Unfortunately, he didn't want her the way she wanted him. Did that mean she didn't owe him? He'd been a good, if odd, friend to her. She hadn't been the same to him.

Holly stood in the small, Spartan waiting room. She could hear Caleb talking.

"I'll have the blood tests back in a few weeks."

"Weeks?"

Her whole body went on alert. Alexei's voice sounded slightly strangled.

"These things take time."

No, they didn't. Caleb often drove into Alamosa and had results the same day.

"I understanding. I, uhm, I do not, uhm, well, thanks to you." Yep, Alexei sounded distressed. "Please to let me know when it is safe to be close to Holly. I care for her. I would not be harming her, not for anything."

There was a long pause. "Okay. Like I said, I'll let you know."

The door to the exam room opened, and Alexei walked out. She stared, studying him for a moment before he realized he wasn't alone. He looked older, more weary than he had the night before. Worry creased his brow and turned that sensual mouth down. His shoulders slumped as he shut the door behind him.

And then it all changed when he saw her. A vibrant smile crossed his face. His body straightened to his impressive six and a half feet, and his entire air took on a sexy, sultry tone. "Holly. It is very good to see you. You look heated today."

Hot. She looked hot. She was starting to hope his English didn't get better. He was adorable when he was screwing it up. "Thanks."

She stood there, not quite knowing what to do. She hadn't dated in forever. Were they dating? Or merely waiting to have sex?

"I have to go to talk to man about job, but would you like to have dinner tonight?"

She actually felt her heart flutter. He was so gorgeous, and he was looking at her like he could eat her up. If they had been alone, she might have suggested that dinner started early and wouldn't he like a piece of Holly pie? Damn it. He had her hormones turned up so high she could barely think when he was around.

But then Caleb walked into the room, his green eyes solemn as he took in the scene in front of him. He stared for the briefest moment before his eyes found the floor. "Uhm, Holly, I'm ready whenever you are."

She nodded, and he backed into the exam room again.

She needed to figure out a way to be right with Caleb. Her heart ached when she looked at him, but Alexei made her feel young and vital. And Alexei wanted her.

"Caleb is stubborn man, *dushka*. If he did not save both lives, I seriously consider coming out of retirement to murder him." Alexei frowned, staring back at the door.

"Oh, god, what did he do?"

"All I know is Russian doctors are not so thorough. A man's backside is sacred in Russia. I tell you, if he tries in bedroom, I will deal with him."

"Huh?" Yeah, maybe she should rethink how adorable his English was.

He reached out and took her hand. "Nothing. Nothing to worry about. I am patient man. Very patient. And tolerant. And no longer violent. So, dinner?"

At least she understood that. "Yes. I would love to have dinner with you. I get off at six. We could have dinner at Stella's if you like."

He shook his head. "No. Not where you work. Let's go to Trio and have nice drink and dance. After I get job, I take you to someplace very nice."

She loved how his hand squeezed hers. "I'm fine going anywhere. There aren't a lot of choices in Bliss."

"When I get job and make the monies, I take you wherever you like to go. But, for tonight, it must be Trio." He brought her hand to his lips, the sensation making her tingle all over. "Now, I must find this place called Roger's Garage. How long will it take me to get there?"

"Long-Haired Roger's place? He's about two miles north of the Feed Store Church, right next to Polly's Cut and Curl. You can't miss it. Polly has a huge pink neon sign with kissing lips on it. It'll take you ten minutes or so by car."

"Car is one of things I must get."

She reached for her keys. "Take mine. I'm going to work straight after this. I don't need it again until I get off. Do what you need to do and then drop it off at Stella's. I have to warn you, it's kind of small."

His smile brightened everything around him. He took the keys and leaned over, kissing her lips. "So many thanks to you, *dushka*. It makes up for the doctor. Be careful. His hand is much bigger than it look. If I could spare you, I would." He brought her fingers to his lips again. "Tonight."

The word held such promise. She was pretty sure the room lost some temperature as Alexei walked out the door.

And now she had to find a way to deal with Caleb.

She decided on a friendly but no-nonsense approach. He was behaving like a protective older brother. She marched right into his exam room. "Why is it going to take weeks to get the blood work back? I happen to know that the hospital in Alamosa will process your samples in a few hours."

His gold and red head didn't move from the chart he was studying. "They do that as a favor to me. I'm not going to call in a favor so Alexei can get some."

She gritted her teeth. "What do you have against Alexei?"

"Well, he's a mobster for one thing." The words came out in a disgruntled huff. He marked the chart, his pen moving across the pages in tense lines.

She thought that was part of the problem. Caleb didn't deal well with violence. "Ex-mobster. And he was only in the mob because he was seeking revenge on the man who killed his brother. I've read all the stories about him. He didn't kill anyone who was innocent. He only ever killed other mobsters. You don't have a problem with Nate and Zane. They basically did the same thing when they were undercover with the DEA."

"Nate and Zane were in law enforcement. They had badges." His tone had gone to a sullen, dark place. His green eyes had deepened as though he was talking about something sacred. "Alexei's a violent man. He's a brutal man, Holly."

"Was. People change."

Caleb leaned against the counter, assessing her as though trying to figure out the best way to give her bad news. "No, they don't. They don't change. When the chips are down, he'll go right back to what he knows best because no one truly changes."

"Really? I know I did. I changed for the worse. At least Alexei changed for the better."

"What are you talking about?" It was the first time since she'd walked in the room that he hadn't sounded sure of himself.

She wished she hadn't opened the line of conversation, but now that she had, she was going to move forward with it. She and Caleb were going to hash this out, and they would either be friends or nothing at all. "I changed after my divorce. Although when I think about it, I suppose it was sometime during the actual marriage that I changed. I couldn't pinpoint the date. It wasn't one specific incident, just a whole bunch of small cuts and bruises on my soul."

His eyes hooded, and he went very still. "Inflicted by your husband?"

She laced her fingers together. Sometimes, even years and years later, the memories were fresh. "And his family. They didn't want Scott to marry me. Scott and I met in college. I was there on a scholarship. He was there because his father had built a wing of the school. It was a ritzy private school. I was the girl from the wrong side of the tracks, and Scott was going through a rebellious stage. We met my sophomore year, his senior. We moved in together pretty quickly. Scott went on to law school, and I dropped out to go with him. I was a stupid girl. I thought I was helping him. Anyway, before he graduated, I got pregnant with Micky, and we got married over his family's very vocal objections."

"What didn't they like about you?" The question had a nasty edge to it, but she didn't think it was pointed at her.

She could still hear her ex-mother-in-law's voice explaining all the things that were wrong with her. She was too fat. She was too stupid. She wasn't well-bred. And Maureen Lang hadn't merely told Holly that. Maureen liked to tell all of her friends, seeking sympathy for the horror of her oldest child's marital disaster. "Pretty much everything. I wasn't cultured enough. I wasn't polished. I wasn't a proper political wife. But Scott didn't want to go into politics at the time. He wanted to open a quiet practice. He was so happy when Micky was born."

"He changed his tune. He's a congressman, isn't he?"

Oh, he was also a rat-fink bastard, but he never let anyone forget that he was a congressman. "Yes. About a year after Micky was born, things started to change. Scott got tired of rebelling, and his father convinced him to move back into the family mansion and run for office. They never stopped putting me down, never let up for an instant. And I changed. I became the kind of woman who pretended her husband wasn't cheating. I became the kind of woman who stopped dreaming. I hated myself. I became the kind of woman who lost her child."

She blinked back tears, but moved on. "Micky was my life. I withered without him, and I don't think I've had a moment where I felt like that girl in college again. I want to. I want to feel like there's something out in the world for me, Caleb. I thought that might be you, but you don't want me that way. I don't know if Alexei is the man who pulls me out of this lonely place I've been in for years, but I'm ready to find out. I'm ready to take a chance. I'm ready to change. So don't tell me people can't change. I need to believe they can."

Caleb was silent for a moment, for so long she worried she'd offended him in some way. She was about to apologize for opening up, for exposing so much of herself to him, when he finally sighed and scrubbed a hand through his hair.

"When I get the test results, I'll call you." He turned back to his file. "Don't worry about it. I won't bug him again. And you can go."

Now she was *really* worried she'd offended him. He'd dismissed her utterly, his walls coming up in an instant when she'd hoped they might come down. A burst of anger threatened to explode. She felt her fists clench.

"Are you telling me you won't do the exam now? You won't even be my doctor?" She had to check the tears that threatened. She was sure her whole face had gone bright red. She'd never been able to control her emotions, one more flaw in Maureen's book.

His head came up, utter confusion sparking his face. "I didn't say that. I don't think you need it. Holly, I've run every test on your blood I could run. I did a workup on you when you had that cold a few months back."

"Yes, that seemed like overkill." She'd had the sniffles, and he'd insisted on blood work.

He took a deep breath and set the folder aside. "I'm thorough. I…I wanted to make sure you were okay. There's this old saying in the medical profession. When you hear horses, don't look for zebras. It's basically a way of telling doctors to accept that a cold is more than likely only a cold. The cold is the horse. Something rarer, like *Streptococcus pyogenes*, would be a zebra. But sometimes zebras can bite you in the ass. I was making sure your cold wasn't something more."

She felt her eyes go wide. "Wow, you're as crazy as the rest of us, aren't you?"

A suspicious shade of red stole across his handsome features. "I'm surprised it took you so long to notice."

"So I suppose I'm clean?" She'd been sure of that. One had to have sex to get a sexually transmitted disease. It had been a long, long time for her. But it seemed unfair that Alexei was the only one who had to get checked out.

"You're perfect." He swallowed again and turned back around.

And that was her cue to leave. So why couldn't she? What the hell was it about this man that called to her? And why did she keep trying? "Caleb, why are you so nice to me when you aren't interested in me physically?"

She needed to understand. She'd been out of the game so long—out of life so long, really—that she wanted to know how and why she'd misread him so terribly.

His eyes came up, and they were harder than before. "You think I don't want you? Not want you? How can you say I don't want you?"

Frustration threatened to boil over. And anger. She was getting angry, too. "Don't play with me. We've done this dance for almost a solid year, and I'm tired of it."

"You're tired of it?" The exam table was between them, and suddenly she was happy for it because Caleb looked predatory. "You're tired of it? I haven't had sex in a year because of you."

"Well, I certainly wasn't stopping you." Actually she'd sort of encouraged him.

His head cocked slightly to one side. She'd been around him long enough to know that slight movement of his head was a sign he was getting angry. "Oh, yes, you did. I couldn't think about sleeping with another woman because the fucking one I wanted was you. Is you."

"I don't understand. I've practically thrown myself at you. I asked you if you wanted to sleep with me. You said no." She'd asked him the first night he'd spent on her couch. Oh, she'd pretended it was about comfort, but she'd hoped that once he was in bed, he would turn to her. She'd wanted to hold him, to know him, to comfort him because he seemed to need it so desperately.

Those sensual lips she loved turned slightly cruel. "I told you I didn't want to sleep with you, and I meant it. I didn't say I wouldn't appreciate a fuck."

Well, that said it all. Tears blurring her eyes, she turned and started for the door. It was obvious he didn't want a friendship. He didn't want anything at all if he could talk to her like that. She wouldn't be treated like a whore again. Not by anyone.

A strong arm snaked around her waist, and she was hauled back against a perfectly hard body. Caleb's body. She could feel his breath against her neck.

"Don't go. Not like this."

The feel of his body against hers was bittersweet. She'd waited so long, and it was only when she was leaving that he thought to hold her. "Caleb, let me go. I'll leave you alone. I promise. I never meant to bother you."

The words tumbled out of his mouth like a waterfall that had been dammed up and finally, finally set free. "And I never meant to hurt you, baby. God, I never meant to hurt you. It's the last thing I want to do. I want you so badly, but I can't get into a relationship. I'm not cut out for it. I would hurt you in the end. Can you understand that?"

Not really, but she had to accept it. "Sure."

He groaned. "Holly, you're the first woman I've wanted since my wife died."

"You expect me to believe you haven't had sex in six years?"

"No. I was like Alexei. Not hookers exactly, but women who didn't expect emotion from me. I couldn't do that to you. You're not like that, so I've kept my hands to myself because I couldn't offer you anything but sex."

But his hands weren't to himself now. They were restless on her skin. The heat of his body was seeping into her own. "I can't believe that of you. You're not unfeeling."

"Maybe." His head rested against her shoulder. He didn't seem willing to let go now that he'd finally touched her. "But I'm unwilling to really try. I'm sorry. I wish I could be the man you need. I wish I could beg you not to go out with that Russian bastard, to pick me, but that would be unfair."

And she wasn't sure she could do it. Now that Alexei was back, she was nervous about seeing him, but she was pretty sure she would regret it the rest of her life if she didn't try with him. And yet the thought that this was the end with Caleb tore her heart up. How had she fallen for two men?

Stupid question. She'd fallen for two men because she'd thought she might be able to have it all. Like Rachel and Callie and Laura. But no. She would have to choose, and either way she went, she would ache with it for the rest of her life. And, in the end, there was no real choice at all because Caleb wouldn't try.

He turned her around, and she could see the agony in his eyes. She'd put that look there. She couldn't stand the fact that he'd blown his precious control for her. He needed his control. She could see that now. "Caleb, I'll be fine. Please. Don't worry about me."

"I think about you every minute of the day and twice as much when the sun goes down." His words were tortured, and his mouth lowered to hers. His lips were briefly hesitant, and then he took over. His hands came up to clutch her shoulders and haul her close. His mouth closed over hers, his tongue teasing at the edges of her lips. She opened for him, and Caleb invaded.

He was everywhere. His tongue played against hers. One hand found her hair, and the bite of his fingers wrapping around her ponytail electrified her skin. He pulled on it, forcing her head into the position he wanted, giving his tongue full access. His other hand skimmed from her shoulder to her waist, the edge of his thumb touching the outer curve of her breast. She wanted it on her nipple, plucking and teasing before his mouth moved down to suckle.

She gave herself over to the kiss, loving the rough feel of his cheek against hers. Caleb seemed to have a perpetual five-o'clock shadow. It was bristly and masculine and made her feel soft and delicate. She sank her hands into his hair. It was so much shorter than Alexei's but just as soft.

Alexei.

She had a date with Alexei, and she was kissing Caleb.

The phone rang as panic hit. Caleb pulled her closer, bringing her into the cradle of his thighs, rubbing his cock against her. He pressed their hips together, proving beyond a shadow of a doubt that he wanted her. She could feel him pulling her in, bringing them closer with the touch of his skin against hers.

She was falling back in, forgetting everything but the feel of him when the phone rang again. The real world was intruding, reminding her of what he'd said before. He didn't really want this. She forced her hands up to push him away.

"Caleb. Caleb, your phone is ringing."

His hands tightened. "Let it ring."

"What if it's an emergency? What if Callie's gone into labor?" He was the only doctor for miles. He couldn't ignore a call, even though her pussy was begging her to rethink her position.

Caleb cursed and dropped his hands. Frustration settled over him. "Damn it. I am not a fucking obstetrician." He took a long, deep breath and then turned away. He grabbed the phone. "What?"

He had the worst bedside manner, and he definitely needed a receptionist. She straightened her T-shirt and wondered how long it would be before she forgot how it felt to be held by him. Should she tell Alexei what had happened? What the hell was she doing?

"It's for you," Caleb said gruffly, shoving the phone toward her. "Apparently Rachel Harper saw you walking in here and told Stella where you are. You should have come in the back way."

She took the phone. "Sorry. One of these days I'll be able to afford a damn cell phone. Not that it would work here. Hello?"

After three minutes and one convoluted story involving a botched gnocchi experiment and a raccoon on the loose in the kitchen, Stella finally got around to explaining that Holly needed to pick up some supplies in Alamosa.

"Sure thing," she said, eager to get off the phone. She hung up and then cursed. "I don't have a car."

"What's wrong? Did it break down again?" Caleb stood as far away from her as he could. Only the wall behind his back seemed to keep him in the room with her.

"I loaned it to Alexei." Alexei, who was out trying to find a job so he could take her someplace nice.

Caleb's hand went into the pocket of his pants. She couldn't miss the fact that he hadn't calmed down. His cock was pressed against the material of his jeans, an obvious and very large monster. He pulled his keys out and tossed them to her. "Take mine."

She caught the keys to his truck. "Are you sure? I'm actually not the best driver in the world."

His hands came up, fingers splayed. "Take the truck. What happened was a mistake, but I don't want us to fight. The last thing in the world I want is for the two of us to not talk."

"You rarely talk."

The right side of his mouth crinkled up in a lopsided, totally gorgeous grin. "Fine, I don't want to not listen to you." His face fell, and she would have done anything to put that grin back. "And I won't stand between you and Alexei. I hope, for your sake, that he really has changed. And don't let the hooker thing scare you. If you think about it, it really is kinder. He wasn't ready for a relationship. His life was violent and unpredictable. It was better to pay for what he needed than to drag someone into it. Especially someone he didn't love."

"So we're friends?" She would take that. It would hurt, but she would be his friend.

He nodded. "Friends. And I'll get the tests back. I think Wolf is going into Alamosa. I'll hop a ride with him. He'll love driving another man's biological samples around."

"It's a little blood. Somehow I think an ex-Navy SEAL can handle some blood."

"And urine. And, well, let's just say I was very thorough. We'll know everything about that man's bodily functions ASAP. Oh, and I took a hair sample to test for marijuana use."

She couldn't help but smile. "Somehow I doubt Alexei has been toking up."

"I can only imagine what he'd call it." That lopsided smile was back, and Holly couldn't help it. She walked into his arms and hugged him.

"Thank you, Caleb."

It took a moment for his arms to close around her, but they finally did. "If you ever need me to find a medical way to torture him, please let me know."

She nodded. "I promise. And I'll bring your truck back."

She walked out of the office with tears blurring her eyes. Her head was down as she walked out the door, and she almost ran into a man.

"Sorry," she muttered as she sidestepped the man.

"No problem," the man mumbled, and looked away, walking down the sidewalk with a quick cadence.

Great. Now she was offending tourists. With a long sigh, she trudged across the parking lot to Caleb's black truck. It was a huge monster, and she had to haul herself into the cab and adjust the seat as far as it would go forward.

The long drive toward Alamosa loomed. She turned east onto 160 and started the drive. Caleb's radio was tuned to a sports channel. She flicked it off because she had enough voices in her head.

She was a mass of confusion. Excitement at the prospect of being with Alexei. Disappointment that Caleb wouldn't be with them. That was what she'd wanted deep down. She forced herself to acknowledge the fact. She'd dreamed of finding what the others had found, of being the center of a happy threesome. She'd fantasized about being between Caleb and Alexei, their big bodies surrounding and protecting her, their hearts loving her and accepting her love back.

She'd bottled it up for so long. She'd shut her heart away because no one seemed to want it. Talking to Caleb had reopened some wounds she'd hoped had long since healed, but then maybe she would never heal from the way her first husband had treated her.

First? Scott would probably be her only husband. She was forty years old, the oldest of all her friends, and the only one unattached. Perhaps that part of her life had passed her by, and all she could hope for was a brief, hot affair with a younger man. There weren't many prospects in Bliss. It was too small a town, and she worked enough that she didn't leave Bliss often. And she wouldn't trade the town or her friends for anything in the world.

She simply wished there was something more for her.

She sniffled and tried to get herself together. Feeling sorry for herself wasn't going to fix a damn thing. She had a date. Just because things hadn't worked out with Caleb didn't mean she couldn't enjoy Alexei. She needed to guard her heart though.

And she needed to slow down. She glanced down at the speedometer as she started down one of the steeper hills. Her speed was picking up way too fast. She was used to her old car with its engine that never seemed quite ready to pick up speed. Even when going downhill, it still sputtered and shook like it didn't want to put forth the effort. Not so with Caleb's shiny new four-wheel-drive truck. It was perfectly happy to allow gravity to increase its forward momentum. It hit eighty with no trouble at all, and the needle kept rising.

Holly put a foot down on the brake. She'd lived in the mountains long enough to know not to shove her foot to the floor or the brakes could overheat. She also knew not to ride them, keeping her foot on the brake over a long period of time, though instinct always told her to do so. A strategic application of pressure would drop her speed and then she would allow it to build back up.

Nothing. They didn't respond at all. Now she was up to ninety and a curve was coming up. She took a deep breath as she passed Mel's cabin at a breakneck speed.

She tried again. Maybe the truck worked a bit differently than her car, and it required more pressure.

Her foot went all the way to the floor, the pedal flopping back with all the strength of an overcooked noodle.

Panic started to set in. The Harper Ranch came and went. The speedometer kept climbing. How fast could the truck go?

She tried again, though she realized there was nothing she could do. The brakes were gone.

Forcing herself to stay calm, she thought about the road. Two more turns and she would be off the mountain and into the valley, where the road was flat and she could see for miles. She could figure out something to do then.

Or she could put the car in a lower gear now. It risked ruining the engine, but it might slow the truck down so she could take the curves.

But it was Caleb's truck. And Caleb would rather have her safe than have his truck. He might not be willing to risk a relationship with her, but she wasn't so foolish that she believed he cared about his truck more than her life.

She would have to find a way to make it up to him.

Wincing at what she was about to do, she forced the gear shift into the slot labeled 1. The whole truck shook, and it took everything she had to control it. The S curve was coming up. She couldn't possibly manage it at almost a hundred miles an hour. No way. She would go right off the road, and there was no guardrail. She would either hit the side of the mountain or she would roll off it.

Finally the truck started to slow, but only to seventy. Gravity was still at work. She had no idea what the incline was this low on the mountain, but it was still steep. And she couldn't see around the curve.

Her heart drummed inside her chest. Her brain played through a million scenarios. She could die right here on the mountain, and she would regret so fucking much. She would regret not trying. She would regret all the years she let slip by because it was easier than fighting and losing. As the curve barreled toward her, all she knew was that nothing, nothing was more important than the fight. The outcome didn't matter. She could lose everything, and it would have been worth it to fight for what she needed.

Why did she only figure that out when death was staring her down?

And why the fuck was she giving up again?

The emergency brake. It was a long shot. She would probably still lose control, but it was all she had.

She pushed the brake in. Exactly like its sister, it went straight to the floor.

And then she saw the sign for the TER. Truck escape ramp. She tightened her hands on the steering wheel. She had to hold on. The TER had only been in place for a few months, and it was meant to slow down eighteen-wheelers that were out of control, but maybe it would work for her, too. The long offshoot of gravel would surely slow her down some. It had to.

At least it gave her a place to go before she hit that curve.

She hit the TER going almost eighty. Between the thick gravel and the level ground of the ramp, she immediately felt the truck begin to ease down.

By the time she'd reached half the distance of the TER, she'd slowed the truck to the point that she was sure she would survive. She rolled gently along until she hit the rail with a thud.

She put her head in her hands and finally cried, happy to be alive and to have another shot at almost everything.

* * * *

Alexei took the only seat available in the small office off the garage. The whole place smelled of motor oil, but that didn't bother him. He liked the cozy work space. But the chair needed some work. It hadn't been made for a large man. He wiggled, testing the sturdiness. It didn't feel like it would fall apart. He hoped not. It wouldn't do him a ton of good to break office furniture during his interview.

Roger, who was indeed bald, had pictures of himself and his wife, Liz Two, that showed off his formerly long, flowing hair. He took the seat behind the desk. "So you're that fellow who nearly blew up Bliss?"

His reputation was not exactly sterling. And thanks to the news reports, everyone knew his story. "Oh, no, no blowing up. I did not set single charge while in Bliss. I merely shoot many peoples."

Long-Haired Roger's eyes went wide, and he leaned forward. "Many?"

And he wasn't helping his reputation along at all. "Well, not too many. Four or five, perhaps. And all of them were very bad peoples. They took over sheriff's department and were going to kill women. I could not allow them to kill women."

In all his time in the mob, he'd never hurt a woman. He'd never struck one in anger or in anything but an erotic fashion. He'd met several women who enjoyed spanking, and he liked it, too, but he'd never treated a single woman with any less respect than he would demand for himself. It had hurt him in his rise in the organization, but there had been things even he could not do for revenge. In the end, his inability to harm a woman had cost him his revenge and helped him regain his soul.

"I'd heard that you saved a bunch of women. And Logan Green, too, though I doubt he thanks you for it."

The deputy was one of the men he owed in this town. Logan Green had taken a beating that almost killed him, and Alexei had been forced to allow it in order to save them all. He'd been outnumbered and outgunned and he'd hated it, but he would sacrifice the young man again if it meant saving Holly and Jennifer. He was going to have to find a way to deal with Logan if he was going to live in this town.

"I am sorry for what happen to deputy. I could not help him without giving myself away, and then we would all be dead." It was a lame excuse. Sometimes at night he came up with a hundred scenarios in which he spared Logan Green from his fate, but at the time he'd gone with the safest course of action.

"That would have been much worse. I don't know what poor Teeny would do without her boy. She and Marie dote on him. He'll be fine. He's got two mommas to look after him. You know, everyone in these parts talked about how you let yourself get all shot up to save Holly. Holly's a sweet girl, and she's the best waitress in the county. The sheriff speaks highly of you, too," Long-Haired Roger said. "I like Nate Wright, even though he's a cranky son of a bitch. He says you saved Callie and Jen, so you're all right with me."

He tried to relax. Maybe this would go better than he'd expected. He was surprised to find himself nervous. He hadn't been thinking about finding a legitimate job all those years before when he'd thrown away the majority of his youth to pursue revenge. Now he had to pay for all the years he should have been in college or starting a career. He had to find a way to make a living in the legitimate world.

"Gene tell me you are looking for good worker." Perhaps once he got settled in, he would find some training school and learn a trade that went beyond racketeering and assassinations.

Long-Haired Roger's bald head nodded. "Yep. I need a new mechanic because my last guy ran off to join the pro-wrestling circuit. I don't think that's going to work out for him, but he wouldn't listen to me. You don't happen to watch wrestling, do you?"

Roger asked the question with a serious look on his face, as though the answer to the question would affect Alexei's ability to be hired. He decided to go with honesty. "No."

He preferred hockey. One day he would sit in his own home with a big-screen television and watch hockey games with his friends. And Holly. Hopefully she liked hockey because he didn't think he would allow her out of his lap once he had her there.

Long-Haired Roger sat back, seemingly satisfied with his answer. "Good. Because I don't need to lose another mechanic to that. Now, do you have experience with cars?"

His brother had taught him much about cars. Mikhail had been forced to learn how to fix his car because they couldn't afford a mechanic. His brother had been armed with only a how-to book and their father's tool kit. After Mikhail had been killed, Alexei had found working on cars to be soothing.

"I am self-taught, but I know what I am doing," Alexei explained. "I will take whatever test you like."

"Do you know about brakes?"

He spoke without thinking, the words rolling from his mouth. He'd spent so many years hiding his true feelings that now he often said far too much. "Oh, yes. I have worked with many brake systems. I know how to cut brake lines of many different types of vehicles. And I was forced to learn how to blow up many mobsters' vehicles. I always studied the different models to know where to place bomb."

Long-Haired Roger's eyes got really wide, and he sat back up straight again. "What?"

Alexei pushed on. He wasn't going to hide his past. Honesty was what worked in America. "It is very important to know how to blow up car and only take out intended target. I was best in Russia. Ten cars blown and not a single innocent victim."

"You blew up cars without anyone in them?"

Alexei shook his head. "*Nyet*. No innocent victims. I did, however, manage to take out some of worst criminals in Russia. Luckily they had pissed off my boss, and that gave me shot at taking them out. They were drug pushers and slave traders. There are many slave traders in Europe and Asia. They look to sell womens to brothels. These womens do not want to go to brothels."

"I can see why not. That sounds like something out of television. And you blew up these fellows' vehicles?"

"Yes, it is best way to take out a person if you do not wish to shoot them. Shooting can get messy, and sometimes people need a bigger demonstration to make them believe you will do what it takes. An exploding car will get many people's attention. But I am careful and always use a device I can control because I do not want the ignition to be turned by innocent person and then they get killed. Only bad person. My partner make fun of me for spending many nights hiding in bushes waiting for my target, but I say it is better to have bad back than bad soul."

Long-Haired Roger's fingers drummed nervously on his desk. "Uhm, I can see you were a very thoughtful assassin. What does your partner think about you now that you've come to the States?"

Ivan had always thought Alexei was an idiot, but then Ivan had been a hard-boiled killer. Ivan had never been his friend. "He does not think at all. He was one of the peoples I killed to save womens of Bliss."

"Okay, then." Long-Haired Roger's face took on a pained expression. "I think you might be overqualified for this job. I really think you should look for something bigger."

Alexei sat forward. "Oh, no. I like small business. I work very hard."

"I...I just don't think you have quite the level of experience I was looking for. Sorry. I really hope you don't blow up my car."

Alexei left with a heavy heart and the sad knowledge that his job hunt was not going to go well.

Chapter Five

Caleb winced as the phone rang, wondering why the landlines couldn't be as crappy as cell service was here in Bliss. The phone kept ringing. Why wasn't a man allowed to drown in his misery in relative peace and quiet?

"And why do I have to be the only doctor?" Caleb asked the only other living thing in the building. Yep. He was now talking to a plant. That was how pathetic his life had become. He was talking to an ivy instead of laying Holly out on his exam table and proving how thorough he could be.

He could still feel that soft, curvy body pressed against his. He could feel the roundness of her breasts crushed to his chest. If he'd had more time, he would have been able to get his hands on them. He would have eased her on to the exam table and pushed her clothes off. The table was a nice height. He could have spread her legs and finally gotten a taste of her pussy. Sweet. She would be sweet with a hint of tangy bite to her cream. That was his Holly. Sweet with enough sass to make it all interesting. He would eat that pussy. How long had it been since he'd enjoyed a woman that way? And he wanted Holly. He wanted her so bad his cock was in a constant state of need.

When he'd eaten his fill, when she'd come all over his tongue, he'd take her. He'd spread her legs and let his cock have its way. He'd fuck her until he didn't have an ounce left in his body. Then and only then would he be satisfied. And not for long.

The phone started up again, an annoying insect that wouldn't let up. It was going to keep ringing. With a growl of frustration, he picked up. "Bliss County Clinic. Who's dying?"

"Caleb?"

He froze at the sound of his brother's voice. "Eli?"

"It's good to talk to you, brother."

He closed his eyes and forced himself not to hang up the phone. He hadn't hidden his location from his family. He'd merely assumed Eli would know he didn't want to talk to him. "What do you need, Eli?"

He could practically hear his brother's frown. He would be tense, his brows coming together. The older he got, the more Eli looked like their father. Damn, sometimes he missed his father with an ache that seemed endless. And sometimes he was happy his father had died before he could see what had become of his middle son.

"Do I have to need something to want to talk to my brother?" Eli asked.

"You know damn well we have nothing to say to each other."

"You have to forgive me at some point. You have to talk to me at some point. I know I fucked up, but I don't want to lose my brother, too."

Then maybe Eli shouldn't have slept with his wife. He held the words in. Arguing with Eli wouldn't do a lick of good. "I'm still alive. Don't be such a drama queen. I've been gone for over a year and you haven't needed to talk to me. You know you were the one who asked me to leave."

Eli's voice softened. "And you sound more animated than I've heard you in years. I would push you out a thousand times if I thought it would save you from the dark hole you fell down."

His hand tightened around the phone. "It wasn't a hole. I was kidnapped. Tortured. I'm sorry that inconvenienced you."

"Damn it. That is always your answer. You think I don't know what happened to you? I've read every report. I had to read the reports because you wouldn't talk to me. You wouldn't see a counselor. You wouldn't try antidepressants. You wouldn't do anything except slowly waste away. I couldn't handle it. I love you, brother. Whatever our differences are, I love you. I had to try something. I was lucky your friend had a place for you to go. Tell me you don't like it there, and I'll come pick you up myself."

Yes, Senator Elijah Sommerville would fuel the jet and have a limo meet him at whatever airport he landed in. Eli was good at using his position. A wave of guilt assaulted him. It had been Eli who had the power to send a SEAL team in after him. If it hadn't been for Eli, he likely would have died in that tiny closet. "I don't want to leave Bliss."

Eli sighed. "I know. You like it there. I've talked to Lieutenant Meyer."

That was news to him. "Since when do you talk to Wolf?"

"Don't get mad. All he's told me is that you're settling in and you're working. I was glad to hear that you're working again. I told you it would help."

"What do you want?" He didn't want to sit here and talk about his life with his brother. There was too much between them. Eli was from a different time. Eli was from "before." Everything was "before" or "after" Africa. It was the way he divided his life.

"Fine. I was calling to see if you would come home for Thanksgiving."

And be reminded of all the ways he'd failed his family? No. "I have patients here. I can't leave."

There was a long sigh. "All right. It's still a couple of months away. We would love to see you. If you change your mind, you know the way home."

Eli hung up. Caleb wouldn't go home for the holidays. He would spend them alone. He would try to ignore the whole season. Colorado winters were different from winters in Chicago. Chicago winters were brutal, but there was a softness to the season in Colorado. A beauty that didn't exist outside the mountains. And Holly always looked adorable bundled up in a parka.

"Are you going to stop talking to me?"

Caleb looked up and saw Wolf's massive form taking up all the space of his doorway. The big cowboy stood there staring at him. He wore his typical uniform of dark-washed jeans and a T-shirt. His boots were worn, but the hat was new. It was still odd to see Wolf out of uniform. "Why wouldn't I talk to you? Oh. You heard me talking to Eli. I don't care if you tell my brother I'm alive. It's fine. If you didn't, he would probably bug me more."

Wolf walked in, his eyes going immediately to the plant. "He wants to know you're okay. He worries about you. Did you make a friend?"

Caleb took a long breath as he zipped up his bag. "It was a present from Nell. She's trying to liven up the clinic. Or she's planning on using it to kill me. I don't know which."

"Interesting." Wolf turned his keys in his hand. "So, why exactly do you need a ride? Something wrong with your truck?"

"I loaned it to Holly. There was a diner emergency." He closed his files and shoved them into the proper folders. He grabbed his keys and led Wolf out the door, locking it behind him.

"Oh, did that matchbox of hers finally give up the ghost?" Wolf asked.

"No. She loaned her car to Alexei. I need to run Alexei's blood work and all the other samples in to the hospital for testing. If I'm lucky, he picked up your mom's Ebola." That was a pleasant thought. The thought of Alexei's organs liquefying before his inevitable, painful death put Caleb in a much better mood.

Wolf's lips pursed. "So Alexei has Holly's car and you gave her yours. Very interesting."

"No, it's not." He took the steps quickly, eager to get out to the hospital and get back. He had rounds this afternoon.

"Yes, it is interesting. The man is only in town for a day, and you've already been pulled into a three-way."

Caleb rolled his eyes and prayed for patience. He hoped that rumor wasn't going around. Bliss ran on gossip, and the citizens lived to get in each other's business. "It's not a three-way. It's a friend helping out another friend who happens to have horrible taste in men. I didn't advise Holly to let Alexei borrow her car. Now are you going to help me out? I promised Holly I would get these in today."

Wolf opened the driver's side door and got in. "Hey, I got nothing better to do, and now it's a four-way. Awesome."

Wolf's sarcasm was one of his flaws. Caleb let it go as he buckled his seatbelt. "Thanks, man. It shouldn't take too long. I already talked to the lab. They're waiting on me. Are you sure James can spare you?"

Wolf had been working with his childhood friend, James Glen, at his huge spread. James had inherited the ranch and herd from his father, but Caleb had heard he was struggling. Wolf couldn't have come home at a better time.

"James is getting to know his new partner. An ex-football player from Texas bought into the Circle G. The paperwork is all done now, and he got into town a while back. He has a wife and brought a friend with him, too. He seems nice enough. Big son of a bitch. James wasn't thrilled about taking on a partner, but taxes nearly killed him. Trev McNamara's his name. He bought in for something like ten million. And it works out for me. I have to go to Texas." He said it with a grimace. There was only one thing in Texas that would make Wolf frown like that.

"You're going to see your brother." Wolf loved his brother, but apparently Leo Meyer made Wolf crazy.

Wolf turned the truck onto the street toward the highway and the mountain road that led out of Bliss. "I'm going to see a man about a job in a club. Unfortunately, it happens to be the same club that my brother works at. If I had a lick of sense, I would find something else to do, but I was never known for my smarts."

Caleb couldn't help but chuckle. "You're finally going to do it, then? You're going to work as a professional Dom? Spanking girls for a living?"

Wolf's massive shoulders moved up and down in a negligent motion. "Well, I shot people for a living, and they won't let me do that now. My request to be reinstated was denied. Apparently a SEAL has to be able to make it past a metal detector, and the rod in my leg makes me an automatic pat down. James doesn't need me anymore. I don't think Mom and Mel need me hanging out at their place. Dear god, *I* don't need that."

"James doesn't need another hand?"

"Well, James's new partner is bringing a built-in hand with him. Some cowboy with a lot of experience. Apparently his brother runs a big spread in Texas. Julian, the man who owns the club I'll be working at, knows him. I'm the one who introduced James to Julian. I got rid of my own damn job."

Wolf hadn't planned on punching cattle for the rest of his life. At least he'd never told Caleb he'd planned it. "Why isn't this cowboy back on his brother's ranch?"

Wolf groaned. "Why would you think? Because he's this Trev guy's partner. They share a wife."

Caleb couldn't help but laugh. "I swear this place is a magnet. We're crazy threesome central."

Wolf shrugged. "There's always room for one more. I think Holly wouldn't mind."

He felt his mood sink. "It's not going to happen."

Wolf turned and started the climb up the mountain. Delicate aspens and stout evergreens were thick along the road. "I don't see why not. Look, I get that you don't want to be in a relationship alone with her. You think she couldn't handle your problems. You don't want to start a relationship with her when you can't move in with her or have a normal life."

At least someone got it. "It wouldn't be fair to her. She should have a man who can be with her all night. Who doesn't fuck her and get up and walk out, or worse, who gets up and goes to sleep in her closet."

"But what if she had someone in bed with her? What if she had someone who could be there at night? Relationships here in Bliss are serious, but the people are a bit more open-minded. You want Holly to get what she needs. You think she doesn't want the same thing for you?"

The idea played at the edge of his brain. It had been playing there ever since Alexei had planted it. But the Russian hadn't really meant it. He couldn't have. He'd said something about Holly being more woman than any one man could handle, but that didn't mean anything. "I think Alexei might have something to say about sharing."

Alexei would never go for it. And he shouldn't. But what if he did? What if Alexei could be the normal, happy boyfriend? What did that make Caleb? The guy who showed up for sex? What good would he be?

And what the hell had poor Holly done that the normal, happy boyfriend was a former Russian mobster?

"I think Alexei might be more open-minded than you think." Wolf handled the turns and curves of the mountain road with the ease of a native.

Caleb shook his head. "I wouldn't be doing it for anything other than sex."

He couldn't allow himself to want more. He wasn't cut out for it. He had too much rage. He was far too damaged.

"Holly needs to feel wanted," Wolf pointed out. "Holly needs to feel like a goddess. I know how to read women. She's been alone for a long time. She's not confident in herself."

"She's beautiful. How can she not know that?" He dreamed about her. Her curves, the sunset color of her hair, the soft silk of her skin. She was the most gorgeous thing he'd ever seen, and it went far past her killer body. When she smiled, she lit up like a lamp that had been turned on and illuminated a previously dark room.

"Because too many people told her she wasn't. She's divorced, right? I bet the guy was an ass."

Caleb would like to get his hands on Congressman Scott Lang. Maybe he should look into the asshole, see if he could fuck up his life a bit. He bet Alexei would be good at that. Alexei would know all the tricks. "He's a politician. Asshole doesn't begin to cover it."

Wolf snorted. "No wonder you haven't told her who you are. I'm sure she doesn't want to get involved with another political family. Look, she's been crazy about you for a while. It's all over her face. She wants Alexei, too. Choosing between the two of you is going to hurt her."

"I didn't offer her a choice." But he had put his hands all over her. He'd held her and kissed her, and now he wondered if he could go the rest of his life without touching her again. "Besides, I can't stand Alexei."

Wolf turned to him, his dark eyes serious. "So you're never going to tell the woman you love how you feel? Man, they won, didn't they? You won't fight for her. You won't share her. You never really got out of the jungle, Caleb. I didn't save you, did I? Your body might have walked out, but the essential part of you is still there. Can't you see that?"

The jungle? Hell, he'd never truly gotten out of the box they'd put him in. He was still there. He moved through his life, but his soul had been killed and buried in the box that had served as his prison. His body moved on, treating his existence as a living purgatory where the things that could open him up were always out of reach because he couldn't get out of that fucking box.

"I can't tell her I love her." He turned his eyes back to the road.

Wolf's voice got low, cajoling. "But you can show her. You can give her the fantasy she's never had. You can make her feel like she's never felt before. How many women get two men utterly devoted to her sexual pleasure? Make her feel like a goddess. Give her back the confidence that was taken from her."

Tempting. So tempting. He could show her how he felt with his hands and his mouth and his cock. He could prove to her how desirable she was. "I don't like Alexei. He's a criminal."

"Former criminal," Wolf corrected.

"Once a criminal, always a criminal."

"He saved Holly. Doesn't he deserve a second chance? He's trying to change the course of his life. I think he deserves some slack. Have you read the transcripts of the trials he testified in? Have you read the workup the justice department did on him? He might have done some bad shit, but it was all to other criminals, and a lot of it was in self-defense."

"He wrote to me." It was the first time Caleb had admitted it. "While he was in witness protection, he wrote to me."

"Really? What did he say?"

"He talked about stuff. His life before his brother was killed. Stuff like that. I glanced through them." It was a lie. He'd read them all. He'd been curious about the first one. It had been an earnest letter that asked for forgiveness and thanked Caleb for saving his life. Caleb wasn't a forgiving man. The rest of the letters had talked about everything from his motel rooms to the television shows he watched to his relationship with his brother. So why hadn't Caleb trashed them? They were still sitting in his desk drawer in a neat stack.

Why hadn't he gotten rid of them?

Wolf sighed. "I don't think it's going to do you any good to stay here and watch Holly settle down with another man. Why don't you think about coming to Dallas with me? There would be any number of places to work in Dallas. And then maybe I wouldn't need to room with my zentastic brother."

And leave Holly? Never see Holly again? And Bliss? He couldn't imagine living anywhere but Bliss. Sure, he complained. A lot. It was his thing. He bitched, but he loved the town. He loved the mountains and the snow. He loved the summers in high country. He'd been to a lot of the world's great places, and not a one of them held a candle to Bliss. He could remember the moment he'd turned off the highway and he'd seen the valley for the first time. He'd stopped the truck because it was so serene and beautiful. The sun had been going down and the whole world had been gauzy and slightly unreal, like someone had painted it. He'd thought this might be a place where he could find some peace—and he had.

"I can't leave. This place needs a doctor."

Wolf slid him a long look. "You're not going to give an inch, are you?"

"What's that up ahead? Is that a person?" He was grateful for the distraction. Someone was walking up the road. It was a dangerous thing to do. The mountain road had curves, and sometimes people drove far too fast. It was a bad idea to walk along the road. The woman, he was sure it was a woman now, trudged up the road, clutching her purse against her side. She needed a stern talking-to. He thought about calling Nate on Wolf's radio.

"Is that Holly?" Wolf's head craned forward.

"Stop the truck." He was definitely having an infarction. His torso felt too tight. His breath sawed in and out of his chest. That was Holly. Her hair had come out of its ponytail, and her skin was pale.

The truck stopped, and Caleb threw the door open. His boots hit the pavement, and he ran.

"Caleb?" Holly stopped and put a hand over her eyes as though trying to figure out who was coming toward her.

He didn't bother to answer. He simply got to her as fast as he could. "What happened?"

Her gorgeous green eyes went wide. It took everything he had not to take her in his arms. "Caleb, I am so sorry."

"The truck?" He reached out and took her hand, turning it over, checking her.

Tears filled her eyes. "Something was wrong with the brakes. I had to use the truck escape ramp. Oh, Caleb, I probably ruined your transmission. I had to shove it into a low gear when the speed got to almost a hundred. I am so sorry."

The brakes had gone out? On this road? He'd recently had that truck serviced. How the hell had they missed that? He didn't stop his instinct now. He pulled her close, crushing her against him. "Are you all right?"

"Sort of."

He heard her sniffle, and then she softened against him. He held her while she cried. No. He couldn't leave Bliss. But he was starting to think he couldn't let her go, either.

Chapter Six

Alexei stared down at the beer in front of him. It was almost empty. Pretty much like his job prospects. Who the hell would want to hire a man who'd spent the majority of his adult life in the mob? He had exactly twenty thousand dollars in an American account. It wouldn't last long. Caleb hated him. He didn't have a job. Had he made a terrible mistake in coming back to Bliss? The last thing he wanted was to end up on Holly's couch with her supporting his lazy ass.

He looked around the small tavern. People were starting to drift in. His marshals were sitting in a booth across from his seat at the bar. They hadn't tried to talk to him, merely nodded his way, though Jessie's eyes strayed to him every now and then. He almost felt uncomfortable under her stare. He hoped they would give up soon and leave.

The door to the tavern opened and a large figure stood there, blocking out the late-evening sun. He wore a khaki uniform and had a Stetson on his head.

"You doing all right, Zane?" Deputy Logan Green asked, his eyes going straight to Alexei.

Logan had changed. Alexei felt his gut turn at the metamorphosis the deputy had undergone. Gone was the lanky, funny kid, and in his place was a big, dangerous man. Logan had filled out, his boyish body gone in favor of broad muscles and a chiseled look. But what disturbed him far more than the change in the deputy's physique was the look in his eyes. Logan had reached out to Alexei even though he was in jail at the time. Logan had been funny and kind. There was no kindness in his eyes now.

"Sure. Why wouldn't I be? It's not even the dinner rush yet." Zane rubbed down glasses, making sure they were perfectly clean. "Lucy and I have everything covered."

Lucy was a sweet-looking brunette with big, sad eyes and a petite frame. Her whole face changed when she smiled. From what Alexei had managed to hear, she was fairly new, brought in to replace Callie. Lucy walked by, giving Logan a wave, which he ignored in favor of giving Alexei an intimidating stare.

"Well, we have some unsavory elements in town right now." Logan stalked close to the bar leaving no mistake who he was talking about.

"Deputy Green, I am not here to cause troubles." Of all the people he'd hurt, Logan was the one he'd worried about the most. Caleb had been damaged long before Alexei had come into town, but Logan was his responsibility. "I am so sorry about what happened to you."

The deputy's eyes flared briefly, revealing the pain that hadn't gone away, but he shut it down, his face going blank. "I'm not here to ask for apologies, Markov. I'm here to make sure you didn't happen to bring any friends along with you. Your friends like to tear up my town."

Zane set down the glass he'd been cleaning. "Stand down, Logan. You didn't come in here to give Alexei a talk. I happen to know that Nate told you to stay away from him. You came in here for a drink, and I won't serve you while you're wearing that uniform. Do I need to call your boss?"

Logan's lips curled up in a grin that didn't even begin to hold an ounce of humor. "No need. I'm off the clock. Having Briggs around has freed me up. And I won't bother to drink here anymore. I'm afraid I don't like your clientele, Hollister."

The deputy turned and walked out the door.

Alexei's heart sank. One more crappy thing in a crappy day. Was he doing more harm than good?

"Something troubling you?"

He looked up at Zane Hollister, who put another mug of beer in front of him. "Many things be troubling me."

Zane Hollister was a big man with a face full of scars. Alexei felt comfortable with him. Probably more comfortable than he did with anyone else. Zane had seen the dark side of life, and he'd still found a way to build a happy marriage. His wife, Callie, was due to have their first child any day now.

"Don't let Logan get to you too much. He's pretty much like that with everyone these days. He won't listen to anyone, and trust me, we've all tried to talk to him. He prefers to listen to Jack Daniel's now. If he can't find it here, he'll go down the mountain to a bar there. I hate the fact that he's going to go to Hell on Wheels, but I can't have him causing trouble in here. We're a family tavern."

Alexei glanced around the space. Trio was a cozy bar and restaurant. There were big windows that looked out over Main Street. Alexei could see people walking by. He wondered if he would ever be a part of this place or if he should pack it in. Caleb didn't want him here. Logan Green definitely wanted him gone. Holly was working at Stella's next door. In thirty minutes she would be off, and he would have to find a way to tell her he didn't have a job and there weren't a lot of prospects for one.

"Jobs are hard to come by here." Alexei had to come to grips with that truth.

"Yes," Zane agreed. "It's a small community. Where did you try?"

"Long-Haired Roger."

Zane snorted and wiped down the bar. "The bald guy? You don't want to work there. Once a year, he and Polly of Cut and Curl fame get into a knock-down drag-out over the neon lips she flashes twenty-four-seven. It can get ugly. Liz Two sides with her husband, but Liz One is a beautician and the things she can do with hairspray will curdle your blood. No. It's best you stay out of that. You could probably get on at the ski resort, but that's seasonal. And you would more than likely have to live up there. I don't suppose you want to live on the mountain on the other side of town for five months out of the year?"

That would defeat the purpose of being in Bliss. He'd come here to be in Holly's bed every night, to form his handpicked family. "No. But I need job."

"Well, I'll ask around. You never know what might come up."

His cock. His cock was coming up because the door opened again, and Holly walked inside. She was stunning. She'd changed out of her uniform and wore a form-fitting black dress with a V-neck that should have been outlawed. Her breasts swelled, the tops round and tempting. She'd curled her hair and put on makeup. She was gorgeous—his wet dream.

"It looks like someone in town is happy to see you," Zane said with a chuckle. "Hey, Holly, you look mighty nice tonight."

She flushed, a smile blooming across her lips. "Thanks, Zane. I have a date."

She did have a date. With a man who couldn't seem to breathe much less speak. "You don't look nice. You are so beautiful, *dushka*. You are sexy and gorgeous, and I do not deserve. I meant to pick you up."

"I got off early. I got dressed in the bathroom at Stella's. I hope I don't still smell like the deep fryer."

He leaned in and took a whiff. She smelled like a woman, just a hint of perfume and her own sweet smell. "You smell good enough to eat. Like a muffin. Sweet."

All thoughts of leaving fled as he got close to her. Anticipation thrummed through his veins. Caleb had called the motel earlier, leaving a message with Gene. All those tests he'd been put through had come back negative, and he was healthy as a horse. He would have her tonight. He would try to take it slow, but he would be in her bed. Perhaps if he had been a better man, he would have backed off, but he couldn't. He needed her. She was his reward for turning his life around. All during the long trials and the attempts on his life, he'd thought about one thing. Holly.

"Let me buy you drink, *dushka*."

"I would like that. I would also like to know what *dushka* means."

He led her to a small booth. He preferred its privacy to the open bar. "It means 'sweetheart.'"

"I like that." She glanced up at Zane. "I'll take a white wine."

Alexei stared at her, unable to take his eyes off her for a moment. Zane left to get the wine. He gave in to his urge to touch her, grasping her hand. "How was your day, *dushka*?"

She smiled brightly. "Good. No trouble at all."

He wasn't sure he believed that. "I would want you to tell me your troubles."

"Nothing at all. It was a completely unremarkable day. How about yours?"

The door opened again, the bell chiming to let everyone know someone else had entered, but Alexei didn't look up. He was too busy staring at Holly.

"Mine was not so good, but night is looking up." Guilt threatened to swamp him. "Some peoples are not happy to see me here."

She squeezed his hand. "I wouldn't worry about it. They'll get used to you."

He wasn't so sure about that. Caleb had seemed confident of his position. "I do not want to harm your place in community."

She laughed. "I think my place in the community is secure. If people don't like it, they can find another waitress."

"Why? Are you quitting? No one told me you were quitting." Caleb's voice let Alexei know they weren't alone.

Alexei looked up, and Caleb was standing right there, his shoulders drawn back, a confused expression on his face.

Holly turned to look at Caleb, obviously surprised to see him standing there. "I didn't quit. I left early. Oh, god. Tell me you didn't do that thing where you walk into the diner like you're going to blow it up."

Caleb's face went blank. "I wish I could."

Holly shook her head.

Caleb turned to Alexei. "I need to talk to you."

Holly scooted out of the booth. "I'll go freshen up a bit. You two behave. Please."

Caleb stood there for a moment as Holly walked toward the restroom.

"If you are to tell me to stay away from Holly, I cannot. Even for you. I know I owe life to you, but I cannot hurt her like that. I don't want to." How could he make the man understand?

"What? I wasn't going to tell you to stay away. Fuck. How do I ask this?" He paced a bit, his boots scuffing along the floor.

"Ask what?" Alexei felt tense. What the hell was going on? After the debacle of this morning's examination, he'd expected Caleb to utterly ignore him.

Caleb put both hands down on the tabletop. "What did you mean when you said Holly was too much woman for one man?"

Alexei stilled. He'd said that this morning, right before Caleb's torture. "I meant she deserve to have the men she want."

"So I'm not crazy," Caleb said, straightening up. "You said that. And if she wants two men?"

"She is enough women for two men."

"See, when you say it like that, it sounds like an orgy."

"No orgies. Just a beautiful woman and two men who could be friends because they care for same woman. Before this place, I would have say two men would fight over woman, but here we don't have to fight. We can care for her together. It is good, no?"

"I don't know, but it does open up some possibilities." Caleb scrubbed a hand through his hair and looked around the bar. It was starting to fill up as the sun set.

"Hey, Doc? You need a beer?" Zane yelled from across the bar.

"Nah, I'm on call. Tell your wife to hurry up and spit that baby out so I can drink again." Caleb went right back to pacing. Alexei watched him, wondering if he should get up and join him. "If I did this with you, it wouldn't make us friends."

Alexei checked his smile. He was pretty sure it would. He'd studied up on Dr. Caleb Sommerville. Since the unfortunate incident that signaled the end of his brilliant career, he hadn't been in an intimate situation with anyone as far as Alexei could tell. He was betting on the fact that Caleb's heart was soft, merely packed under layers of protective ice. He simply needed to be thawed out.

Alexei knew the feeling. He shrugged. "We do not have to be friends. Merely partners in her pleasure."

"All right. I want to make sure I have this perfectly straight—you were inviting me to join you in having sex with Holly?"

Sometimes Caleb could be a bit obtuse. "Not only the sex. Also the relationship. You only want to have the sex with Holly?"

Caleb's face held a hint of a smile. "See, that sounds weird. I don't know what I want. I know I want to give her what she needs. I know I want to make her feel as special as she is. I don't know if I'm capable of being a normal boyfriend."

He'd rather thought that was the problem. "She does not need normal. I think she needs something different. So you can relax. You can be as involved as you like. As long as you treat her well, you will be welcome."

"Why would you offer this? You have to know you could have her to yourself. You could waltz right out of here, and she would probably follow you."

He doubted that. Holly had a home here and many friends. She was entrenched in the community. "I do not wish to leave Bliss. I want to make home here for myself and any family I become blessed with."

Caleb went a little pale. He was obviously scared by the idea of a family. "Still, you don't have to share her. She'll go with you."

"Because you do not fight for her. If you choose to fight, she would hesitate."

"And she would be miserable." Caleb stared at the floor, his hands on his hips.

"Yes, I think she would be. My solution is best. Happy woman. Happy men."

His eyes came up, staring at Alexei. "I don't know if I'll be happy, but it's more than I expected. I was freaked out by her accident today."

"Accident?" The word fell out of his mouth. "She tell me nothing happened to her today. She say she went to work and then come here for date."

Caleb's eyes narrowed. "She lied. She nearly died on the mountainside when the brakes went out on my truck. And before you get pissed off at me, I had that truck serviced last month. There was nothing wrong with the brakes."

"Did they go out all at once or slowly?" He didn't like the sound of this. It was rare for brakes to go out on a modern vehicle with no warning. Suspicion began to creep along his spine.

"I didn't think to ask her. I think she would have noticed if they were giving her trouble. She was on the mountain. If the truck escape ramp hadn't been there, if there had been another car on the mountain…" Caleb let the sentence trail off, but the implication was clear.

She would have died. She would have been killed before he'd had a chance to truly hold her, to love her.

He could hazard a guess at what had happened. "The brake fluid slowly drains out. You would not notice it at first. Brakes would work normally. I suspect we will find that computer system was tampered with as well."

"What are you trying to say?"

"Brakes don't go out on their own. Not in that fashion. Do you know of any reason someone would attempt to harm you? It was your vehicle." Of course, Alexei had stood at the truck. He'd stood there for nearly half an hour before he'd walked into the office. He'd leaned against it, thinking about how to break through to its owner. Surely no one thought the truck was his.

"No. And don't jump to conclusions. Brakes do go out. We'll know more once Long-Haired Roger takes a look at it."

Long-Haired Roger, who was still down a man because he couldn't deal with Alexei's past. "We will see. And then we will talk." The truth of the situation hit him. "She did not tell me, but she tell you."

Caleb's head shook sharply. "No. She didn't call me or anything. It was chance that I know anything at all. I found her walking back up the fucking mountain. She'd passed the Harper Ranch, but she didn't want to bother them. She apparently was going to walk right by Mel's place, too. She was walking all the way back to Stella's."

"This is no acceptable behavior in woman with two mens." It wouldn't be acceptable if Holly only had one man, but it seemed especially wrong that she'd cut two men out of her trouble. She hadn't even tried to call for help. What good were they if she didn't lean on them?

"No, it is not," Caleb agreed. His arms crossed over his chest.

At least they were in agreement on one thing. "What are we to do about this situation, Caleb? I do not believe she will listen to a stern lecture."

"You think I didn't already try that? After she stopped crying, I yelled for a good thirty minutes. I gave it my all. I can really yell, man. She didn't seem bothered by it at all. She apologized and told me she needed to get to work."

"We need to work on the controlling scenes with Holly," Alexei explained. This was what he'd wanted. A partner. Someone to discuss strategy with. Someone who knew what it was like to care about Holly.

"Scene control, buddy. We need scene control."

And it helped that Caleb could translate for him. "I think she deserves spanking."

Caleb stared at him for a moment. "Have you been hanging out with Wolf?"

"I do not know any wolves. Though I would be all right with a dog." Why was Caleb talking about pets?

Green eyes rolled slightly. "Dude, Wolf is a friend of mine. He drove me out to the hospital after we picked up Holly. Do you want to know what he said I should do to Holly?"

"If he is smart man, he tell you to spank her."

"Well, you would think he's incredibly smart. He also thought I should tie her up and then spank her and then…well, he's a creative guy."

Alexei would like to meet this man. "So, we are in agreement?"

"I'm not saying no to it. I just want to make sure she doesn't get hurt."

Alexei smiled. "She will not be hurt, but she will learn the lesson."

"To talk to her men."

"To rely on her men."

Caleb finally scooted into the booth across from him. "Maybe we should make out a schedule. You know, one of us takes her to work and one of us picks her up. This town can be very dangerous. Serial killers. Biker gangs. Your friends."

Was he ever going to get over that? "No more friends. All dead or in jail. And they were not friends."

"You get my point. Bliss can be a dangerous place. And Holly runs around all on her own. She's out there running around like a huge cupcake, and all the criminals are hungry. They're starving. Do you know what I mean?"

Alexei had no idea, but he nodded anyway. Perhaps Caleb wouldn't prove to be the best translator.

Caleb continued. "And did you say anything to her about that dress?"

"I tell her dress is beautiful." He knew how to tell a woman she was beautiful in any language. "Dress is sexy."

Caleb pinned him with a stern stare. "No. Dress is naked. Dress needs more material. Dress needs a turtleneck. Look, man, if I give on the spanking thing, I want you to stand by me when I tell her to not walk around with my boobs hanging out for every man in the county to salivate over."

"Our boobs." Caleb needed to get it right if he was going to ask for solidarity.

"Fine. Our boobs," Caleb conceded. "The point is those boobs are supposed to be ours. We have to protect them."

He tried to imagine that talk. It seemed to him that it would likely end in nonerotic violence. "I worry she take spanking better than a lecture on her clothing."

"Maybe. But if we're going to do this, we have to present a united front."

Great. They would both get slapped. But Alexei smiled anyway. "Yes, we do."

"Or she will eat us alive."

He planned on her doing just that, but he didn't point out the fallacies in Caleb's plan. He wasn't about to stop the man now. When Caleb had started talking, he'd talked about merely hanging around for the sex. Now they were making rules together.

Yes, Caleb only wanted sex. Sure he did.

Caleb leaned forward. "I don't know how good I'm going to be at this. I haven't dated a lot. I haven't been celibate since my wife died, but I haven't cared about anyone either. I certainly haven't been in anything that vaguely resembled a relationship. What if I fuck this up? This is why it's better if I'm only here for sex. I won't fuck up sex."

Alexei leaned forward, too. Finally the man was softening. He was talking about the problem instead of simply saying no. "It will be okay. No one knows how a relationship will go. Not a single person in the world know how a relationship will end when they begin."

"I certainly know that." A haunted look passed over his face, and Alexei knew he was thinking about his wife. When would Caleb trust him enough to talk about her? And to talk about why he was hiding his identity?

"We can only care about her. We can only try to protect her. That is all we can ask of ourselves." He knew all too well how the world sometimes had its say. "So, you are in, my friend?"

"This still doesn't make us friends," Caleb shot back, but the words sounded stubborn, as if only forced from his mouth from long-standing habit. Caleb was silent for a moment. "You honestly believe this is her fantasy?"

"Yes, it is."

The answer had come from Holly. Alexei stiffened, praying she wasn't going to be upset. Her voice had been quiet, so she must have been close. How much had she heard? "Holly, we were only talking."

"You were negotiating, Alexei." She stared at both of them and made no move to take a seat. She clutched her purse.

Caleb's eyes went straight to her chest. The man might not like the dress, but he certainly seemed to appreciate it. "Maybe we don't want to be like everyone else in Bliss."

A single eyebrow arched over Holly's lovely, wide eyes. "Really?"

Caleb sputtered for a moment as though trying to navigate in uncharted seas. "No, it's not like everyone else here. They go into it willy-nilly. Do you think Max and Rye talked it out before they went after Rachel or did they all simply fall into bed together? Alexei and I don't have some weird psychic twin thing. We have to talk."

"Holly, your wine. It sounds like you're going to need it." Zane handed her a glass of white wine. He did it with one hand. His other hand held the receiver of a phone, its corded length stretching halfway across the bar. "And could y'all talk louder? Callie's having trouble hearing." Zane put the phone back to his ear. "I asked them, babe. Yes. Alexei and Caleb. And Caleb's already acting like a bossy asshole. He thinks he can do this better than the rest of us."

Alexei could actually hear a peal of feminine laughter escape from the phone.

Holly took a long swig of her wine. "Great. Now everyone knows."

"I don't think I'll do it better than everyone. I'll just do it a bit more cautiously," Caleb said with a frown. "I don't jump into things."

Zane shook his head. "Dude, six years. It took me and Nate six whole years. It took Rafe and Cam five. Sure it took Max and Rye like fifteen minutes, but they're the only ones you beat, so get to the back of the line on the 'thinking things through' show."

"Zane Derek Hollister, that is not a thing to be proud of!" the voice from the phone yelled.

Alexei felt the whole thing spinning out of control. Caleb started to argue with Zane, who was trying to hold two conversations. Holly went bright pink and looked like she might ask for the whole bottle of wine. The door opened, and Laura walked in with her two men. Her eyes lit up, and she started toward Holly.

Holly took off like a shot. Laura was right there, opening her arms to her friend. Cool blue eyes looked across the bar like lasers attempting to acquire a target. Him. Laura Niles gave him a look that could have frozen off his cock.

His blissful night was slipping away, and no one was going to save it.

No one except him.

He stood. "Caleb, I am taking conversation back to Holly's place. There are too many cooks in kitchen."

"No, there's only me since Callie got too big to work. That's something I thought I could talk to you about, Alexei," Zane said. He put the phone back to his ear. "No, babe. You're not that big. Oh, baby, you're so beautiful. You know I still think you're sexy." He pulled the phone away, cradling it against his chest. "She's crying again, Doc. Maybe you should go take a look at her."

"No." Alexei stood up. He was done. If he didn't set boundaries, then everyone in Bliss would walk all over him, and he would end up sleeping alone at the motel listening to two US marshals going at it again all night long. *No* was Caleb's favorite word. Alexei would adopt it as his own.

"No?" Caleb asked, a hint of a smile on his face.

"No. Callie is fine. Does water break?"

Zane shook his head. "No. She's not in labor."

Excellent. Then they shouldn't have any problems. "Good. Then have your partner go home and rub her feet. Make her feel sexy and beautiful. We will do same for our woman."

Caleb seemed to take it as his cue. "Zane, Callie's fine. She needs affection more than she needs a doctor. And gossip. She lives on gossip. If she goes into labor, I'll be at Holly's house. But, man, she better be in labor, if you know what I mean."

Zane nodded and got back on the phone with his wife.

"I am going to get our woman and make a few things very clear to her." A bit of outrage thrummed through his system. She thought she could run to her friend instead of talking it out with him? She was angry at him for attempting to provide her with exactly what she wanted? "Women. I do not understand them."

"Don't look at me, man. I would have thought she would be happy we were talking about it." Caleb stared at her, too.

If she was already angry, then Alexei had nothing to lose. "Let me show you how it is done in Russia."

He turned and stared across the room. Holly's eyes widened as though she finally understood he wouldn't be put off. A deep sense of satisfaction flooded his system. She was aware of him. She was the tiniest bit scared of him. He watched as Laura's arm went around her friend's shoulder, a protective wing for Holly to hide under. They slid into a booth and began talking.

That was unacceptable.

And Alexei finally noticed that every man in the bar seemed to be staring at the gorgeous redhead and her beautiful breasts. "You are right. Dress needs more material."

Yes. They would discuss that, too.

"Maybe we should talk about this. She looks pissed," Caleb said.

Alexei ignored him as he started across the room. Caleb would follow or he wouldn't. He'd done everything he could to make Caleb welcome. It was up to him now. He wasn't waiting another night to get inside the woman who had turned his world around.

Chapter Seven

"What's wrong, sweetie?" Laura asked, opening her arms wide and wrapping them around Holly.

Holly sniffled, well aware that she was now the focus of everyone's eyes in Trio. Sure the tourists would mostly ignore her, but not the locals. She counted them. Rafe and Cam had taken the adjoining booth, their backs to Laura and Holly. In true male fashion, they left plenty of space between themselves and the crying female. James Glen sat at the back of the tavern with his girl of the moment. It looked like he'd finally convinced Serena Hall to give him a shot. Serena was a lovely brunette who acted with the rep theater in Creede. Just across the bar, Hope, the secretary at the sheriff's office, sat with a half-eaten sandwich in front of her, staring longingly at James. Poor thing. At least Holly's scene would give Hope something else to think about because James Glen was one man who wasn't about to be tamed.

"Tell me," Laura urged. "And tell me fast because I think those men are getting ready to come over here. Wow. Is that Caleb with Alexei? Should we call Nate?"

She shook her head. "No. They're not fighting. It's worse. They're negotiating."

Laura's head straightened up. "Negotiating? What on earth are they negotiating?"

She took a deep breath, sniffling again. "How to share me."

"Are you serious? That is the most unromantic thing I've ever heard."

Thank god Laura understood. "I know. I walked away for a couple of minutes, and when I came back I overheard Caleb telling Alexei that he only wants sex, and Alexei was okay with that. But they don't like my dress. It's my only good dress. I don't have another one."

Laura patted her back. "Oh, sweetie, I'm so sorry. You look beautiful. I think what they don't like about the dress is the fact that your boobs are hanging out."

"They are not."

Laura looked back at Cam and Rafe. "Boys, what do you see when you look at Holly right this second?"

"I see you, *bella*. Only you," Rafe said with a smooth smile.

"Boobs. Lots of boobs," Cam replied at the same time. His face reddened. "And you, babe. Yeah, I was talking about your boobs."

Laura rolled her eyes. "I can always count on you, Cam." She winked at them both and then turned back to Holly. "See. They're not being assholes. They're being *possessive* assholes. There's a huge difference. And you need to think about this. Caleb Burke, isolated freak, is sitting over there talking to a former mobster about how to make love to you. If you think about it, it's kind of sweet."

"Caleb doesn't like to talk to people at all, much less Alexei." What was wrong with her? This was everything she wanted. Sure, it wasn't exactly how she'd pictured it happening, but they were talking. Why had she walked away? Why hadn't she given them both a sexy smile and invited them back to her place?

"You're scared, honey," Laura said.

Yep. She was suddenly terrified. "It's just sex."

Laura's head touched hers. "Not for you it isn't. You need to decide if you can handle this."

"Caleb only wants sex." She'd heard him say it. She'd hoped when he'd walked up that he'd come to his senses. She'd gone into the bathroom and touched up her makeup with a sense of hope. She'd fantasized about sitting in the tavern and having a nice dinner, the three of them together.

Then she'd walked out to Caleb saying he just wanted sex and Alexei agreeing to it. Was that what she'd wanted?

"Caleb lies to himself a lot, I think," Laura said. "He says he wants sex, but he never goes after it. That man is so stinking hot he could have had sex with almost anyone he wanted, yet he lives like a monk. Did you know that Lisa Alvarado, the ski instructor at Elk Creek Lodge, came in for three gyno visits this winter? Seriously? Caleb finally had to tell her that her vagina didn't need more prodding."

Holly felt her fists clench. Lisa Alvarado was a pretty twenty-five-year-old with a perfect body and a quick wit. She'd liked her right up until five seconds ago.

Laura continued, every word firing her jealousy. "And I heard that he gets hit on by ski bunnies all the time. They call him Doc Hottie up at the Lodge. Of course they run the minute he opens his mouth, but let's face facts—the man is hot."

"Could we move this conversation along?" Cam asked, poking his head around the booth where he sat with Rafe behind them. His eyes were narrowed with irritation.

"Fine," Laura said with sarcastic glee. "Let's talk about how sexy Alexei is."

Both of Laura's men groaned and yelled to Zane to bring them a round of beers.

"He's a beautiful man." She looked back where Alexei had a ferocious look on his face. She'd seen that look on his face before. It was the look he'd had right before the bullets had started to fly on the day he'd saved her life. Whatever he was about to do, he was serious about it.

"He's gorgeous," Laura agreed. "He's the type of man who could have any woman he wanted."

Yes, Alexei had probably had many beautiful women. He was a sexy monster of a man. And she hadn't even seen him with his clothes off. In clothes he was devastating. What would he look like when he stripped down and wore nothing but smooth skin and hard muscle? And Caleb? Caleb was no slouch in the muscle department. Both of the men were beautiful and ridiculously masculine.

What the hell was she doing? She wasn't in their league.

Laura reached out and touched her hair, commanding her attention.

"Calm down. I can feel your anxiety from here, and if Scott Lang was in this bar right now, I would beat him to death with my shoe. Look at me. You're beautiful. So beautiful. Did you know that Wolf Meyer told me he wanted to ask you out, but he cared too much about Caleb to hurt him that way? That's three ungodly gorgeous men who want you."

Both of Laura's men snorted and started talking about what a douchebag Wolf Meyer was. As Wolf had been dating Laura before they came back, Holly could forgive them.

"Did he really say that?"

"Ask him yourself," Laura challenged. "Though I wouldn't ask him when Alexei was around. That man looks scary. And, again, hot."

Alexei stood, his tall body matched only by Zane's, who seemed to be struggling with his telephone. Alexei barked something toward Caleb, who got out of his seat, too, and stood beside Alexei, both men staring across the bar toward her.

And then Alexei began walking. There was no doubt where he was heading.

"He's going to tell me he's leaving," Holly said, her heart aching. She'd fucked everything up.

"It has been a long time since you had sex. Your instincts are way off." Laura shook her head. "That man is not leaving, but don't be surprised if he doesn't bother to wait until you get home. You yell if he gets too rough with you."

Laura slid out, standing by the bench as Alexei approached. "She's all yours, buddy. Break her heart and I'll feed you your balls on a skewer."

Alexei nodded briefly at Laura, who crossed the short space between booths and slid in next to Cam. Alexei turned to Holly. "You will to come with me."

"Alexei, say what you want to say." She knew when she was about to get dumped. It was better to get it over with. It would be a relief. "Say it and leave, okay?"

Caleb walked up behind Alexei. They both loomed over her. "What did she say?"

"It doesn't matter. Anything she say now is fear speaking, and I will not listen." His hand came out and grasped her wrist, pulling her toward him. She was pulled out of the booth, her heels hitting the ground. Like gravity forcing her forward, she landed in Alexei's arms with a thud.

"What are you doing?"

He said nothing, simply leaned over and shoved his right arm under her knees, hauling her up like she weighed nothing at all.

She hooked an arm around his thick neck for support and looked over his shoulder at Caleb, who appeared to be following along. "Caleb, what is he doing?"

Alexei walked toward the exit. She looked around the tavern, but no one seemed to be willing to help her out. Rafe and Cam each stood and put an arm around Laura as they smiled at Alexei. Nope. No help there. Zane was still on the phone. Hope looked up, her face open and wide, but she didn't stand.

"Alexei, you should put me down." Everyone was watching her.

Alexei's face closed. He gave her absolutely nothing. "If you wished to have say, you would not have walked away. You will learn. I love Bliss, but I will not allow the chaos to change my plans for evening."

"Caleb, talk to him." She looked over Alexei's shoulder. Caleb was following behind them.

"I can't. We discussed this. We decided to form a united front. It's the only way to survive and thrive, sweetheart."

"Are you serious?" He looked serious. He looked really serious. Caleb's face was set in stark lines as Alexei kicked open the door and walked out into the night.

"I'm dead serious. We have to stick together. I don't know how this whole thing is going to work, but I do know that the guys need to stick together or the girl will make us crazy."

Holly felt her mouth open. Was that what they had really been talking about? Had they been strategizing about how best to handle her? "You said you only want sex."

Caleb stopped, distance growing between them because Alexei kept walking. She could see Caleb's face fall and wished she hadn't asked the question.

"Are you trying to drive him away?" Alexei asked, his voice tight.

"I don't like the idea that he only wants sex." It hurt her heart.

"He can't give anything else now. He needs time. He needs to ease into relationship. You are earning much punishment, *dushka*." Alexei's words were clipped, his walk a staccato rhythm. "I worked hard to get him here and you push away. Ten more."

Holly felt her eyes go wide. "Ten more what?"

"Punishments. Holly, I am man. I will be indulgent but can only allow you to push so far. Make decision now. Spanking here or at home. If at home, then you will go and talk to Caleb. You will make him happy and invite him to come with us."

Caleb stood by the door, looking like a gorgeous puppy that wasn't sure if he should follow the pack or stay behind and die. "I'll talk to him. Are you really going to spank me? Don't I have a say in that?"

"No. You have no say in punishment. Are you going to tell me you didn't lie about what happened today? Caleb lied? You didn't almost die in car accident?"

Crap. She hadn't told him about that because it didn't matter. "I'm fine. I didn't want to bother you."

Every step they took brought them farther away from Caleb. He stood at the door, watching them. Panic was starting to set in. He wasn't following them. He was staring but not following.

"Bother? You bother me. Tell me how you would feel if I almost die and don't bother to mention it to you? Someone try to shoot at me but I tell you no problems today. I don't care enough to worry you. How would that make you feel? People who care don't treat each other with so little concern."

Okay. She hadn't meant it like that. God, why was Caleb standing there? "Please let me go talk to him."

Alexei stopped and looked down at her. "Why? You didn't want him. You don't want me."

Oh, she'd seriously fucked up. "I want you, Alexei. I'm worried that you don't want me."

His face was a block of granite. "You are one who walked away. I change whole life because of you. You can't question me. Caleb change because of you. He talk to me because he wants you."

What had she done? How much would Scott cost her? Laura was right. She was allowing her disastrous marriage to affect her current life. "Please, let me down."

"No. I'm not going to let you go." His arms tightened around her.

"Please. I won't go. I'll take what you give me, but let me get him." She couldn't stand the thought of Caleb being left behind. She couldn't stand it. This was what she'd dreaded. She couldn't make the choice. She needed them both. She needed two men—both of whom were out of her league. Caleb had stated plainly that he only wanted sex. Alexei was too beautiful to stay. She couldn't keep Scott, and he didn't come close to Alexei.

But Scott would never have risked his life to save another human being. He wouldn't spend his days saving people who couldn't pay him. Maybe it was time to understand that Scott had nothing on Alexei and Caleb. He didn't have their heart. He didn't come close to their souls. Maybe she had to believe that there was more to life than the way a person looked. Maybe she had to take into account the life a person had lived. The choices a person had made.

Caleb had chosen to be a doctor. He'd chosen to help people who couldn't pay him. Alexei had given up fifteen years of revenge to save a couple of women he hadn't even known. He'd turned his life around because he couldn't lose his soul.

What had she done? She'd hidden from life. She'd run from the fight. She'd taken what was given to her and never thought to question it. She hid from the good things in life.

"Please let me down."

Alexei set her on her feet. "Don't cry, *dushka*. I will stop. I will be gentle."

Her heels hit the pavement. She immediately put her hands up, cradling his face. "Please don't. I want you. I want the real you. Spank me. I'll take it. I want the freaky you who can't speak English and isn't sure how to deal with American women. I want that Alexei. And I want Caleb, who's too much of a dumbass to know he wants more than sex."

He did. He wouldn't be standing there with that sad-sack look on his face if he didn't. He would have walked away. Was her insecurity worth more than their feelings, their affection? Maybe it would fall apart. Maybe they would each find someone else—but tonight they wanted her. What did it make her if she didn't even try?

A coward.

Tears pricked at her eyes. "I want you, Alexei."

His whole stance softened, as though her words had power over his physical state. "I want you, Holly. I've dreamed of you. I've longed for you."

She couldn't fucking ask for more than that. What was she doing? She'd asked the question a thousand times since he'd walked back into her life. Why hadn't she asked herself the question that mattered? Did she want him? God, yes. Was she brave enough to try?

She went on her tiptoes. "Forgive me."

"Always, *dushka*. I will always forgive." His hands threaded through her hair. "You will find me very forgiving."

She touched her lips to his. "Thank you. I need to talk to Caleb."

His lips curved up. "Yes. Bring him home."

She turned, Alexei's strength uplifting her own. She was through letting Scott and his family win. She was through allowing the past to rob her of her future. She was scared. She was out of her mind scared, but she couldn't leave Caleb standing there. She couldn't.

Heels grinding into the gravel, she walked toward him. His face was frozen in a blank stare, as though he would accept whatever she offered him. It hurt her heart. She'd probably had that expression a thousand times. Maybe she understood Caleb better than she thought.

She came to a stop in front of him, staring at his gorgeous face. He was male-model beautiful, and he wanted her. Maybe he just wanted her for sex, but it was more than he seemed to want from anyone else. It struck her suddenly that she couldn't control him. She could only give what she was willing and pray it was enough.

There was something lovely and amazing about that.

She was jumping off a cliff and hoping he would catch her. If he didn't, she would fall, but at least she would have tried. She wouldn't regret the attempt. She would regret never trying.

She held out her hand. "Caleb, please come home with us."

She used "us" because that was what she wanted. She wanted Caleb and Alexei. She wanted a family. She'd told herself she wanted Alexei for a hot affair, but she threw that notion to the wind. She wanted him forever. She wanted both of them. She might not get them, but damn, it wouldn't be because she hadn't tried.

"I'm not good at relationships." Caleb's eyes found the ground beneath his feet.

"I have a divorce under my belt and nothing serious since. I've had two lovers my whole life, Caleb, and one of them was a drunken hookup with my high school lab partner. I don't know anything about this except the fact that I want you. I want Alexei, too. I want you both. I might not be any good at this, but I want to try."

His eyes softened. "You can't believe that."

"I do. Caleb, I haven't had a relationship with any man since I got divorced, and to tell you the truth, I don't think I was very good at sex. My own husband didn't want me." He'd wanted everyone else. Secretaries. Nannies. Hotel maids. Never his own wife for the last three years of their marriage.

He reached out for her hand, his callused fingers sliding against her own. "You're wrong. You're so fucking gorgeous, Holly. I want you so bad I ache with it."

"I want you, too, *dushka*. I need you." Alexei was suddenly behind her, his heat sinking into her body. His hands found her hips. "Let us take you home. Let us show you how we feel."

She leaned back against him, her eyes still on Caleb. "Please, Caleb."

He moved forward, his body crowding hers. "I don't want to hurt you."

Never knowing what it felt like to be between these two men would hurt her. "If we don't even try, I'll regret it. I want you. It has to be enough for now."

His mouth was so close. "I'll try, but I'm damaged. I'm not whole, and there's nothing you can do to fix me."

She would see about that. "Kiss me."

"I can do that." Caleb leaned forward, and his lips met hers, gently exploring. His hands moved from his sides and found her hips. His tongue teased out, licking at her lips before she opened and allowed him in.

Strong hands reached from behind and boldly cupped her breasts. Her nipples immediately sprang to life as Alexei's fingers brushed them. His body pressed against her back while Caleb's pushed at her front. She was caught in between them, neither giving her an inch of space. She could feel two hard cocks straining. Caleb's pressed against her belly. Alexei rubbed his along the small of her back. He leaned over and nuzzled her ear, his hot breath causing her to shiver. His tongue played along the shell of her ear, and he murmured low, sexy words in Russian.

"What does that mean?" Holly asked when Caleb finally let her mouth go to explore the skin of her neck, kissing and nipping her flesh.

"Let me translate for our Russian comrade," Caleb offered. He pulled her hips to his and stared down at her chest. There wasn't any hesitation left in Caleb's eyes. Those green eyes were predatory now. He wanted her, and he would have her. She could feel it.

"Please do." Alexei chuckled. His hands cupped the undersides of her breasts and pushed them up, as though offering them to Caleb.

"He says he wants to fuck. He says you're the sexiest woman he's ever seen, and he can't wait to get inside you. He wants to shove his cock deep inside that pussy of yours, and he never wants to leave. He'll live there. He won't want to eat or drink or even breathe. He'll do nothing but fuck you for the rest of his life."

"He is right, *dushka*. I take back all thoughts that Caleb would be bad translator. He is very good. Now let me tell you what he is thinking. He is wondering why he waited so long. He's wanting you from the moment he lay his eyes on you, and he can't stand the thought of going one more day without being with you."

"You're not a bad mind reader, Alexei." Caleb sank his hand into her hair. "Are you sure you want this? I don't think I'll be able to stop if we go much further. Two men can be demanding. If you want to take this slow, tell us now, and we'll back off and go at whatever pace you want."

It was obvious to Holly that Caleb needed a firm hand. "I want it. Take me home and make love to me now."

"Yes, take her home," a deep voice shouted.

Holly came out of her haze and realized they were standing right outside of Trio. The lights from the tavern spilled out into the twilight, and Nate Wright stood by the door, his big, authoritative presence a reminder to her they weren't alone. And that her nipples were probably showing.

Maybe Caleb was right about the dress.

Caleb pulled her forward, pressing her chest into his, protecting her from embarrassment. Alexei slipped from behind her and stepped forward. She noticed the sheriff wasn't the only one looking at them. There were at least ten faces pressed against the glass, looking out at the action.

Nosy busybodies. Including her best friend, who gave her a big thumbs-up. She giggled against Caleb's chest, her embarrassment rushing away. They would gossip in Bliss. The whole town ran on it, but they would be happy for her, too. No one would look down on her. They would cheer her on.

"Do I need to give you a ticket?" Nate's head turned, and his eyes narrowed. Cam stood beside him. "Damn it, Briggs, are you a deputy or not? You were going to let them go at it in the middle of Main Street? Don't you know how these things go around here? If you let this threesome get away with it, Max and Rye are going to start jumping Rachel in public just to prove they can. It'll be a free-for-all."

Cameron Briggs grinned. "Sorry, Sheriff. What can I say? I believe in the power of love between one woman and her chosen men. Besides, I thought if we gave Doc there time to think, he'd talk himself out of it."

"No." Caleb loosened his hold and then leaned over, scooping her into his arms.

Holly smiled because she knew that "no" meant "yes" to her. She wrapped her arms around his neck. There was no way to mistake the warm satisfaction on Alexei's face as he looked at them.

"Hey," Nate said. "You can't say no to a ticket."

"No." Caleb proved he could.

"Go. Take her back to car. I'll deal with sheriff." Alexei winked at her. "Try to wait for me."

"No." Caleb had started walking toward her clunker of a car. He shouted the word over his back toward Alexei, but there was a smile on his face as he said it.

"Hurry!" Holly called out. Alexei's big body got smaller as Caleb walked further away.

When they got to her car, he set her on her feet and held out his hand for the keys.

"It's okay. I can drive."

"No."

She sighed. "Caleb, you can't tell me no all night."

He pulled her close. Now that he'd touched her, he seemed to want to be really close. His face rubbed against her hair. She reveled in his affection. She'd expected that Alexei might be deeply sensual, but Caleb's obvious need for contact softened her heart. She brought her hands up to his waist.

"I won't tell you no all night. But we're going to have a talk about this dress. I can see your nipples. It makes me want to tear off what little material there is and get those breasts in my mouth. I will say no to this dress, Holly."

His voice was thick and rich, like molasses, clouding her senses. Even the way he told her what to wear seemed sexy. "I can't let you dictate to me."

"Really? Then you won't care if I run around without a shirt on or if I choose to join the Naked Man March. I hear the women of the town are going to set up lawn chairs and cheer the biggest penis."

"No." She gave him back his favorite word. She really didn't want him to do that. Once a year, the men of the Mountain and Valley Naturist Community marched through town on their way to the Wild Man Retreat that was supposed to bring them back to their masculine selves, apparently by showing off their junk. The sheriff had tried to arrest a few of them last year but rapidly discovered a distaste for dealing with that many penises. Nate Wright took that day off to go fishing.

"See, we can compromise." He kissed her again, making her forget her argument.

Alexei jogged up behind them. "Let's us to go. I got us out of ticket, but we need to take her home."

Yes. It was time to go home. It was time to be with her men.

* * * *

Vince took a slow sip of beer and tried to disappear into the background. He slumped down, trying to disguise his height. He was a tall man. People tended to remember his height. In New York, no one noticed his Italian dark looks. He blended. It was hard to do here. Everyone knew everyone else in this weird town. And they seemed to have the strangest relationships. It was very difficult to figure out who was with whom.

And his target seemed to like to draw a fucking crowd. And to switch cars.

His first attempt had failed. It gnawed at him. The truck had been perfect. Even if the yokels had figured out someone had cut the brake line, allowing the fluid to slowly drain, no one would ever think it was the sunny tourist who smiled but didn't talk much. He was nothing but another granola-loving hiker.

But his target was still walking and talking and apparently about to have three-way love. That was unexpected. He'd counted on a lover, but certainly not two. They had to separate at some time. And now the threesome seemed to be down to one car. Maybe he could try again.

A big guy with scars marring his face stood over the booth Vince occupied. He'd been tending bar when Vince had come in. There was a waitress walking around. She seemed like a mouse of a woman, young and pretty, but nothing impressive. She hadn't studied him the way this big guy did.

"Get you another beer?" the big guy asked.

If Vince had to guess, this guy had experience. There was something about the eyes and the way he held his own. Cop. The big dude had been a cop once. Vince put on his best "man of the people" smile.

"Sure. I'm on vacation after all." He opened his face, allowing his eyes to go wide. "This is a great little town you have here. I'm staying in Pagosa Springs, but they told me there was some great hiking out this way. And the sand dunes are incredible."

He'd picked up a bunch of pamphlets touting local attractions at the motel in Creede. He'd learned the lay of the land. Locals, he'd discovered, usually got bored talking to tourists. A couple of minutes of gabbing about how pretty everything was and their eyes glazed over, any suspicion giving way to the need to get on with their lives.

"Yes, they're beautiful. And there are a lot of romantic places around here. I'm sure your wife probably loves it."

Yep. He would rather have dealt with the waitress. The big guy was probing. It was time to start lying. "Girlfriend. She was a little tired today. She stayed back in the motel. I had to get out a bit."

"Long drive from Pagosa. Guess you heard about how good the beer is. I'll get you another." The big guy turned, but not before giving him another long look.

Fucker. This was supposed to be a simple job. Now some fucking ex-cop had stared at him long enough that he could probably draw his face from memory. He thought about leaving before the guy could get back, but that would look even more suspicious. He was stuck.

And now the sheriff was here. Awesome. And he wasn't some round-ass rural jerk who couldn't get his head out of his anus. He looked lean and sharp. And he was talking to the big guy.

Damn it.

His cell phone vibrated, signaling he'd received a text. Yeah. That was what he needed. This job was rapidly devolving into a clusterfuck that wasn't worth his money or time.

The target is still moving.

No fuck, the target was still moving.

He was ready to leave. There would be another job. He typed back as he prepared to get the hell out of Bliss. He'd head back to New York where no one bothered to look at the people around them. He could fade into blissful anonymity.

Sending back the down payment. Job not worth it.

The ping back was almost immediate.

500,000 more.

Someone really wanted the target dead. Damn it. He couldn't turn it down. His fingers hovered over the keys.

Done. Second attempt tomorrow.

He nearly cringed as the big guy walked back with a beer in his hand. He didn't like to drink on the job, and there was no question that he was on the job. It would be his single biggest payday to date. He couldn't walk away. He needed a few days to learn the target's habits. He'd hoped for an easy job, but it was more complicated than he'd imagined. It didn't help that the target had two people close all the time. He might have to take out all three of them. It would cause more scrutiny than he would like, but he could leave the country for a while.

"Thanks. Everyone's so friendly around here."

The big guy smiled, but it was a feral thing, a showing of teeth. "Yeah, we are." He looked down at the smart phone in Vince's hands. "Don't rely on that too much. Cell service here has been spotty for months. You're lucky you can get a text. It looks important. I'll let you get back to it."

He turned and walked away. Vince drank his beer and plotted his next move.

Chapter Eight

Caleb brought the car to a shuddering halt in front of Holly's small cabin. He wasn't sure how much she'd paid for the tiny vehicle, but if she'd laid out even a dollar, he was pretty sure she'd spent too much.

He managed to get the car in park. The sun was beginning to go down, and soon the night would be blanketed with stars. The cabins that dotted the valley were lit with warm yellow light, giving each house an inviting glow. He was going to Holly's cabin. He was about to spend the night in Holly's cabin, and not on her couch this time.

His heart thudded in his chest. He was really going to do this. He was going to make love to Holly with another guy present. How did it work? Did they take turns? They had to take turns. Right? Maybe he should call someone. Wolf was a freak. He would know. The rumor was James Glen liked to share, and he and Wolf had spent the summer playing freaky-deaky games with some of the women in the area. Yes, Wolf could Cyrano de Bergerac him through this.

A soft hand squeezed his arm. "Caleb, it's all right. You can drop me off. You can even have the car. I'll get Cam to give me a ride into town tomorrow. I think our schedules coincide this week."

"No." He turned to her, panic threatening to overtake him. "Why? Have you changed your mind?"

His dick wouldn't accept it. Oh, he would force himself to walk away if she didn't want him, but he was pretty sure his dick would shrivel up and fall off his body. He was so fucking hard.

She smiled slightly. "No, but I was worried you had. You've been sitting here for a couple of minutes."

Crap. Sometimes he lost track of time. His brain flitted about, and he didn't realize how long he'd been thinking.

A harsh groan came from the backseat. "Please to get out of car. I think my back is seizing. I turn into pretzel."

Alexei. Alexei was trapped in the backseat of Holly's rolling hell on wheels. Caleb thought he was uncomfortable in the front. Even with the seat back as far as it would go, his knees were still practically up to his chest. Alexei had to force himself into the back. Holly had tried to convince him to sit in the front, but Alexei had insisted.

Maybe he wasn't the world's worst asshole. Alexei had been incredibly courteous to Holly.

Holly was out in a shot, pushing her seat forward. Alexei looked like a hulking beast in her backseat. He took up every square inch of space and then some. Caleb couldn't help but laugh. He got out of the seat as Alexei was stretching.

"Next time you be one in back." Alexei's brows had come together, the first sign of impatience he'd seen in the man. Thank god. He was beginning to think Alexei was perfect. He seemed to always be patient, and he was willing to share his toys. It was intimidating. "I have very rough day. First the examination that we will never speak of again, then humiliating job interview, and then deputy hate me. I am not in mood for more ping-ponging. Are you in or out?"

That was as plain as he could put it. "I'm in. I wasn't changing my mind. I was wondering how this was going to work."

"Oh, god," Holly said, her eyes widening in horror. And her breasts were still hanging out, though now that they were alone, he sort of liked the dress. "Are we back to the negotiation thing? Couldn't you two jump on me and let it all sort itself out?"

Alexei ignored her, turning his serious eyes on Caleb. "It is simple. We make love to her. We show her how beautiful she is."

"Yes, what he said." Holly took her keys and went to open the door. Her heels made a snapping sound against the wooden steps.

Caleb still had some questions. It was better to get them all out of the way. "Look, despite the town I live in, I've never had a three-way. I mean, how do the logistics work? Are we going at her at the same time? Do we draw straws to see who goes first?"

Alexei leaned in, his voice going low. "One in pussy and one in ass. I have brought condoms and lube. This is how it works."

"I'm not stupid, Alexei. I know that's how it works in the end, but there's a huge problem with your scenario," Caleb pointed out. "She hasn't had sex in…how long has it been since you had sex, babe?"

Even in the fading light of the evening, he could see her cheeks flare. She leaned over the railing of her porch, her voice a low hiss. "Like seven years or so. Do you have to yell it? Callie's cabin is right across the street, and her hearing is excellent."

"Sorry." Caleb lowered his voice. "I was trying to point out to Alexei that anal sex is not possible tonight."

"Oh my god." Holly opened the door and put a hand to her cheeks before pocketing the key.

"I have had sex with many anuses. I know what I am doing." Alexei's face was scrunched up as though he was trying to figure out a problem. "I never had problem before. You lube it up and go. Women enjoy."

Yeah, he bet Alexei had done many anuses. Damn, they needed to work on his English phrases. He was sure the hookers Alexei had paid hadn't had the same problem Holly would have. "You've had sex with experienced women. Holly's not experienced. She hasn't had regular vaginal sex in years. I doubt she's been giving dudes across the county some backdoor action. She's probably a virgin there. That asshole of hers is going to be very tight. So fucking tight. You see the sphincter muscle is…"

Holly stamped her heeled foot on the porch. "Don't you dare go into an anatomy lesson, Caleb Burke. Get in the house. We are not discussing my anus in my front yard."

Alexei's face lit up. "You are in trouble, friend. Take my advice and stop thinking. You are allowing your brain to control this when your heart should be in control."

His heart? That was a scary prospect. He'd prefer for his cock to be in control. "All right, but we have to get her ready for the whole anal thing. We have to go slow."

"I will bow to your expertise if you will listen to me about the heart. No more thinking. Just to feel."

Caleb nodded his head. There was a big part of him that was screaming inside. What the hell was he doing? Did he honestly think for a second that he could fuck her and then go home? Sleeping with Holly would change things.

And what about your life right now do you love?

Not a goddamn thing.

Alexei turned and walked into the cabin, and Caleb followed him. Maybe Holly had the right idea. If this were left up to him, they would all sit down and stare at each other awkwardly until they had sufficiently talked it all out and knew where everyone's hands were supposed to go.

He thought about Caroline. She'd been a virgin when he'd first slept with her. That was exactly what they had done. They had discussed it, planned for it, set an appointment. It had been scheduled almost right down to how long she should take to have an orgasm.

He could barely remember what she looked like when he was awake. He'd taken her virginity, married her, neglected her, and gotten her killed, and the only time he could recall her face was in his nightmares.

"Don't." Holly walked straight up to him. She put her hands on his face, pulling him back in to the real world. "You're here, so now you're mine. I won't take a silly *no* this time."

Fuck, he didn't have to worry about not remembering Holly's face. He saw it nearly every second of every day. Passion. He felt so much passion for her it scared him. He'd never felt that for Caroline, and it was one more pound of guilt to weigh him down. It was there, but he couldn't give in to it. He needed Holly more than he needed to give in to his guilt.

He pulled her to him. God, he loved the way she felt. She was soft against him, so fucking feminine that everything male inside him responded. He'd married Caroline because it had been expected of him. She'd had the right breeding, the right social connections, the proper education. She'd fit into his world. But Holly *was* his world. His whole fucking world.

"I'm crazy about you." He couldn't say the "L" word. He might never be able to say the "L" word again. He'd said it before, and it had been utterly meaningless. But she should know he thought about her always.

She smiled, the sight lighting up the room. "I like you, too, Dr. Burke."

Fuck. She didn't even know his real name. How long could he hide that from her? Had he been out of society long enough that everyone had forgotten? His family connections were moot. He never intended to walk in that world again.

His cock throbbed in his jeans. She was so soft, so fuckable. He'd never wanted a woman the way he wanted Holly.

"Take your clothes off, *dushka*. Show him what he's been wanting to see." Alexei's deep voice reminded him that he wasn't alone.

And that didn't freak him out the way it should. Knowing Alexei was here, that he would stay beside her all night, gave Caleb a sense of peace. Holly deserved it.

She took a step back, and her hands went to the shoulders of her dress. Her fingers were shaking a little. Her breath came out in a ragged puff.

"You're beautiful, *dushka*. So lovely. Let me see all of you. Show me how gorgeous you are. Do you know how long I have waited for this moment?"

"I think that's why I'm worried. I'm not twenty anymore, Alexei." She looked vulnerable standing there. Did she think she needed to hide from him?

It was time to shove all his shit down and be what Holly needed. She didn't need an anxiety-ridden freak. And she didn't need perfection. He'd been wrong about that. He'd stayed away because he had this vision of the perfect man for Holly. But what if all she needed was honest desire? He had that in spades.

He put his hands on her shoulders and let his fingertips play under the edges of her dress, skimming softly along her skin. Her scent filled him. He wanted to inhale her. He pushed the dress off her shoulders, her bra straps coming into view. They were thick and wide.

"Sorry," she said, her face flushing. "It's not exactly sexy. It's what I wear to work. I don't have a lot of lingerie."

"Stop." Alexei came to her side. His face was set in harsh lines. "No more apologies. Be still and let Caleb undress you."

"Hush, Holly." He pulled at the strap, pushing at the dress along the way. He exposed her shoulders. Her skin was silky smooth under his fingertips. "Look at that."

He let his fingers trace the line of her throat and the graceful curve of her shoulders.

"She is beautiful." Alexei took a place at Holly's back. He took her hair in his hands and brought it up before bringing his head down to kiss the nape of her neck. He ran his face along the back of her shoulders. Holly's eyes closed, and she leaned back.

She didn't look like a woman who was worried about her bra anymore.

Her arms relaxed, and the dress slid down. Alexei's hands disappeared, going behind her back. Her bra loosened, and Caleb pulled it off. Her breasts bounced free.

Fuck. He hadn't thought it possible to get harder. She was sexier than he'd dreamed. Her breasts were round and real. They were porcelain, tipped with good-size pink-and-brown nipples. Her skin was so pale, with a sweet dusting of freckles here and there. He stared at her for a moment. He could see the faint lines of veins and blood vessels, each one tracing a path to her heart. He touched a very faint blue line that ran under the skin close to her nipple. Anastomotic veins. They fed the nipple and ran into the veins under the superficial fascia of the breast. He knew every function of the breast, could recall every piece of anatomy he'd learned—but he wouldn't be able to put into words why he was so fascinated with this breast. Caleb reached out and took one in hand. He chuckled with satisfaction as the nipple puckered, begging for him to play with it.

Alexei growled from behind Holly, his head peeking over her shoulder. His eyes were on her breasts. "Pluck at the nipples."

Alexei was going to be bossy. He could deal with that. Alexei was the reason he was here in the first place. And, damn, but he wanted to play with those nipples.

He let his thumb flick across one and then the other. Holly shivered at his touch, her eyes coming open. Her gaze met his, the desire in the green orbs almost overwhelming. Her breasts swelled in his hands, and he couldn't wait to taste her. He fell to his knees, and her breasts were exactly where he needed them to be. He nuzzled her, letting his nose find the valley between her breasts, burying his face until he came into contact with her sternum. He breathed her in.

Her dress had caught around her hips, leaving the curve of her belly on full display. He kissed his way down to her navel, his hands worshipping every curve. He could smell her arousal, knew she was getting soft and wet, but he wanted to wait. He wanted to lavish her with all the affection she'd missed.

He licked his way back from her navel up to one plump breast. Alexei's hands came around and cupped her breasts, holding them up. It put them in the perfect position. Caleb leaned forward and pulled the nipple in his mouth. He sucked on her breasts, licking and biting gently before tonguing them. He switched back and forth, withholding nothing. Alexei's hands held her in place, giving him the opportunity to explore.

He cupped her ass, his fingers sinking into soft flesh and giving her a squeeze. Her ass was round and heart shaped. He stared at it as often as he could. He dreamed of spreading her gorgeous ass and fucking her asshole. He wanted every part of her. He wanted to sink his dick into her every hole. The soft wet heat of her mouth. The tight hole of her ass. The perfection of her pussy. He would leave no part of her untouched.

"Oh, Caleb. That feels so good." Holly was getting restless under his hands. Her skin was heating, flushing with arousal. Blood would be rushing to her vagina, making it plump and soft as it prepared to receive a cock.

His dick twitched at the thought. He knew all the functions of the various systems, knew why his balls were tight against his body, why his cockhead was most likely weeping. But it was different, so different than the other sexual experiences he'd had. He wanted to taste her. To really taste her. He wanted the juice of her arousal to coat his tongue.

He pulled at her dress, tugging at the underwear under it. The dress fell to the floor, and he dragged her white cotton underwear with it. He stared at the flesh he'd uncovered. Holly was a natural redhead, and she was as aroused as he'd suspected. The neat hair covering her pussy glistened with her natural lubrication. He reached out a hand to touch her.

"Caleb, stop."

He looked up, and Alexei's face was hard with arousal. Holly hissed slightly as Alexei pinched at her nipples.

"We still have not to discuss problems of earlier."

Bastard. Son of a bitch. Motherfucker. He wanted to go into that now? Caleb was ready to forget the whole damn thing. "Can we talk about this later?"

He wanted to fuck. He wanted to spread her legs and eat her pussy and then shove his cock deep, but Alexei wanted to give Holly a lecture. No. Not a lecture. A spanking.

Yeah, that was kind of hot, too.

"I don't want to talk." Holly reached out to Caleb. "If you have something to say, say it later."

Alexei's face went positively arctic. He looked down at Caleb, and for the first time, Caleb could really believe that this was a man who had survived in the Russian mob for years, seeking revenge. This was a man who had killed in defense and revenge. He'd read his file, but everything he'd seen of Alexei had been a smiling man who laughed and joked, or a repentant man, asking for forgiveness. But this was a part of Alexei, too.

"No. We need to be discussing now. Caleb, when would you prefer to talk to her? After the fucking? When she is perfectly satisfied and tired? She will not listen then. She will merely say yes and turn over and go to sleep, and more than likely will do same thing next time."

"What are we talking about? What did I do?" Holly tried to squirm, attempting to cover herself, but Alexei held her fast.

Shit. The big bastard was right.

Caleb got to his feet. "You didn't stop and get help. You didn't call either one of us."

"Today? When I wrecked the car?"

Caleb sighed. Why did she go there? Maybe they were better matched than he thought. She seemed to be a worst-case-scenario girl, not unlike himself. "You didn't wreck the car. You saved your life by properly driving it. I'm not pissed off about the truck. I'm pissed off that you thought you had to walk down the mountain when you could have stopped at a friend's house and called someone to come get you."

She shook her head. "I didn't want to bother anyone. Besides, Nell doesn't have a phone and Laura's busy."

Alexei's hand wound into her hair. His dark eyes found Caleb's. "You understand why I do what I do?"

Did he understand why Alexei was about to spank her? Sure he did. "She didn't even mention calling one of us. That road is dangerous. You could have been killed walking down it. You had another mile to go. You could have mitigated the risk by calling one of us from the Harper's place or Mel's. Even if you couldn't reach one of us on the phone, you could have called Stella's or The Trading Post and someone would have found us. Everyone knows everyone else's business in this town. Would you rather get hit by a car on that mountain than risk bugging one of us with a call?"

He did understand Alexei's anger now that he thought about it. What good were they to her if she didn't bother to rely on them?

Alexei stared down at her. "I need to have place with you, Holly. I am not smart man like Caleb. I am not sweet like you. I do not have place in this community. I need place in relationship. I will treat you like princess. I will treat you like queen. In normal life, I will be your lapping dog, but here, in the lovemaking part of life, I will be king and you will obey." He pulled her head back gently so she was forced to look in his eyes. "If this scares you or you are not interested in this part of me, then I will leave you to Caleb. I can't ignore these needs I have. I can only promise to be careful with you, to take care of you. Caleb, if you are bothered by it, I will leave, too."

It was obvious that Alexei wouldn't compromise. Oh, he would share and he would give on many things, but he understood who he was at heart and couldn't compromise.

Caleb respected that. Caleb wanted that for himself.

"Over his knee, Holly. Discipline is important."

Alexei smiled.

Crap. They had just become partners. And maybe they could actually be friends.

* * * *

Alexei sighed as he realized he'd tackled one mountain. Caleb was in. Holly stood still in his arms, her backside brushing his rock-hard cock. She was soft everywhere. He wanted to crush her against him and show her how different they were. He could have her on a bed, legs spread and penetrated faster than she could take her next breath, but that wouldn't start the relationship off on the proper footing.

He'd meant what he'd said. He would trail after her, playing her ever-doting suitor. He wouldn't care what anyone thought. But in private and when she was in trouble, he needed to be in charge. He needed this.

He let go of her though his every instinct screamed at him to keep her close. It had to be her decision. He would die if she said no, but he wouldn't force her. He'd never forced a woman in his life. He wouldn't start with the only one he'd ever truly cared about.

"Come." He sat down on her overstuffed couch and patted his knee.

She looked so vulnerable standing there, her arms covering her breasts. He would break her of that habit, too. She was beautiful. She should be proud of her body. He knew he was proud to have a woman as lovely as she was.

"Holly, satisfy the big guy so we can move on to the fun part." Caleb's hands cupped her shoulders. It was obvious that his partner was no longer thinking about the mechanics of the situation.

"Okay," she said, her voice shaking slightly.

Caleb pulled her close, his hand sinking into her hair. He caught her mouth with his.

Alexei watched, his cock threatening to bust out of his slacks. They were beautiful together. How had he managed to become involved with not one, but two redheads? He could almost hear his father's voice. He'd constantly teased Alexei's mother about her hair. Redheads were more volatile, more passionate, more trouble. Then his father would disappear behind closed doors with his "trouble" for hours. Yes, these two were trouble, and he was looking forward to it. Caleb's red and gold hair contrasted nicely with Holly's richer hue. Caleb's skin was tan against Holly's exquisite porcelain.

Where did he fit? Caleb had everything. Brains, money, a powerful family. He'd simply had a terribly traumatic experience. Alexei had decided after he'd learned of Caleb's past that the way to repay the doctor was to help bring him back to himself. When Caleb was healed, would he even need Alexei anymore? When Caleb was whole again, would Holly even look at Alexei? What would she need with a former criminal who couldn't find a job?

Caleb's hands cupped her breasts. Holly's moans and sensual cries were going to make him crazy. He let go of his worry. There would be time enough to worry about the future later. For tonight, he wanted to revel in the fact that he'd won. He'd gotten the three of them in a room together. He'd brought them together.

Holly practically melted in Caleb's arms. Their tongues mated. Their hands explored each other's bodies. Caleb's hands bit into the flesh of Holly's ass, bringing his cock in hard contact with her. Alexei watched. He would enjoy watching them make love. He was surprised to discover he didn't feel any jealousy. He'd worried about it, but Holly needed this. And Caleb, whether he ever recognized it or not, needed Alexei. It was good, so good, to be needed.

Caleb let her go and turned her in Alexei's direction. He gave her ass a little pat. "No more stalling, baby."

She walked toward him, her breasts bouncing slightly. Her lips were swollen from Caleb's kisses, and her skin flushed a pretty pink. He was going to make her skin even pinker. "You're going to spank me because I didn't call you?"

He shook his head. She should understand. He was not an unreasonable man. "No. I don't have phone yet, *dushka*. I'm spanking you because you didn't call Caleb. He would have been easy to reach. He would have taken care of you. He would have made sure you were safe."

Her eyes narrowed. "I don't know how I feel about this, Alexei, but I'm willing to give it a try."

"If you want me to stop, then I will stop, and we will come up with other punishment." He didn't want that. Any other punishment would make mutually satisfying sex impossible for a while. Any other punishment would involve withholding her orgasm. He didn't want that. His hands were itching to touch that gloriously round ass.

"I think I can handle it. Well, I hope I can. Jen seems to like it well enough, and I've heard Rachel and Callie mention something about it. I think I can handle it if they can." She took his outstretched hand and let him place her over his lap. She was awkward at first, but she sighed finally and relaxed.

And he was left staring at the prettiest backside he'd ever seen. The globes of Holly's ass were round and perfectly formed. He touched the dimples in the small of her back. They dipped gracefully and curved into her cheeks. She shivered under his hands.

Caleb came to stand in front of them. He pulled the T-shirt over his head and tossed it aside before getting down on one knee. He had the tube of lubricant Alexei had purchased earlier in the day at The Trading Post along with the condoms. Alexei had been surprised at the wide variety the small store carried.

Caleb was staring at her ass. "We're going to have to prepare her if you want to share her properly."

Properly? There was nothing proper about what he wanted to do with Holly. He wanted to fill all of her holes. He wanted to possess her in every way possible. But Caleb was right. She needed to be prepared. And he needed to find out if Holly would like his particular kink.

He brought his hand up and down in a short, quick arc. The sound snapped through the room.

Holly's whole body tensed and a shriek came out of her mouth. "Damn it, Alexei! You have to warn a girl."

The little *dushka* didn't understand who was in control. He was more than happy to teach her. Five quick slaps, alternating cheeks. Her lovely ass was curvy but firm. On the final slap, he rubbed her cheeks, reveling in the heat of her skin. She tried to come up, but he gently pressed her back down. "You do not make rules here. I make rules here and rule one is to call one of your men when danger is around you."

Another five. Her ass was pinkening up beautifully. Her legs kicked a bit, but she didn't fight him. If she had, he would have stopped immediately. He loved to play the game, but he never wanted to hurt her. Only little bites of pain to make the pleasure more overwhelming.

"Look at that." Caleb's hand came out and touched the now hot-pink cheek. He didn't look disgusted with the process. He looked like he might start to drool at any minute. He was certain Caleb could give a million and one medical reasons for why an erotic spanking was stimulating, but his mouth was silent for once.

"She owes me five more. You wish to give?" He'd made his mind up to share with Caleb a long time before. He wouldn't back down now. If Caleb wanted to play these games, he would cede a bit of control to him.

Caleb swallowed. "I don't know. I don't mind watching, but I think I'll sit this part out. You can be the one who spanks her. I'll be the one who shoves a couple of fingers up her ass afterward."

"Gee, thanks, Caleb," Holly said.

Two more. The flesh of her ass quivered, and she moaned. Each strike of his hand against her flesh caused his cock to tighten. "No sarcasm when punishment is happening."

"I don't think he should shove fingers up my ass." Holly's voice was strained, her breath rasping in and out of her mouth.

He stroked her bottom, letting his fingers trace the crack of her ass. One day he would part those cheeks and force his dick in. She would take him. She would welcome him into the most intimate parts of her body. "I wish I could tell you he will be gentle, but I think he did not do well in this part of his school. He obviously miss day they train doctors in gentleness."

Caleb's face split in a wide grin and he laughed, his head falling back. It was a full-throated laugh, unselfconscious. He'd never heard that sound come out of Caleb's mouth. It was good to hear the man laugh, even if it had been a humiliating experience. "I promise to treat Holly's sweet little rectum with far more gentleness than I treated yours."

"What?" Holly practically came off his lap.

Two more slaps and she calmed down. She obviously needed a firm hand. "Our friend was very thorough in examination. He say I must to do every year, but I think I find different doctor."

"You checked his prostate so he could have sex with me?" Holly asked, trying to turn her face up.

Caleb's hand stroked her hair. "No, I checked his prostate because that's what doctors do when they're pissed off. It's a perk of the job. I'm going to very gently work my fingers in your ass because eventually I want to shove my cock up there without too much discomfort to you. I have to stretch you out. I'd prefer a plug, but fingers will work for tonight. But Alexei probably does need a check done every now and then. Do you have any history of colon cancer in your family?"

Caleb was such a frustrating man. Alexei had to get him back to the job at hand.

"No to the doctoring now. Please to prepare fingers for ass." Alexei slapped her one last time and rubbed the spot he'd hit. So hot and pink. He let his fingers travel lower. He could already smell the musk of her arousal, but he wanted to feel it, taste it. She'd liked the spanking. He could play with her. He could gradually introduce her to more exotic forms of play. He could see her bound and waiting for his pleasure. "You are not angry with me for spanking?"

She groaned as he lightly touched her pussy with teasing strokes. "No. Please, Alexei. The spanking was nice, but I need more."

She was wet. So wet. His fingers slid easily through her juices. He let his middle finger slip inside her pussy. Her delicate muscles clenched around his finger. He fucked that single finger in and out of her pussy. He could practically feel her vibrating with frustration.

"You will get more," he said, feeling a smile cross his face. "But not until you work for it."

Chapter Nine

Holly was ready to scream. Work for it? She was going crazy. What Alexei had called punishment had felt like the most exquisite torture. At first the pain had stung and bit into her skin. But then she'd been struck by the erotic quality of it. She'd felt small and vulnerable across Alexei's knee. It had been a long time since she'd felt delicate and feminine. She'd found herself breathlessly waiting to see what exactly he would do.

And it had been possible for one reason and one reason only. She trusted him. She was shocked to find that she trusted this man implicitly. Maybe it was the earnest, heartfelt letters he'd sent every month they were apart. Maybe it was the fact that he'd been willing to sacrifice his life to save a group of strangers, but she knew deep down that this was a man who she could rely on.

She could love him if she let herself.

She wasn't going there. Way, way too early for that.

Alexei's legs spread wide and she found herself being shifted from his lap to the floor between his legs. The rug beneath her was soft from years of use. Her hands came up on Alexei's knees for balance.

"You do very well, *dushka*." Alexei's dark eyes seemed unbearably hot. His hair had fallen over his forehead. He looked like a gorgeous angel, fallen from heaven. So dominant.

"You did spectacularly well." Caleb's hand found her head. She sighed at the feeling.

Alexei's voice brought her attention back to him. "But now it is time to take care of me. You will take care of me while Caleb prepares you for later. Take my pants down. Take me in hand."

She had to remind herself to breathe.

"I'm going to need your ass in the air, baby," Caleb said.

She turned and felt her heart skip a beat. Caleb had taken off his shirt. He was wearing nothing but a faded pair of Levi's, and even those were unsnapped, leaving a view of his spectacularly cut torso. There wasn't an ounce of fat on the doctor. She'd heard he ran every day, but it looked like he lifted weights, too. A lot of them. His body was lean and tight. He was like a sleek, predatory jaguar, built for speed and agility.

She forced herself to look away because she worried actual drool might be coming next. And when she turned back, Alexei had unbuttoned his shirt.

If Caleb was a jaguar, Alexei was a full-blown tiger. His chest was broad and covered in muscles that tapered down to a six-pack and lean hips. His eyes narrowed as he looked at her. The tiger, it seemed, was awfully hungry.

"Are you going to do as I asked? Or do you need another spanking? Perhaps this time I will bind your hands and feet. I will tease that little pussy of yours, but you will get nothing."

Nope, she didn't want that at all. Her hands trembled as she reached for the button at the top of his slacks. She unbuttoned it, slipping the round disk through the hole and moving down to his zipper. She could feel the hard line of his cock struggling against the fabric of his pants.

She pushed the front flaps of his slacks aside. He wore cotton boxers. The tip of his cock strained at the opening, the head peeking out.

"Don't be shy." Alexei stared down at her, decadent anticipation in his eyes. "Touch me. Take me in hand and stroke me. I want to feel your mouth on my cock."

How long had it been since she'd given a blow job? Forever. It had been forever since she'd touched her tongue to a man's cock.

She pulled the waistband of his boxers down, and his cock escaped its confinement. It also looked like cocks had gotten way bigger since she'd been out of the game. Alexei's cock was huge. Long and thick, so thick. It lay almost flat against his perfect abs. She reached out and touched it. Soft skin covered the hard muscle. It was beautifully formed, with a mushroom-shaped head and heavy, round balls. She was fascinated by the deep *V* where his cockhead met the thick stalk of his penis.

She couldn't help it. She reached out and touched her tongue to the place.

Alexei groaned, and his head fell back, relaxing against the couch.

"She doesn't listen very well." Caleb's hands gripped her hips, reminding her of what he wanted.

She came up on her knees, giving Caleb her backside.

"That's better." Caleb's hands slid over her slightly sore backside. Even that slight pain seemed erotic.

She was between two Greek gods, and she suddenly let go of all that insecurity. If they didn't want her, they wouldn't be here. Alexei wouldn't be thrusting his cock toward her face and Caleb's hands wouldn't be worshipping her ass. There must be something attractive about her if these two men wanted her.

"Lick me." Alexei's accent had gone deeper and thicker. He muttered something in Russian. The words were like an aphrodisiac. She didn't need to know what he was saying. He was telling her to take him in her mouth. He wanted to fuck her mouth.

She brought her tongue to the bottom of his cock where the soft skin flowed into his balls. She started at the base and licked a line up. He smelled good, masculine and clean. He tasted good. His flesh was an amazing mix of baby-soft skin and rock-hard muscle. She teased the *V*, lavishing it with affection.

She felt Caleb pulling apart the cheeks of her ass.

"Are you ready for me to play a bit? God, this is a perfect example of an anus. Mmmm. Look at that."

"Suck me inside. Stop playing." Alexei's fingers wound into her hair. "Suck me until I am dry."

There was a drop of arousal on the head of his cock. It sat there like a treat waiting to be lapped up. She swiped it up with her tongue. Salty. She sucked his cockhead into her mouth just as she felt something wet touch her.

"Pucker up now, sweetheart. When I'm done, you'll open right up for me." Caleb's voice had gone dark, too.

She couldn't help but jump the tiniest bit as Caleb massaged the lube into her ass.

"She is tight, no?" Alexei asked.

"Fuck, yeah, she's tight. Tell me something. You ever done this before? The three-way thing?"

It was nice that they could hold a conversation. It really was. Of course, she couldn't join in. Alexei thrust his cock up, as though tired of her shallow play.

"Open up, *dushka*. Take more. To answer your question—no and yes. Yes, I have done the ménage, but in Russia, this is done with many women and only one man. It sound very sexy. The truth is a cock gets tired after a while and womens can be demanding. And they do not want to watch the hockey games afterward. You Americans are smarter. Best to please woman and then have friend to hang."

"*Hang out with*, Alexei. It's hang out with. I'm hoping you don't hang me. And don't call this an American thing. This is a Bliss thing. It only happens in Bliss."

Holly shuddered as Caleb rimmed her asshole. She tried to talk around the cock in her mouth.

"Don't talk. Suck."

Bossypants. She could finish this. If Alexei thought he was going to talk sports or something with Caleb while she worked on his cock, then maybe it was time she distracted him. It might have been a long time since she'd sucked a cock, but the instinct didn't go away. She was still a woman, and a woman knew how to get to a man.

She cupped his balls, rolling them up against his body as she sucked him deep. It was hard. He was so big. He filled her mouth. She had to relax her jaw, but she finally managed to get that whole monster in her mouth. She sucked at it in long, luscious passes, whirling her tongue around the stalk.

Alexei groaned, and the Russian words began to flow.

"She's giving it to you good. Fuck. I can't wait to try her mouth." Caleb pressed his finger in, little forays into her ass that had her clenching. "Relax. Let me in. Let me play with your ass."

It burned. That finger made it hard to concentrate on the cock in her mouth. She forced herself to suck. Caleb kept at it. He fucked her ass, pressing in and then stretching the rim. He finally sighed, and Holly felt his finger sink in.

"So fucking tight." Caleb pushed in. "This is what you wanted, Holly. Two of us inside you. Wait until it's a cock inside this tight ass and not just fingers, sweetheart. Then you'll know who you belong to."

Caleb Burke was such an idiot. Only sex? There was something possessive in the way the man made love. Maybe she was misreading him. Maybe she was on her way to heartache, but it felt like more than sex.

She felt closer to them than she'd felt to anyone in the longest time. She loved her friends. Nell and Laura had been her support system for so long, her strength, but this was something even sweeter. This was pure intimacy. She opened herself to them and gave.

"*Dushka*, a little more. You will swallow me, no? I want to give this to you."

And she wanted to take it. Holly took a long breath and went deep. She grasped his stalk and squeezed gently while she took him to the back of her throat. She swallowed while breathing through her nose and felt the moment his orgasm began.

Warm fluid spat in her mouth while Alexei's hands wound in her hair. He murmured what sounded like loving phrases to her in Russian while he filled her mouth. She swallowed him down, the saltiness strangely sweet on her tongue. She was full of him. It was enough. Holly finally let the cock go, kissing it with great affection.

Caleb added a second finger, and she couldn't help the groan that came out of her mouth. The sensation burned, but it was so intimate she couldn't deny the appeal. Alexei's hands softened in her hair. He petted her, praising her the whole time. He told her how beautiful she was, how sexy. He promised her he'd never had a better blow job, although he called it a blowing job, and she couldn't help but giggle at that.

"She is opening up?" Alexei asked, looking over her head. He didn't move to fix his clothes. He seemed perfectly comfortable with that gorgeous cock of his hanging out as he watched his partner fucking her ass with his fingers.

"She's tight, and she's going to stay that way, but it will work. I think we need to get her a plug. I'll get one tomorrow."

She came off Alexei's lap as far as the fingers in her backside would allow her to. "I am not running around town with a plug up my ass."

Caleb shrugged. "Yes, you will. All the other women do it. Trust me, half the women in this town are playfully accessorized. Come by my office tomorrow. I'll take care of it. I won't touch you back here until you're properly prepared. I want you to love this. I won't hurt you."

He wouldn't. Caleb wouldn't be capable of hurting her physically. Her heart was another matter, but she'd decided to risk it. "All right, Caleb."

"You see, she learns to obey in the bedroom." Alexei sounded awfully pleased with himself.

Holly groaned as Caleb pulled his fingers out. She felt his lips kiss the small of her back.

"That's probably going to be the only place she obeys, and thank god for that. I'll be right back." Caleb left, walking over to her small bathroom.

Alexei hauled her up to his lap. He pulled her face to his and kissed her, his lips eating hungrily at hers. "Thank you, *dushka*. Thank you for pleasing me and for being the open, beautiful woman that you are. I dream of you every night. Tonight, I will not need to dream. Tonight, I will sleep beside you."

She would sleep cuddled between them both. It would be as good as the sex. She'd never been very good at sex. She was thrilled Alexei was happy with her. Now she had to hope Caleb was happy with her, too. She would get on her knees in front of him when he returned, and she would see how he tasted.

Alexei's mouth journeyed over and around her face to her neck. His hands were even bolder. One wrapped around her waist, but his other hand delved between her legs, teasing at the lips of her pussy. She spread her legs to give him access, and he skimmed over her clit. So close. She was close to that heavenly place that always seemed to elude her. She'd brought herself to climax a couple of times, but this felt so different.

"Please." She wasn't above begging. She wanted him inside her. She could feel his cock against her hip. He was already hard again.

"*Nyet*. This I cannot claim."

"Because it's my turn." Caleb stood over her, his face granite hard. He'd shucked the rest of his clothes. He was leaner than Alexei, but his cock was just as big. Two. She had two gorgeous men. "He's had a moment with you, and now I want my time."

He reached down and plucked her out of Alexei's arms. Alexei smiled a slow, sexy grin and winked at her. "I did promise to share my toy."

Caleb's arms went around her waist and under her knees. He didn't look down at her. He simply walked off, taking the few steps to get to her bedroom. "Turn on the light for me. I want to see her."

It wasn't said to Holly. It was tossed over his shoulder toward Alexei, who was already getting off the couch. She watched as he pushed his slacks down, shrugged out of his shirt, and followed them, completely naked.

Thank god everyone was naked. It was every bit as bad as she'd thought it would be. They were so far out of her league, it was ridiculous, and yet they were here. They were with her.

Caleb stabilized himself on her quilted queen-size bed and placed her on top. He got to his knees and towered over her, taking her legs in each hand and pressing them apart. He was so lovely, his face stark in the dim light.

The light came on as Alexei entered the room. "Let me help you."

Caleb looked up and nodded, his face almost unreadable. Alexei's weight forced the mattress to dip. He placed a hand on her cheek and smiled down warmly. Caleb ran a hand down her torso.

"I think I want to taste you before I fuck you," Caleb said.

Just like that, her heart started to pound. Caleb inside her. Alexei inside her. Even if it all went to hell tomorrow, she would have this night to remember forever. She would have loved them. She'd been alone for far too long. "Please, Caleb. I need you. I need you both."

"Then you'll have us." Caleb leaned over and kissed her throat. He kissed his way down her torso, pausing to suckle on her nipples and to dip his tongue in her navel. Alexei stroked her hair and kissed her forehead, her cheeks, the tip of her nose. Their lips were soft, playing against her skin, making her feel more wanted than she'd ever dreamed of feeling.

"Tomorrow, when you come to my office, I'm going to shave you. I want to be able to really enjoy this." Caleb's finger slid into her pussy. She was so wet. She'd never been so wet. Anticipation was going to kill her.

Caleb forced her legs apart and stared at her pussy. Alexei had stopped his exploration, and he stared down her body as well.

"She's beautiful, but it will be even better when she's completely bare. How about we split the duties? You take care of discipline, and I'll see to her grooming and preparation. I'll make sure she's always ready for pleasure." Caleb sounded so different. In control. Sure of himself. It was undeniably sexy.

His eyes were on her as he got on his belly and breathed in the scent of her arousal. When he reached out and swiped her pussy with his tongue, she nearly came off the bed. Alexei reached down and gripped one of her nipples.

"Stay still, *dushka*." His fingers tightened almost to the point of pain. It was a sweet bite that caused her whole body to clench.

"Whatever you did, she liked it." Caleb nipped at her pussy lips, feasting on her. He tortured her with his tongue while Alexei pinched at her nipples. Alexei repositioned himself so he could get his mouth on her breasts. One hand twisted on the nub while he bit gently on the other nipple. All the while, Caleb sucked and licked her pussy. He blew on her clit.

"I have tricks, baby. I'll play them all on you before I'm through. I made a very thorough study of the female reproductive organs. These are a lovely example of labia majora. The outer lips." Caleb kissed them, sucking each side into his mouth. "And your clitoris has more than one part, of course."

He was killing her. She wanted to buck up, to force him to fuck her with his tongue. That muscular, talented tongue of Caleb's hovered over her clit, but he kept talking, his breath hot on her flesh.

"You have the hood." He reached to the top of her mound and gently pulled back on her clitoral hood. "It's a hiding place for the good stuff. This is the clitoral glans. Look at that, baby. Yours is full of blood. It's begging for some affection, isn't it?"

Dying was more like it. "Please, Caleb."

He licked at her, but it was a teasing touch. "You have a very beautiful clitoral crus. So pretty."

He was maddening.

Alexei chuckled. "Caleb, my friend, you are much better at discipline than I am. If we ever want to torture our pretty woman, we will set up one of your anatomy lessons."

"Well, I think I should prove that I know how to do more than just name the lovely thing." Caleb pulled the hood tight and sucked her clit into his mouth.

Holly nearly came apart. The orgasm was stronger than anything she'd ever felt. It raced through her veins and all along her skin. Alexei's lips tugged at her breasts, bringing them into the sensation. She felt the pleasure flow to her fingertips and toes, radiating from her pussy.

Caleb continued to lick at her clit. Every time he touched her, she nearly jumped, the pleasure threatening to start all over again. Caleb laid one last kiss on her before getting to his knees.

"I don't need help with this part, Alexei." His voice was hard and commanding.

Alexei kissed her one last time. He got up off the bed. "I think you do. You forget."

Alexei tossed him a condom. Oh, god. He was going to fuck her. Caleb Burke.

Caleb shook his head and stared down at the condom like he needed a minute to recognize what he was holding. "Yeah. I should wear this."

"You want me to leave?" Alexei asked.

She stayed quiet. She hoped Caleb wouldn't shut Alexei out. Somehow it felt right to have him here. It felt perfect to be with the two of them, but if Caleb needed it, she would learn to compromise.

"No. You can watch." Caleb seemed to struggle for a minute with the condom, tugging it over his cock and rolling it down.

Alexei settled himself into the small chair she used for reading at night. He was a huge hulking presence, making her chair seem more delicate than it really was. He sat back, utterly relaxed, with the singular exception of his cock. It strained upward. Alexei guided his hand up and down the gorgeous monster, his other hand toying with a condom. He was waiting his turn.

But Caleb had found his footing again. He wet his dick in her juices, sliding it all over. The nerves in her pussy lit up again. She'd been pretty damn sure she couldn't come again after what he'd done with his tongue. She'd been perfectly willing to lie back and let them do their worst, but now she reached up to clutch at Caleb's shoulders as he placed his cock at the edge of her pussy.

"Baby, you're so tight. Even here. Shh. I don't want to hurt you." His dick teased at her entrance, shallow thrusts that made her want more.

"You're hurting me now. Fuck me." His caution was going to kill her.

"You should give woman what she wants, my friend." Alexei's hand kept up the slow drag on his dick.

"Demanding thing, aren't you? How the fuck did you hold out for years, baby? You're too hot to languish. Well, we can make up for lost time." Caleb gripped her hips and started to thrust.

Oh, fuck, he'd been right. She was too small. Even as the burn hit her, she pushed down on him, trying to take more. She didn't care that he was too big. She wanted him inside. She wanted to know what it felt like to have him.

He was ruthless. He held himself up as he worked his dick in. Shallow thrusts that gained more territory every time he moved. She tried to pull at his hips, to get him to go deeper. She'd never felt so wild. She'd been a good girl all her life. She'd been the one who always did the right thing no matter what it cost her. She'd been faithful to a man who had cheated on her with most of the female population of Denver. When they had needed money because his family had cut him off, she'd quit college to put him through school. When she'd gotten pregnant and his family had finally taken him back, she'd gone and endured their insults because she'd made vows. She'd promised, and she'd held herself to that promise right up until the day the world was torn out from under her.

No more. Now she could see the half life she'd lived. Always afraid to make waves. She wanted this.

"Holly, calm down."

"No, I want this." If Caleb refused her, she wasn't sure what she would do.

He stopped and pulled out. Her heart threatened to break. He didn't want her. She'd screwed up.

Caleb rolled over on his back and tugged on her hand. "Come on. Take me. Take me however you want, baby."

His body was laid out for her. Every inch of his six feet two inches was waiting for her.

"Caleb, I..." She wasn't sure what to say.

"Kiss me."

She leaned over and kissed him, her heart coming back to life. He was doing this for her. For all of Caleb Burke's gruff ways, he was a compassionate man. She could see that he wanted to dominate her, but he gave her what she needed.

"I love you, Caleb Burke." She loved him with her whole heart. She had almost from the moment she'd seen him.

"Holly." He swallowed as though there were words in his throat, but he would never let them out.

She placed a finger to his lips. He didn't need to say a thing. He was damaged, brutally so. He'd lost his wife. That was all she really knew. He might never love again, but he should know he was loved. She would give him what he needed. A pass. "Hush. You don't have to say it back. I just needed to say it."

She mounted him. His cock thrust up between his legs. She gripped him gently and placed his dick at her entrance. So good. He felt so good. Every muscle rippled as she let gravity do its worst. She lowered herself onto him inch by delicious inch. Caleb's hands clutched the bed sheets under him as though he was trying hard not to take control.

She worked her way down. She was so wet that despite the size difference, she slid onto his cock. He was big and thick inside her. She was already full. What would it be like when Alexei was with them? She let her head fall back as she took him as far as she could go. Every inch of her pussy was filled with Caleb Burke. She experimented a little, bouncing up and coming back down.

"Oh, god, you feel so good. More. Holly, fuck me harder."

It briefly flashed through her brain to tease him the way he'd teased her, but she wanted him too badly. She ground down on him, loving the groan she elicited from him. His hands found her hips, seemingly unable to stay out of the game for a minute more. He circled her waist and forced her down on his dick.

"God, that's it, baby. Fuck me hard. Ride me."

She balanced herself on his chest and took off. She fucked him, letting his hands steady her. She felt wild and free, powerful for maybe the first time in her life. She found the perfect angle and worked it. His cock slid over some place deep inside her as she ground down on him, her clit hitting his pelvis in perfect harmony. She went off like a rocket, the second orgasm even more powerful than the first. She was barely starting to come down when Caleb took over. He rolled her on her back, rearranged her legs, and thrust back in.

"You know how hot you are? Do you know how hot you make me? Fuck, baby, watching you come is the hottest thing I've ever seen. Don't for one moment think you aren't beautiful." Caleb didn't hold back now. He pounded into her. He reared back and shot forward. He leaned down and joined their bodies, cock in pussy, belly to belly, her nipples pressed against his chest. He kissed her and completed the circle of their bodies, his tongue thrusting in her mouth, and he came. His body stiffened, and he lost control. His hips hammered, but she could taste herself on his tongue. He ground down against her, and pleasure flared to life again.

She might have been frigid before, but there was nothing cold about her now.

Caleb's body stiffened one last time before he slumped on top of her as though all his strength was gone. He kissed her, his tongue playing, but it was a lazy thing now.

He finally rolled off her. "Do you feel better, baby?"

"Thank you." He'd given her exactly what she needed.

But that look was back in his eyes. Now that the sex was over, it seemed Caleb was back. "I'm going to go clean up. I'll get you a hot towel."

"If you want to go, you can. It's okay." She'd play it his way for now. He'd given her what she needed. If he needed space, she would give it to him.

He seemed to come to some decision. "No. No. I want to stay. Alexei got to watch. I want to watch, too."

"I am thinking I should be the one to go, *dushka*." Alexei's voice was still deep, but he sounded smaller now.

God, she'd told Caleb she loved him.

Caleb rolled off the bed. "I'll leave you two alone for a minute. I don't think you should go, Alexei. I don't want that. I thought I would, but I don't." He walked out after a momentary pause but left the door open behind him as if he needed the reminder that he was welcome.

"Why would you leave?"

"*Dushka*, you love him. It is plain. He is foolish man who is allowing hurt to silence his mouth. He loves you, too. Perhaps it is better I leave you to work out."

And just like that, she finally understood that this wasn't a game for Alexei. He honestly thought they could make this whole thing work. He wanted it to work. He wanted her, and not for a little while. He wasn't biding his time.

"Nothing has been real for you, has it?" She thought about what his life had been like. He'd told her in his letters. He'd written long passages about what his life had been like since his brother had been killed. Every moment of his adult life had been a lie. He'd lied to go into the mob, and he'd hidden huge pieces of himself to stay alive.

He shook his head sadly. "No, my *dushka*. It has not been real. *This* is real to me. I want for your happiness. I see you with Caleb, and you are so happy with him. You are in love with him. I will take that as consolation. I cannot be the third. I cannot be the one who is merely here for fun."

He meant every word he'd said to her. She'd discounted him because he was so much younger, but he knew what he wanted. He'd said he wanted her, and he'd meant it. He didn't play games anymore. He needed something real. He wouldn't accept less. She finally got it.

She had power over both these men. She would never abuse it. It was a gift she'd waited for all of her life.

She didn't bother to cover herself up now. The instinct had been strong an hour before, and now it fled. It was right to be naked in front of Alexei. He was hers. He'd offered that huge heart to her on a silver platter, and she'd been too insecure to see it. She wasn't stupid enough to turn him away. Beneath his rough, gorgeous exterior was a man with a breathtakingly beautiful soul. "Alexei, I love you, too."

He shook his head. "No. You do not have to say."

She took his face between her palms. "Alexei, I love you. I love you. I love you. I'll say it until you believe it."

He looked up at her, his eyes so serious. "I love you. I never say this to any woman except my mother. No woman but you."

She took his hand and led him to the bed. She lay down and pulled him on top of her. "Make love to me."

"With much pleasures, *dushka*."

He spread her legs and worked his way inside after rolling a condom on his cock. Holly sighed as the pleasure built, and she vowed she would do anything to keep her men.

Chapter Ten

Caleb gingerly rolled out of bed, praying he didn't wake either of the people currently sleeping under the soft quilts. Holly was exhausted. And probably sore. Yet she hadn't turned them away. Caleb had taken her twice followed each time by Alexei, as though neither of them could stand to not take their fair share out of her gorgeous hide.

She'd welcomed them. She'd held out her arms each time and welcomed them into her body. It had felt like coming home.

She loved him.

What the fuck had he done?

He glanced at the clock. It was almost two in the morning. He couldn't stay in bed. He was too antsy, his eyes constantly going to the door. There was a thin line of light coming from under the door, taunting him. It had taken everything he'd had to lie there and wait for them to fall asleep. He'd simply watched the door, waiting for it to open and something terrible to crawl through. Something terrible always came through.

Wolf was right. He'd never really left that damn box.

He scrubbed a hand through his hair and wished he were a better man. He glanced back and Holly was lying there, the moonlight hitting her face. So fucking gorgeous. She turned as though she realized he wasn't in bed any longer and sought the other source of warmth. Alexei's arms came around her, and she sighed as she settled back down. They nestled together, obviously warm and happy.

They didn't need him. He was free to go. He'd done exactly what he'd promised. He'd given her a night of passion. He'd given her a fantasy. So why did it feel like it had been his own fantasy that had come true? One he didn't even realize he'd had. For those hours, he'd been happy. He'd been focused on her. He'd belonged.

As quietly as he could, he walked across the floor, closing the door behind him. He made a beeline for the bathroom. He turned on the light and washed up as best he could. He didn't want to shower. He smelled like her. How long could he go before he ran patients off?

He looked up in the mirror and stared. When the hell had he stopped trying? The man who looked back at him seemed older, gaunter than he remembered himself being. He was sleepwalking through life, and he couldn't quite make himself wake up.

He loved Holly. He couldn't say it to her. He felt it in his soul, but she deserved more. And maybe he deserved far less.

He hadn't thought about Caroline once after he'd started making love to Holly. All of the other women he'd fucked had somehow morphed into her. She was a ghost who constantly clung to him. He hadn't loved her. He'd thought he had in the beginning, but they had become two completely separate people. She'd begged him not to go into the jungle. She'd told him he would die out there.

She'd been the one to die. How was he supposed to be happy after he'd caused so much misery?

It was better to leave. Alexei had offered him everything he could have hoped for. He could enjoy Holly in the only way he was capable of. He thought briefly about leaving town permanently, but he was honest enough with himself that he knew he wouldn't. He would come back as often as they would let him. He would be their third because it was all he would allow himself. He would watch as they moved in together, built a life together, and he showed up for sex. It was pathetic, but he would do it because he couldn't walk away. He needed this place. He needed her.

And he needed to leave.

He slipped out of the bathroom and started to look for his pants.

"You leave so soon?" Alexei's voice startled him. Caleb nearly jumped out of his skin. Which was also all he was wearing.

"Damn it. You can't do that to a person." Now that there wasn't a woman in the room, two dudes talking with their junk hanging out seemed weird to him. He skipped the underwear and went straight for the jeans, scooping them off the floor and stepping into them as quickly as he could.

"You sneak out, I sneak up. There is no difference." Alexei didn't seem bothered by the whole nude-dude thing.

Crap. He wasn't expecting to deal with Alexei. Alexei was supposed to be perfectly happy to see his ass leave. Alexei should have stayed curled around Holly. "Go back to bed, man. I'm going to head home."

"You have trouble sleeping?" Alexei's eyes narrowed thoughtfully.

"I don't sleep much, no." He looked around for his shirt. The room was littered with hastily tossed off clothes. Holly's dress had been thrown across the long sofa. Her shoes had made it to the tiny kitchen. There was a bra on the fireplace. He located Alexei's slacks hanging over the TV and tossed them his way. "If we're going to have a conversation, put on some pants, man."

"Americans." Alexei pulled his slacks on while shaking his head. "We will not mind if you toss and turn. Come back to bed, my friend. In morning, we make love to Holly all over again."

They might mind when he woke up screaming and in a cold sweat. They certainly might mind when he punched and kicked, trying to get out of the cage he found himself in every night when he closed his eyes. He could hurt Holly. He hadn't actually hurt anyone in a while, but it could always come back. He couldn't risk it. "No."

A long sigh came from Alexei's mouth. "Yes, that would be answer. You say no a lot, Caleb. We must find things for you to say yes to."

He made it sound so damn simple. "I'm not saying I won't come back."

"You simply will not to sleep with her. Or is it me?"

This was so awkward. "You seriously think I would fuck with you in the same room, but I won't sleep in the same bed? No. It's not that. I don't like to sleep with anyone."

There was a long pause, as though Alexei was trying to figure out how to deal with him. This was precisely why Caleb had stayed out of relationships. He didn't want to be figured out.

"Is it because of what happen in Sierra Leone, Dr. Sommerville?"

The words stopped him in his tracks. It was as though Alexei had pulled the pin on a grenade, and now Caleb had to wait to see if it was going to go off and kill them all. "You know who I am."

The Russian shrugged. "I had not much to do in witness protection. Your family is very celebrated. It was not difficult. There were many, many articles about the Sommervilles. One of US marshals I worked with thought she recognized you in the hospital. I have a cousin back in Russia who is excellent at investigating. He sends me much information. Why do you hide this? You are hero, Caleb."

Some fucking hero. He'd led ten people to their deaths. His wife. Two nurses. Three local aid workers. Five patients who had come to his clinic seeking anyone who could help them and their children. They'd all been slaughtered because a group of criminals had seen a spectacularly heady payday.

"I don't want to talk about it." He never talked about it.

Alexei shook his head. "I do not be understanding. I know what happens in Africa was bad, but it was not your fault. You were victim."

"I took those nurses there. I took my workers there. I brought the patients in." He'd led them into hell.

"You take workers there to help people," Alexei insisted. "You take them to bring medicine and healing to people with no hope. You help patients."

Yes, he'd set up the clinic to help, but the situation had been far more complex. He'd also done it to get away from a marriage that wasn't working. His charity work had become his world. He'd ignored everyone and everything because it was easier to focus on people who only needed him for his skill as a doctor. He should have known that Caroline would turn to another man. If he'd had half a heart, he would have freed her before he went into the jungle. If he'd done that, she wouldn't have come after him in search of her divorce. "You don't know anything about it, Markov."

"Then explain to me. Maybe you should talk about it."

He fucking thought about it all the time. He didn't want to talk about it. Anger started to simmer inside him. Alexei thought he could walk back in and put him through some weird kind of therapy? Or was there something more sinister at work? Maybe Alexei wasn't as friendly as he seemed. It wouldn't be the first time someone had gotten close to him in order to feed off his family. "And I was beginning to think I was wrong about you. Tell me something, are you planning on telling Holly?"

Alexei leaned against the wall. "I don't understand why you hide this. She would understand better if you tell her your story."

"Yes, she would love it. I chose to go by my mother's maiden name a long time ago. I don't live in my brothers' world. I don't fit there. I never did. So, let's skip all the small talk and get to the shakedown portion of the evening. How much?"

For the first time, Alexei didn't look totally self-assured. "I don't to understand."

God, that whole "I don't get English" thing was probably a scam, too. "How much to keep your mouth shut? How much to get you to leave? Money. That's what we're talking about. How much of the Sommerville pie do you intend to get your hands on? It's a big fucking pie. I'm sure you think you're entitled to a slice. I have to say, I appreciate your tactics better than the last fuckers who got some cash out of me. At least you didn't kill my wife and shove me in a cage. The sex thing was a much better way to start your extortion play. Did they teach you that in the mob?"

Alexei stood up straight, his face opening. "What are you talking about? This has nothing to do with mob. This is one friend trying to watch after another friend."

"Sure it is." Why hadn't he seen it? He'd let his lust for Holly blind him. Holly. Alexei had seemed to want her so badly. She was going to be hurt, too. Motherfucker. "Did you think about her for one second? Did you think that she would fall in love with you, or was that part of your plan, too?"

Alexei's eyes went cold. "Do not bring her into this. And do not question my feelings for her. I know who you are. I am not one keeping secrets from her about myself. I have not told her about you. I will not tell her, but how will she feel when she realizes you did not trust her?"

He trusted Holly. At first he'd simply wanted some peace, and that had meant pretending he wasn't a Sommerville. Wolf had promised him that this was a place where he wouldn't have to worry about reporters and where almost no one would know or care who his family was. Stefan Talbot had known, but he'd promised to keep quiet. The town had needed a doctor. It had seemed like a place where he could do his work and be alone.

And then he'd met Holly. And the more he knew about Holly's past, the deeper he realized he was in. Holly had gotten the shit kicked out of her by one political family. How the hell would she feel about the fact that he had a brother in the Senate, two cousins in Congress, and a father who had served as the Secretary of the Interior. The Sommervilles made the Langs look like tiny gnats. She would flip out at the prospect of dating a Sommerville.

And perhaps at one point in time she would have been right to do so, but Caleb was done with the whole scene. And his family wasn't like the Langs, but the time that he could have made that plain to her was past. He couldn't explain to her that his brother wouldn't look down on her. His brother would simply be happy that he was dating someone, anyone. Dating would be normal, and Eli would probably dance a jig if he knew about it. As for his younger brother, Josh would probably fight him over Holly. Holly was exactly Josh's type.

But she didn't have to know anything about his family until fucking Alexei came along. "It doesn't matter."

"I agree. You are not your family. But I wonder. You do so many good things. Why do you hide them?"

"I don't want to talk about this."

Alexei held up a hand. "Then we will not."

Caleb opened his mouth to tell the fucker that he wouldn't pay him a dime, but Alexei stopped him.

"Don't to talk anymore. You will only make me angry, and nothing will be helped. I am not going to blackmail you. I don't want your money. Though I do not understand why, I want your friendship. I found out who you are exactly the way I say I did. Nothing more. Nothing less. I admire your work. I am grateful for your work. It saves my life. I would not to repay this with blackmail. I have done nothing that would make you believe me. I can only live and prove I am not the man you think I am."

But Alexei *had* done something. More than something. He'd heroically saved Holly and then offered to share her.

Caleb wasn't sure which Alexei was more dangerous—the

criminal or the man who acted like a saint. He had two choices. He could believe Alexei or he could watch him with suspicion.

He might do a bit of both. "If I find out…"

Alexei held up a hand. His whole body seemed to go on full alert.

"What?" He'd barely gotten the word out when Alexei hushed him and reached down to pick up his shirt. He lifted it, and Caleb caught sight of a big, shiny object. "Holy shit. Is that a gun?"

"Shhh." Alexei hefted the gun—yep, that was a big fucking gun—and clicked off the safety. His voice was low as he came close. "Someone is outside. I hear car, and now someone is moving."

Caleb stopped and sure enough, he heard it, too. Someone was outside the cabin. He heard footsteps on the porch. They stopped and then began again, this time moving around to the side of the house. Still, he wasn't sure about that gun. "Is that necessary?"

Alexei's brow lifted. "Yes, it is necessary when many peoples wish to kill you. Stay here. I will take care of intruder."

"No fucking way. I'm coming with you." He might have to stitch someone up. "You need to be careful with that thing. It could be Mel looking for aliens. Or Laura checking in on Holly. We're not alone out here, you know."

But Alexei was moving along the floor toward the back door. Holly's cabin was small, with the front and back doors in sight of each other. Alexei moved almost silently, a genuine feat for a man his size on old hardwood floors. The door squeaked quietly as Alexei slipped out.

Someone was out there, and Alexei was taking it seriously. It was probably someone they knew, but then again, Holly'd had a close call earlier. Adrenaline started to pump through his system, giving him an edgy energy and making everything seem sharper, more visceral. Alexei thought someone had cut the brake line. What if the same person had decided to try again?

Who could be after Holly? He was suddenly damn glad that Alexei had the gun. Maybe it was a necessary accessory in Bliss. His heart began to palpitate as he followed Alexei. He wasn't sure what he would do, but he meant to be there. It seemed wrong to let him go alone.

The night was oddly silent around him, the only sound the gentle rush of the Rio Grande. The moon illuminated the yard. Holly's back door led to a small porch and a single set of steps. Somehow Alexei managed to make it to the grass without a sound, but Caleb's every step squeaked and groaned, the wood shifting under his feet.

Alexei turned and sent him an intimidating look. All Caleb could do was shrug. He'd never gone to "sneak up on someone" school. He crossed the porch as fast as he could.

Alexei held out a hand, stopping him from moving further. They both pressed against the side of the cabin. Alexei poked his head around and quickly came back. He held up a single finger.

One.

He quickly cupped his junk. Caleb nearly rolled his eyes but got the silent message.

One man.

There was a strange man walking around outside Holly's cabin.

He didn't like this feeling. His stomach spasmed, and for a moment, he could have sworn he heard the sounds of the jungle, felt the heat of that sun on his skin. His vision blurred, and in his mind he saw a canopy of green, and the antiseptic scent of his clinic washed over him. He kept it clean, so clean. He shivered. The jungle was always so hot, but this was Bliss and the night was cool.

And he wasn't alone.

He forced himself to return to the present.

Alexei nodded and then he was off, a silent wraith taking down his prey.

Caleb followed, rounding the corner in time to see a slender male trying to open the guest bedroom window. He couldn't see the man's face but realized quickly that he and Alexei were far from alone.

Zane Hollister charged in from the side and Cameron Briggs from the front. Each moved the same way Alexei did—with silent, predatory grace. And each man held a gun in his hand. They seemed to have some silent language of nods and hand motions. Alexei took charge. He grabbed the man by the back of his neck.

"Hey!" the man yelled as he found himself jerked into the air and then tossed to his back. There was a resounding *woof* as he hit the ground and suddenly three guns were pointed straight at his face. All three men stared down at the intruder.

Caleb caught a glance of his face. Not a man at all. Despite his height, it was easy to see this was a teen. His wide eyes had a youthful roundness. And the teen was utterly terrified.

"You will to tell what you are doing here attempting to break into house." Alexei's voice was a low growl.

Caleb moved in, trying to get a better look.

"Rafe is already looking up his plate number." Cam gestured back toward his cabin across the way from Holly's. "We caught sight of him driving up."

"Nate's running his plate, too. Get his wallet. We need an ID," Zane said. "Once we figure out who he is, Nate can take him into town."

The kid was completely still, holding his hands up in an obvious plea to not get shot. "Uhm, am I going to die? Has anyone ever mentioned that you guys are hot? Wow. Seriously. Hot. I think I already died and went to heaven. Please don't shoot me."

"Guys, I think you can back off," Caleb said. The young man on the grass didn't sound anything like a dangerous stalker. His voice shook as he spoke.

"Or at least get rid of the guns and then we can talk," the kid continued. "I always knew I would love this place, but I never expected to be greeted by a cadre of hot guys who don't like to wear shirts. I really hate to say this because I'm going to completely shut out my chances of making out with any of you, but maybe we should wake up my mom, and she can convince you to spare me."

Fuck. He'd known the kid looked familiar. He pushed Zane aside and got a really good look at him. He'd seen the face before in various stages of growth. Holly kept pictures of her son all over the house. "Micky?"

His head turned slightly. "I prefer Mick, but seriously, we'll go with whatever keeps this gorgeous head on my shoulders. I'm too young and hot to die."

"That's Holly's kid. Holly's son." Caleb pushed at Alexei, who immediately backed off. Zane and Cam stood down. Caleb reached out a hand to the kid on the ground. He was a lanky teen with dark hair and Holly's eyes.

"God, you're hot, too. Is there something in the water here?" Mick asked as he reached out and took Caleb's hand, allowing himself to be hauled up.

Nate Wright showed up, jogging over from his cabin. "Guys, that car is registered to Scott Lang. Isn't that Holly's ex?"

Rafe came around the corner. "Yes. Her ex. What the hell is he doing here?"

Mick put his hands together and looked up toward heaven. "Thank you, god, for sending me down this rabbit hole. I promise to be the best Alice ever."

"You are Holly's son?" Alexei stared at the kid.

Mick took a deep breath. "Yes. I know how late it is, and she wasn't exactly expecting me. I didn't want to wake her, but I couldn't find my key. I've only been out here twice and that was years ago, but I remembered the window in the guest bedroom didn't lock."

It didn't lock? And she'd left it like that for years?

Alexei looked at him as though he could hear his thoughts. "Yes, we will start a tally for punishment sake. I will fix this tomorrow."

"How did everyone get here so fast?" Caleb asked. There was a good amount of space between the cabins. "Do you guys have a neighborhood watch?"

Cam shrugged. "I'm a paranoid weirdo. I hear a car, I check it out. We don't get many sports cars up here."

Zane flipped the safety on his gun, his big shoulders relaxing. "And after the whole serial killer thing, we can't be too careful. Besides, Rafe and I had a bet as to the time when Doc there would slink away. I think I lose. I had him running before two, and it's five 'til."

Rafe laughed. "That's fifty bucks, Hollister."

Alexei shook his head. "No. Zane is winner. He was doing the bail. If son does not show up, he would have been gone."

Nate and Zane exchanged a high-five. Caleb frowned at all of them.

"Hey, I gotta buy diapers. Do you know how much a small-town sheriff makes?" Nate asked.

Probably around what a small-town doctor made. He didn't get paid to have everyone make bets on what time during the night he would fuck up, but that was small-town living. "You all suck."

Now that he seemed fairly certain he wasn't in danger, Mick relaxed. "So, I'm sensing that no one is going to horrifically murder me. Tell me something, are you all couples or is this a free-for-all swinging singles kind of thing?"

Caleb felt himself flush. Mick was under a serious misconception. "They're not couples. Not the way you think."

Alexei turned to the boy. A huge grin came over his face. "No, no. No couples. Only trios and only about the women. Beloved women."

Mick frowned, his whole face turning down in an exaggerated pout. "That is typical."

"Micky? Oh my god!" Holly ran out of the cabin, Laura following hard behind. "What are you doing here, baby?"

She had thrown on a robe and it was obvious that while Cam and Rafe had been taking care of the intruder, Laura had been checking on Holly. Holly put her hands on her son's face and looked him up and down as though checking for injuries. Holly was a good foot shorter than her baby boy.

Nate and Zane stepped away.

"I can see you three have this under control," Nate said, nodding at Caleb. "Good night. And Rafe, we'll expect that in cash tomorrow."

Rafe grumbled, but they too left, Laura promising to talk to Holly in the morning.

And he was alone with Alexei, Holly, and Holly's son. Holly's son. It had been an easy thing to forget that she had a kid. Holly had responsibilities that he didn't begin to understand.

Holly fretted over the teen, her hands fluttering. "What's going on, baby? Why are you here? Did you drive all the way from Denver? Is something wrong?"

Mick smiled down at his mom. "Slow down, Mom. I'm here because I wanted to see you. I needed to see you. Yes, I drove from Denver. And everything is fine. It's great. But I might have told Dad I'm gay, and he might have kicked me out of my palatial homeland. So, yeah, it looks like I live with you now. Surprise."

Mick Lang stood in the yard, his sarcasm belying the vulnerable set of his shoulders. He might be seventeen, but he wasn't close to being a man yet. He needed his mother.

Holly hugged him fiercely. "Yes, you do, baby. Of course you can live with me. You might not have been here, but this was always your home. Oh, sweetheart, come inside. So do you have luggage, or did your father kick you out with nothing?"

Caleb saw the way her fists clenched. He understood. It was a good thing Scott Lang wasn't anywhere close. What kind of man tossed out his child?

"Oh, no, I managed to get a couple of things." He gestured toward his car. The red sports car gleamed in the moonlight. And it was stuffed with suitcases.

Holly smiled. "Good. The boys can get them. You don't mind, boys, do you?"

"Not at all, *dushka*," Alexei said with a gracious bow. "I hope that son will forgive me for tackling him."

He didn't mention the gun, and it had conveniently disappeared. In fact all of them had disappeared. The men had quickly hidden the weapons the minute they'd heard Holly coming. Alexei's gun had gone in the pocket of his slacks. Caleb kept his mouth shut.

And so did the kid. He merely nodded Alexei's way. "No problem. It was a dumb idea to try to sneak in. I haven't been smart lately. I appreciate the fact that you were looking out for my mom. And I was joking about the whole gay thing. Not the me part. That's real. But I knew you weren't of my persuasion. My gaydar is nearly perfect, and it doesn't go off around you. It's a loss to my kind. Are you my mom's boyfriend?"

"Micky." Holly sounded horrified.

Alexei merely put an arm around the kid. If he was embarrassed to get caught sleeping with the boy's mom, it didn't show. "I am, indeed. I care very much for her. I am so glad to meet you. Your mother is proud. She tell me all about you in her letters. You are good boy."

"That whole accent thing is so hot. And what about Red over there?" Mick asked, his eyes narrowing on Caleb.

Caleb felt pinned by those eyes. "I, uhm, care about your mom, too."

Mick grinned. "Everything I heard about this place is true, isn't it? I think my grandma calls it a 'den of iniquity.' I always thought it sounded like fun. I can't wait."

Mick walked into the cabin with his mom, chattering away about all the things he wanted to do now that he was in Bliss. Caleb stood in the yard feeling like his whole world had changed.

Alexei slapped him on the back. "Come. Let's to help out the kid. You cannot leave now. You have to see this. Holly needs us."

It would probably look pretty bad to run out. And after everything the kid had heard, he wouldn't think much of a man who used his mother and walked away. Fuck. He had to stay. It was going to be a really long night.

157

Alexei hefted a trunk and passed it to him. Caleb groaned under the weight. It felt like the kid had managed to sneak the kitchen sink out of his dad's house. There was a ton of stuff.

Alexei's wide grin mocked him. "It is good to have family, no?"

Family. He'd run from his, and somehow, someway he'd found another one.

Chapter Eleven

Holly stared out of the tiny window of her kitchen into the yard and wondered if she wasn't already fucking up her second chance. Her son had been home for less than twelve hours, and she'd already exposed him to her suddenly kinky sex life. And to a bunch of men with guns. Yeah, she wasn't an idiot. They'd all looked so innocent after she'd rushed out, but she'd caught sight of the bulge in Zane's jeans, and despite rumors, she seriously doubted his thingy wrapped all the way around to the small of his back. She doubted any of them had been unarmed. Not a single one of those men would run around in the dark of night without some form of weapon.

"Good morning, *dushka*." Alexei's arms came around her waist, lifting her slightly as his face nuzzled her neck.

She'd woken up wrapped around him, utterly safe in his arms. She wouldn't be cold as long as Alexei was in her bed. And she'd missed Caleb because he hadn't gotten back into bed with them.

She was perverse.

"Good morning." Doubt crept back into her head with the morning light. He was so beautiful.

"Your son, he is all right?"

Her son was still asleep. She'd tucked him in last night after making him a cup of tea and trying to get him to talk. He'd said little past the fact that Scott had kicked him out after discovering his sexual orientation, and his stepmother had done nothing to help him. That hadn't been a big surprise. Connie was a cipher. She'd been handpicked by Maureen Lang to be the perfect political wife. She'd immediately spat out two genetically perfect kids and never disagreed with Scott. She wore what she was told to wear. She had a life filled with teas and events. Holly didn't envy her.

"I think he's fine. Well, he's as fine as a kid who had his whole life ripped away can be." Rage still threatened to choke her. Asshole. How could he have done that to their son?

Micky had told her a long time before that he thought he was gay. He'd known when he was a kid, and no matter how much football his father made him play, he couldn't help the fact that he preferred boys. She could still remember the night he'd told her. He'd cried because her big response had been to ask if he had a boyfriend. Why couldn't Scott have been the same way?

Alexei ran his nose through her hair, the sensation making her shiver with pleasure. She loved how affectionate he was. "I do not know, *dushka*. He seem to be very happy."

She threaded her fingers through his. "He wouldn't talk about it. He only wanted to talk about finishing high school online and where he's going to go to college. How am I going to send him to college? I don't even have a savings account. I've lived hand to mouth forever."

Because she hadn't really tried. She'd spent the last eight years getting by. She loved Stella, but did she want to waitress for the rest of her life?

He squeezed her close. "Do not to worry. We will deal with all things. We will find a way."

He was so stinking good to her. She couldn't argue with him. She couldn't point out that he didn't have a job and hers didn't pay well. They weren't exactly a power couple.

"I have to be going. I will make rounds in Bliss and then perhaps move on to Creede if no one is hiring here." He kissed her forehead. "Don't forget you have to see Caleb today. He will expect you in his office at noon. Do not to be late."

Caleb wanted to shave her and prepare her ass for anal sex. Or did he? He'd seemed pretty freaked out. She wasn't sure if he was anxious about the relationship or if the idea that she might have a son living with her made him rethink everything. She wouldn't blame him. It was causing her to rethink. "I don't know if that's still on."

Alexei slapped her ass, the sharp pain making her shriek. "You will go. Do not to be disappointing me. Caleb stayed. He did not leave until morning. He stay on couch, but it's progress. So go."

Maybe. But she also had a kid to think about. "I'll talk to him."

Alexei stepped back and grabbed her keys off the kitchen table. "You will obey him or deal with me." He winked, but there was no way she could miss the command in his voice. "I take car. Is okay? Caleb walked back to town. When do you need to be at work?"

"I'm off today. Feel free to take the car. If I need anything, I can get Laura to take me to town."

"Or I could do it." Micky stood in the doorway dressed in a T-shirt and flannel pajama bottoms. He looked younger than his seventeen years. Her heart threatened to break. He was so young and so precious to her. She couldn't fail him.

Alexei leaned back in, but she moved away. She couldn't make out with her boyfriend in front of her son. Alexei's eyes darkened, but he stepped back. "We will talk about that later, *dushka*. Good-bye, Mick. I will be looking forward to seeing you later. Take care of your mother."

"Always."

Alexei left, waving good-bye, and she was alone with her son.

"Don't you dare do this to me." Micky crossed his arms over his chest and stared at her, a spark of rage in his eyes.

God. She'd already made him uncomfortable. What had she expected? He'd come looking for his mom and found her with two men. It was normal in Bliss, but Micky hadn't grown up here. What must he think of her? Tears blurred her eyes. Just as she found some small measure of happiness, she was going to have to give it up because her son came first. "I'll talk to him. Don't worry about it, baby. This is your home. I won't have you uncomfortable."

"And you don't understand me. I wasn't telling you to dump your ungodly hot boyfriend. Seriously? I need to go to Russia. And Red is weird, but totally hot in a geek-chic, I've-got-PTSD way." Micky shook his head and walked to her. "I didn't come here to wreck your

161

life. I came here to be with my mom."

Every word seemed to cut through her. "And I should focus on you."

Micky's hands came up in frustration. He had some of his father's coloring, but she could see her dad in Micky's eyes. He had that same expression her father had always had when he thought she was doing something dumb. "No, you shouldn't focus on me. You should be happy. What have you always told me you wanted for me? When Dad was putting me through every honors class and pushing me to achieve, what did you want for me?"

Micky had been under so much pressure to be perfect. "I wanted you to be happy."

"You said happiness was the only thing that mattered. You told me to be true to who I am and what I want. To be kind to those around me and to love—to really love. Don't you dare think I want less for you. I will be so mad if you break up with those gods of masculinity because you think I don't know what sex is."

Maybe he was more mature than she'd thought. She touched his face. God, she remembered how small he'd been, how he'd clung to her like a little monkey. He'd been such a sweet child, and he was almost a man. She'd missed him. "I wish I'd been with you."

He softened. "You were, Mom. We talked every day we could. I never stopped hearing your voice in my head. I never thought for one second that you didn't love me. You just picked the wrong man to marry."

"I am going to kill your father. He had no right to do this to you." She felt her fists clench.

"Don't. Mom, please, don't call him. It's over, and I'm cool with it. I'm good. I want to move on." He hugged her. "He wasn't all bad, you know. I know he was a horrible husband. Still is, by the way, but he wasn't a terrible dad."

"How can you say that? You came out to him, and he kicked you out."

"I'm not surprised. I was kind of hoping he would. Mom, I went into that room knowing he would probably do it. I'm a campaign liability. I'm good with this. Let it be. Come on. I have one year and then I'm off to college, and I don't want you to worry about that, either. I want to enjoy this year with my mom. Can we do that?"

She nodded. "I don't want you to be uncomfortable. I care about Alexei and Caleb, but I know it's weird. I think a lot of people would think raising a teen around a ménage relationship would be wrong."

"Yeah, well raising a kid around politics is way worse. Trust me—all the backstabbing and double-dealing has warped me way worse than your crazy sex stuff ever will. Don't worry, Mom. According to Gaga, you were born this way. And we should all listen to Gaga." He grinned and walked around the living room. He picked up something that had fallen behind the couch. "But seriously, they're slobs. We have to work on that."

Two pairs of underwear. Alexei's and Caleb's boxers. Embarrassment flashed through her. She was beyond happy that Micky was okay with her relationship, but she didn't want to push it in his face. She grabbed the undies from him. "I'll make sure to note your preferences."

He laughed as he looked around the cabin. She was well aware it wasn't anything like the estate he'd grown up on. He simply straightened up the pile of magazines on the end table. "Good. And I'll get ready for breakfast. Take me into town. Show me around. I want to see everything, starting with where you work. I have two weeks before I have to start sending in assignments. And before you freak out, I left all the information on the table. It's a perfectly licensed school. Every college will accept the transcripts. It's in California, but I can send everything in remotely, and my teachers will do conferences and lectures over the Internet."

He'd figured it all out. She was beginning to be intimidated by her son's competence. She played with the pamphlets he'd left. "I'll look into it."

Micky winked. "Do that. I'm going to take a quick shower. Hopefully the big dude didn't take all the hot water."

"All right." She took a deep breath as he disappeared into the bathroom.

The phone rang as she sat down to read the material he'd left for her.

"Holly?" There was no mistaking the smooth, douchebag tones of his voice.

"Scott? You asshole. How dare you call here." She practically growled into the phone. If she could have reached through it and ripped

163

his throat out, she would have.

He snorted. "Yes, I'm not the one with nerve, sweetheart. Let's agree that it's a family trait. I want to make sure Micky got in okay. He left late last night."

Now he was worried about their son? "You have no right to even ask about him. You kicked him out."

He chuckled. "Damn, I love that kid. If that's the way we're playing it, then fine. I've always been the bad guy in your head. All right, I'll allow that I *am* the bad guy. Is he okay?"

"He's in one piece." No thanks to Scott.

"Good. I hope he's getting what he wanted." There was a long pause. "You tell him to stick to our deal."

The line went dead, and she was left wondering what was going on.

* * * *

Caleb stood outside the store, staring up at it. He did that sometimes. Sometimes Bliss was so weird, he had to stop and take the moment in.

Technically the Guns and Biker Stuff and More Store was halfway between Bliss and Del Norte, but damn the place definitely felt like Bliss. The building was a long cabin-style structure, and a big dude with a beard that any pirate would envy sat on a rocking chair on the porch rocking back and forth and drinking a beer at ten in the morning. If he was upset Caleb was standing and staring, he didn't show it.

The purr of a truck caught his attention and he turned. Wolf was here. Thank god. He wasn't sure he would actually be able to go into that place. It could be a trap. He would send Wolf in to get the items he needed.

What items did he need? Condoms.

How the hell was he going to buy condoms here? Did they sell them next to the revolvers? Did you get a discount for buying both? When he thought about it, they were actually similar. One protected a dude from assholes and the other from tiny humans who would need him far more than he could handle.

Did Alexei want kids? Did Holly want another one?

Stop. He wasn't going there. That was a mighty big leap to take when he'd slept with her once.

"You just going to stand there?" Wolf came to his side.

"He seems to like standing," the dude with the long beard said as he rocked. "He's the doc, right? The one from Bliss? Seen him around. Folks say he's weird. They're right."

The screen door opened and a tiny woman strode out. "Willie, don't be rude. Wolf is a wonderful customer and this man is his friend."

Willie shook his head at the newcomer. "Wasn't being rude, baby. Just stating plain truth. Doc's been standing in the parking lot for a good ten minutes. If Mel was here, he would say the aliens got in his head."

"This is a parking lot?" It was a yard, and not particularly well kept. He'd gotten a ride from Cam, who'd dropped him off with a grin. "And I was waiting for Wolf. He's the expert here."

The expert on sex toys. Though he couldn't be much of an expert if he'd brought them to a gun store to buy sex stuff. Unless Wolf was way kinkier than he thought…

The woman, who wore capri pants and a bright pink blouse, smiled. Caleb pegged her in her early sixties, with a bounce in her step and wide brown eyes. Her salt and pepper hair was wrapped in a coronet around her head. She glided down the steps and held out her arms. "Hello, Wolf. How is your mother?"

"Mom is great, Deb." Wolf hugged the tiny woman with the ease of a man who knew how to connect to the people around him. Wolf wouldn't have stood out in the "parking lot" staring at the hand-painted sign and wondering what the hell he was doing. Wolf would have strode in boldly and proclaimed what he needed.

"I'm here for a butt plug."

All eyes were suddenly on him. Willie even took off the mirrored sunglasses that covered his eyes.

Wolf probably wouldn't have put it like that.

A laugh huffed from his friend, and that seemed to break the moment. Deb and Willie both had a nice guffaw at his expense, but the truth was it wasn't all that costly. He didn't have a real sense of shame when it came to the crap that came out of his mouth. He'd grown up in a household where he'd been expected to be politic all the time. He'd never been any good at it.

165

Willie stood up. "Well, I think that's my cue. You gentlemen join me when you're ready. I'll have a selection for you. Is this for you? I have a very manly set that came in just the other day."

Of course he did have a nicely stocked sense of pure embarrassment. "I'm sorry, what?"

Wolf's grin was as big as the sky. "Dr. Burke is not training his own anus, Willie. This is for his lady."

"Ah, he finally got into Holly's undies," Willie said and then his eyes went steely. "Or is this for some other woman?"

He got the feeling that if he answered incorrectly, his access to anal plugs might be closed in this establishment. Or limited to ones with spikes or something. "My..." He'd been about to say girlfriend. "I like Holly."

And he was absolutely certain he was going to love her asshole. That was really all the commitment he could make now.

"Then I'll bring out our feminine line." Willie disappeared into the store, his beer still in hand.

"I know I shouldn't ask this," Caleb began with a sense of trepidation that didn't quite overcome his curiosity, "but what are the differences between male and female butt plugs? Technically the tissue is the same. The muscles are the same."

Wolf shook his head. "I believe he's talking about presentation."

"Well, I was planning on presenting it to her with lubrication."

Deb's hand went over her mouth, obviously holding in her mirth. She took a deep breath and became the competent business owner once more. "I believe he's talking about size and color, and Willie has a few with some interesting attachments. He'll walk you through it all. Come on in when you're ready. I've got blueberry muffins just out of the oven. We're expecting the OG Pack MC coming through this morning, so I added extra fiber. Don't let the name scare you. It's not original gangsters. It's Old Geezers. To become a prospect you have to show your AARP card. I'm going to put some coffee on. They get cranky without caffeine."

And they called him weird.

"So you did the deed last night." Wolf looked at him with approval. "How are you feeling?"

"Perfectly well," Caleb replied. Sex had taken his stress level down briefly, but then the normal anxieties had come back. "My blood

166

pressure is normal. Nose is a little stuffy but I bet that's allergies."

Wolf groaned. "I meant emotionally. How do you feel about the fact that you had a three-way."

"I did not have a three-way." He needed to put that rumor to bed now. "I had a one-way and Alexei had a one-way, and Holly was kind of the intersection. But our cars didn't have a rear ender, if you know what I mean."

Wolf stared at him. "You are insane. You know that, right?"

"I think the definition of sanity should be more fluid," he admitted. "I didn't enjoy the psychology courses I took. Now explain to me what biker stuff is. I get the guns. I'm curious about the more. Why biker stuff?"

Wolf shrugged. "Willie watched *Sons of Anarchy* and his guns and more store became a place to buy biker stuff. Not like motorcycles, but they have all kinds of accessories. I don't know, man. I don't actually go into that part of the store. Deb is an expert on firearms and ammo and Willie is the toy maker. Not that he makes the plugs, but he's an excellent artisan when it comes to paddles and floggers. Now tell me how you feel."

"I feel like you're way weirder than me because you know these people. I thought Nell and Henry were the odd balls. Not that there's anything wrong with that. I also feel I should stick with the butt plug because Holly might become concerned if I came home with paddles and floggers." She might use them on him.

Wolf stared.

And stared.

Caleb let out a groan of frustration. "Fine. It was great and I care about her. I do. I didn't even hate Alexei being there. It felt oddly normal."

"Then why did you try to run?" Wolf asked.

Damn gossip mill. "Because it felt oddly normal. Because I liked it too much. Because Holly told me she loved me and for a minute I wanted to say it back."

Wolf put a hand on his shoulder. "That's good."

"I didn't say it back." He couldn't.

One big shoulder shrugged. "Well, we're taking baby steps. I heard her son is in town. How did that go?"

"Seems like a nice kid." Mick had handled finding his mom with two men pretty well, considering. "A little sarcastic, but I can deal with that. I think Holly was embarrassed though." Maybe he should think about this.

"Stop right there," Wolf ordered. "Don't even go there. You're all adults and her kid is in his last year of high school. She deserves to have a life. No one in Bliss is going to blink an eye."

And Mickey had seemed cool with it. "I'm trying. Like I said, it was nice. It was probably the best night I've had in a long time."

The trouble was he wasn't sure he could trust it. Not because he didn't trust Holly. It was the universe he didn't trust. He'd come to understand that life was a capricious thing that tossed him one way or another like a boat in a storm.

Of course a boat was better handled when there was a crew on it rather than a singular captain trying to do everything. Maybe that had been why he'd felt so comfortable with Alexei. He'd known if things went off the rails, there was someone else there.

"I'm glad," Wolf said, starting toward the store. "If there's anyone who deserves a good night, it's you. Now let's go look at some butt plugs. We need to get a whole training set, and Willie experiments with some exotic lubricants. Don't worry. Nell tests them all for parabens, whatever those are. She's pronounced them organic and cruelty free. Well, not the ginger one. She said that one stung."

Yep, Nell was a freak. It kind of made him more comfortable around her. Next time she threatened him with endless rounds of conversation he would inquire whether or not she was wearing a butt plug that day. That might mess up her game play.

Excellent. He wouldn't be unprepared for their next round.

The growl of motorcycles rumbled through the air as a swarm of Harleys made their way into the "parking lot."

Wolf waved for him to get inside. "Come on, man. You do not want to mess with those guys."

There were about twenty bikes being parked, and six of them had more than one rider. The helmets started to come off and Caleb couldn't help but stare. The men were all wearing leather vests that proudly proclaimed them the Old Geezers of the Rockies.

"Yeah don't mess with us, young man," a guy who had to be in his mid-nineties said, reaching out his hand for his...yep, that was his old lady. She was maybe eighty-five on the generous side, and she was wearing a tank top and no bra. "We're one percenters."

The woman at his side grinned, and when she did that she proved that age should be judged on so much more than a mere number. "He calls us that because we've got about one percent of our lives left."

"Then we should party!" another called out.

There wasn't a single one who could possibly be under seventy-five.

Caleb smiled. These people were living. They were giving a big old finger to the world and gave not one fuck what anyone thought.

Alexei would think they were cool.

He'd just thought about calling Alexei and telling him about the experience.

"That big old truck yours?" one of the OGs asked Wolf.

Wolf nodded gamely.

"Get out of your cage, son," the man said. "Get a bike and see the world. Time's a wasting."

It was. And suddenly Caleb didn't want to miss a minute of it.

He jogged to the steps. He had a set of butt plugs to buy.

* * * *

Three hours later, Alexei parked Holly's tiny torture device in the back of Stella's and began to walk up Main Street. Useless. The whole morning had been useless. He looked up as he heard another car stop.

"Hey, we lost track of you last night. I take it things went well with Ms. Lang?" Jessie asked, getting out of the white SUV they'd rented. She'd changed into slightly different colored slacks and a pristine white shirt.

"I tried to tell her that you're a big boy now," Mike said, shutting the driver's side door. His loafers crunched against the gravel. "But she was worried. The appeals court hands down its verdict any day now."

Yes. He'd forgotten about the appeals. The thought of having to go back into court was not pleasant. "I am fine. Nothing to worry about."

Jessie looked around. "I don't know. I've heard some crazy stories about this place."

"It is nice place." Bliss was the nicest place he'd ever been.

"Nice enough for a Sommerville. I saw him last night at that bar. What the hell is Caleb Sommerville doing in a place like this?" Jessie asked. She'd been the one to recognize him that day so long before.

Alexei turned to her. "Please to not be telling that around town. He is hiding."

Jessie sighed. "After what happened to him, I can't blame him. You know they shot his wife right in front of him. By the time the State Department finally found him, he'd been held captive for months. They said he'd been held in what looked like a box."

A box. Caleb had been caged in a small space for a long time, his body encased, surrounded. For most men, it would make them claustrophobic. What if it had the opposite effect on Caleb? What if he needed to feel surrounded to be comfortable? An idea started to play in his mind.

Mike shook his head. "Poor bastard. Well, at least he had someone as powerful as Eli Sommerville on his side, or he would have been left there to die. Guess he didn't deny his family name then, did he?"

"He has a lot of friends," Alexei said with a frown. "If he wishes to be anonymous, this is his choice. I suggest you to be leaving him alone. I would not take it kindly if his secrets get out when he does not wish them to."

"You're close to him?" Jessie's eyes assessed him.

"He is my partner."

"I would listen to him if I was you." A tall, dark-haired man turned the corner. He'd obviously heard a good portion of the conversation. "Caleb here is Alexei's partner. We take partners real damn seriously here in Bliss."

Caleb stood with the other man. He stared a hole straight through Alexei. "You aren't going to blackmail me, are you?"

He was so stubborn. "I tell you this."

The dark-haired man held out his hand. "Wolf Meyer. Nice to meet you. And I spent a good twenty minutes of my life explaining that to Caleb. He's got a thick head. I tried to explain that if a man like you wanted money out of him, you would put a gun in his face and demand it."

It was good to know he had a reputation. "I would not to hurt Caleb for the world. He save my life."

"Yeah, I told him that, too." Wolf turned to the other two. "Feds?"

Mike looked offended. "US marshals."

Wolf rolled his eyes. "Same shit, different uniform. Caleb, you have everything you need?"

Caleb nodded. "I think I can handle it from here." Wolf walked away, but Caleb stayed. "Are they your handlers?"

"Not any longer." At least he hoped that was true.

"We're in town to make sure he's okay. There are two men he testified against who are up for an appeal. I'm nervous they might come after him. These are powerful men with long arms, if you know what I mean," Mike explained.

Caleb turned to him. "Impatient bastard."

Alexei shrugged. "I wait long time."

"Dr. Sommerville, will you talk to him?" Jessie asked. "It would be better for everyone if he stayed in protective custody."

"My name is Caleb Burke. If you insist on formality, you can call me Dr. Burke. I changed my name a long time ago. It's legal. Use it. As for Alexei going back into witness protection, that's not a good idea. He has responsibilities here. Don't worry, if someone shoots him, I know how to stitch him back up." Caleb gestured toward the town square. "Enjoy your stay in Bliss. Come on, Alexei. Walk with me."

Alexei waved good-bye to his handlers. Maybe they would get the idea that he wasn't going back.

"How did the job hunt go?" Caleb asked gruffly.

He sighed as they passed The Trading Post. It was the one business in town he didn't have the courage to go into and ask if they were hiring. The neat storefront was one of the mainstays of the town. They sold everything from groceries to books to sporting goods in the multi-story structure. It was also run by Logan Green's mothers.

"I will keep searching. I will try other towns this afternoon."

"Yeah, you keep right on walking, buddy. Maybe you should try some other states." Logan leaned against the side of his county-issued Bronco, his eyes narrowed.

"Just keep walking." Caleb nodded at the deputy but didn't speak to him.

Alexei stopped. "Logan, perhaps we could talk."

He needed to figure out a way to make this right with the deputy.

"I think I'll pass. I remember what happened the last time we talked." The deputy's eyes were rimmed with red. It was obvious he hadn't been sleeping much.

"I am so very sorry for the pain you went through. I would do anything to make it go away."

Logan stood up, his stance predatory. "You didn't do much when that fucker was trying to kill me, did you? I believe I would have been termed an acceptable loss in your books. Tell me something, asshole, did I play my part? Was I a good distraction? Did me getting my ass tortured buy you the time you needed to save your own sorry self?"

"I did to save Holly and later Jennifer." It was his reason, but the words felt hollow in the face of Logan's obvious pain. How could he tell the deputy that he still had nightmares? He could still hear the low, animal moans Logan made as his life was altered forever.

"Yeah, I'm sure that helps you sleep at night." Logan slammed his fist onto the roof of his Bronco.

Caleb took a couple of steps closer to the deputy. "Have you been drinking?"

"You know what, Doc? That's none of your fucking business." The deputy took a step back.

Caleb wouldn't let it go. "It certainly is if you're both on duty and driving around. You carry a gun, Logan. You can't do this. And what's wrong with your eye? Is that a contusion? When did it happen?"

"Don't touch me, Doc. It's fine. I got in a fight last night. You should see the other guy." Logan stepped out from behind his car. "You should remember that, you big Russian asshole. I'm not a kid anymore. I'm not a pushover, and you won't be able to use me again."

Yes, he could plainly see that Logan's youth had been taken from him in a brutal way. And he might not live for long if he kept getting drunk and fighting.

Logan looked at his car but pocketed his keys. "I think I'll avoid the doc calling my boss. I've had about enough of this town's interference in my life. And Markov, you should leave. There's nothing for you here. Not a damn person is going to hire you, and Holly will wake up one day and see you for the criminal you are."

Alexei watched as he took the steps of his mothers' store two at a time.

"He should get that contusion looked at." Caleb was shaking his head as the door to The Trading Post opened and closed.

He felt utterly helpless. There was zero chance the deputy would ever accept help from him, but it was so obvious he needed it. He knew the look on the young man's face. He'd seen it a thousand times on his own. It was the look of a man who had nothing to lose and wouldn't mind going out in a blaze of glory.

"Holy shit, you really aren't tricking anyone, are you? You honestly give a shit that Logan is hurting." Caleb stared at him as though seeing him for the first time.

"I cause him pain."

"No, some asshole named Luke caused him pain."

"Luka." He could still see Luka as Stefan Talbot killed him. So much death. So much pain, and he was still causing it.

"You couldn't have spared him. What would that mob boss guy have said if you had told him, 'Hey don't hurt the cop who arrested me. I think we should be a kinder, gentler mob?'"

He had a point. "I don't think Pushkin would have liked that."

"Nope. It wouldn't have gone over well. He would have shot your ass, killed Logan, and I don't like to think about what he would have done to Holly." Caleb's face went pale. "You can't imagine what a man can do to a woman."

Alexei could. He'd killed a man once, a member of his own group who had tried to rape a young woman. He'd managed to cover it up by letting the woman flee and blaming the whole thing on her. Alexei had given her money and helped her disappear. But he didn't talk about it with Caleb. Caleb was lost in his own nightmare. Caleb's nurses had been raped. "They were trying to do good, Caleb. They knew it was a risk."

"They were dumb kids."

"Yes, well, sometimes dumb kids change whole world. And sometimes they die. Why am I not responsible for Logan, but you are for nurses and wife? You did not pull trigger. You did not rape. You did not offer them up to save yourself."

"How do you know that?" He asked the question between gritted teeth. "How do you know I didn't beg them to take the women and not me?"

"Because I study you. You are man who walks away from wealth and privilege to help others. You are man who saves someone when it would be better for you if he die. I did not only come back for Holly, Caleb. I came back because I falls down for Holly, but I also came back because I admire you. I think you are lost and you are worth being found again." He might turn away. Caleb could run. Caleb could think he was playing a game. For all Alexei knew, Caleb could think he was coming on to him. But he wasn't going to lie to the man.

"You fell for Holly." Caleb's voice was tight, thick with some unnamed emotion. "The other way makes it sound like you're clumsy, and we both know you aren't that."

Alexei didn't smile, but he felt a little joy in his chest. Caleb wouldn't respond by offering him affection, but not fighting him was the way the man gave acceptance. For all that the confrontation with Logan hurt, Caleb's lecture on English warmed him.

"Are you going to come with me?" Caleb asked, putting a hand on his arm. "I'm supposed to meet Holly at the clinic in fifteen minutes."

He should go into Creede. He should continue his job hunt. But the thought of being with Holly again, of watching Caleb preparing her... He needed to see her. "Yes, I will join you."

Alexei stepped out into the street. The clinic wasn't far away. He could consider it his lunch break. After he'd spent some time with Holly, he would feel better about finding a job.

Caleb stepped out with him. "I had Wolf tell me what to buy. I don't know what kind of training the SEALs give out, but it obviously covered sex toys."

He heard the squeal of tires just before he felt a sharp shock of pain and the whole world went black.

Chapter Twelve

"I can't believe how big you got!" Stella stared down at Micky while she poured coffee into Holly's mug.

Her boss was dressed in her typical uniform of jeans, a ridiculously over-the-top Western shirt, and white boots embroidered with loud red roses. She'd left off her cowboy hat, but her helmet of blonde hair was on full display.

Micky grinned up at her. All morning he'd taken everything in with an eager embrace. "Well, I couldn't stay a kid forever, Ms. Stella. I had to go and turn into a whole heap of man. I hear you recently got married. That's a shame because I've had a crush on you ever since that day I tried your butterscotch pie."

Micky might like guys, but he knew how to butter up a woman, too. Holly remembered that day well. It was one of two times Micky had been allowed to come to Bliss. He'd been twelve.

"Don't even try your flirtatious ways on her, baby," she said with a smile. "She got married to a billionaire."

Micky laughed. "Seriously? Yeah, you probably don't want little old me. Tell me something, Ms. Stella, why are you still here? Shouldn't you be jet-setting to some exotic location?"

Stella waved him off. "Sebastian likes it here. He waited a long time to come home. Now I can't get that old man out of Bliss. Oh, we took a nice long honeymoon, but in the end, this is home. And I wouldn't stop working. What would I do with myself? And who would feed these people? Zane Hollister? I don't think so. He thinks his wings and bar food beat my waffles. He is wrong. And the man has no idea how to make a chicken-fried steak."

Stella walked off to serve another table, vowing revenge on Zane. The two had gotten into a friendly rivalry. There was talk of a chili cook-off.

"This place is different, you know." Micky finished off the coffee in front of him.

"I know."

He shook his head. "No. You've been here too long. You don't see it anymore. I've wanted to live here all my life. At first it was because it seemed simpler, and I missed you so much. But I found Great-Granddad's diary one day. It was stuffed away with some other papers in Dad's office. Did you know Great-Granddad built the cabin you live in with his own hands?"

That was surprising. She hadn't thought a Lang would know how to hammer in a nail. That kind of work was left to servants. "I know your grandmother thought he was crazy."

"He built it back in the forties. It was a fishing cabin back then, but the community started building up in the sixties."

"Yes, I'm sure the venerable Judge Lang adored all the hippies moving in."

Micky wagged a finger her way. "See, Dad being an asshole made you prejudiced. Judge Albert Lang was my great-grandfather, and he had a lot to say about this place. He was retired by the time the commune, as he called it, came to town. He loved it. He loved the people. He loved how the cowboys and the hippies somehow got along. He used to go to the weekly protests with a lawn chair and a beer and cheer on the craziest sign. And the protesters courted his vote. He said this place was magical. He was a judge for thirty years. He saw horrible things in his courtroom, but he would come here and he would feel clean again."

She would love to read that diary. But she also didn't want Micky to have misconceptions about Bliss. "Terrible things happen here. It's not paradise."

"I know. It wasn't back then, either. And what's with all the alien sightings? Granddad talks about him and some young vet putting down an alien invasion back in the sixties. I think he might have been going senile by then."

Not the way Mel told it. "We have some characters around here."

"Yes, and I want to be one of them. I want to be who I am and not apologize for it. I want someplace where I'll be accepted and relied on not because of what my last name is, but what I'm willing to do to help out."

She loved his enthusiasm but couldn't help but think about his future. "Micky, baby, I don't know how much of a future there is for you here. It's hard to find a job. There aren't a lot of opportunities."

"There's a college in Alamosa," he explained. "After that, we'll see. I only know that I don't want to go back to Denver or Washington. I want to figure myself out. I want the world to be big and small at the same time. Big enough that I can lose myself in it, and small enough that I can find my way home. Here, Mom. With you."

She reached out and grabbed his hand. She'd had so many dreams for him. From the moment he'd been placed in her arms, she'd had big plans for his future, and now she saw clearly that he dreamed better than she ever had.

Happiness. Family. A place to call home. Those were what mattered.

It was all in reach. It was past time to grab it.

"I'll support whatever you want to do, baby."

Micky's eyes had gone wide and they were staring past her. "Oh, god, that man is hot. And there's two of him. Support me in finding my own crazy, hot cowboy ménage. Please, Mommy. Buy me those two."

And he was slightly demented. "Try to remember, I'm your parent. I do not want to hear about your sex life. I wouldn't want to hear about it if you were straight, either."

He had the most mischievous look in his eyes. Holly was well aware he played it straight around his father. Now he was indulging in being himself. Way too much. "That is the hottest cowboy ass I have ever seen."

She winced. It was great that Micky was enjoying his newfound freedom, but this was still a small Western town. She turned to see who the recipient of her son's admiration was.

Everyone in the café had stopped as though waiting to see if the

177

bomb was going to go off. Stella's mouth sort of hung open, and she stood very still. The whole café reminded Holly of a collective possum in the presence of a large predator. They held still in hopes that the predator wouldn't eat them.

Max Harper turned and stared at Micky, his eyes narrowing. Rye stood beside his brother.

"Did you hear what that kid said?" Rye asked.

Max frowned. "Yeah. Yeah, I did."

Oh, fuck. The baddest-tempered man in town was staring at her sweet, apparently way-too-sexually-precocious baby boy. Max liked to start fights. He really liked it. Max was at least two hundred pounds of pure muscle. And Micky was right. He had a great ass, but Holly wasn't sure he wanted to hear that from another man.

Max started to stalk toward their booth.

Holly stood. How would Rachel handle this? Rachel was the only one truly capable of handling her husband. "Now, Max, he is seventeen years old. You can't beat him up."

Max ignored her. "What did you say to me, young man?"

Micky turned a nice shade of green, proving that he had a healthy sense of self-preservation. She tried to get in between her baby and the tiger whose tail he'd pulled.

"I said you had a nice backside, sir." Micky sounded like he gulped a little between words.

"You are not helping." She sent her son what she hoped was an intimidating stare.

"And you're of a homosexual persuasion?" Max asked, his voice low.

"Yes, yes, sir."

"Max Harper, I swear, if you touch my son, I will cut off your balls." That sounded a little Rachel-like.

Max finally looked to her, his handsome face a mask of confusion. "Why would I beat him up? He complimented me." Max swiveled and showed off his backside. "Rachel never compliments my ass. Do you know how hard I work for this? I try to keep myself attractive for her, but she never even mentions it. It makes a man wonder."

He turned back and around, and the whole café seemed to deflate with the knowledge that no one was going to be murdered.

"It's not right," Max said, shaking his head.

Rye groaned behind him. "She's not ignoring you. She's tired because Paige has had an ear infection, not because she doesn't think your ass is pretty."

"See, if you were with a gay guy, he would worship you for that ass. Nothing would get in the way." Micky was right back to grinning.

Holly could see he was going to be a handful. She might need to start a "sarcastic teen" support group.

Max crossed his arms over his chest and smiled, smug satisfaction evident in his stance. "I told you I would play well with our homosexual brethren. This is one hot piece of man meat. It plays across all sexual orientations."

Rye slapped at his brother. "He wasn't talking about you, idiot. It was obvious he was talking about me. No man is going to put up with your shit."

"Oh, I could find plenty of people who would put up with either one of you," Micky assured them, putting his chin in his hand and enjoying the show. Max and Rye argued over who had the better butt.

They were identical twins. Rachel would one day be nominated for sainthood. Two men were twice the work. Twice the laundry. Twice the cooking.

Twice the amazingly hot sex.

Twice the love.

Yeah, she could handle the laundry.

Holly glanced out the huge front windows that overlooked Main Street as Micky suddenly found himself the arbitrator of their argument. She felt her whole body heat up as she saw Alexei standing in front of The Trading Post talking to someone. His shoulders were so broad. He'd taken up most of the space in the bed, but she hadn't minded. She'd been warm and happy.

Alexei turned and she could see who he was talking to. Caleb. Caleb had changed his clothes and looked relaxed as he talked to Alexei. He stopped for a moment, his face tightening. Emotion was evident on his beautifully imperfect face. Caleb's face was an odd combination of harsh features and gorgeous eyes. Everything about it was masculine. And he had obviously been deeply affected by something Alexei had said.

She got out of the booth again. Were they having an argument? Were they going to fight? She doubted it would be like the friendly throwdowns Max and Rye got into. Damn it. This couldn't work if they didn't get along. Everyone would be miserable.

"Baby, I'm going to go talk to someone for a minute. Will you be okay?"

Micky sighed. "I think I can handle it. Can you catch a ride back with one of the hotties? I want to drive around a bit." She nodded, and Micky turned back to the cowboys. "I don't know. It's a close race. You both have really nice asses."

Holly began walking for the door when Caleb put a hand on Alexei's arm and nodded toward the street. Alexei smiled. They weren't fighting. They were talking, really talking. They looked like friends. Hope bloomed in Holly's chest. She stepped out of the diner and started to cross the street.

And then she heard it. It was the squealing sound of tires trying to keep up with an engine that was running fast. She smelled the burning rubber as she stepped onto the street and saw a flash of black coming her way. She suddenly knew what it felt like to be a deer in the headlights. She was strangely frozen by the sight of the car coming her way. She had to move, but she knew there wasn't any time. God, she'd just gotten her son back. She'd found her men.

"Whoa!" someone yelled, and an arm wrapped around her midsection, hauling her back. She fell with her savior, hitting the ground behind them.

She looked up into the eyes of James Glen. His ever-present cowboy hat had fallen off, revealing his longish, golden-brown hair.

"What was that?" she asked, barely able to speak.

"That was some asshole tourist," James replied. "Are you okay? Logan is supposed to be catching speeders. Where the hell is he? Trev, did you get a plate number on that asshole?"

Holly looked up, and there was a gorgeous slab of cowboy looking down at her. She was pretty sure she knew who he was, though. Trev McNamara, professional football's bad boy and, if rumor was true, James Glen's new partner in the Circle G Ranch.

"No. It all happened so fast. Are you all right, Miss? Should I get a doctor?" Trev asked, reaching a hand out. He had her on her feet in no time. "I think we need to call one. It looks like he missed you, but he caught that other guy."

Holly's heart nearly stopped. "Alexei!"

She raced across the street where Caleb was kneeling over Alexei's body. She nearly screamed when she saw the blood on his leg.

Caleb looked up, his eyes rising to meet hers. "He's fine. He got clipped across his thigh, but it's not broken. The worst we're looking at is a hematoma."

"I am fine, *dushka*. Caleb pull me back in time." Alexei took the hand Caleb offered, and they got him to his feet. "I should have watched what I was doing."

"It wasn't only you," James said, striding up with his friend. "Holly nearly got it, too. That asshole came out of nowhere."

If Alexei had been counting on Caleb for support, he would have fallen to the ground. Caleb was all over her like a monkey momma checking for bugs on her baby. His hands were suddenly everywhere.

"Where are you hit? Are you bleeding? How bad is it? Should I call an ambulance? There's nothing an EMT can do that I can't, but they can get us to a hospital faster."

Well, she couldn't trick herself into thinking he didn't care. "I'm fine. I didn't get hit. James pulled me out of the way then softened my fall by hitting the ground first in a gentlemanly manner."

James had his cowboy hat back on. He tipped it and winked. "Ma'am, it was all in a day's work."

Caleb picked her up anyway. He simply leaned over and scooped her up, hauling her to his chest. "Come on, Alexei. We need to check her out. James isn't a doctor, so you'll excuse me if I don't take his professional advice. No offense."

James's eyes sparkled with amusement. "None taken, Doc. I never would. I know you have a tranquilizer gun, and you know how to use it."

Trev McNamara's eyes went wide. "Tranquilizers? You people run around shooting each other?"

"Just Mel. How did I get this reputation?" Caleb asked. "Alexei, could you pick up the bag? It's got the plug and lube and stuff in it."

"Caleb!" Holly shouted, feeling her skin flush. The man had not one ounce of discretion.

All the men around her laughed.

Trev slapped James on the back. "Damn, I like it here. I can't wait to tell Bo this story."

James picked up the bag—which was apparently filled with sex toys—and passed it to Alexei. "Yeah, well, I think you're going to fit right in."

She had to wave over Caleb's shoulder. He strode down the street toward his small clinic.

Alexei smiled as he tried to keep up. "I will have to remember to not get injured while you around, *dushka*. The doctor plays favorites."

"Caleb, he's hurt."

"Are you hurt?" Caleb yelled over his shoulder.

"This, I will survive," Alexei answered.

"See. He's fine." He leaned down and managed to get the door to the clinic open. He strode to the exam room and tenderly placed her on the small table. His hands immediately started to unbutton her shirt.

"I told you, I'm fine."

"I'll decide that." He pushed her shirt off her and smoothed his hands across her shoulders. "You have an abrasion right here."

She hissed as he touched it. "I scraped the sidewalk."

"Alexei, there's a wound kit in the second cabinet. Get it for me and then take your pants off." Caleb looked back at him. "And no arguments. I'm the boss in this office. You're limping."

"It is nice of you to notice." Alexei said it with a smile as he did as he was asked. He passed Caleb the kit and then started on the button of his slacks. "I hate this man who drives too fast. He ruin perfectly good pair of slacks."

"Take off your bra, sweetheart," Caleb ordered. "He could have ruined your life. I find it interesting that he nearly managed to mow down two people, but he drove straight as an arrow afterward."

She frowned his way. "Caleb, I don't need to take off my bra."

Caleb tore open the packaging on some gauze. "Alexei?"

Alexei placed his folded slacks on the counter and walked around her back. He had her bra unhooked faster than she could protest. "*Dushka*, do not disobey doctor. He is boss here. If you disobey, he will not give you lollipop. You will be bad girl. You know what bad girl gets."

Bad girls tended to get cock. What were they playing at?

Caleb shook his head. "You had to bring in the pervert, didn't you, Holly? You couldn't have chosen someone perfectly normal to complete our threesome?"

She hissed slightly as he cleaned the teeny tiny wound she'd taken.

It was so small that it hadn't even bled much. It shouldn't affect her abilities in the least. It certainly shouldn't stop either one of them from showing her some affection.

"Tell me you don't want to play doctor. That is what you call it, no?" Alexei's finger traced her spine. She leaned into his touch.

Caleb continued to work on her. "Yes. That's what we call it. But only after the pretty patient proves herself fit for play. And we should talk about that car."

Alexei's voice went deep and dark. "We will talk about it. Later."

"As long as we get around to it," Caleb said. "That didn't feel like an accident to me."

She sat up straight, his words sending a chill through her. "What do you mean it wasn't an accident?"

"Shhh." Caleb dabbed at her wound. "I said we would talk about it later and we will. For now, I want you to lie back."

She sighed. He didn't sound like he was going to move. Sometimes Caleb turned into the rock that bumped up against a really hard place. She lay back on the padded exam table. Alexei loomed over her.

"Everything will be all right, *dushka*. Your men will take good care of all your parts. We will let no one be taking you from us."

But she could think of someone who might want to take a lot from her. "Do you think it's Scott? Do you think he could get so mad about Micky he would try to run me down?" It seemed incomprehensible. Scott was a jerk, but he wasn't a killer. Of course she also would have guessed that he couldn't possibly have tossed their son out into the cold.

"It was probably some asshole. And I don't think anyone would want to hurt you, sweetheart." Caleb's hands worked the button of her jeans. "You weren't the only one who got hit."

She tried to get up. Alexei gently pushed her back down. "You think someone wants to hurt Alexei?"

Both men laughed. It annoyed the hell out of her.

Caleb ran his hands along her abdomen, pushing in lightly, feeling all along her torso. "I think there are several people who would love to see Alexei in two pieces."

"You are wrong," Alexei corrected. "They would love to see me in many pieces. One threatened to put body in wood chipper and fertilize yard. And I have had many, many threats to death."

"Death threats, buddy. You've had a ton of death threats. Take a deep breath, Holly." Caleb had his stethoscope out.

The chill of metal hit her skin as he placed the instrument to her back. "How can you two be so calm?"

Caleb sighed. "Because we're not sure. And because whoever it was didn't succeed. And we're really not sure."

Alexei rubbed his chin thoughtfully. "If I were going to kill me, I would to use gun. It is easiest. It is quick. I wouldn't bother with trying to make accident. This person is not best assassin, if there is one at all. So calm to the down. It will be all right. We will talk to sheriff and keep eyes on the open sign."

Caleb shook his head. "I'm not even going to correct that one. Another deep breath."

The bastard wasn't going to give in. She forced herself to calm down. They were right. Alexei was a controversial figure, but they couldn't jump to conclusions. "Should we go talk to Nate after you decide I'm fine?"

"Holly, do you understand anything about adrenaline?" Caleb asked. He turned to Alexei. "Take off the shirt, too."

She turned her head so she could see Alexei shrugging out of his shirt. His big, muscular chest came into view. Caleb put the stethoscope to Alexei's chest, moving it around with a deep competence.

"I know you get a rush of it when you're in danger." That was all she knew about adrenaline. Now sexual arousal was a different matter. She was learning all about that watching the two gorgeous men. The room suddenly seemed too small. And intimate. How many fantasies had she had about Caleb that involved an exam that got a little handsy?

"Let me tell you about the effects of adrenaline on the human body. Adrenaline is a hormone produced by the adrenal gland. It's located behind the kidneys." Caleb got to one knee and began examining the scrape on Alexei's upper thigh. "Its purpose is to heighten the body's response to stress, to make your senses more capable of reacting during dangerous situations. However, it tends to linger even after the situation is gone. Hence, that thing. Dude, do you mind?"

He gestured toward Alexei's enormous erection. It strained against his boxers. Alexei grinned down. "I believe you explained why I have this hardening on. It does not help that I can see Holly's beautiful breasts. And you are not without hardening yourself."

"I am hard as a rock, but I'm not shoving it in your face," Caleb complained.

"It is one of the dangers of being doctor." Alexei turned his hips to the side.

Caleb washed down the scrape with antiseptic. "I guess you could say that. They don't warn you about it in medical school. And you're fine. So we can move on to the part where we burn off some of this adrenaline. One of the aftereffects is a need for physical activity. We could have a nice time with you or we could go out back and punch each other."

"This is not good idea. I do not wish to break doctor." Alexei seemed supremely secure in his physical prowess.

Caleb didn't look so sure. "I don't know. I'm way meaner than I look, and I know all the best places to hit. One good blow to the kidneys and you'll be pissing blood for a week."

Holly needed to put a stop to that. She would not have her men end up like Max and Rye. "I think we should fool around. Definitely." She didn't want them fighting. Playing a few games with them would be a much better way to deal with the problem.

Caleb got back to his feet. "You're not where I left you. Look, sweetheart, you're the patient. I'm the doctor. You need to trust me. Can you do that?"

He wanted to play doctor? She could do that. Her skin already felt warm. "Yes, Doctor."

"Excellent. I need to perform a thorough examination." Caleb smiled as he said it. "If anyone wants to start humming a little 'bow chicka wow wow' music, it would be fitting. This exam could get freaky. I could go over my privacy practices, but you should know that what happens in the doctor's office stays in the doctor's office."

She loved the fact that he joked now. He never used to. He'd been so serious. It was all Alexei's fault. She couldn't take credit. They needed Alexei. "Is this your assistant?"

Caleb winked at her, a mischievous look in his eyes. "This is my nurse."

Alexei frowned. "I am not liking to be nurse."

Caleb slapped him on the shoulder. "Then go to med school,

buddy. For now, open up that bag and prepare my instruments. We wouldn't want to miss a thing, would we?"

"I'm not going to be able to keep a straight face." She already felt the laughter bubbling up inside her.

"Then my nurse will have to administer discipline. He's good at it." His hands went to the bottom of her jeans. "I'm afraid these are going to have to come off."

Well, she would be surprised if they didn't. She tried to look around to see exactly what Alexei was doing. She wasn't sure about the whole anal plug thing. She needed to sit down with some of her friends and talk this out, but it didn't look like that was going to happen. Alexei was washing something. She couldn't quite see what it was, but she had her suspicions.

Caleb pulled her jeans off with a quick tug. "I'm afraid the underwear is going to have to go, too."

He hooked his thumbs under her cotton panties and dragged them down as well. She was left naked and vulnerable on the table. Caleb stood at the end of the table, his hands on her knees. He was still dressed, but his erection was thick and wide, pressing at the denim of his jeans. With a quick flick of his hand, he moved the stirrups from below the table into place. Holly allowed him to place her feet in the stirrups, opening her up. Her pussy was on full display. She could feel cool air on her folds. So vulnerable. She felt vulnerable, but it was all right with these men. She could explore this wild, sexy self she'd never imagined was inside her because neither of these men would hurt her.

"You look healthy enough." Caleb was good. He wasn't even smiling.

He stood between her legs, his handsome face serious. She loved the deep line that came between his brows when he concentrated. She had seen it a hundred times as he sat in the café, drinking coffee. She'd always wanted to kiss him right where the line was deepest, as though she could kiss away his cares.

"But I would be remiss if I didn't check everything," Caleb continued.

She was ready to laugh, but then his finger came out and traced a line from her sternum to her navel to her pussy, and she decided to play along. "I feel healthy, Doctor."

He stared at her body, his eyes getting hot. His palm ran across her skin, touching one leg and then the other. He started at her hip, skimmed past her pussy with maddening care and ran down to her toes. "I intend to make sure you stay that way. Now, young lady, we should talk about certain practices that will ensure your continued good health. Nurse, are you ready?"

"Can we call me assistant?" Alexei passed him a wet cloth.

"Fine. Assistant." Caleb took the cloth and placed it directly on her pussy. She sighed as the warm, wet cloth covered her mound. He cupped her, sending heat flooding through her system. Alexei brought over a small bowl of water, a razor, and shaving cream. "While I handle this, perhaps my assistant would like to give our patient an oral exam?"

Alexei's lips turned up in the sexiest smile. "I believe I would like to do this."

Caleb pressed the cloth down as Alexei loomed over her. If all nurses looked like Alexei, more people would come into the doctor's office. He should have looked ridiculous standing there in nothing but his boxers, but all she could see was perfect skin and sculpted muscles. He leaned down and pressed his lips to hers, softly molding his mouth to hers, his palm covering her breast.

She felt Caleb begin to cup her pussy, spreading cool gel across her before he began to shave her.

"Lie still, *dushka*," Alexei commanded against her lips. "Allow the doctor to do what he does best."

"He's best at shaving pussies?" Maybe Micky had come by his sarcasm honestly.

Alexei twisted her nipple to just the point of pain. She hissed as the sensation bloomed across her skin.

"You are asking for another spanking." He bit at her lips, tugging her lower lip into his mouth and sucking. He peppered her whole face with kisses.

And Caleb stroked her. The sensation floated up from her pussy. He softly ran the razor across her skin, making the entire event a sensual experience. The razor played along her skin as Caleb manipulated her, making sure he got every inch. Alexei's tongue delved deep as a single finger pressed in.

"This is a lovely pussy, Ms. Lang." Caleb's deep voice rumbled out of his chest.

He was far dirtier than she'd imagined. She'd always known Alexei had a filthy mind. One look at the man and she could tell he would do disgusting, nasty, sexy things to the woman who caught him. But Caleb was a revelation. She would never be able to think about a physical again without feeling his hands on her body, playing, teasing, tempting.

"Are you finished?" Alexei asked, coming up for air.

Caleb waved for him to come look. Holly knew she should feel weird with two men staring at her pussy while her legs were spread wide, but all she seemed capable of feeling was impatience. She was going crazy. She gripped the sides of the table, her nails sinking in. The paper that covered the table crinkled under her skin.

"Much better." Alexei reached out and touched her. He and Caleb touched her at the same time. Caleb's fingers went low, playing inside her pussy while Alexei ran his thumb over her clit. She lifted her hips, seeking more from them. "Now she will be able to feel everything."

"Ah, I believe our patient has shown that she's ready for the next procedure." Caleb had the most decadent grin on his face.

She wanted to howl as they both pulled their hands away. How could they stay in control? She felt so out of it. She was desperate.

"I think I'm going to enjoy playing with you from this position." Caleb stood between her legs and brought his finger back to her pussy. "You're so wet. You seem to have a healthy sexual appetite. Of course, there's only one way to make sure this is normal."

He got to his knees. She could feel the arousal coating her pussy. She knew what he was going to do.

His tongue did a long, slow slide though her labia. She moaned at the feel. Her whole body had started to pulse with arousal. It was so different than before. Before he'd shaved her, he'd only licked at her labia and clit and deep inside her. She hadn't thought she needed more. But now he put his whole mouth on her, encasing her in heat. She felt devoured—in the most decadent way.

She was so sensitive now without the encumbrance of pubic hair. Caleb's tongue licked all over. He stroked her from the top of her mound all the way down almost to her asshole. He pulled away before touching it, and she ground her teeth in frustration. She wanted to curse.

"I think our patient is beginning to understand that she's neglected a few of her erogenous zones." Caleb's hands held her ankles like manacles. She had a sudden vision of being tied down and open to these men. Maybe she would spend time in Stef's playroom. "I think she wants me to lick her asshole."

"Caleb! Do you have to be so blunt?" Heat flushed through her system. At least Alexei was a bit more discreet.

Caleb simply continued his delicious assault on her flesh. "Nope. I decided when I got to this town that the only way to fit in was to be as blunt and obnoxious as possible. I'm too old to change now."

He was thirty-seven. He wasn't old. She had some work to do on the man, but she kept getting distracted by his tongue. He speared her pussy, making her moan and shake.

"Doctor? This is ready. Perhaps you could use a second opinion on whether or not she is healthy in this place. I have some experience in this." Alexei's impatience dripped from his mouth. He stood over them, watching everything Caleb did to her.

"Bastard, you want to try my treat." He grumbled the words against her skin.

Alexei's eyes narrowed. "I have not been able to taste treat. Last night you kept treat all to self. You are treat pigger."

She felt Caleb laugh. "Yes, I'm a treat pigger." He gave her one last lick and got up.

Alexei immediately took his place. "These things should be fair. We have to share our treats. I like the way these things hold her legs open. We should to be getting some for home."

"Home?" Holly asked.

"I think you'll find you have a houseguest, sweetheart." Caleb shoved his jeans down, freeing his cock. "We talked it over, and we don't think you should live there alone. There are too many crazy things that happen in this town."

And everyone looked out for everyone else, as evidenced by the activities of last night. She lived in between a bunch of former federal agents. They were always on the lookout for someone or something to pull a gun on.

She could barely breathe as Alexei started a long, slow exploration of her pussy with his tongue. "I'm not alone. I have Micky now. He's just a kid."

"She is worried I will not get along with her son?" Alexei asked

Caleb.

Caleb shook his head. "No. She's worried Micky will get the wrong idea."

"He will get the idea that I love his mother and wish to have much sex with her," Alexei said.

Caleb pointed to his nose, letting Alexei know he'd gotten it right. "Yeah, I think she's worried that he'll catch on to that last part."

She was pretty damn sure Micky already knew about that. Still, she was a bit uneasy. Micky had said he was fine with it, and he was seven months away from being considered an adult.

"The boy knows. He is smart boy." Alexei was obviously not buying that argument. "He only has to look at the way I eat his mother up with my eyes to know that passion is between us."

"Well, I think he'll be okay with it as long as there's also a condom between you." Caleb walked to the counter, showing off his spectacular backside. He turned back around and had what appeared to be a fully-lubed anal plug in his hand.

"Alexei, you can't simply move in. We should talk about this." But she didn't want to do that right this moment. She wanted to forget about everything that could possibly come between the three of them and simply feel.

His head came up. She could see the juice of her arousal on his lips. "You do not wish me to be with you?"

He looked like a sad puppy who hadn't expected to get kicked.

Caleb looked startlingly similar. "We did talk about this. Alexei and I talked about it and decided that he should move in with you. Did you expect him to live at the Movie Motel forever? Gene only changes out those movies once a week, and he has a strange thing for Doris Day. Having to watch those movies twice a night is cruel."

Alexei shook his head and started to get to his feet. "I do not want to impose. If Holly feel uncomfortable, then I will wait."

Oh, she couldn't turn down that gorgeous face. And Micky did seem to be strangely okay with it. Maybe after years of living with a cold stepmother, he was looking forward to an odd Russian and a slightly deranged doctor for stepfathers. Oh, god. She'd thought it. She'd thought about marrying them. She'd had a vision of the three of them together forever.

She'd promised herself she wouldn't get in too deep, but that ship

190

had sailed. She loved them. She couldn't imagine the future without them.

"I'll have a list of improvements for you. If you're going to live with me, you can help me keep the place up."

Alexei's smile was slow and sure. "I will be pleased to do these things for you. And I will be good to your son. I will make you happy. It is my job."

Caleb handed the plug to Alexei. "It's his only job, so expect him to be good at it." He looked down at her. "He'll take care of you."

But Caleb didn't make the same pledge himself. "And what about you?"

A cloud passed over his face. "I told you, I can't do serious. I made that clear."

She could practically hear his panic. She reached up to touch him. He had his demons. She couldn't force him to confront them, but she also couldn't leave him alone with them. "You can come and go as you please. You'll always be welcome."

"This is everything I can give you right now." He touched her face, smoothing back her hair. His mouth had turned down, and she would do anything to get the playful doctor back. "I promise I'll try. I wouldn't have been able to do this a couple of months ago. Holly, I—I haven't cared about anyone the way I do you. Anyone."

Not even his wife. It was all she could ask for. "I think I feel a pain, Doctor."

His breath hitched. "Really?"

She knew what he was asking. He wanted to know if she could handle his quirks. He was blunt when he talked and taciturn the rest of the time. He was enigmatic and so hard to read. He was hardheaded and yet his soul was so generous. She could handle him. "Yes. I have a terrible pain."

"You should tell the doctor all about it. My assistant is ready to help, too. Now where is this pain? Is it here?" Caleb leaned over and brushed his lips over hers.

She shook her head. "No. Lower."

"Ah, then it must to be hurting here." Alexei kissed one of her toes.

"No," she replied. "Higher."

Caleb kissed her neck. Alexei licked her ankle. Holly kept up the play, sending Caleb to suckle her breasts and Alexei to torture the backs of her knees. They worked their way down and up her body, leaving no inch unkissed, unloved. Finally Alexei kissed her inner thighs, and Caleb's lips softly touched her clit.

"I think we have to go deeper," Caleb said, shaking his head.

Alexei got to his feet, plug in hand. "You should hand me the lubricant. I will work in the toy."

Caleb handed him the lube and came back up to the head of the table. "And I'll deal with the oral portion of this exam. I need you to turn over, sweetheart. We'll flip the stirrups down for this part. It's going to work best if you stand on the floor with your legs wide apart. You need to be still while we assess you. While my assistant works on your sweet asshole, I need to feel your mouth on me."

She pulled her feet out of the stirrups and flipped over on her belly. There was no point in fighting. They would only talk her into it. And she wanted them both. She wanted to know what it felt like to be in the middle, to know that even while they fucked her, they could feel each other deep inside her body.

She laid her cheek to the side and looked at the gorgeous monster Caleb thrust at her face. Caleb's cock was already coated with cream.

"Open up, sweetheart. I need to test your mouth."

She fought not to giggle but stopped entirely when she felt Alexei dribble lube on her ass.

"This is beautiful, *dushka*. I dream about fucking this sweet hole. So tight. You're going to be so tight." He pressed a finger in, rimming her.

Caleb rubbed his cockhead along her lips. "She'll be even tighter with one cock in her pussy and another in her ass. She'll be tighter than anything I've ever felt before. Open up for the doctor, sweetheart. I need you to say *aahh*."

She opened her mouth slightly, and Caleb pressed in. He pushed past her lips and her teeth and forced the head of his cock into her mouth. He tasted clean and salty. Even when they held her down and played the dominant cavemen, she'd never felt as powerful as when they made love to her.

"That's right, sweetheart. Oh, your mouth is so hot." Caleb put a hand on her hair, holding her down gently for his use. "I think you're giving me a fever. Fuck. I won't last long."

She felt something harder than a finger pushing at her asshole. The sensation was dark and forbidding.

"You must to relax, Holly. You must let me inside," Alexei said.

"Fuck it in, Alexei. Short thrusts. Don't let up. Let that sweet little asshole know who the boss is. Let it know it can't keep you out. You're going to take it. You're going to make it yours." Caleb's words were soft, almost gentle, but the dominance behind them made her fists clench. He wouldn't let her keep him out. Not out of her mouth or her pussy or her ass. He would keep on until he'd claimed every part of her.

"That's right, *dushka*. Relax. You look beautiful like this. So open, so trusting." Alexei did exactly what Caleb had told him to do. He pressed in and pulled out, making tiny circles every time he gained some ground. He twisted the plug, forcing her open. "Do you know what it does to me? Watching you take his cock? I am possessive man, but it is right to share with him. He is partner. It is right for you to submit to us. We take care of you. We live for you. Open for me. Let me in. Let me have you so we can all be together."

She looked up at Caleb's face. His eyes were closed, but the look on his face was more peaceful than she'd ever seen. He was calm and set to his task. She'd given him that.

She relaxed, opening herself to everything they had to give to her.

* * * *

Alexei sighed as the plug finally slid home. The light purple plug looked sweet squeezed into her tiny asshole. So beautiful. Holly was a delight in every way. She was the inexperienced one, and yet she made him feel like an untried youth. Every moment he spent with her felt new, as though he was finally discovering what it meant to live.

He'd never had to prepare a lover to take him. It had been an easy exchange of money or simple pleasure. The women he'd been with had wanted something from him. They had wanted cash or the thrill of sleeping with a mobster. Those had been the most unsatisfactory encounters. He'd often needed sex to burn off the terrible things he'd seen or done.

With Holly he felt clean, even as he thought the filthiest thoughts about her. It would be right and good to do anything he wanted to her because love flowed between them. Such a sweet feeling to belong to someone. This was what washed away his sins, his pain. This was what made him whole.

And he could see it was starting to work on the good doctor as well.

"Fuck, you feel so good. Take more of me. I want to feel the back of your throat." Caleb pumped into her mouth, obviously lost in the sensation. Alexei could remember it. Her mouth was small and tight. Hot and welcoming. The way she'd used her tongue on him still made his balls draw up.

He caressed the globes of her ass. Her skin was creamy and white, the pink of yesterday fading back to her natural color. She'd liked having her ass spanked. She would like it when he tied her up and forced his dick into any hole he wished. He would make sure she knew how much he appreciated her trust, her love, her submission.

And he needed her. Now.

He walked to the counter and reached into Caleb's small bag. The doctor had spent his morning shopping for all manner of helpful items. In addition to the plug, lube, and shaving accessories, he'd purchased condoms and a set of nicely padded handcuffs. Alexei preferred rope, but he would take the cuffs.

He grabbed the condoms and the cuffs.

Her hands had come out to grab at Caleb's backside. Bad girl. She hadn't been given permission to do such a thing. Caleb needed a few lessons in how to play doctor. He got lost in the sex and forgot the rules.

"Holly, you are only allowed to use mouth on doctor. Please to give me your hands." He took her left hand and pulled it behind her back.

"Obey Alexei." Caleb pulled his cock out, his face in an unholy grimace. "This better be good, man. I'm close."

"She is not. And she is trying to take over," he explained.

"No, I'm not," Holly shot back.

He smacked her ass with a hard, sharp swat.

"Oh, my god!"

Alexei chuckled. "It feels different with plug?"

"I don't know if I like it. I don't know. It feels so sensitive." She wiggled her ass as though trying to get used to the sensation.

He intended to make sure she liked it very much. "We will see how it feels when I take you. I must make thorough examination of all your lovely female parts. And I don't want you to move. You must let experts have their way."

Caleb's voice came out in a frustrated huff. "Give him your hands, Holly. He's back in boss mode. Neither one of us is going to get off until he has you exactly the way he wants you."

Holly's hand came around and rested on the small of her back. Alexei took her hands in one of his and with the other snapped the cuffs on.

"You see how pretty she is like this? She is beautiful. And she will not fight with you. *Dushka*, are you afraid or uncomfortable in any way?" If she was, he would take off the cuffs. "We don't have to do anything. I just be wanting to explore."

Holly turned her smart mouth on him once again. "I am damn uncomfortable, Alexei. I have a plug up my ass and no one will fuck me."

He smacked her ass again, making her moan. "Just know, *dushka*, that all of this is for pleasure. The minute it does not be pleasing to you, it will stop. I would not hurt *moy* angel."

His angel. She was his angel.

"I'm fine, babe. I'll be sure to let you know if I'm in pain. I'll probably do it really loudly. I don't know about looking pretty though. I feel awkward." She twisted on the exam table.

"He's right. You look lovely, sweetheart," Caleb reassured her. "Now mind the doctor. Let me use your mouth. I need to fuck your mouth. I think my partner is going to take care of your pussy."

Yes. He would take care of her pussy. Caleb began feeding her his length, the sight tightening Alexei's cock. He'd never imagined how intimate it could be to share a woman. This was what he'd longed for all those lonely nights in strange hotel rooms. He'd longed for a family.

He got between her legs and made a place for himself. He tested her pussy. Wet. She was soaking wet. She'd enjoyed their play.

He'd enjoyed it, too. His cock was hard as a rock, jutting from his core and practically banging at his belly in an attempt to get what it wanted. He fisted himself, pumping a few times before opening the condom and covering himself. One day he would take her with nothing between them. He would convince her to make a baby with him. She was so caring. She loved her son and regretted not being with him each day. Another baby would be good for her. Good for him. He wanted a daughter with Holly's red hair and green eyes. A baby girl he could pour his love into, or a boy he could teach as his father and brother had taught him. A child to share with Holly and Caleb.

He couldn't wait any longer. He could see the plug he'd worked into her ass peeking out at him as he pulled her cheeks apart. He lined his dick up and thrust in.

She moaned around the cock in her mouth.

"Oh, that's right. Suck me hard, sweetheart. You suck that cock." Caleb pushed in and out of her mouth. He exchanged a dark look with Alexei. An intimate look. They were sharing a woman, and it connected them. They weren't alone in loving Holly, in taking care of her. Caleb turned his eyes back down. He never let up thrusting his cock, but he seemed to be watching. Alexei knew what he was doing. He'd done the same thing the night before. Caleb was watching for any sign of distress. She was their woman. They would take her safety and pleasure seriously.

And it was his turn to make sure she was pleasured. He pulled on her hips as he forced his cock in. Her pussy was tight, and he could feel the hard drag of the plug in her ass. It lit up his cock, threatening to make him blow.

"She's so tight," he murmured in Russian, not caring they wouldn't understand him. He was lost in the feel of her pussy wrapping around him. Her muscles clamped down on his dick like a vise tightening to the point of sweet, sweet pain. He pulled out a little, just to the head, and started it all over again. Her pussy sucked at him. Her hips bucked back up as though trying to take him deeper. He pumped into her, enjoying the penetration. He watched as she sucked Caleb's cock, her pink tongue lashing at the head when he pulled out.

"I'm going to come." Caleb's breath sawed in and out of his chest. "I'm going to come down your throat, baby."

He glanced up at Alexei, a desperate look in his eyes.

"I will make her come, too." He reached around and felt for her clit. The bundle of nerves was swollen and needy. "Poor *dushka*. She is wanting."

He drove his dick in as he pressed down on her clit, and she spasmed around him.

Caleb moaned. "That's right. Take it. It's all for you. Only for you."

Holly's pussy tightened, the muscles milking him. It was far too much. Between the sight of Holly sucking down his partner and the tight fit of her pussy, he lost it. He drove into her over and over, pleasure suffusing every inch of his body. He felt his balls draw up and had to hold on as the orgasm rushed over him.

So good. Sex had never felt like this before. His every sense was engaged. He loved the smell of their mixed arousals, the sight of Caleb stroking her hair as he came down, the feel of her skin beneath his hand, the sound of her practically purring.

She looked up, a silly grin on her face. Her eyes were glazed with satisfaction. "So, am I healthy, Doc?"

Caleb's grin just about matched Holly's. So different from the frozen man he usually presented to the world. This man was happy, open, capable of emotion. "I think you've passed this particular test. But you should know that I intend to keep a very close watch on your health."

Alexei flipped her over. She struggled a bit with the cuffs but settled into his arms. "I think our pretty patient needs some rest."

Caleb nodded. He didn't even reach for his jeans. He simply stretched and yawned. "Take her upstairs. I have a bed. Not much else, but the mattress is good. Mine is actually bigger than her bed."

"Join us." Alexei turned toward the door.

Caleb looked like he could use a nap, but his face suddenly closed, and he shook his head. "No. I have to clean up in here. I might have an actual patient at some point in time. I need to think about hiring a real nurse."

Alexei opened his mouth to speak. A job was a job.

Caleb shut him down. "Someone with credentials, buddy."

"Is anyone going to get me out of these handcuffs?" Holly asked.

"Not for a while, *dushka*." Alexei left Caleb standing in his exam room. He took the steps to Caleb's apartment two at a time, carrying his precious burden the whole way.

He'd made headway with the good doctor. It was time to see if his living space would give up any of Caleb's secrets because Alexei didn't intend for Caleb to come and go as he pleased.

But first he had an angel to take care of. He laughed as he tossed her on Caleb's big bed.

Chapter Thirteen

Caleb heard the racket as he disinfected the exam table, wiping it down and rerolling the paper.

Someone was yelling out on Main Street and whoever it was seemed damn serious about it. He hoped the noise didn't disturb Holly. She'd had a long night and was probably ready for a nap after all that physical exertion. She didn't need to listen to screaming. He was about to charge out and do some yelling of his own when the phone rang.

He needed a nurse, and maybe a receptionist. He hated answering the phone. He didn't like cleaning up, either. He wouldn't have any problem with telling his staff to reset the exam room after he'd fucked his wife on the table.

Caleb stopped. Holly wasn't his wife. Holly wasn't going to be his wife. Husbands slept with their wives. Husbands told their wives everything. He'd been a horrible husband, and he had no intention of wrecking Holly's life. And Holly had a kid. He'd be a terrible father.

But Alexei would be a good one. Was he going to be able to watch Alexei get Holly pregnant and start a family? Would he be able to take care of her? There wasn't another doctor for fifty miles. Even if he forced them to go to another doctor, there wouldn't be an obstetrician. There weren't enough people to support a specialist. They would have to go to Alamosa, almost two hours away. It was the precise reason he was the one taking care of the pregnant women in Bliss. He could send to them a specialist for specific appointments, but for the most part, their care fell to him.

He stopped and took a deep breath. He was borrowing trouble.

And he suddenly knew why he hadn't hired a nurse. Deep down, he hadn't expected to stay. He'd expected to move on because that was what he did. Even as a kid. He'd moved with his father and brothers between houses in Chicago and Washington and boarding schools, never making deep connections with anyone but Eli and Josh. He hadn't even connected with Caroline.

He'd expected to get sick of Bliss and leave one day, but the place had wormed its way into his heart, warming him where he'd thought he'd had nothing left but cold.

He had to get his shit together. He loved Holly. Hell, he was even beginning to be fond of the big Russian.

He couldn't leave. Not when he'd found his home.

And his home was really loud.

The phone continued to ring as though the person on the other end of the line knew he didn't like to pick it up and wouldn't take no for an answer. What was he thinking? He had to answer the damn phone.

He picked up. "Bliss County Clinic."

"Hey, Doc. I was wondering if you were there. This is Roger."

"Long-Haired Roger or Roger?" They got pissed when you confused them, and without the visual confirmation of hair, he found it difficult to tell them apart.

"Oh, this is Roger from the shop. I was calling about your truck."

Ah, Long-Haired Roger. The bald one. "Got it. What's the word?"

"Well, it's the strangest thing. The brake fluid leaked out."

He'd figured that out already. "And how did that happen?"

"Well, it looks like someone cut the line. Or it was a real careful critter. You know, sometimes monkeys can use tools. I saw that on a nature documentary the other day. But we don't have any monkeys around here. And I don't care what Mel says. I won't believe we have a Sasquatch until I see him. And Sasquatch is probably really big. Someone would have noticed him under your truck."

Long-Haired Roger, who might also be called Rambling-On Roger, continued, but Caleb didn't really hear him. Someone had cut his brake line. Someone had tried to kill him and nearly gotten Holly instead. What the hell was going on?

"Leave the truck. The sheriff needs to see it." He was going to have to pull Nate Wright into this.

"I already called him. I thought it was real odd. I know Holly was in the truck. Now, Caleb, I know you're touchy, but I thought you liked Holly. Everyone around here is taking bets on when you'll finally ask her out."

He closed his eyes in frustration as he heard a siren go off. "I didn't try to kill Holly. Holly is my…my girlfriend. Look, just fix the truck when the sheriff releases it and send me the bill."

He hung up and walked to the door. The siren had gone dead, but he could see the faintest hint of red and blue lights filtering through the blinds. He prayed Nate hadn't jumped to the conclusion that the town doctor wanted to murder his café crush. It seemed incomprehensible, but nothing was impossible in this town.

He couldn't make out who was yelling, but they were damn serious about it. He put down the antibacterial spray and went out to the waiting room. The ivy Nell had left looked sad and lonely. It was the only bit of color in the white and gray room. He'd bought a painting because Holly had talked him into it, but it had been taken into evidence after the Russian mob incident, and he hadn't looked for another since.

He lifted one of the blinds, hoping Nate wasn't storming the clinic. The sheriff of Bliss stood in the parking lot, his hands on a woman's elbows, locking her arms into a pair of not-padded handcuffs. What the hell?

Caleb strode out of the clinic, not bothering to put on his boots. He was happy he'd felt weird cleaning in the altogether, or Nate Wright might have been getting to see more of him than he wanted to. As it was, he'd only put on his jeans. He was sure he looked like a disheveled crazy as he jogged across the thin lawn toward the parking lot.

"Nate, what the hell is going on?"

Nate looked up, a frown on his face. "You know this woman?"

He turned her around. She was a slender woman with brown,

plainly cut hair and yes, she was familiar. He searched for the name Alexei had called her. Jessie. She'd been with a dark-haired man. If he had to guess, he would have bet they were a couple. "I met her a couple of hours ago. I think her name is Jessie."

She'd also been in Trio the night before. He'd noticed her. Her eyes had almost constantly been on Alexei, though she'd held hands with the man she'd sat with.

"Yes, my name is Jessie Wilson, and I was with Alexei Markov." The woman didn't plead. She sounded pissed off. "It's kind of my job. If you will check the badge in my back pocket, we can clear this up."

Nate nodded and Cameron Briggs came up behind the suspect. He quickly pulled a wallet from the woman's back pocket and opened it up.

"The badge claims she's Jessica Wilson, and she's a US marshal," Cam said as though he didn't quite believe it.

"Sheriff, the aliens know all the best forgers," a familiar voice said.

Caleb turned and suddenly Mel was standing beside him. The older man wore coveralls, a thermal shirt, and sneakers. He was never without his trucker hat. It was lined with heavy-duty tinfoil to keep the death rays away.

"She's an alien?" It was a decent bet. Mel assumed most outsiders were aliens.

"No idea. I don't think so. She doesn't have the look. And I didn't see her wearing one of the amulets the Els wear. She could be an Anakim. You would know them better as Elders. You see, the Elders are actually about nine to eleven feet tall, but they wear these amulets that molecularly condense them down to regular size. I don't see the amulet. And she's neither reptilian nor one of the Grays. I think she's a real, live human asshole." He turned toward Caleb expectantly. "Although we should probably check her just in case. You could do an exam. Check for a prehensile tail."

Sometimes being the only doctor in Bliss county was a hassle. "I am not checking anyone's tail, Mel. She's human."

"Hey!" Jessie's partner ran across the street, holding his hands up in the universal sign for "don't shoot me." "My name is Michael Novack. I'm a US marshal. That's my partner, Jessica Wilson."

"I tried to explain to this small-town asshole that I'm doing my job. I was waiting for you when I saw someone playing around with

201

that piece-of-crap Ford over there." She gestured back to the parking lot where Alexei had parked Holly's car.

Caleb felt his stomach turn.

Michael managed to convince everyone to let him pull his badge out of his pocket. He flashed it around. "We're Alexei Markov's handlers. We followed him when he left Florida because there's still some danger to him. Even though technically he left the program, Jessie and I wanted to stick close to him until the appeals court hands down its verdict on two of his cases. We've been following him around. Though we're supposed to keep a low profile."

Jessie practically snarled at him. "Do not blame this on me. Alexei drove that car around all day. Was I supposed to let some asswipe mess around with it? He was suspicious."

Nate turned to Mel. "Did you see this man?"

Mel shrugged. "I only saw her, but that doesn't mean I couldn't have missed something. She was under the car."

Jessie groaned, obviously frustrated. "Because the man had run off. I'm not sure if he was a bad guy or not. I couldn't exactly chase down a tourist who was tying his shoe. I had to check. I think he did something. It looks like there was something attached to the bottom of the car."

The door to the clinic opened, and Alexei stood there. Caleb didn't miss the way his right hand snaked behind his back. There was little doubt that his partner was hiding the gun he carried. Alexei reholstered the weapon and strode out. Caleb saw the slats to the blinds open.

"Holly, it's safe. You can come out," Caleb yelled.

"I tell her to stay in bedroom. Our woman needs her hearing checked." Alexei caught sight of the marshals, and his face fell. He turned to Nate. "I can explain."

Nate waved him off with a roll of his blue eyes. "I can take a wild guess. You couldn't keep your dick in your pants long enough for the US legal system to work its way through all the fuckers you put in jail. The marshals are trying to keep you alive."

"Alexei?" Holly walked up to Alexei, her feet bare and her hair still tousled. "Is that true?"

Alexei turned to Holly, his face grave. "That is truth, what sheriff say. Though I was going to grovel a bit more. I would not have come for you if I do not think is safe."

"Well, we might have to rethink that," Nate said as he uncuffed the female marshal. "I had a nice talk with Long-Haired Roger. Someone tampered with Caleb's truck."

Holly's hand was suddenly in his. He heard her startled gasp. "Oh, god. Someone tried to kill me."

"Or Caleb." Deputy Briggs pulled out a tablet and started making notes. "It was Caleb's truck. And now Holly's car in front of Caleb's clinic."

"But I be driving car around." Alexei's accent had gotten thick again. Caleb was starting to get his tells. When Alexei got emotional, his accent was almost too thick to understand.

"You didn't drive my truck," Caleb pointed out.

"No. But I stand by it for almost an hour before I walk in yesterday morning. I watched Nell walk in. I was afraid to be talking to you. What if someone saw me and thought it was my truck? What if there is someone in town trying to get to me? What if they learn how much it would hurt me if they got to Holly or you instead?"

Caleb squeezed Holly's hand, noting Alexei was holding her other hand. It felt right.

"Sheriff, she checks out." Logan swaggered onto the scene. He seemed to have gotten control of himself, but there was a red rim to his eyes that bespoke of many nights' lost sleep. "She is who she says she is, though her boss was surprised to find out she was in Colorado."

Jessie took back her badge. She shoved it in her pants and glared at the sheriff. "We're doing this under the radar. I think it's too early to take him out of the program. Look, we spent a lot of time with the big guy. He was supposed to settle down in Boca Raton under the name Howard Solev. He had all his papers. He was supposed to be a recent immigrant working for a security company. We worked hard to set up a safe life for him. Imagine our surprise when he disappeared. I knew he had someone he cared about here. Arrest me for giving a crap."

Nate stared down at her, giving her the same look Caleb had seen him give speeders and other minor irritants. "Look, Marshal, here's what I know. I know that someone deliberately tampered with Dr. Burke's truck."

"Don't let Long-Haired Roger discount my Sasquatch theory. I think they're rising up against industry and big business, Sheriff. I don't think they like gas-guzzling trucks," Mel said seriously.

Nate's expression never changed. "I will keep that in mind. Cam, be sure to place environmentally friendly Sasquatches on the board of suspects."

Cam grinned. "Will do, Sheriff."

"What is wrong with you people?" Jessie asked.

"Not a damn thing," the sheriff replied. "Now, my second problem is that I have US marshals in my town who don't do me the courtesy of informing my office that they're here and working a case. Don't give me that bullshit about caring about him. You're carrying a gun, and you're more than willing to use it. You owe me the courtesy of letting me know what's going on."

"Yes, we do, Sheriff." Michael seemed to be the more reasonable of the two. "We're sorry. We honestly didn't think anything would happen to him. We've been keeping tabs on him from a distance. This town seems pretty good about protecting its own. We didn't even have to step in when Ms. Lang's son showed up. He almost immediately had six men on him."

"I liked that part."

Caleb looked to his left. Mick stood there with a cup from Stella's. He took a long drag from the straw. Caleb noted that the Farley boys were with him.

Mick grinned at him. "Look, I made friends. They're showing me all the cool spots."

"Like the place where all the girls bathe naked because they think no one can see them," one of the brothers said.

Mick shook his head. "Yeah, I wasn't so interested in that one. And the nudists are way funkier than I would have thought. But I liked the Feed Store Church. And there were a couple of people miming their distaste for Wall Street on the square. That was pretty awesome."

So that's what Nell and Henry were up to this afternoon.

"What's up with the feds?" Bobby Farley asked.

"They're here about Alexei." Will looked over and waved at the Russian. "Hey, man! We're glad to see you. We need a coach for little league hockey. I should warn you, it's only me and Bobby. You wouldn't have much of a team."

Alexei warmed immediately. "We do not need many peoples. We merely need to be meaner than the rest. This I can teach you. If I am not dead."

Bobby looked to the sheriff, a thoughtful expression on his face. "Yeah, the sheriff is worried about that, too. Though he also thinks it could be Holly's ex-husband, because he's a son of a bitch, or Caleb's family. He has a whole board of suspects."

Nate Wright's eyes widened. "You two little shits. Did you bug my station house again? I swear to god, I am talking to your mother."

Neither boy looked particularly intimidated. Will shrugged. "We didn't bug the station house. We just invented a machine that amplifies sound. We didn't even have to use the full range. You can be really loud, Sheriff."

Mick pointed to both kids. "I love these kids. If only I'd had you on my side a year ago. But there's no way Dad would hurt Mom. He's a dickhead, but he wouldn't hurt her."

Just as Mick said the words, there was a horrific boom and fire shot to the sky. It came from the parking area not fifty yards away. The sound cracked, splitting the air with a terrible roar. That sound seemed to be everywhere—invading his consciousness and making the world seem unreal.

Caleb's ears flared with pain. *Too loud.* And then everything was muffled by an odd ring. They would be ringing for hours.

Alexei leapt into action, covering Holly with his big body, and Caleb took the kids. He felt the blast from the explosion heat his skin as he tugged at the kids, trying to protect them with his own body. He covered Mick's head with one hand and pulled the twins in with the other.

When it was over, he looked to Mick, who had lost his "perpetually amused with the world" expression. His eyes were wide with terror. He stood and tried to brush away the smoke that seemed to be everywhere. An acrid smell permeated the air.

Caleb was well aware he was speaking far too loudly as he talked to Mick. "Take care of the boys. I need to check on your mother."

Holly's son nodded and immediately took the twins under his wing. He moved them away from the site to the other side of Main Street. Logan was moving Jessie and Michael to the other side, too. Cam checked on Mel.

Nate was already on his radio. "Hope, get the fire department out here. Yes, we had a bomb go off. Try like hell to keep people away from the area."

But they were already streaming out of homes and businesses. Well-meaning citizens were suddenly everywhere. Chaos. It was chaos. Caleb was far too well acquainted with chaos. Holly. He needed to get to Holly.

"I don't think the Sasquatch did that, Doc," Mel yelled. "They're not real good with electronics!"

Caleb ignored him and moved to Holly. Alexei had her on the ground, his big body covering every inch of her. She was struggling beneath him, but he wouldn't budge.

"Is danger passed?" Alexei asked, yelling a bit.

It was a good thing because Caleb's ears were still ringing. "We're good."

It was also good to know that Alexei had her back even when she was fighting him.

Alexei let her up.

"Micky?" She looked around for her son.

He finally got his hands on her, assuring himself that she was all right. "He's fine, sweetheart. I think we're all fine."

"My ears are ringing," she said, calming visibly once she could see her son.

"Mine, too," Alexei said, pulling at his ears.

Caleb slapped at his hand. "It's tinnitus. It'll go away. Don't pull at them."

Nate walked over. "I think we need to take this to the station house. Logan and Cam are going to stay here and see if we can get anything off the car—once it's not a flaming ball anymore. We need to talk. All of us."

Mick stepped up, his face white as a sheet. "I should come, too. I'm worried maybe my dad might be more involved than I hoped."

"What?" Holly asked, taking his hand.

"Well, I might be blackmailing him, and he might be really pissed off."

Yeah, it was definitely time to talk.

* * * *

Vince was almost ready to call it a job. A fucked-up job. A big, old pile-of-shit job. He'd never before screwed up the way he had in this town.

He trudged through the woods, cursing nature at every turn. Where had he parked his Jeep? He'd seen an opportunity to get at one of the vehicles the target used. It seemed to be the only car left between the three of them, and if he got one of the others, his employer was okay with that. Collateral damage.

But he'd been made. Oh, they might not know exactly who he was, but they knew someone was after one of the townspeople. It wouldn't take them too long to figure out who was the target. They only had three fucking choices.

And the sheriff seemed much smarter than a local yokel. The whole fucking town was a bastion for former feds and conspiracy nuts, and every goddamn one of them had a gun.

Life was easier in New York.

He'd blown the car because he was afraid he'd left something behind. He knew he'd done a hack job on it, but he couldn't get at the damn car while it was parked at the woman's cabin. Last night had proven that. He'd watched as six huge men had shown up to take care of one skinny-ass kid.

No way. No how.

The parking lot of the clinic was away from the street. It was surrounded by a concrete wall. He'd watched the three of them enter the clinic after his botched attempt to take out the target with the car he'd stolen after hiding his Jeep on the mountain. He'd listened and heard the freaks all having sex. After deciding they would be occupied for a while, he'd decided to give it a go.

And that dumb bitch had found him. He'd barely gotten the device in place when she'd called out to him like they were old friends or something. She'd said hi and he'd taken off.

He'd barely made it over the wall when the sirens had started up.

He felt sick to his stomach. He wasn't this guy. He wasn't the guy who screwed up. He should never have taken the job. He should have known how many goddamn eyes would be on the target.

But he wouldn't quit. He would simplify finish the fucking job. No more accidents. No more close encounters.

The target was getting a bullet to the brain the next chance Vince got.

He was going to end this.

Chapter Fourteen

Holly stopped her pacing long enough to stare down at her only child.

"Dad told me to get a hobby." Micky sat back in his chair with a shrug. He had a cup of coffee in his hand and looked distinctly uncomfortable to be sitting in the Bliss County Sheriff's Office.

They occupied the main room, all of them. It was getting crowded. The US marshals Alexei had neglected to mention to her sat together watching the scene play out. They leaned against the back wall, talking to each other in low tones. Alexei looked as uncomfortable as Micky did, though Holly was sure it was for different reasons. The last time Alexei had been in this room, he'd nearly died. He'd been shot in the gut, and only Caleb's sure hands had saved him. She remembered how it had felt to clutch him and know she couldn't hold him together. It had been horrible, and she hadn't even been in love with the man then.

Now she wasn't sure she would be able to survive it. She tried to give him a reassuring smile before she turned back to her baby boy. She didn't smile at him. "Please explain to me how blackmailing your father is a good hobby. I think he was talking about something like stamp collecting or reading. I doubt he meant for you to dabble in crime."

Micky leaned forward. "It was photography. It seemed like a good idea. And Dad made an excellent subject. I mean, he didn't know at the time that he was the subject, but he was good."

She put her head in her hand. He was so stubborn. "Please tell me you didn't do what I think you did."

"I think the boy catches father with many womens." Alexei sat back in his chair and gave Micky a look of deep respect. "This could ruin career. How much did you get?"

"Don't encourage him," she said Alexei's way. The last thing Micky needed was a partner in crime. He seemed to be doing quite well on his own.

Caleb leaned forward, joining the other two men. "It wasn't money, was it? You wanted out. You wanted to be free of the whole 'political family' thing. I can understand that. It's hard. Everyone's always looking at you. You can't be yourself. You have to live up to the family name."

Micky pointed to Caleb. "He gets it. I did it to get away from my dad, but I also took a lot of money. Hey, I wanted to be free, not dirt poor."

"Holly, I know you want to throttle the boy, but how about we hear him out?" Nate asked, sitting on Hope's desk.

Micky seemed to suddenly remember they weren't alone. "Crap. Is that really a crime? Am I going to be arrested? I don't look good in orange."

Oh, she hadn't even thought about that. "You can't arrest him."

Nate waved her off. "If what I've heard about your ex is true, then I should give the boy a medal. But this is a serious situation. Someone blew up your car. If the congressman is involved, I want to know."

Marshal Michael Novack shook his head. "If this is about Ms. Lang, the US marshals would leave this completely in your hands, Sheriff."

Jessie gave Micky a thumbs-up. "Give 'em hell, kid. I never did like politicians."

At least Micky had the law on his side on this one. It didn't look like anyone would be hauling her baby boy off.

"I think it probably be me. Not Holly," Alexei said. "Many peoples wish to be killing me. I should not have come to town. I should have stayed and been Howard."

Michael crossed his arms over his chest. "You wouldn't have been happy. We knew that."

Nate sighed. "Okay, so it could be Holly or Alexei."

Caleb's hand came up slowly. "It wouldn't be the first time someone tried to kill me."

That was news to her. "Who would want to kill you?"

Caleb's face went oddly blank. "Have you met me?"

Every damn man in her life was made of sarcasm.

She turned to the marshals. "Do you guys think this is about Alexei?"

"I would bet on it," Michael said. "He put a lot of dangerous men in jail. Two of those men are trying to wrangle their way out of convictions. If they get their cases overturned on appeal, well, it would be better for them if Alexei couldn't testify again."

"But just so you know, we haven't received any specific threats," Jessie continued. "We're playing the odds here."

"Marshal Wilson gave a detailed description of the subject to Hope. Turns out she's a hell of an artist. We should know something soon. Zane is coming in because he got a bad feeling about a guy who hung out at Trio the other day. I've learned to trust his instincts. We'll see if the two match up," Nate said. "Although I wouldn't bet on it. She says the guy was short and very pale. I don't think they're going to match. The man Zane talked about looked Italian American to him."

"Scott is the only person who might want to hurt me. But I don't get it. I didn't even know about Micky's side business, which is going to stop now." She couldn't have her son blackmailing his father. The three men in chairs all started talking at once.

"Holly, you need to listen to the kid. Do you have any idea how hard this could have been on him?" Caleb's face was earnest, his hands tight on his thighs.

"Boy is tough. Boy does what he needs to do." Alexei went on praising her son.

"Mom, I can't go back. I won't."

She held a hand out to silence them. To her great surprise, they all fell in line. Maybe she was missing something here. She got to one knee in front of her son. "What happened? Have you been thinking about this for a while?"

Her son's face flushed with emotion. "I thought about it all the time growing up. Don't get me wrong. There was a lot I loved…still love…about being incredibly wealthy. And Dad isn't the world's worst dad. He's a terrifically horrible human being. Seriously, don't vote for him. But he loved me."

"He didn't kick you out." She took an odd comfort from that. Guilt had been gnawing at her ever since Micky had shown up. When she'd been thrown out of his life, she'd at least thought that Scott loved him. For all his douchebag ways, he'd genuinely cared for their son. Just not for her.

Micky sighed, putting the coffee down. "No, Dad didn't throw me out. And when I threatened to leave, he threw a fit. He told me if I stepped one foot out of his house before college, he would make sure I didn't touch my trust fund."

That sounded like Scott. "Baby, what did he do that made you want to leave?"

"I met a boy."

Her heart ached. She knew where this story was going, but he needed to tell it.

"His dad worked for mine," Micky said. "Not as anything big. He was on security detail, but they lived in the guesthouse. His name was Tristan. Mom, I think I loved him. I know I never felt that way before. I know I joke about how hot guys are, but it was different with him. I could talk to him. I could tell him everything. He was my first kiss. My only kiss."

She reached up and wiped the tears at his eyes. She didn't bother with her own. "Baby, I'm so sorry. Did your dad fire his?"

Micky shook his head. "No. It was worse. Dad gave him a promotion, but only if Tristan never contacts me again. They moved to DC two months ago. Tristan is a good boy, at least. He won't return my calls or my e-mails. I guess he's enjoying his dad's newfound wealth."

Caleb's face had gone red. "You can't let that get you down. You have to push those types of people out of your life. They'll just use you."

"Well, he didn't seem that way before my dad bribed his family." Micky took a deep breath and shook it off. "Anyway, I realized I couldn't take it anymore. I had to get out. I'm not stupid. I know all about Dad's penchant for sleeping with his aides. All I had to do was follow him for a day or two and I had everything I needed. I presented it all to him in a beautifully polished PowerPoint presentation. I even made a graphic representing how his dick was going to cost him voters."

Scott must have been livid. For the first time, she had to consider that he might have been mad enough to come after her. He might have suspected she was the one behind the scheme. After all, he'd done the same thing to her once.

A steely look came into her son's eyes. "Mom, I won't take it back. I can't go back to being that person. I need to be me. I need to be whoever I turn out to be. I can't play the game anymore. Not one more second. I love you. I want to spend time with you. I want to find a nice liberal arts college and get a degree that wouldn't get me a job at a fast food restaurant. I'm thinking creative writing. I want to do stupid shit because I think I'll figure out who I am. Not Mick Lang, the congressman's son. And not your little Micky. But me. Just me. I hope you'll let me do that with you. But I'll do it without you, Mom."

God, he wasn't a kid anymore. He'd made a decision it had taken her most of her adult life to make, and he hadn't needed two lovers to do it. She nodded. "Blackmail the son of a bitch until he can't see straight."

Caleb slapped his hands together. "Yes!"

Alexei sat back, crossing one foot over his knee and looking very much the dangerous mobster. "We need to make sure your master negatives are in safe place. We will talk."

Micky's eyes went wide. "I love my new daddies."

"Okay, that made me terribly uncomfortable." Caleb went back to staring at the floor.

"He has a very bent sense of humor," she acknowledged. She turned to Nate. "Is there any way you can manage to get my son-of-a-bitch ex to come in for questioning?"

"I'm working on it," Nate replied.

The double doors to the station house opened, and Logan and Cam walked in. Cam had a big grin on his face, but Logan merely stared at Alexei. Scott Lang walked in between them. He wore his thousand-dollar suit with casual grace, and his eyes almost immediately found hers.

"He came in quietly once we told him his son was involved," Cam explained. "We were lucky. He was at a political rally in Pagosa Springs about thirty minutes away."

"Son, what happened? Are you safe?" Scott hadn't changed in years. He still looked every inch the immaculate politician. He was perfectly groomed, perfectly dressed. Not a single hair dared to stray from his chosen style. His features had been built for TV.

Alexei was too dark, too brooding. He was gorgeous, but he'd had a hard life and it showed in his eyes. Caleb's hair was twelve kinds of out of place. And his T-shirt was never tucked in. It was only a miracle it wasn't wrinkled.

Scott was perfect, and now she wondered what she'd ever seen in him. Her men were the perfect ones.

"I'm fine, Dad. Not a singe on me, thanks to Mom's boyfriend." Micky seemed to take particular delight in pointing to Caleb.

Scott turned to Caleb. "You look incredibly familiar. If you saved my son, I thank you."

Caleb got up and mumbled as he turned away. "No problem."

"Logan, Cam, we need to run a 703. This could get messy." Nate hopped off the desk. "Cam, you know what to do. Logan, behave."

The deputies walked around the back of the group.

Nate faced off with Scott. "Congressman, I don't know what my deputies told you, but someone blew up your ex-wife's car today. And yesterday she nearly died in an accident that seems mighty planned to me."

Scott's hands dropped. "Are you serious? I thought this was something Micky had come up with. He's a devious one. Is this a joke? Did someone actually try to kill Holly?"

If he was acting, he was spectacular.

Micky stood up and faced his father. "Yes, Dad. I was there. Someone blew up Mom's piece-of-shit car. She needs a new one. I think you should buy it."

Scott shook his head. "Don't try my patience, son." He turned to Holly, his voice going deep. It was the same tone he used to let voters know he felt their pain. "Are you all right?"

She nodded. "Yes."

And just like that his sympathy evaporated. "What have you gotten yourself into? Who is this boyfriend? What's he into? If he's dangerous, I don't want him near my son. Micky, our deal is off. You

213

can get your ass in the car. You're coming home. And don't throw those pictures in my face. You want to ruin my career, go ahead. I won't save my fucking career in exchange for my son. Holly, you get in the car, too. We're leaving. You can stay in the guesthouse."

Both of her men started toward Scott, and Holly finally understood what a 703 was. It was code for "keep the douchebag alive." Cam put a hand on Alexei, and Logan stood in front of Caleb.

"You are not taking our woman anywhere, *dolbo yeb. Zhopa!*" Alexei went off in a litany of Russian, most of which sounded like curses.

"You touch her and I will find a horrible way for the Russian to kill you," Caleb promised. "I took the Hippocratic oath. He didn't."

Scott looked between the two men. "I thought the ginger was your boyfriend. Oh, god, Holly. Not you, too. This town is just wrong."

Holly stood her ground. It was long past time to make a stand. "It isn't wrong, and I'm not leaving. And yes, they are both my boyfriends. And Micky knows."

Micky grinned. "Total thumbs-up, Mom. They are hot! Dad's still doing the political equivalent of the pancake waitress."

"Micky!" Holly and Scott managed to say it at the same time.

And she realized something.

"You love him."

Scott's face went softer than she could remember seeing it in decades. "Of course, I do. He's my boy."

"He's gay, Scott." There were still people who could have a problem with their son's sexuality. It could cost him votes.

"Yeah, I figured that out when he was six and asked for Cher to sing at his birthday party. I've always known," Scott admitted. "He thinks I got rid of Tristan because he was a boy. I would have gotten rid of a girl at this age, too. He's too young. He's way too young to even think about settling down. Damn it, he's my son. He can't know what he wants at this age. He thinks he's in love, but in the end, he'll love his career more and he'll end up wrecking someone's life. Someone he loved. Just…just not enough. Is it wrong that I wanted to spare him that? To spare Tristan that pain?"

She shook her head. She would never forgive him for what he'd done to her. But she didn't need to brood over it anymore. "Scott, he's not you. And he's not me."

Scott took a step toward her. "Babe, you know you're the only woman I ever loved."

Cam got into a defensive position. Alexei went off in Russian again. Caleb simply stared at Scott.

Holly held out a hand, trying to let her men know that she had this one handled. "Oh, Scott, your love wasn't worth much, was it?"

He didn't even look offended. "No. Which is why Connie and I work and you and I didn't. She doesn't give a crap as long as I keep her in Prada. But you, oh, you needed more. I hope these assholes are giving it to you. Our son is the best thing I ever did."

"He blackmailed you." Holly was a little surprised at the way Scott talked.

Scott smiled, a fierce turn of his lips. "That's my boy. He's ruthless. I've never been more proud than I was the day he took down the old man. My other two kids are bleating sheep. They're tax deductions. Nothing more. But our Micky, he can be anything because he won't accept less. I'm proud to be his dad."

"Yeah, that's going to go over so well with your little old lady supporters and the church groups," Micky pointed out.

Scott sighed. "Well, I wasn't going public with my support. Son, fuck whoever you want. Just do it in private. And for god's sake, don't do it like your mother. She has it all wrong. It's two girls and one man. Though I will admit, your mother is certainly pretty enough for two men."

"She's not going to sleep with you, Dad," Micky said, groaning a little.

"Ewww! I am not." Holly wouldn't touch Scott with a ten-foot pole.

Scott shrugged. "You can't blame a guy for trying. You look good, Holly."

"*Yob tuvoyiu mat!*" Alexei pressed against Cam.

"Uh, Sheriff, he's really strong." Cam looked like he was one of those tackle dummies football players used.

"Alexei, down!" Caleb snapped. "Holly made her choice. She chose us. She isn't going anywhere. He's doing nothing but making an ass of himself. And, unfortunately, I don't think he tried to kill her."

"Kill Holly?" Scott turned to the sheriff. "Sheriff, I'm an asshole. I'll sign the paperwork proclaiming it, but I would never physically harm Holly. I love her. As much as I'm capable of love, I love her."

She looked at her men, who appeared ready to do everything they had promised. "He's not capable of much. But I'm pretty sure he didn't try to kill me."

Nate frowned. "He was in Denver yesterday?"

"Yeah. He was in Denver at a rally and then Pagosa Springs today," Cam replied, eyeing Alexei like a tiger who was about ready to pounce. "But he probably wouldn't do this himself. I ran his financials on the way out to pick him up. If he paid someone, he did it from a secret account."

Scott's foot tapped impatiently against the floor. "I didn't try to kill my wife. Ex-wife. I wouldn't do that."

Nate's eyes rolled. "Fine. You can go. I sincerely suggest you get the hell out of my town before the Russian decides to take your head off. I think Doc there will let you get by, but the Russian has gone a while without killing someone. I'm worried about him."

"Doctor?" Scott looked at Caleb, his mouth dropping. "Holy shit. You're Caleb Sommerville."

"Damn it." Micky frowned at his father. "She didn't know that."

Caleb flushed, his skin turning a dark red.

"What?" Holly asked. "You're wrong. His last name is Burke."

Jessie put her hands up. "Alexei, you can't blame me for this one. I didn't let the cat out of the bag."

"What are you talking about? Alexei?" She turned to Alexei, who seemed to know something she didn't.

Alexei's rage seemed to flee in favor of a deep guilt. It was written in the lines that creased his face. Cam stepped back as though realizing the threat had passed.

"*Dushka*, everyone in Bliss hide something," Alexei said. "Caleb does not like his original name. That is all."

Oh, but it wasn't. Alexei might be an excellent liar, but he didn't seem capable when it came to her. There was something else going on, but she let it go. She turned to Caleb. She still wasn't sure what was such a big deal. Alexei was right. A lot of people came to Bliss because they wanted to forget something. "Sommerville is a little stuffy, babe. I like Burke better."

"You're okay with it?" Caleb asked. Every muscle seemed tense.

She shrugged. "Why would I care? Lots of people change their

216

name. Laura changed hers. Rachel did, too. Nell went through a phase where she called herself Moonbeam Laughingstick. I should have changed my name, but I'm way too lazy."

Micky slapped his hands together. "Good, excellent. Then we're all happy. Dad, you should ship out. Don't you have voters to defraud?"

Scott's eyes narrowed, speculation plain in the blue orbs. "She doesn't know."

"Dad." The word sounded like a warning coming out of Micky's mouth.

Holly got a sick feeling in the pit of her stomach. Micky knew something, too. Everyone knew except her. She looked at Caleb. "What are they talking about?"

He seemed to find the floor behind her endlessly fascinating. "Nothing that matters. I'm Caleb Burke."

Scott rubbed his hands together as though something pleased him greatly. "No, you're Caleb Burke Sommerville of the Chicago Sommervilles. Holly, darling, if you think you couldn't handle the Langs, you really should meet the Sommervilles. Talk about old money and power. They invented the terms. That family came over on the Mayflower, didn't they? Well, it didn't take them long to become one of the premiere families in American politics, and they've kept it that way for a couple of hundred years."

"You're an asswipe, Dad." Micky's fists were clenched.

Holly looked around the room. "Micky, you knew who he was?"

Micky's eyes turned down. "Yes, Mom. I lived in DC long enough to know who the power players are. I knew who he was the minute I laid eyes on him. And I knew he was different. He wouldn't be in this town if he wasn't."

Scott laughed. "If you think my mother is a monster, you should meet his brother, Eli. He's in the Senate. There's talk of a run for the presidency. How is that going to look? The heat's going to be on, Holly. The great Elijah Sommerville isn't going to like the fact that his sainted brother is involved with a waitress, and apparently a foreigner. This little ménage of Caleb's might be exactly what my party needs to bring him down."

It was happening again.

"*Dushka*, calm down. Caleb has his reasons." Alexei's eyes fairly

217

pleaded with her.

"He managed to tell you." An icy stubbornness was settling over her.

Alexei shook his head. "No, I discover on my own. I discover what an amazing man he is. Yes, his family is wealthy and powerful, but he choose to be doctor to poor people in Africa. He choose to save peoples. And he choose to come here. He choose you. He might be too stubborn to admit to this, but he loves you."

Not enough. Never enough. "He didn't even tell me his real name."

Caleb's eyes were flinty stones staring at her. "This is my real name. This is who I am."

"Why didn't you tell me?"

His jaw hardened, and he looked back at the floor. "Because it doesn't matter."

"If it doesn't matter, why didn't you tell me?"

His eyes came up, and they were cold. So damn cold. "Because I've had too many women who were interested in my family and not me."

She felt her hands shaking. She was right back where she'd begun. She was twenty and in love and under fire. "You thought I was a gold digger. Just like my ex-mother-in-law."

Scott laughed, a smug, satisfied sound. "If he doesn't, I assure you his brother will. Caleb Sommerville is worth about fifty million dollars. That's what your trust is worth, right? And Eli is worth probably a billion. Believe me, Holly, you don't marry into that family without some heavy vetting. His first wife was a socialite. Caroline Hanover. Good stock. My mother would have approved."

"Congressman, I think we've had about enough of you. Please feel free to go." Nate gestured toward the door. "My deputies can show you out."

She'd heard enough. "I think I'll go, too, Sheriff. We can all agree this is probably not about me. I'll be at my cabin if you need me."

Caleb reached out and grabbed her arm. He pulled her close. So close. She could feel the heat of his skin. "I'm not through."

She wasn't about to let him manhandle her. "But I am. I've played out this scene before. I won't put myself through it again. I thought the reason you wouldn't commit was because you hadn't gotten over your first wife. I can see now that you would never commit to someone like me. Scott told me once that I was excellent mistress material for a man like him. He's a bastard, but at least he was honest with me."

Caleb wouldn't let go. His face tightened. "You pulled me into this. I wanted to stay away. I wanted to be alone, damn it. You made me care about you. Don't you dare walk away from me now. You sit down and talk this out."

She pulled away from him. "I think I'll pass, Dr. Sommerville. You can find some other cheap lay."

"*Dushka*, don't go." Alexei didn't touch her, but she could feel his will.

She turned away from him, too. "You knew, and you didn't bother to tell me. I don't want to talk to you, either."

She strode out of the sheriff's department, Micky hot on her heels.

"Mom," he called out.

He was the one man she was mad at who she absolutely couldn't get rid of. "Could you please drive me home, son?"

His face fell. "Sure. But you're making a huge mistake. He's not like Dad."

"I don't want to talk about this with you. I want to go home. You can't understand what it's like. You belonged. You had Lang blood. I can't do it again. I can't be the person everyone looks down on. Caleb can talk all he likes, but in the end, he'll want to be with someone his family will approve of. You heard your father. His wife was a socialite. She fit into that world. When he chose a woman, he chose one who fit into his social network. He's told me for a year he wasn't good for me. I should have listened."

Micky followed her across to Stella's parking lot where his car was parked.

She was so stupid. Micky was driving a hundred-thousand-dollar sports car, and she'd bought his whole "Dad kicked me out" routine. She also bought Alexei's sad puppy eyes. He hadn't even bothered to mention that he had two US marshals tailing him. No one told her anything. That was how much she meant to these men.

Her son she could forgive, but Alexei and Caleb? She wasn't sure. She'd been an idiot thinking this would work out.

She'd barely opened the door to the Benz when Nell came rushing up. She was still in her mime face paint, but her mouth was moving a hundred miles a minute.

"Oh, my god, Holly! I just heard that Sasquatches blew up your car. I mean, I know it was a person. Even Mel knows that now, but are you okay? How did it happen? What went wrong? Do you know who I should protest against?"

Nell's hands fluttered as she spoke. Holly caught them in her own. Nell immediately calmed.

"I'm fine. Everyone's fine except my car. My car is now evidence. Don't worry about it. I think I'm out of the line of fire." But Alexei wasn't. Caleb wasn't. Someone was still trying to hurt one of them. Indecision bit at her. She looked back at the station house. Was she making a mistake?

What the hell was she doing walking away when they were in trouble? But how could she trust them when they'd lied to her?

"Do you need anything?" Nell asked.

Time. She needed some time. "No."

"She needs a friend with a good head on her shoulders to kick her in the ass," Micky said, frowning. "She just dumped both of her boyfriends. Can you kick her ass?"

Nell shook her head. "No. I am bad at that. I can hold her hand and pat her back and agree with everything she says. But I think I know just who she needs."

Before Holly could protest, Nell was in the backseat of the car. She sighed and got in, wondering all the while if Micky wasn't right.

* * * *

The door to the station slammed shut, and Holly was gone. Alexei wasn't sure how everything had gone so wrong in such a short period of time. A few hours before, he'd been perfectly happy. Holly had been in his arms. He'd laid her in bed, and she'd immediately fallen asleep. He'd listened to her breathing, and that was when he'd caught sight of Caleb's closet. It had been left slightly open and there was a pillow and sleeping bag inside. He'd stared at it, a sadness in his heart.

He'd figured out Caleb's sleeping problem and come up with a plan to fix it. He knew what he wanted to try. He'd crawled back into bed with Holly, utterly content. Everything had been falling into place.

And now it had all blown up as surely as Holly's car had.

Scott stared at Caleb, a decidedly satisfied look on his face. "Dr.

Sommerville, it's been a pleasure to meet you. I assure you my party is going to be interested in what I learned on this trip. You know, I always thought that one day I would get back together with Holly. I really did care for her. Oh, not in an official capacity, of course. She isn't political wife material. But I thought I would have her again. I suppose not. You seem to have hurt her as much as I did. I don't think she'll give either of us another chance, so I'll take what I can. Yes, I think outing you will make up for losing Holly."

He turned and walked out the door.

And Caleb stood there. Alexei checked his need to punch something. There would be time enough for that. For now, he had to deal with his partner and fast.

"Go after her."

Caleb seemed frozen. Only his lips moved. "She made her choice."

"It was wrong choice. You need to fight for her. Can't you see that's what she needs? It would have been different, very different, if you had been one to tell your story—your name. But it came from the man who broke her once before. Can't you see? She needs you to fight."

"She walked away," Caleb's voice was hollow. "She walked away when I asked her to stay. She didn't really ask me anything. She heard my name, and she judged me. She doesn't want me. I was right to have stayed away in the first place. And now I have to leave town. I can't blow my brother's career up over a failed romance."

"It only fail if you allow. And do not worry about your brother. I take care of this. Stay. Think." He turned, hoping Caleb would still be there when he got back, but he had to take care of something first.

"Alexei!"

Alexei turned at Nate Wright's sharp bark.

"Don't you kill that man in my parking lot."

"I will not kill. But he might wish I do." Alexei turned and strode out the double doors. Rage churned in his gut, but he checked it. Beating the shit out of Scott Lang wouldn't solve anything. It would make things worse. In this case, the threat was worth far more than the act.

Scott Lang stood by his Audi, his keys in hand.

Alexei stopped in front of the man. He was pleased when Scott let the hand holding the keys fall to his side.

"What the hell do you want?"

"You know who Caleb is, but my question now is do you know who I am?" It was time to introduce himself.

Lang gave him a once-over. "You don't look familiar."

"Do you know the name Alexei Markov?"

His eyes widened slightly. Alexei was pleased to see fear begin to creep onto Scott Lang's face. "You're the Russian who turned on the mob."

"And several politicians," he admitted. "I do not discriminate."

Scott's hand went to the door of his car. "I'll ask again, what do you want?"

He wanted many things. He wouldn't get most of them, but there were a few that were truly worth fighting for. "I want to turn back clock and make sure you never open that mouth of yours. I cannot be doing that. But I can explain a few things to you. I really am everything the press says. I really did everything they say. I did it for my brother. For revenge. I spend years pursuing this revenge. I give up life for it."

"Yes, I read that." Scott swallowed as he spoke.

"I do not give up revenge until I meet one woman. Holly." He leaned against the Audi. "I am only alive because of Caleb Burke. You should understand that I consider these two people my family."

"Are you threatening me?"

He smiled, though he knew it was the smile of a hungry wolf. "I am explaining the truth of the world to you. You think your wealth will protect you. You think you can hire enough guards to be buffer between you and my revenge. This is not true. If you tell world about Caleb, Holly, and myself, you will never be spending another night in restful peace. You can put walls between us. You can put men between us. It will not stop me. I will come for you. I will be there one night even if it is long in the future. I will be the last face you see before blood leaves your body. I vow this. If I have my way, Caleb will marry Holly. I will be happy to be the secret. I will be happy to be anything they allow me to be. I will not be the reason they are taken down. If anyone be finding out, I will hold you accountable."

Scott's face had gone a pleasing shade of stark white. "I can't promise that. I can keep my mouth shut, but it could still get out."

"No. If it does, I will come for you."

"Damn it, man," the politician practically whined. "You can't hold me accountable."

"I will come for you." He stepped away from the car. His point seemed to have been made. "Remember this. You can tell whole world, and I will come for you. You can tell single friend who tells someone else, and I will come for you."

Scott straightened his shoulders, but his voice was still whiny and small. "Don't you think you scare me."

"You will make decision. If wrong decision, then I will come for you. I will come for you because I will have nothing left. I will watch you, Congressman. I will always be watching you."

He turned away to see Caleb standing there, his hands on his hips. Alexei felt himself flush. Damn it. He hadn't wanted Caleb to see that part of him. He'd been careful to always be the smiling Alexei around Caleb. He knew Caleb had read the stories, but he hadn't seen the truth of him.

The Audi peeled out of the parking lot like the devil was chasing it.

"I think the congressman might have peed himself." Caleb said the words, but Alexei didn't see any humor in them. His friend stood there, grim-faced and hopeless. "You didn't have to do that. My brother is a big boy. Trust me, he can handle himself. It wouldn't be the first time someone tried to use a scandal to bring down a Sommerville campaign."

It would be the first time Alexei had been used in such a way. He wouldn't stand for it. "It is my problem to handle. Not his."

Caleb ran a hand through his hair. "I don't understand you. Why the fuck would you think that? I don't get anything about you. Why the hell are you here?"

How could he make Caleb understand? This didn't work if they didn't watch out for each other. "I love Holly. She is better part of me."

"Then why the fuck didn't you go after her?" Caleb asked, his eyes straying down the road where Holly had taken off.

Alexei took a long breath. This was a gamble, but he'd never been known for playing it safe. "Because you are part of me, too."

Caleb shook his head, his eyes returning to Alexei. "God, you're confusing."

He sighed. Caleb couldn't seem to see the truth. "I am not. You are simply not as smart as you think."

Caleb stopped and stared, and then a smile crossed his face. He

223

laughed from deep in his belly. He laughed, doubling over. "I'm definitely not as smart as I think. I'm stupid. So fucking stupid."

Caleb's laugh turned into something sad. Alexei felt it in his heart.

"I don't know what to do," Caleb admitted. "I know what my instinct is. I should leave."

"Your instinct is stupid."

"She doesn't want me."

"She is scared," Alexei explained, though he thought it should be evident. "She need you. And you need her. Please to be thinking about this. She thinks you loved your wife."

"I didn't," Caleb replied, his voice hard with guilt. "And I hate myself for that. I did what was expected of me. I did what I'd been taught to do. I married Caroline, and then one day I knew I needed something more."

"Will you need more than Holly?" Alexei knew the answer, but he wanted to hear Caleb say it.

Caleb didn't even hesitate. "No. I love her. Fuck. I said it. I love her. I don't think I deserve her though. My brother is capable of giving me hell. I don't think he will. I think as long as I stay out of the spotlight, he won't care what I do as long as I'm happy. He's not a monster, but he could say something. He could make her feel bad. I can't promise that some pushy reporter won't find out. I knew she would feel this way, and I took her anyway. I need to leave. I need to let her be happy with you."

They really did need him. He'd worried about his place, but it was obvious now. Caleb was a brilliant man, a kind man. He was the type of man the world needed, but he'd been broken in a way that left him incapable of trusting himself. He needed someone who didn't mind kicking a little ass—even his.

The good news was he was great at kicking ass. "You not go. You will stay. You will stop with the aching belly and begin to grow back your balls. This is not worthy of you. Our woman is out there. She is alone, and yet you stand here worried that she will not forgive. Make her forgive. Give her something. Give her your story. Tell her why you are afraid. Tell her why you don't sleep with her."

Caleb's eyes came up.

"Yes," Alexei explained. "I see closet. I am man with curious nose."

"You're nosy," Caleb corrected. "You're a nosy bastard. And I'm not bellyaching. I can't change who I am."

"So stubborn. You already change. You change when you agree to be with her. And don't be telling me you were only there for the sex. You were in love, simply not man enough to say. Be man, Caleb. Be man you were when you decide to walk away from wealth to help people. Be man you are in your soul, not the one who is too scared to reach out for what he needs."

"I sleep in a fucking closet because I can't stand to be in the open." His hands went to his hair, shoving it back even though there wasn't enough of it to fall in his face.

Alexei shrugged. "This we can handle. We make nice closet for you. We tuck you in and close door."

"Damn it. You don't get it. You make this sound easy, but it isn't." Caleb practically growled his frustration.

He found himself oddly calm. He understood Caleb far better than his friend could know. "No, you make hard because it easier to live with than to let go. You cling to pain because you know it. It is familiar. It is blanket. You think I do not understand? When I close eyes, I see my brother. I do not see him as he was. I see him dead. I see the blood as though that was only thing that mattered about him. Blood. Everywhere. One bullet reduces him to a mess on the floor that someone had to clean up. I see this when I close eyes at night. And I force myself to think one thought of him. I think about day he teach me to skate. I replay that day in my mind. The air is crisp and cold around me, but my brother's smile is warm. He is patient. He teach me what he knows. That was my brother. That was his life. He was taken from me. I take him back. You had something taken from you. Are you strong enough to take back?"

"You're a fucking bastard." Caleb's eyes closed, and when they opened again, there was a suspicious moisture there. "I love her. I don't want to let her go. I don't want to let this go."

Alexei reached out and gripped his friend's shoulder, something deep inside falling into place. "Then don't let go."

"You know you're using me as a substitute for your brother. You have to see that."

Maybe he was, but it couldn't hurt anything. He saw Caleb for what he was. Caleb was nothing like Mikhail with the exception of the fact that Alexei cared for both. "It is more than that, but even if it was, I am good brother. I would be good brother to you. I would not be letting you down."

A gleam of hope entered Caleb's green eyes. "I can't ask for more than that. Alexei, I sometimes walk in my sleep. I hit the walls. I kick at the furniture. It's more complicated than sleeping in the closet."

He'd wondered if a lot of Caleb's problems didn't stem from this. This was an easy thing to fix. "No, it is simple. When you get out of bed, I will wake you and put you back in. Your body will learn."

"And if I hurt Holly?"

There it was. He could see it now. This was Caleb's greatest fear.

"I will not allow it. You have to trust me or this will not work. You have to know that I will protect her, even from your demons."

Caleb finally nodded. "Yes. Yes, I want this. I'm pissed at her right now, though."

"I am angry myself. She walk away. She is not allowed to do such a thing. I believe a spanking is in order." His little *dushka* didn't know what she'd done. He'd practically begged her not to walk away. He'd been willing to grovel, but it appeared she needed something more.

"I think she does deserve a spanking. And a good one," Caleb agreed.

Alexei turned and saw Logan Green staring at him.

"You really believe that shit you just spit?" The deputy's voice was tight.

This was the chance he'd been praying for. "Yes, I believe. And it apply to you, too. Something bad happen to you. You are the one allowing it to change you. You are the one allowing it to beat you. I let this darkness inside beat me for years and years. I let it take my youth. You are on same path. You can hate me all you like, but this I know."

"You don't know shit, man." Logan stalked past him and pulled the door open and slammed into his Bronco, gunning the engine. He backed out without bothering to look behind him, the wheels peeling away.

"You tried." Caleb's hand was on his back.

"We've all tried." Nate Wright and the marshals stood on the steps of the station house. It was obvious they had heard more than Alexei would have liked. The whole town had a curious nose.

"Alexei, I think you should come with us." Jessie frowned down at him. "This isn't about the doctor. This is about you."

His stomach twisted. "I cannot leave. This is home."

"Yes, and you're endangering everyone in this town," Jessie pointed out.

The sheriff snorted. "I wouldn't count us out yet, Marshal."

"He needs to be in witness protection." Jessie's face was set in mulish lines.

"Jessie, you know why he's here. He's in love with the woman." Michael turned to his partner, his lover, his voice going low. "I thought we talked about this."

Her head shook. "I changed my mind. He needs to come with us. He's too valuable to risk."

"I can't go. I can't to be leaving." If he left, Holly and Caleb would fall apart. He would fall apart. He knew it was selfish, but he couldn't leave.

Nate stood tall, settling his hat on his head. "Stand down, Marshal. I already put out a call. Every person in this town is going to be looking out for Alexei. He's one of ours now. We protect our own. Now, unless you're willing to take him into protective custody, I think you should let him go. I got a call from Callie a couple of minutes ago. The women of Bliss are currently descending on Holly's cabin."

Caleb went a little white. "Are you serious?"

"Why are they going to Holly's?" Alexei asked.

Nate frowned. "It's called 'Break Up Patrol.' Every woman who can will rush to the recent dumpee's house to offer support. It's an estrogen fest of the highest order. No man who wants to keep his balls on will go in there, but I think you two are going to have to. Unless you want to end up groveling for the next year or so. And I would appreciate it if you would break that shit up. Callie insisted on going. She needs to be in bed. I have some riot gear if you need it."

Alexei shook his head. "I can handle these womens."

Caleb pointed to him. "He can handle the women. I'm going to hide behind him."

"Good thinking." Nate tipped his hat. "Alexei, you carrying?"

"I carry much." He could carry many things. He was very strong.

Caleb's head shook. "He wants to know about the gun you stuff down your ass."

"I do not stuff gun in ass. I have it in small of back. You need to

227

reread anatomy book." He realized what he'd revealed and winced. "Sheriff, I need gun."

"You also need a permit to carry concealed. Congratulations, I just certified you as a training instructor for Bliss County's safe gun program. Cam will get all the paperwork done. Until then, don't conceal the fucker. And Caleb, it might be a good idea for you to carry that tranq gun. I know you don't want to kill anyone, but if you don't have a problem shooting Mel on a regular basis, I don't see why you can't tranq an assassin." Nate tossed Caleb a radio. "And keep this on at all times. You see anything shady, you call."

"I think I can handle that." Caleb put the radio in his pocket.

And they could handle Holly. If she thought they would let her walk away, she was in for a surprise.

Chapter Fifteen

"What the hell is wrong with you?" Laura asked, throwing her hands up in the air as she paced across Holly's living room floor.

If she'd expected sympathy from her BFF, she'd been wrong. Laura had charged in like a lion and started to roar.

"He lied to me," Holly explained, though she'd mentioned that fact more than once.

"About his name," Laura shot back.

"Yes."

Laura pointed at her. "I lied to you about my name."

"That was different."

"I lied about mine, too." Rachel Harper came to stand beside Laura.

Holly turned to Nell, who held Rachel's baby, Paige, on her lap. Nell looked completely innocent even though she was the one who had instigated this horror show. "Why would you do this to me?"

"I didn't lie about my name," Nell said with those wide eyes of hers.

"That is not what I am talking about, and you know it." She wasn't going to let Nell be obtuse about this.

"I did what any friend would do when she sees her friend jumping off a cliff. She calls in her stronger friends to pull you back." Nell bounced the baby on her knee. "If it were left up to me, I would jump off with you. I'm not the best person to handle this sort of thing. But Laura is really good."

"So is Rachel," Callie added with a bright smile. "Rachel is excellent at telling me when I'm doing something silly."

Callie sat on the recliner with her hand over her huge belly and her feet up.

"Well, why don't you join in, Callie? You want to let me know how stupid I am?" Holly was getting frustrated with her houseguests.

She shook her head. "Oh, no. I'm just happy to be out of my house. I thought Zane was going to have to roll me over in a wheelbarrow, though. If I don't have this baby soon, I think I'm going to pop. But if you're asking me, then I do think you're making a mistake."

"Caleb lied to me." She would say it over and over again until someone understood.

Callie looked at her sympathetically but shook her head. "So did Rachel and Laura."

"That was different." Apparently everyone was planning on acting obtuse today. The situations were completely different.

"How?" Callie asked.

"They were trying to hide from something." Laura had been on the run from a serial killer and Rachel from a stalker. It made total sense that they would change their names for protection.

"So is Caleb." Laura sighed and sat down. "I'm sorry. I'm coming on way too strong. Holly, I love you, but I think you're wrong. I changed my name because I was running from my past. I didn't want Rafe and Cam to find me. I also didn't want the serial killer to find me, but it was about Rafe and Cam, too."

"And I was on the run." Rachel's mouth became tight as she obviously thought about her life before Max and Rye. "I still don't go by my old name. I changed it because I'm not that woman anymore. I'm Rachel. I'm the person I found here in Bliss. I think Caleb is the same. He smiled at me yesterday. Do you know how little that man smiles?"

"Did you ask him why he didn't tell you about his name?" Laura sat back.

"He said he couldn't be sure I wasn't a gold digger." She could still feel the humiliation that had flared.

Rachel snorted. "Idiot."

Laura's eyes narrowed. "Is that what he said? Or what you heard?"

"No," Micky called out from the kitchen where he was making coffee. "He said he'd had a lot of women who were more interested in his family than him." He walked in carrying mugs of coffee. "And I understand that. I get him, Mom. When you're a member of an incredibly wealthy family, you have to wonder why people are around you. I don't think he thought you were a gold digger for a second. I think you scared the crap out of him."

No one understood. She felt frustrated tears pricking at her eyes. "I seriously doubt that. I know you think you know how he feels, but I want you to think about how I feel. I was married to your father for years. It was a huge mistake. The Langs ripped me apart. I can't do that again. I don't even want to try."

"It's not like his family is here all the time," Rachel pointed out. "I didn't even know he had a family. I knew his wife died, but that's about it. If Jen weren't on her honeymoon, I would put her on this. Trust me, Stef Talbot knows something about Caleb and his past. No one comes into his town without a file. I wonder. I bet he has an actual file."

"Rachel, you can't break into the Talbot Estate," Callie said.

Rachel's strawberry blonde hair shook, and her eyes lit up the way they always did when she was planning something nefarious. "I wasn't going to break in. I was going to walk in and then, whoops, I didn't mean to go into Stef's office. I got lost. And I certainly didn't mean to have that file folder fall open."

"Or you could ask me." Micky sat down in front of her. "You must be very isolated if you didn't hear his story. Dr. Caleb Sommerville was working with a charity group providing medical attention and surgeries in some of the world's worst places. He walked away from his wealth. Does that sound like Dad? I bet that the Sommerville family wasn't thrilled that he chose to practice in Africa."

"He went through something bad, didn't he?" Laura asked.

Micky nodded.

"I thought so. I recognize the look on his face from time to time. I

231

see it in the mirror." Laura's voice had taken on that far-off quality she used when thinking about her former life.

"I see it on Zane's face." Callie's hand smoothed over her belly. "It's hard for him to talk about what happened while he was undercover. Can't you give Caleb a chance?"

When had she become the bad guy? "I thought you guys were supposed to support me."

Nell leaned toward her. "We are, sweetie. But we wouldn't be very supportive if we let you make the biggest mistake of your life."

Was it a mistake? How could she trust him again? And what else hadn't he told her?

And did any of it matter? Or was she letting her past ruin her chances for a future?

"I can't live that life again." She said it more to herself than anyone else.

"I don't want you to. I don't want that life. That's why I'm here." Caleb stood in the doorway, his hands in the pockets of his jeans. His face was lined with care, as though the last moments had aged him.

Alexei stood beside him.

How much had they both changed for her? What had it cost these possessive men to decide to share her?

"I'd like to know your story." She said it simply, though it meant the world to her. If he wouldn't talk to her, she wasn't sure there was a chance.

He nodded, but no words came out.

"Could we be doing this in private? Ladies, I appreciate your love for Holly, but we need time alone." Alexei opened the door.

Laura stared him down, never one to let a little thing like a six-foot-five-inch, slab-of-muscle renowned-for-his-former-violent-tendencies man intimidate her. "You better take care of her."

"Laura, they will. That's why they're here." Nell stood, looking perfectly happy with the outcome of the afternoon. She settled Paige on her hip. "Come on, guys. Let's get Callie home. She's going to bring another beautiful soul into the world any day now. We should make sure her house is ready. I want to bless the baby's room and invite the goddess in."

Rachel held a hand out to Callie. "Ugh, I hope you don't mind some smelly herbs, Cal."

She shook her head. "I don't mind. But I'm pretty sure I'm never having this baby. I know it's Zane's because it's so big. I think this baby weighs thirty pounds. He planted a giant inside me. And I swear this sucker has more than four limbs."

"Uhm, I can do another ultrasound." Caleb put his hands on Callie's belly. "How about tomorrow morning? You're not due for another two weeks, but if the baby is big, we might need to schedule a C-section."

"Oh, no, Callie," Nell said, her eyes wide. "Maybe we should call the shaman back in."

"Nope," Callie said. "If the doc wants to split me open right now, I'm up for it. I'm done with being pregnant. And I will happily let you take another look at my boy."

Rachel snorted as she lifted her baby from Nell. "Doc is a good man, but he's not the greatest at reading a sonogram. Is he, baby girl? He thought you had a penis. You don't have a penis. No, sir. Callie's baby won't have a penis, either. She's going to be your best friend."

"Now, we need to talk about this," Nell said, her skirt fluttering around her ankles as she ran after the other women.

Laura gave Holly a long hug. "You just holler if they give you trouble. I think I'm going to have to save Nell. Rachel can get touchy about drugs and childbirth. We're going to be over at Callie's making casseroles to freeze so Zane doesn't have to cook after the baby comes. Why don't you come with us, Micky? You can get to know your new aunts, and I think Rafe and Cam are going to be doing some yard work. We can pull up lawn chairs and whistle until they take off their shirts."

"I think I'm going to love my new uncles," Micky said with a smile. He stopped in front of Caleb. "Talk fast, man. I'm pulling for you."

The door closed behind them, and they were alone.

"Cheap lay?" Caleb asked, obviously ready to get to the fight. His face was tight.

She wasn't about to let him make her the bad guy by throwing her words back in her face. "You're the one who lied, Caleb."

"I didn't lie." Caleb's words were clipped, short, revealing his frustration. "I've gone by my mother's maiden name for years. I didn't like everything that came along with being a Sommerville, including the money. I like living simply. The only time my money has come in

233

handy is when you needed things, like a roof. Which wasn't cheap."

She put a hand on her hip. "Oh, so now you're owning up to that? I asked you before and you wouldn't answer."

Caleb scrubbed a hand through his short hair. "I didn't want you to feel beholden. You think I didn't look into your past? I knew who your ex-husband was. I knew what he did to you. I might not have known all the details, but I could make some great guesses. You obviously didn't want to leave your son behind when you got divorced."

"Of course I didn't."

"Your husband used his money and power to separate you from your son." It wasn't a question. Caleb said it with a familiar disgust, as though he'd seen it before.

She took a long breath. "Yes, he did. Actually he managed to come up with some damning photographs of me with his head security guard."

"Bastard," Caleb cursed. "What did he do? Hire someone who looked like you?"

She stilled. She hadn't told him she wasn't guilty. So why did he assume she was innocent? "Maybe he simply followed me, Caleb."

"Bullshit. You wouldn't cheat. I know you. You wouldn't cheat on him no matter how big an asshole he was. He was the father of your son. You took vows. You wouldn't cheat."

Tears pooled in her eyes. "How can you know that?"

"*Dushka*, he knows for same reason I know. He sees your soul. Why can you not see his?" Alexei stood by the door, his face grim. He watched the argument with dark eyes and a flat mouth.

It struck her that Alexei had as much to lose as either of them. Though he wasn't a part of this argument, he was involved. He was part of this. She could yell at Caleb all she liked, but it wouldn't help the three of them.

"Explain why you wouldn't tell me your name."

Now it was Caleb's turn to calm down. He paced a little. "Because after I found out about your ex-husband, I was afraid you wouldn't like me. And I wanted you to like me."

"Why?" Holly asked.

The words burst from his mouth like a cork popping from a champagne bottle. "Because I loved you from the minute I saw you. I walked into the café and you smiled at me and I felt like the sun had come out after years of rain, and that scared the shit out of me. It still scares the shit out of me. But I've figured out that something else scares me more. Losing you."

She stood there in her tiny cabin—the very place where she'd been exiled—and realized that she could believe him or not. She could pull the mantle of past pain around her and be safe. She could go on as she had before. She could even keep Alexei. She didn't need Caleb. Caleb would always have ties to a world she hated, a world that could come back to hurt her. Alexei would stay with her.

And they would all be living a half life because this weird thing between them worked. It was beautiful and odd and worth fighting for. And it was far past time to put her fear aside.

She didn't speak. Words had always failed Caleb, but his actions spoke volumes. He'd taken care of her when she'd needed it. He was damaged, and she didn't exactly know why. It didn't matter. It didn't matter if he never healed. She would take him damaged and broken. She would try to heal his hurt.

She put her hands on his face. "I love you, Caleb Burke."

Not Sommerville. Micky was right. This was who Caleb wanted to be.

His green eyes were solemn as he looked at her. "I love you, too. I just don't know that it means much."

Holly put a finger to his lips. "You don't have to tell me anything. I don't need to know. I love the man you are now."

"And you would love the man he was," Alexei said quietly. "He is very stubborn. He always has good heart."

"I want to tell you. You need to know." Caleb looked so miserable standing there, as though he was sure she would reject him.

She'd put that fear in his eyes by walking out. She should have yelled, fought with him. She should have stayed. She was well aware that if Alexei hadn't been there, there was a great chance that Caleb wouldn't have come to her.

They needed Alexei. She held out her hand.

Alexei hesitated. "*Dushka*, perhaps you two should be alone."

Caleb shook his head. "No, I want you to hear, too. You should understand. I know I said I would be happy to just be around for the sex, but that was bullshit. I want this thing to work, and you're a part of it, Alexei."

Caleb stepped away. He started to pace again, and Holly could see how this would go. He would tell her in his clinical way, detached and outside himself. She didn't want that. She wanted him to know that he was safe with her. She'd taken that from him when she'd walked away. He should know she wouldn't do that again.

Holly pulled off her shirt and let it drop to the ground. Without hesitation she pulled off her bra.

"What are you doing?" Caleb asked, his eyes going straight to her breasts.

"She is getting ready to talk." Alexei smiled warmly at her. He could read her mind. He worked the buttons on his shirt, exposing his chest.

Caleb turned between the two. "We're going to talk naked?"

She pulled her hair out of the ponytail holder she wore. "Yes, consider it our first family tradition. When we have terrible things to talk about, we do it in bed, naked. I want to hold you, Caleb. Will you let me?"

He stilled. "I can't do this if you're going to walk away every time I upset you, because I'll probably upset you a lot. I know that maybe isn't fair, but I can't handle not knowing where I stand. I can't play games. I'm not any good at them."

He wasn't. He was horrible at hiding his feelings. Alexei was good at it, but she didn't want to play games with either of them.

There was only one way she could think of to prove that she was in. Without bothering to cover her breasts, she went to the phone. "What's your brother's number?"

Caleb's head came up. "What?"

"Eli? What's his number?" The only way to prove she could handle him was to throw herself into the fire.

"Holly," Caleb started.

"Give her number." Alexei had gotten down to his underwear. She was never going to get used to that body. It was beautiful. It matched his soul.

"Do your clothes just fall off you?" Caleb asked, shaking his head.

Alexei shrugged. "It is skill. Now give Holly number. I am intrigued to see what she will do."

Caleb rattled off a number, and within seconds the line was being answered.

"This is Sommerville. Who is this? I don't recognize this number. This is a private line for family only."

He sounded gruff, a man who knew his place in the world and wouldn't appreciate it being questioned. Holly had no desire to question Eli's place in the world, but he was going to understand hers as well.

"Eli. I'm going to call you Eli because I think we'll be family soon enough. My name is Holly Lang. I live in Bliss, Colorado."

There was a brief pause, and then he sounded almost amused. "I know your name, Ms. Lang. I keep tabs on my brother."

Well, of course he did. "Then you know we're seeing each other."

"I know he's interested. My brother likes to move slowly. He's the tortoise of the dating world."

He really was. Luckily Alexei was the hare who had pushed Caleb forward. "Well, his slow ass finally crossed the finish line. I'm going to be honest with you, Eli. I'm in love with your brother. And I'm keeping him. You can send in your spin doctors or image consultants, but it won't make a difference. You can't turn me into some perfect political wife."

"Well then, it's a good thing you're planning on marrying a doctor." There was zero question of his amusement now. She could practically hear him smiling.

But she hadn't told him the whole truth yet. "I don't have a college degree. I'm divorced with a son who recently came out. I live in a town known for its unconventional relationships."

"And apparently its aliens," Eli interrupted her.

Holly continued. "And you can't run me off. I will have you know that my son is accomplished at blackmail. And Caleb and I have a friend who knows a thing or two about getting what he wants. A very good friend. A partner."

There was a long pause. "Oh, fuck. Seriously? Caleb's gone native?"

Finally she'd managed to get a rise out of him. "Yes. It's perfectly acceptable here in Bliss. And our partner used to be involved in a crime syndicate, but he's gone straight now. So if you want this relationship of ours to remain private, you better keep the press off us. But you can't get rid of me. I love your brother, and I won't be bought off or scared off or blackmailed off. Do you understand?"

Eli's voice was warm as he spoke. "I think I do, Holly. I'm going to call you Holly since we're going to be family soon enough. Consider me properly intimidated. Now that I know who the boss is, perhaps you can get my brother to call his family more often. We miss him. And Josh wants to come see him soon."

"I think we can arrange that. Your brother says hello. He'll call you later, but for now he has some things to do." Before he could reply, she hung up. She turned to Caleb, her heart racing. It had gone far better than she could have imagined. It still could all go to hell, but she'd made her stand. "There, now we've started on the proper footing."

Alexei smiled at her, his cock already straining at his boxers. "That was very sexy, *dushka.*"

Caleb's hands came out in supplication. "He won't try to break us up. Eli isn't your ex. Are you sure about this? Eli can try to keep us off the radar, but I can't guarantee that we won't have nosy reporters sniffing around. I can promise that I'll protect you as best I can. I can promise that no matter what anyone says, I'll be here."

She couldn't ask for more. "Then take off your clothes and meet me in bed. You can tell me your story, and I can apologize for walking out. But Caleb, no more secrets."

"I don't have any more." He followed her into the bedroom, Alexei on his heels.

Holly shed her jeans and underwear. She was painfully aware of the plug that still resided in her ass. Alexei's hand caressed her there, reminding her that he was the one who had worked it in.

"You are still wearing plug?" Alexei asked, his voice deep and dark.

She nodded. "I didn't take it out."

She'd found it oddly comforting. Even as she'd walked away, she'd kept the toy deep inside. Every time she'd felt it, she'd pretended it was a caress. How could she think to walk away from them? She needed them.

Alexei put his hands on her hips, drawing her close. "You are never allowed to walk out again, my *dushka.* You can get mad, yell all you like, but this is a family. We can't to be walking away. Family is too important. This is too important."

She wrapped her arms around his waist, loving the feel of his muscles playing against her. He was a gorgeous monster, and his heart was as big as his body. "I love you."

"I love you, too." He tilted her head up and took her lips in a soft, sweet kiss.

Caleb was suddenly at her back, his hands on her skin. She felt so good surrounded by them.

Caleb swept her hair to the side and kissed her neck, a tender touch of lips to skin. "I'm sorry I didn't say it before. I can only tell you I was scared. I love you, Holly."

She turned to him, knowing how hard a confession that was. "Oh, babe, you won't regret it."

His hands came up, brushing her nipples. His mouth was against her ear, the warmth of his breath soft on her skin. "I'll tell you everything you want to know, but after. I want to make love. I want to be inside you."

"Yes." She didn't want to wait. She wanted them, needed them now. "Please, Caleb. I want you both."

"I think we can handle that." Caleb's cock was thick against her backside.

"You are ready for this?" Alexei asked.

"Yes," she and Caleb said at the same time. She laughed. She wasn't sure who Alexei had been talking to, but he'd gotten the answer he wanted. He dropped his boxers, tossing them aside. His big cock bounced free, jutting up.

"I'm ready," Caleb said, squeezing her. "I want to make love to our woman."

Caleb let go of her, and she could hear him rustling behind her, his clothes coming off.

Alexei put a hand on her head and pushed with a gentle pressure. "On knees, Holly. I want to feel your mouth."

Holly got to her knees, clenching her ass to keep the plug in. His dominant commands made her feel ridiculously sexy. When Alexei's voice went deep and he got bossy, her pussy responded as though it knew who its master was. She took Alexei's cock in hand and ran her tongue across the head. He hissed slightly and sank his hands into her hair. He leaned back, giving her full access to his dick.

"God, that's pretty." Caleb stood beside Alexei, looking down at the place where his cock disappeared into her mouth. "I think I want some of that."

His thick cock pointed her way. Caleb pumped himself a couple of times.

She never would have imagined that Caleb Burke would stand right next to a man he'd once considered a criminal waiting for his turn at a little oral. They were her men. A deep feeling of possession settled in her chest. These men were hers, and she was never going to let them get away. They had given themselves to her, and she intended to keep them.

She turned her head, allowing Alexei's cock to pop out of her mouth, and licked at Caleb. She took both her men in hand and licked them in turn. Her tongue flicked back and forth, teasing them. She curled her tongue around Alexei while her hand tightened on Caleb. She sucked Caleb into her mouth, playing with Alexei's balls with her free hand. They stood together, their hips touching, and she'd never felt sexier. Two hands played in her hair. Two voices groaned and told her how hot she was.

She licked the ridge of Caleb's cock, carefully sucking at the *V* on the underside. She worried it with her tongue, glorying in the cream that seeped from the head. It drenched her tongue with the taste of him. She switched to Alexei, mingling their flavors. She lapped at them, not able to get enough.

She sucked Alexei deep. One, two, and three passes before switching. Caleb groaned as she pulled him in. He pumped his hips toward her. She ran her tongue up and down his length. He pulsed in her mouth. He was close.

"Don't you come," Alexei growled.

Caleb pulled out with a moan. "Bastard."

"We take our woman together."

Caleb's eyes darkened. "Yes. I want that. Holly, get on the bed. Hands and knees. I want your ass in the air."

And he called Alexei bossy.

Alexei helped her to her feet as Caleb opened the nightstand and pulled out condoms and lube. He tossed them on the bed and then winked at her. "Stay here, baby. I have a trick I want to try."

"And I have some discipline to administer." Alexei directed her to the bed. "Did you think I would let you walk away with no punishment? You have been bad girl."

She felt like a bad girl, and it felt good. She didn't hesitate to get on her knees, lifting her ass in the air. Alexei's discipline always seemed to end with her crying out in pleasure. She intended to be bad more often.

Alexei's hand came down instantly, the smack ringing through the air. Holly cried out. The smack made the plug shift, lighting up every nerve in her ass. It was a jangled, oddly erotic sensation that made her fists clench around the comforter under her hands. She held on because Alexei seemed damn serious about punishment. His hand rained down on her ass, leaving not an inch untouched. Over and over he smacked her in short, unrelenting arcs. Each time she winced and ground her teeth and let the pain turn into heat blooming across her skin.

He stopped suddenly, and she groaned as he ran his hand across her ass.

"So pink and pretty. And I love the way this looks." He pressed lightly on the plug, playing with the base. Holly couldn't help her whimper. She could feel her pussy pulse with every touch.

He pulled on the plug with one hand while his other hand played in her pussy, light, teasing touches that made her crazy for more.

"You like this, *dushka*. You love my discipline. You will love it even more when I tie you up. You'll be helpless. I'll tie your hands and feet to the bed. You'll be open to us, our pretty love slave. We'll take care of you. We'll clamp your pretty nipples and torture you with our tongues. You'll beg, my darling. You'll beg for a cock, but we'll hold back. You'll get nothing until we decide it. We'll play with you to our hearts' content."

It sounded like torture. It sounded like heaven.

He smacked her again, making her cry out. This time he left his hand over the site as though imprinting himself on her.

"I will try many things with you. You are my pretty slave in bedroom. I am your slave everywhere else." He kissed the small of her back, wrapping his arms around her waist. "Mine."

"Bastard, you told me you would share." Caleb emerged from the bathroom. He winked at her as he joined them on the bed.

"I share. But she is ours. She will not to be looking at other men." Alexei smacked her ass again—a definite warning of things to come.

Holly piped up. "It's going to be hard, boys. My dating life has been so active up to this point."

Another smack, this one hard. He wasn't playing around with that smack. Holly groaned and forced herself to breathe.

"No joking," Alexei barked. "I need to know that you are mine. Ours. I need to know that we will be together."

"Always, babe. Always."

She felt Caleb's hand tracing the curves of her ass. "And it's going to be hard for her to keep her eyes off other dudes. We have a lot of naked dudes running around Bliss. She might have to go around blindfolded."

Alexei's face came into view. He gave her the sweetest smile. "As long as she is ours, then perhaps she can look all she likes. We will have to make sure we are most sexy of men."

They wouldn't have to work hard. They were the sexiest men she'd ever met. It went beyond their perfect abs or handsome faces. It was bone deep. "No one can hold a candle to you two."

"That's good to hear because I think Alexei here is going to need a lot of praise. He seems very vain," Caleb said.

"I merely wish to be lovely for my *dushka*. She deserve most beautiful of mens." Alexei pointed to Caleb. "You could use a haircut."

Caleb's laugh filled the room. "Don't even go there, buddy. How about you be the beauty and I'll be the creative one. Damn, she's so wet."

"She like her spanking. I think her ass will be spanked often."

She felt Caleb's lips on her skin. "Poor baby. He did a number on you. Your skin is all pretty and hot and pink. So lovely. I think after taking a spanking like that, you deserve a treat. Spread your legs, sweetheart. He's the stick. Let me be the carrot."

He was so much better than a carrot. She widened her stance, pushing her knees out for Caleb to slide underneath. She shuddered as she felt his hands on her thighs. They were big and warm, and she knew what was coming.

"Holly, I'm a doctor and that means I've made a thorough study of female anatomy. I can say with great confidence that this is the prettiest pussy ever made. It's perfectly formed. Plump and juicy and ripe."

"And she smell so sweet," Alexei added. He got on the bed next to Caleb. She felt his hands on her ass, his finger tracing the valley between the globes.

"Yes, she does."

She shuddered as she felt Caleb's nose run along her pussy.

"I've also studied a little chemistry, and I happen to know the effect of menthol on a woman's pink parts." He licked at her, a long, slow stroke of his tongue.

Something wicked and crisp made her pussy swell. "Oh my god, Caleb, what did you do?"

He chuckled. "It's a fun little trick. I brushed my teeth. I spit, but I didn't rinse. The menthol from the toothpaste creates a tingly feeling. Do you like it?"

She couldn't breathe. Her pussy felt like it was swelling but in a delicious way. It was like her skin was open to all sensation. As though she'd been plunged into freezing water and emerged with every pore open and ready for pleasure. Her pussy felt alive.

Alexei began to torture her ass with the plug. He pulled it out a little ways and then fucked it back in.

"Hold still," Alexei commanded, putting a hand on the small of her back.

"I can't." She felt too much. It was too much pleasure. Caleb was eating at her pussy, lighting it up. Alexei filled her ass with the plug, making the nerves there flare to life.

"You will hold still or we will to be stopping," Alexei promised.

"Holly, be still. He really will make me stop. I don't want to. You taste so good, sweetheart." Caleb swiped at her clit. She felt her eyes go wide. "And this will work on us. You can suck our dicks like this, and we'll go crazy."

She could imagine it. There didn't have to be boundaries with these men. She could explore to her heart's content. She could try every wild thing she'd ever dreamed of and a few things she hadn't even thought she wanted. She wouldn't have said she could ever submit in the bedroom. She'd thought Jen was crazy for wearing Stef's collar, but she got it now. She could submit to Alexei, and he would take care of her. Alexei was the dominant one in the bedroom. Caleb was the softie. She could have the best of both worlds. She could have it all. She only had to be brave enough to reach for it.

"Besides, our *dushka* needs to learn to be quiet. We have an impressionable boy in house now." Alexei pulled the plug out almost to the tip before driving it slowly back in. "We must try to set example."

She knew some people would tar and feather her for having a

relationship like this around her son, but he'd been so deprived of true love, she couldn't see how this hurt him. He wasn't the norm. He would have a whole world that told him he was wrong. Maybe by seeing his mother refusing to accept someone else's morals in exchange for her own happiness, he would know that love was love no matter what guise it came in. It was real and precious and so rare that it would be wrong to turn it away. Love didn't always come in the conventional way. It didn't always mean a white picket fence, but this love was worth fighting for.

She was worth fighting for. If her men had taught her one thing, it was that she was worthy.

"I think we set a fine example." She was proud of her men. She wouldn't hide them. Caleb made her cry out, lashing her clit with his tongue. The cool tingle of the menthol spread all around. "But I will be quieter."

She bit her lip. She wanted to scream. They were killing her. Caleb speared his tongue high into her. He pressed his mouth over her mound, surrounding her with his heat.

Alexei fucked her ass with the plug, never letting up on the sensation. "My friend, I believe she is ready. Perhaps you can make her come. I want her soft and willing when we take her together."

"My pleasure," Caleb said against her lips. She felt him tighten his hands on her thighs right before he sucked her clit into his mouth.

The sensation washed over her like an icy wave. She'd never felt anything like it before. Her pussy seemed to have taken over her body, becoming the center of her being, and Caleb and Alexei commanded it.

Her whole body shook. The only reason she could stay on her knees was their hands holding her in place.

Caleb let go of her clit but continued to tease her, sending shocks through her system. She sagged against Alexei's supporting arm.

"Yes, that is what I wanted. I wanted a perfectly satisfied woman who we can please all over again." Alexei pulled the plug from her ass. She sighed and felt oddly empty without it.

Caleb pushed his body up the bed through her splayed legs until she straddled him. His cock strained against her pussy. "Get me a condom, buddy."

Before Alexei could pass it to him, he pulled her down. She was grateful to let her body sink onto his. He kissed her, letting her taste her own juices on his tongue. He ate hungrily at her mouth. She could feel his desire. His hands roamed across her body as his tongue dominated.

Holly let him take over. She felt like she was floating, tethered only by his strong hands and the silky glide of his tongue against hers.

"I love you, Holly," Caleb whispered against her lips. "I love you so much. I feel so lucky to have found you."

Tears pricked at her eyes. "I love you, too, Caleb."

He needed to hear it. She could see it in his eyes. For all his wealth and privilege, he needed what every person needed—to know he was loved and accepted for himself.

She pressed her lips to the line between his eyes, the one he got when he concentrated on a problem. It would get deeper with age, and she would always love it. It was a part of him. His oddness and lack of social grace were endearing because they came with such an open, caring heart.

"Don't forget me, *dushka*." Alexei's weight caused the bed to dip. He passed Caleb a condom. His big cock was already sheathed. He pulled her up, freeing Caleb to work the condom over his dick. Alexei kissed her, cupping her head in his hands.

Caleb gripped her hips. "Come on, baby. I need you."

She needed him, too. She leaned down, letting her breasts rub against his chest. She loved the differences between them. He was so hard, making her feel soft and feminine. Alexei got in behind her, placing a hand on her back.

"Are you in?" Alexei asked.

Caleb thrust up, joining them in a single move. She groaned and let her head find Caleb's shoulder. He felt so good. His dick was thick inside her pussy.

"Oh, yeah. I'm in. She feels perfect. Tight and hot around me."

"She will be tighter in moment. Hold her for me." Alexei moved behind her. His hand stroked down her back. "*Dushka*, my little love, you will tell me if I hurt you. We can go slow. I want you, but I want it to be right."

So dominant, and yet her big Russian was a teddy bear. He could talk all he wanted, but he melted for her, and she was grateful for it. She reached around to touch him. "Take me, Alexei. I want to be with my men."

"As your wishes go," Alexei replied.

Caleb laughed, shaking his head. "I'm going to make a list of all the ways he screws up sayings. Really, we could do a whole website."

"Hush, Caleb. Make the funs later." Alexei parted her cheeks. "This is serious business."

Caleb held her, his hands tightening around her waist. His eyes went hot. "Yes, it is. Very serious. Holly, let Alexei get in your ass, sweetheart."

She wasn't sure she had a choice about it. She needed to know how this felt. She needed to be between them.

She buried her head against Caleb's chest as Alexei worked the lube in. She listened to the strong beat of Caleb's heart as he worked a finger in.

"Let him in, sweetheart. We want to fill you up." Caleb's words caressed her.

She relaxed against him, giving over to Alexei. Before she knew it, something far larger than a finger was seeking entry.

"Yes, *ti nuzhnA mne.*" Alexei's Russian was thick, rolling out of his mouth like the sexiest of songs. Holly had no idea what he was saying, but every word out of his mouth sounded like sweet seduction. "*Ne magU zhIt' bes tebyA.*"

"I'll translate for him," Caleb offered. "He needs you. Or rather he be needing you. He needing you so bad."

"I will not forget, my friend," Alexei said, but she could hear his amusement. "But you speak Russian fairly well."

Caleb shook his head. "No, I speak Holly well. I know what a man in your position would say. I feel the same way."

Holly took a deep breath as Alexei pressed in. Pressure built. She closed her eyes.

"It's all right, baby," Caleb whispered. "It only feels like it's going to tear. It won't really. The sphincter ani external muscle is an amazing thing. It's called a voluntary sphincter. It opens when you let it. It's sensitive, like the perineum. Anytime you want to lick my perineum, feel free."

"Alexei, make him stop the anatomy lesson." He would go on forever if they let him.

"This I cannot do, *dushka.* Our partner gets turning on when he talk about body parts. We must be getting used to this."

"Hurry up," Caleb said. "I'm dying here. The sphincter might be a patient muscle, but my cock is dying. She's so fucking tight."

"A little more. Just a little more." Alexei's voice sounded strangled.

He thrust in and around her asshole, forcing his cock inside in gentle pushes. Every move made her burn in amazing contrast with the cool sensation of her pussy. In and out, Alexei worked her ass, opening her and making her ready.

She heard him groan and felt him slide deep inside her ass, the walls finally broached. She was open to them, completely vulnerable.

Alexei flexed inside her. "Oh, *dushka*, this is what I wanted. This is what I need. I can feel everything."

It took her a second, but she realized what he was saying. He could feel Caleb. He could feel Caleb's cock sliding along his and he could feel her. The three of them together. It was so intimate, more than she could have imagined. It was more than the physical. It was sharing.

They began to thrust in earnest. Caleb pushed up while Alexei dragged his dick out. Every nerve in her backside lit up.

She pushed toward Alexei, trying to get that dick back in her ass. Caleb pulled on her hips, filling her pussy. Any way she went was another intimacy, another pleasure. She rode the wave. She rocked back and forth, forcing her pussy onto Caleb's cock. She shoved back and got an ass full of hard dick. She moaned and wailed her pleasure, feeling every inch of them, glorying in the fact they were deep inside her. They belonged to her. She, Holly Lang, had two men, and they were magnificent.

"Please. Please." She was so close. The need grew like a wave about to crash. Caleb pumped up and Alexei thrust in, the seesaw effect jostling her back and forth between them. She rode it, letting her body find the rhythm. In and out, back and forth, every inch of her felt on fire. Alexei's hands gripped her hips and Caleb's her thighs. She could feel them brushing against each other, working together to keep her in place. She felt possessed, beloved, wanted.

"I am close. Her ass is so tight, so good." Alexei flexed inside her.

"I've never felt anything like this." Caleb looked up at her, his eyes clouded with emotion.

"Please, I can't stand it anymore. I need to come." It was driving her wild. She was so close to something powerful.

And then she felt a hard pinch to her clit, and she went over the edge. She felt her men go wild, pumping into her, grinding as they came.

She slumped forward, letting her body rest against Caleb's. Alexei's cock came out of her ass as he kissed her back and let his head find her shoulders. He pulled them all to the side, but kept them close, the heat of their bodies surrounding her.

Caleb's eyes opened. She could still feel his cock nestled against her pussy. His arms went around her.

This was what she'd wanted. To have him wrapped in her arms. "Tell me what you need to tell me."

Chapter Sixteen

Caleb realized why she'd decided to have this conversation in bed. He felt different already. Before when he'd thought about telling her, he'd felt frozen. But there was no way to feel frozen when her arms were around him and he could smell her and feel the warmth of her skin. He reached down and slipped the condom off his cock, rolling it in a tissue and tossing it in the trashcan across the room. He settled back in, surprised at how comfortable he was with the big Russian snuggling in behind Holly.

He was happy Alexei was here. Somewhere along the way he'd grown to give a damn about the man.

Holly's hands strayed to his hair. The early evening light filtered in, making the room seem soft and intimate. It was a small room. No more than a bed and a chair and a dresser. He wasn't sure how all three of them would fit, but he knew they would try.

"Caleb?" Holly asked.

He couldn't put it off any longer. He cuddled against her. It was easier this way. He didn't feel alone, and he realized how long he'd felt that way—forever. Maybe right up until this moment.

"I married Caroline because it seemed like it was time. I had graduated from med school at an early age."

"Like the Doogie," Alexei said.

Caleb thought about groaning but laughed instead. Since he'd started taking the Russian at face value, he'd learned that Alexei kept him from being so damn serious. "Not exactly Doogie Howser, but I was nineteen. I was a bit of a prodigy. I finished my residency when I was twenty-five. I was supposed to open a practice in Chicago. I did what was expected of me. I married the right woman. I opened an office in the right part of town. I was empty inside, and I didn't know why."

Alexei sat up, watching him with an encouraging smile on his face. Holly simply waited. She'd waited a long time for him to talk. She'd been so damn patient with him.

"I got invited by a friend to do some charity work in Africa. It was six weeks in Sierra Leone. I immunized babies and performed some surgeries in conditions I wouldn't have believed possible. I administered a lot of AIDS meds. I watched a lot of people die. And I felt something. It was different than the upscale patients I saw who complained about scars and talked on their cell phones the whole time I was examining them."

"They needed you." Holly's hand smoothed his hair back.

"I guess so. I was always the smart one. Eli was our dad's shadow, and Josh was the rebel. I got lost in the middle somewhere. But in that tiny clinic, I finally felt like someone needed me. Not because I was a Sommerville, but because of what I could do. I finished my six weeks, came home, and immediately announced I was starting a clinic and moving to Africa for at least two years."

"Your wife, she did not like?" Alexei asked.

He could still see the look on her face. "No. She did not."

"But it would be an adventure." Holly's eyes narrowed in confusion.

She would see it that way. Holly would have packed up with him and followed him. She would have stood by his side, his partner in all things. Hell, the Russian would have gone with him, standing guard over those he held dear. How had he gotten so fucking lucky?

"Caroline didn't see it that way. She rarely left Michigan Avenue. She liked to shop and throw parties. She liked being a doctor's wife, but she greatly preferred being a Sommerville. I didn't realize it until a few years in that she thought I would change my mind and go into politics. She was disappointed to say the least. She let me go to Africa. She told me she wasn't coming with me. I explained that it was something I had to do. I walked out on her. I left her with the house and the money and walked out."

"Caleb, did she come after you?" Holly asked. "She can't have loved you too much if she didn't come after you. I would have hauled your ass back home if I couldn't follow you."

"I didn't see her for almost a year. I set up my clinic in a township. There were always skirmishes going on. The blood diamond trade had completely torn the country up. There were always groups of soldiers coming around, some of them as young as nine and ten years old. They would come through and take what they wanted, and I would start over again. And then one day they decided they wanted me."

Holly gasped. "They figured out who you were."

Caleb sighed. "A magazine ran an article on me and my clinic. It wasn't a huge leap to know that my family would pay a lot of money to keep me safe. The day I was kidnapped, Caroline showed up with divorce papers. She'd been having an affair, and she wanted to leave me. She told me what a pisspoor man I was and how much better my brother was than me."

"Your brother takes your wife?" Alexei asked, horrified.

So he didn't know everything. "Yes. Eli had an affair with Caroline. I don't even know how angry I am with him anymore. Josh barely speaks to him. It wrecked our family, and I didn't even love her. Eli loved her. He lost a lot. It doesn't excuse what he did, but I can't hate my brother any longer. I have to find a way to move on."

"Caroline was there when the soldiers came?" Holly's eyes had filled with tears.

Even as he told the tale, he felt his soul lifting. He felt the burden being split, pieces of hurt being taken on by these people who cared about him. The horror still closed in on him, but he wasn't alone. "They killed her. They shot her in the back. They took my nurses and raped them before killing them. I had to listen. I still hear them sometimes."

"Oh, baby." Holly's arms tightened around him as though she could protect him. His fierce Holly would have tried. She was a precious gift, and he was suddenly damn glad to have a partner. Alexei

251

would never let anything happen to her. It gave him great peace.

"How long did they keep you?" Alexei asked.

Forever. "A few months. Eli got the ransom message through the embassy. He thought it was a joke at first. Then they found the clinic and Caroline's body. He paid the ransom, but they weren't satisfied with it. They came back for more. They moved me around a lot. Then they settled into an abandoned government shelter. They locked me up in a closet. I stayed there for at least six weeks. I hated it when they took me out. It was always to beat me or force me to do something. They would throw shit at me. Come up behind me with bats."

He could feel Holly's tears on his chest. He soothed a hand through her hair. It felt right to share it with her. It felt right for her to cry because he finally realized what it meant to love. It meant sharing the burdens of his soul. It meant Holly could cry for him when he couldn't. She had the right to cry for him, to ease his mind the same way he had the right to protect her. These exchanges were sacred, and to deny them lessened the love between them.

"I was so scared, baby. I wanted to die. I was more scared to live than I was to die. When Wolf found me, I could barely walk."

Her head came up. "Wolf?"

He nodded. "Wolf Meyer was a member of the SEAL team that rescued me. He found me. He got me out of the jungle."

"He gets banana bread." Holly cuddled closer. Holly made the world's best banana bread. It was her gift for people she cared about. It looked like Wolf Meyer had just made the list.

"Eli was waiting for me. He'd aged ten years in the months I'd been gone. He'd spent millions of dollars, used every favor he had to get me back, and I couldn't look at him without wanting to kill him. What kind of man does that?"

"A man who has been betrayed," Alexei replied. "No matter what he did, he still betrayed you, Caleb. You had right to be angry."

"I don't want to be angry anymore. I just want to be here. I want to live here in Bliss and take care of my patients and have a life. I want that so badly, but I can't even sleep in a bed. Holly, baby, I sleep in my closet. It makes me a freak, but it's the only place I feel safe."

"We can make it work. We can expand the closet," Holly assured him.

Alexei snorted. "We are not all going to sleep in closet, *dushka*.

Caleb will heal, but for now I have plan."

He got out of bed. He didn't bother to cover up, simply walked across the room without a stitch on. Caleb envied Alexei his comfort. He was a man who didn't have a problem with his own skin. He couldn't help a little smile as Holly's eyes strayed. He could tell he was going to have to amp up the workouts if he wanted to keep up with his partner.

He tightened his hold on Holly, reveling in their closeness. He was so tired. Weary even, but he felt light at the same time. He wouldn't leave tonight. He would stay with her. He would pace the floors, stare at the ceiling. It didn't matter. He wouldn't spend the night away from her. He could do this. He could handle it.

He was startled as the bed jerked and moved. Holly's head came up.

"Alexei, what are you doing?" Holly asked as the bed slid across the floor and bumped against the wall.

"I am fixing problem." He climbed back on the bed, sliding under the covers. "Caleb, put your back against wall. Holly, you will press against his front. He will be surrounded."

He already was. He could feel the wall against his back and Holly turned over, scooting back against him, wriggling that gorgeous ass until it nestled against his cock.

"I appreciate this," he said, his cock already stirring. "But I don't think it's going to work. How am I supposed to sleep when all I want to do is fuck her again?"

"You will get used to this. Close eyes. Try." Alexei settled in, lying close to Holly. They were all snuggled together with Holly in the middle.

"I'm not going to need my electric blanket this winter." Holly sighed as she slid her hand over his waist. "I hope this works. I like being in the middle."

"Get used to it, *dushka*." Alexei settled in.

Caleb wrapped his arm over Holly's waist. It wasn't late, but she could probably use a nap. He would hold her while she slept. He would lie here and get used to the feeling. He could still see the door. No one could come up from behind him. Maybe he could be okay.

He closed his eyes, breathing in her scent. He let his mind wander as Holly's breathing evened out. Now that his secret was out, maybe he could pull money out of his trust fund and build a bigger cabin for the three of them…four of them. Mick would be here, too.

He should build a bigger cabin and expand his clinic. He needed better equipment. Maybe an MRI. If he had an MRI, then he could shove Holly in it when she got sick.

He fell asleep to the thought of a bright, shiny new imager.

* * * *

Alexei rolled out of bed. The evening had slid into night. The room was dark, but there was no doubt that the doctor was finally getting some sleep.

Perhaps he shouldn't worry about getting a job. He should go to school and become a therapist.

If he lived that long.

He found his jeans and pulled them on. As quietly as he could, he left the bedroom and started toward the kitchen. They would be hungry when they woke up.

Was he doing the right thing? Jessie's words came back to him. Was he putting Holly and Caleb at risk?

"Hey. Is all the crazy make-up sex done?"

He turned and saw Mick coming in the back door. He liked the young man. Despite the fact that Mick's coloring was different, he reminded Alexei so much of Holly. It was in the way he smiled and held himself.

"The up making is finished. We are fine. I was going to make dinner. You are hungry?"

Mick smiled. "Not exactly. The women around here like to feed a growing boy. I've had lasagna and brisket and enchiladas and a whole bunch of cookies. I was the official taster. Remind me not to taste for Nell anymore, though. She puts tofu in everything. And there was a woman there who thought I should eat beets. I didn't think beets were real. I kind of thought they were something parents told their kids about, like the boogeyman. They're real and they're horrible."

"I will not cook beets, then." He actually liked them, but they were obviously not for Mick. "I will make something you like."

The phone rang. Alexei answered it quickly, not wanting to wake Caleb.

"Hello?"

"Alexei, thank god." Jessie's voice sounded small over the phone line. "I've been worried about you. Look, we got some information about the man I nearly caught this afternoon. We have a credible source who claims that Angelo DiStefano hired a hit man to kill you."

He gripped the phone and tried not to show his anger. DiStefano was one of the men he'd put in jail. Would it ever be over? "I understand. Do we have identifications on this man who has been sent?"

"I got a look at him. Hope at the sheriff's department sketched him. The sheriff faxed it back to our office, and we're going to see if we get anything, but you have to see that it's time to come in, Markov. It's too dangerous."

"What does Michael say?" He knew what Michael would say, but he was drawing out the conversation, putting off the moment when he had to leave them. He couldn't stand the thought. "Can I talk to him?"

"No," she said suddenly. Her voice calmed. "Not right now. He's in the shower. He thinks we need to get you in hiding. Tonight."

Of course he did. "I will come and talk to you. I need to get my things out of motel anyway. I will be there in twenty minutes. You can meet?"

"Absolutely. I'll be there. Alexei, I'm sorry about this, but you're doing the right thing."

He hung up. He wasn't so sure about that.

"Was it the cop again?" Mick asked.

"Yes. I need to go see her."

"No, you don't."

Alexei shook his head. "It is not so simple."

"It's very simple. She wants you to go back into hiding. You can't do that. You owe my mom. Don't leave her."

How did he make him understand? "I owe your mother safety, too. I don't want to leave. I love her. I love the family we are to be building, but I can't make her target."

"I think the men of this town can handle it. I didn't get more than a foot inside my bedroom before I had six guns aimed at my head. Some of the women are scary, too. Remind me never to piss off Rachel Harper." He crossed his arms over his chest. "If you walk out, I worry they'll fall apart. You're the glue that brought them together.

Everything in life is a risk. I think my mom would rather take the risk than be safe and not have you."

But how could he live with himself if anything happened to her?

"I don't know what to be doing. I love your mother. I want to be marrying her and spending my life in Bliss, but I think all I offer is danger. I don't even have job."

"Uh, that's where you're wrong." Mick grinned and looked pleased with himself. "I talked to the big, superhot guy. Wait, that could be anyone here. Do you people know how to grow them ugly? Anyway, the big guy who runs the tavern."

"Zane."

"Yes, that's him. Anyway, he was talking to his wife, the super pregnant one, and he said he needed to find a bartender to help out because he wants to spend more time at home once the kid shows up. I negotiated for you. He's a cheap bastard, but I think you'll find the salary works."

"I have job?"

Mick nodded. "You have job. And we're going to work on your use of articles in sentences. Naw, it's actually kind of cute. Anyway, you start on Friday, and if Zane asks, you've worked at many functions. You graduated from the Bartending School of Eastern Moscow."

Alexei laughed. "I think Zane know my history. He will not believe, but he is man who will give points to you for creativity."

"Hey, I'm a man who gets the job done. So you can't leave."

His heart hurt. He would love to work at Trio, talking to people and becoming part of the town. "I think it still might be best."

Mick sighed. "Fine, then go and talk to this woman, but you take Mom and Caleb with you. You can't cut them out of this decision. That's not what family does. If you're going to walk out on them, they should have their say."

Alexei looked at the door to the bedroom where his partner and woman lay sleeping. It would be easier to walk away. Simpler.

Family was not simple. With a heavy heart, he went to wake them.

Chapter Seventeen

Holly clutched Alexei's hand in hers, threading their fingers together as Caleb drove out of their valley toward the motel.

Caleb talked in rapid staccato bursts, betraying his anxiety. "After we talk to the marshals, we need to meet with Nate. I want to see what they've come up with on this guy."

Holly wished they were still in bed. When Alexei had awakened her, she'd reached for him, hoping for a kiss. She'd immediately known something was wrong by his frown and the sad look in his eyes.

Alexei's hand squeezed hers. "I don't want you or Holly hurt. I hate that we cannot leave Mick in house alone. Perhaps I should go so you would be safe."

Holly had asked Laura to watch Mick. Despite the fact that he was seventeen, she couldn't leave him there alone when someone was stalking one of her men. The assassin didn't seem to discriminate, either. Whoever this killer was, he didn't mind who he hurt. He'd nearly killed them all at one point in time. She couldn't risk her son. But she also couldn't imagine her world without Alexei in it.

"No." There was nothing anxious about Caleb's pronouncement.

There was a determined finality to his favorite word.

Alexei sighed. "You cannot be saying no. No is not an argument. We need to be talking about this."

"No." Caleb's eyes focused on the road ahead of him.

Despite the seriousness of the situation, she couldn't help but smile. "I don't think he's going to relent on this one, babe. And I agree with him. And Alexei, you're forgetting that the good doc there has some serious connections with the justice department. I don't mind calling Eli Sommerville and telling him exactly what I think he should do. We can get these people to take threats to you seriously. And if we can't find the proof, I bet Micky can fabricate it."

Her son was damn fine at manipulating situations to his liking.

"I need you to understand that I must be keeping you safe," Alexei said.

"How exactly are you planning on doing that from some cheap motel room in the Midwest? Or will they take you back to Florida, and you can go back to being Howard? Is that what you want?" Caleb asked, looking at them through the rearview mirror. His eyes were narrowed, and Holly could practically feel the frustration pouring off him. He'd been so peaceful before, as though something had finally fallen into place, and now he'd had it snatched from his grasp.

"I do not wish any of this. I thought this was over." Alexei turned his head, looking out into the night.

"It is over," Holly insisted. "We just have some cleanup to do."

"And when the next person comes after me?" Alexei asked.

"We handle it," Caleb insisted.

Holly was glad she and Caleb were presenting a united front. "We deal with it. But we don't walk away. Anything could happen to any one of us. We stay vigilant, but we don't let fear ruin our lives. I'm willing to talk to the marshals. I'm even willing to leave town for a while, but we will all go."

"We can go to Chicago if we have to," Caleb offered. "My family's compound is well guarded. We'll talk to the marshals, and then we'll pack up Mick and head there for a while. Alexei, you can play referee for me and my brother. Holly, I know you don't want to deal with my family, but this is better than breaking up."

"I can handle your family." She could. She wasn't the same girl who had gotten torn apart by the Langs. She was sure of herself now.

She'd built a life and a home and found love. She had more work to do, but she could handle anything the world threw at her. Anything except losing her men.

Alexei put a hand on Caleb's shoulder. "You would do this for me?"

Caleb was silent for a moment. "I would. I know you think you owe me, but I owe you, too. I wouldn't be here without you. I wouldn't have Holly without you. I would have gone on the way I had been. If you leave, I'll take care of Holly. I won't go back to the man I was before, but we will be incomplete. You have to see that. And don't give me a bunch of bullshit about how you don't have a job and I'm smarter than you. I don't want to hear that crap. You can go to school. I'll take care of it. You can figure out what you want to do. And so can Holly."

"Really?" She hadn't thought about it. She'd lived paycheck to paycheck for so long that the idea of finishing college hadn't even occurred to her. But she could. She could go back to school. She was forty years old, and she felt like the world was new again.

Caleb's eyes were warm in the rearview mirror. "Yes. I would love it if you studied nursing, but I won't tell you what to do."

She might enjoy being a nurse. "Maybe I'll be a doctor and give you a run for your money, Caleb Burke."

Caleb's whole face fell. "Oh, god, no. I don't even want to think about that. My point is I don't want to listen to Alexei whine about his lack of a job. It's not an excuse to walk away."

"I have job. I am to be tending the bars at Trio. But I can go to school at same time." Alexei turned back to her, and there was a confidence in his eyes that hadn't been there before.

"That's great, babe." Up ahead she could see the Movie Motel, its lights blinking, announcing a vacancy. The movie was apparently in full swing as Holly could see the light from the screen illuminating the night.

Caleb turned into the parking lot. Holly could see the marshals' SUV up ahead. "While we're here, we can check you out of the motel. I think we should all stay at Holly's until we're ready to go to Chicago." He pulled into the parking space and turned back to them. "Do you have your gun?"

Alexei nodded. "I go nowhere without."

Caleb nodded. "I put the tranq gun in the back."

"Do I get a gun?" After all, everyone else had a gun.

"No," they said at the same time.

She should have a gun. She'd talk to Laura about it.

There was a sharp knock on the window. Holly startled but then looked up. Logan stood there glaring down.

"I want to talk to you," he said, staring at Alexei.

Alexei nodded slowly and stepped out of the car. "What do you be needing, Deputy?"

Logan's eyes were hard. "I need you out of my town. I figure you owe me, Markov. I took a lot of pain so your ass could live."

"Logan," Holly started. She felt for Logan. She'd known him for years, since he was just a kid, but she wasn't about to let him run Alexei out of town.

The deputy turned on her. "Stop. I don't want to hear it from you. I'm sick and tired of everyone telling me to be tolerant. I don't have to be tolerant. He doesn't belong here. He's the one who brought those mobsters here, and now he's brought another killer along with him. You might like to fuck him, but I'm not going to let my town go to hell because Holly Lang needs to get some."

Holly Lang had had just about enough of Logan Green. She knew he'd gone through hell, but it was time for him to start coming out of it. "You back off. You have no right to try to run him out of town. If it hadn't been for Alexei, you would be dead. I would be dead. I can't imagine what you went through, but you're alive."

"He doesn't want to be." Caleb's eyes had softened as he looked at the deputy. He placed himself between Holly and Logan. "And I know what that feels like. You're not just mad at Alexei. You're mad at everyone who walks around like the world is the same place it was before you were taken into that room. You hate every one of those fuckers who don't get what you know—that the world is a fucked-up place just waiting to tear you up."

"They don't even see it. They expect me to get over it because the wounds scabbed over and the broken bones healed." Logan's face was drawn in pain, but his eyes still stared at Alexei. "They don't get that it could all happen again. Which is precisely why assholes like this guy shouldn't be allowed in our town. I'm going to get rid of you one way or another. If you won't leave on your own, then I can make your life hell."

Her blood started to boil. She heard everything he'd said, but he was pushing her too far. "You back off and do it now. Everyone in this town has been putting up with your crap for months. Don't pretend that everything will be fine if Alexei is gone. You were drinking and fighting and endangering everyone in this community before he came back. You need help and everyone has done their best to give it to you, but you just tell everyone you're fine and go back to the bar. It can't go on. You're a cop. You can't be out of control."

Logan laughed, a bitter, nasty sound. "We're all out of control. Don't be stupid."

"You will use nicer tone of voice when you speak to woman. And don't ever call her stupid." Alexei's tone had deepened. She was getting worried that he'd had enough of Logan's bile, too.

Instead of backing down, Logan's lips turned up in a feral smile. "I'll call her whatever I like, asshole. What are you going to do about it?"

Caleb's hands came out. "We're not doing this. Logan, back off."

One of the motel room doors came open, and Holly saw Jessie standing there. She wore jeans and a T-shirt, her shoulder holster on display. There was a shiny gun resting against her left side. She quickly closed the door behind her and surveyed the group. "What the hell is going on? Alexei? I thought we agreed you would come alone."

Alexei's eyes widened as he looked over her. "I never say such thing. Where is Michael?"

"Busy," she said shortly. "I'm in charge right now, and I don't think your friends should be here."

"He's not going anywhere alone as long as someone out there is trying to kill him." Caleb pointed to Jessie. "And you're not taking him anywhere without us."

"See," Logan said with an ugly grin. "Everyone wants you gone, asshole. And take Holly and the doc, too. We don't need them."

"You need many things, Logan," Alexei said with a shake of his head. "I don't think you will accept anything good I could give you, though. You will have to have patience because I am not going to leave. I live here now. I have a family here, and I will not leave them."

"We'll see about that." Logan didn't move, but he seemed to realize there were more people than he wanted around.

Jessie crossed her arms over her chest and gave a long-suffering sigh. "Alexei, we need to talk, and I don't think we should do it with an audience. Dr. Sommerville, I mean Burke, why don't you take Ms. Lang home, and I'll talk to Alexei. I promise you, I can keep him safe."

"Where is the other one? The other marshal?" Caleb asked.

"Michael is working on the case with the sheriff. He should be back any minute. We need to get you someplace safe. If you two are serious about going with him, then you should go home and pack a bag. Time is of the essence," Jessie said, her eyes going back to the door of her room.

Logan stiffened, his eyes narrowing, confusion plain. Holly saw his shoulders straighten and then relax as though he'd figured something out. He exchanged a look with Alexei, their eyes meeting and something passing between them. "Yeah, maybe you two should go do that."

"I can handle all of this. I will deal with marshals, and then we can do what we planned on doing," Alexei said, pulling a key from his pocket. He leaned over and brushed his lips against Holly's. "*Dushka*, everything will be fine." He turned back to Jessie. "Allow me to gather my things and speak to Holly and Caleb. I will return in moments."

Her face tightened. "All right. You're stubborn, you know. Maybe you should all go down to your room and discuss this. You're putting them in terrible danger. You're going to realize that soon."

"I guess I'm not needed here anymore. Looks like you got this under control, Marshal." Logan stepped back, tipping his hat with a mocking smile. "And Alexei, hope your trip goes well. Be sure to watch out for strangers. You never know when one is going to come up from behind—or in front."

"I am going to talk to Nate about him. He's lost his damn mind," Holly grumbled. She turned and saw Logan jogging out toward his Bronco. She noticed that he passed it by and ran around to the front of the motel. What kind of trouble was he going to cause now?

"Don't to be worrying, *dushka*." He took her hand. There was an air of urgency about him. He tugged her along, his eyes watching as Jessie went back to her room. "Caleb, let's take her to my room, and we can talk."

Alexei led her to the next door. His protectors had apparently wanted to keep a close eye on him.

Caleb talked in a low voice. "I don't know why, but I don't like this. Let's call the sheriff when we get in the room. I think it would be best if we don't tell the marshals what we're planning. The first chance we get, we pick up Mick and haul ass for Chicago. Once we're there, my brother can protect you. Until then, I worry they might haul you into protective custody. We wouldn't even know where they had taken you."

Alexei pushed the key into the door and turned it. He looked down and gasped. Holly couldn't see anything to be worried about. There was just a piece of string lying in the doorway. She could see it plainly because the door faced the movie screen, as all of the motel's doors did. The whole parking lot was lit up as Doris Day searched for love. But Alexei's face went stark white, and he ducked to his knees. "Caleb, protect her."

The door exploded as a bullet crashed through. Caleb tackled her just as she felt it whizz by. She hit the concrete with a crash, pain flaring along her skin. Alexei got to his feet and knocked in the door with one kick. He immediately started firing, the sound cracking through the air, exploding all around her.

Her heart nearly stopped. Alexei had walked in there.

"Don't." Caleb put an arm around her waist and rolled from the sidewalk to the cement of the parking lot, positioning their bodies between two cars. "He knows what he's doing. We need to get to my gun, sweetheart. It's in the trunk of the Benz."

Alexei came back out of the room, firing as he stumbled backward. Blood coated his shirt. Holly felt the scream build inside her chest.

Alexei dove for the protection of the parked cars, coming to Caleb's side. "I'm hit by bullet."

"No shit," Caleb said, getting on his knees. "That's what happens when you walk into a room where a dude's got a gun."

"I thought you said he knew what he was doing. God, Caleb, you have to fix him." Her heart was in her throat, panic threatening to take over. Had the danger passed? They had to get Alexei out of here. The blood looked like it was everywhere. Was he dying? God, he couldn't die.

"I am only hit in shoulder." Alexei popped up over the car for a moment, and two quick shots rang out. He came back down. "I had to see how many. There is only one man. I do not recognize. I hit him in leg, but he get me, too. I thought it best to retreat. The sheriff should be here soon. I have no doubt that everyone has called."

He grimaced as he took two more shots over the hood of the car.

"Caleb, where are you hit?" Alexei asked.

Holly gasped and looked down at Caleb. He had blood on his pants.

Caleb's voice was steady as he talked. "It's a through and through. He got my left gastrocnemius muscle. It hurts like hell, but I'll live. I can't run though."

Calf. He was talking about his calf muscle. She was the only one who wasn't shot. She slipped her hand into Caleb's pocket and pulled out the keys. "I'll go get the other gun."

"No, you will not. You will sit here. Help is coming." Alexei grabbed her arm. "You will be obeying me now."

She wanted to, but the air split around her as whoever had been in that room fired again. "I don't think this guy is going to wait for Nate. We need another gun. Why isn't the marshal taking this guy down?"

"Because she sells me out. Logan didn't like what she say about Michael meeting sheriff. That was why I wanted to get you two into my room before I confront her. She is one who wanted me out here alone." Alexei's eyes clouded with pain. "Caleb, you need to get Holly out of here."

"I might be able to walk," Caleb said. "But I told you, I can't run."

They were trapped.

Alexei held the assassin off, firing another shot over the car. He yelled at his assailant. "The police are on their way. You should be running. Do you wish to be caught?"

"I'm getting this job done, Markov," a deep voice yelled. "I can take you out alone or get your friends, too. But one way or another, I'm finishing this tonight."

Holly put a hand on Alexei as though she could keep him there. She wasn't about to let him walk out and sacrifice himself. "You are not going anywhere. Put that out of your mind."

Alexei fired again. "Start moving back. We need to get somewhere where we can protect our backs."

"We need to stop your bleeding," Caleb argued.

Alexei shook his head. Even in the low light, she could see he was getting pale. "No time."

Holly crawled to the back of the car, the concrete under her knees biting into her flesh. Ahead of her she could see the drive-in playing the movie of the week. Doris Day fluttered on screen, but all she could see was another woman creeping behind the row of parked cars. Jessie Wilson had that gun out now, and she was making her way toward them.

"She's coming," Holly whispered, terror making her heart pound.

They would be surrounded with nowhere to go.

"I am be coming out!" Alexei dropped the gun and stood with his hands up.

"No!" Holly shouted. She tried to reach for him, but Caleb pulled her down.

"Don't. Don't make this harder on him," Caleb whispered fiercely in her ear.

There was a solitary shot that split the air. Holly screamed against Caleb's chest, his arms tightening around her. He held her so close she could barely breathe.

Alexei slumped down, his hand reaching for her. His eyes were bright, and a smile covered his face. "Can you reach gun, *dushka*? Can you give to me?"

Caleb looked him over. "Where are you hit?"

"I wasn't," Alexei said with a tired smile. "Assassin is dead. We have a savior."

"Just because I saved your ass doesn't mean I like you, Markov," Logan shouted from somewhere behind them. "It means I'm still a cop no matter what anyone says. And I know you're in on this, Marshal. Nate is home with Callie. I talked to him five minutes before I got here. There's no way you met with him. Is your partner dirty, too?"

"Michael doesn't know anything," Jessie called out. She sounded close. "I drugged his beer tonight so he wouldn't give me trouble. I didn't want to do this. I didn't mean to be the one to pull the trigger, but you know what they say. When you want a job done, do it yourself."

"You're going to jail, Marshal. You can't kill all of us," Logan said. He sounded like he was on the move.

Holly picked up the gun. She tried to hand it to Alexei, but he shook his head.

"My arm is numb." He tried to move it but it lay against his chest.

"He's lost a lot of blood." Caleb pulled his shirt off, balling it in his hands before he put it on Alexei's shoulder, covering the wound. "I don't like the color of his skin. I think he's going into shock."

The gun was heavy in her hand. Alexei couldn't shoot. Caleb was busy. She was the only one left.

"You want to tell me why?" Logan called out.

Jessie's voice sounded closer. "You know what a government job pays, idiot. I got nothing. I bust my ass for years, put myself out there, and I get nothing. Why should I turn down a hundred grand to look the other way? All I was supposed to do was make it easy for the pro, but no, nothing is easy in this piece-of-shit town. But I have to finish the job or DiStefano will finish me."

Caleb looked back at Holly. He pressed down on Alexei's shoulder, putting his weight behind it. "We need to get him out of here. Maybe I can get him into the room now that the hired guy is dead."

Where was Logan? Holly couldn't see him. From where she was sitting, she couldn't see anything. Her heart was pounding. That adrenaline thing was threatening to take over. Caleb and Alexei were counting on her.

"And it doesn't bother you that you're killing a man?" Logan asked.

Holly turned and realized she could see Logan creeping along. The lights from the movie screen shone down on the parking lot, illuminating it. She could see him in the shiny hubcaps of the SUV they were hiding behind. He was watching for the marshal, his gun in hand.

Jessie didn't seem to mind the game of cat and mouse Logan was playing. "Markov is a criminal. I don't give a fuck that he turned around. He should be in jail, too. I'm more than happy to off the asshole. My partner is a good lay, but not a smart man. He never did see things my way or this would have been easier. Ah, there you are."

A gunshot rang out.

Holly stifled a scream as she saw Logan's body fly back and blood bloom across his arm.

It was all going to hell. Logan was down. She couldn't tell if he was dead or alive. Caleb couldn't run, and he wouldn't even if he could. Caleb's hands were on Alexei, trying to save his friend. In the distance she could hear a lone siren. There was only one siren wailing in the night, but she doubted Nate Wright was by himself. Soon every able-bodied man in Bliss would descend, but it would be too late.

"No one to protect you now, Markov. I guess you should have taken up with someone scarier than a doctor and a waitress." Jessie's boots thudded against the concrete. She came into view in the mirrored surface of the hubcap. She drew down every time she reached a new car. Two cars separated them. Two more cars and she would be on them.

"Holly, I want you to run," Caleb whispered. "Give me that damn gun and get out of here."

And leave them behind?

"No." It was Caleb's favorite word, and she gave it back to him. She was pretty sure he understood it.

Jessie was one car away. Holly found herself strangely calm. She'd never fired a gun before, but she would do it now. She would do it because if she didn't, she lost so much more than her life. She lost her love, her heart, and her soul. Alexei was pale, so pale. Caleb couldn't run. Logan wasn't moving.

It was up to her.

Jessie took a step toward the car. "Nowhere to run, you piece of shit."

She hated to do it, but Holly moved to the other side as quietly as she could. She couldn't see Jessie in the hubcap anymore. If she stayed watching the marshal, she couldn't shoot her. She could only see what was coming from behind her. She had to give up her line of sight in order to be ready to shoot.

Holly shifted, her eyes meeting Caleb's.

"I love you," he mouthed. He held on to Alexei, giving this job to her.

She felt his strength. They were united. He had his job to do and she was left to this. She would save them or they would all go down together. Not a single one was willing to leave the others.

Holly braced herself. She straightened her back against the SUV, protecting against the inevitable kickback. She might not have shot anyone, but she'd heard all the lectures.

She forced herself to focus. Only one thing mattered. One moment.

"I think this is the one, you piece of shit," Jessie said. "Your running is over."

The minute the marshal came into view, Holly pulled the trigger. She kept her eyes open and fired at the largest part of the marshal's body.

Jessie's arm dropped as blood blossomed across her chest. Holly watched as the gun the marshal held slipped from her hand and hit the ground. Jessie stared at her for a moment, a weird recognition on her face before her eyes went blank. She fell to her knees and slipped away.

"Holly, baby, don't you ever do that again! I love you. I love you so fucking much, but don't do that again." Caleb kept his hand on Alexei's chest, but there was no denying the horror in his eyes. "I'm going to let him spank the hell out of you. When Stef gets back from his honeymoon, we're going to talk about paddles and whatever the hell that thing is with all the tails. That's what I'll use."

"Thank our woman." Alexei managed to bring his head up. "Caleb, stop yelling and thank our woman."

Holly's hands shook as she let the gun go. She crawled to Alexei. They could thank her later. "Logan got shot. He's down. I don't know if he's alive."

Caleb reached for her hand. "Use your weight on this. Don't be afraid to put a little force behind it. We have to stanch the bleeding until I can sew him up." He looked down at Alexei. "You don't go anywhere. You understand me?"

Alexei smiled up at him. "I will live to annoy you, Doctor."

Caleb nodded and forced himself to get to his feet. He grimaced as he moved, but he was obviously determined to see about Logan. He held on to the car above them as he hobbled away.

"I am so sorry, my *dushka*. I should not have come here." Alexei placed his good hand over hers.

She pressed against his shoulder, praying she could keep the blood in his body. "No. No more of that. I love you. Caleb loves you. No apologies, and if you think you can run, you're wrong. You're never allowed to leave."

He smiled. "I must listen to such fierce woman. I wouldn't want to be on side of you that is so bad."

She didn't bother to correct him. He would never really be on her bad side. "I love you."

"And I you. I will not go. I will never to go."

His eyes closed, and Holly prayed he could keep his promise.

Chapter Eighteen

Two weeks later

"Doc, I am never listening to you again. You are the worst baby deliverer ever!" Zane Hollister said with a grin from his seat on the sofa in his cabin. The Hollister-Wrights had just gotten home from the hospital and settled in. He cradled a tiny baby boy in his hands. Little Alexander Grant Hollister-Wright was perfect.

And so was his brother.

"Stop your bellyaching, Zane," Nate said, patting Charles Stephen's back. "He did a fine job delivering the babies. But he can't read a sonogram."

Holly laughed. Caleb was bad at that. "He's going to work on that because I don't think the women of Bliss are anywhere close to being done with babies."

Caleb shrugged. "I told Stef I wasn't an obstetrician."

"You are great doctor," Alexei said, slapping his partner on the back. "You save many lives. You cannot help that one boy hide behind the other."

Caleb's face went red. "Well, I might have seen an extra leg in there somewhere, but to be honest, given everything I've heard about Zane, I thought the kid just had a really big penis."

Callie's laughter pealed through the room. "I can see where you would make the mistake, Doc. I don't mind. I'm just glad all my boys are healthy."

"Hello to the house!" Rachel said, knocking on the door as she entered. Jen and Stef were with her, along with her husbands.

"You had to show us up, didn't you?" Rye asked as he walked inside.

Caleb's arm went around Holly's waist, and he hauled her close. "You think you ever want to try something like that?"

"A baby?" She was too old. She looked at the sweet babies in the room. Screw that. Age was just a number.

Caleb's voice was warm against her ear. "Yeah, the big guy and I have been talking about it, and as soon as we make an honest woman out of you, we thought we might give the baby-making thing a try. I really like Mick. I think I might like to have a family."

She leaned into him. He would be an incredible dad. He and Alexei had already proven to be good to Micky. "I think I would like nothing more."

"And I will enjoy the practicing." Alexei pressed against her other side, leaning in to kiss her cheek.

She looked up at him. Alexei wasn't back to a hundred percent, but he was getting there. Caleb was the most thorough of doctors. And all thoughts Alexei had about leaving them seemed to be gone. Eli Sommerville had brought down a ton of hellfire on DiStefano's head. It would make anyone who considered revenge on Alexei think twice.

"Look here, little guy, we're going to have a talk, you and me," Max said to one of the boys. "I catch you looking at my daughter, and we're going to have trouble."

The baby yawned, his tiny mouth opening and forming a perfect *O*. He didn't seem intimidated by the big man threatening him.

"Max, you leave those boys alone." Rachel held their daughter, who was doing her damnedest to reach for the baby closest to her. Paige babbled and reached out her chubby arms as though trying to get to the boys. "I think Paige is the one we should watch."

Max shook his head. "That's not true. Paige is perfect. It's those boys who are going to cause trouble."

"You know it, Harper," Nate said with a big grin. "The Hollister-Wright boys are going to be hell on wheels."

Holly sighed as the men started arguing good-naturedly. The small cabin was filled with friends and family and love. The thought of kids running around Bliss made her heart skip a little beat. She was forty. Did she really want to start again?

Hell, yeah.

Alexei announced that it was time for him to go and open up Trio. Good-byes were said and hugs given. Holly and Caleb followed him out of Callie's cabin. They opened the door and found Logan standing on the front porch next to Wolf Meyer. Logan was pale and paced nervously. His eyes came up.

"Logan, are you all right?" Caleb asked. "Are your stitches okay?"

Caleb had dug the bullet out of Logan's lung. It had been touch and go, but Logan was strong. At least physically. He looked a bit frail as he began to talk.

Logan shook his head. "I'm fine, Doc. I wanted to talk to you three. I wanted to apologize."

Wolf held out a hand, shaking both Alexei's and Caleb's. "I've been watching out for him, Doc. He's good. He's been following orders. His moms have taken great care of him, but he insisted on coming here."

Logan swallowed. "I know I was an ass. I've been in a bad place for a long time. I know I have to find a way to get out of it, but I don't think I can do it here. Alexei, I hope you can forgive me."

"There is nothing to forgive." Alexei's words sounded choked in the back of his throat. He'd been worried about Logan. He didn't want the younger man to hurt.

Logan cleared his throat. "Thanks. I appreciate it. When I heal up, I'm going to Texas with Wolf for a while. Nate's giving me some time off. Maybe a lot of time off. Wolf's moving down to Dallas for a job. His brother lives there. According to Wolf here, his brother is good at dealing with guys like me."

Wolf smiled. "My brother is a shrink. He loves this shit. Bringing Logan to him is like giving him a present. Leo's going to talk to Logan for fifteen minutes and think I gave him a trip to Disney World. It might actually make him not be a douchebag for a day or two. I wish I could take that other guy with us. He's a ball of torture right now. Leo

271

would eat him up."

"Michael?" Holly asked, frowning.

Wolf nodded, his face turning grave. "Yeah, I'm joking about it, but that guy is in pain. He rented out a cabin on the mountain. He hasn't left it yet."

Holly could remember the look in Michael Novack's eyes when he'd stumbled out of his room right as Nate had placed a sheet over Jessie's body. He'd practically howled. And then when he'd heard the story, a terrible silence had come over the marshal. He'd gotten up and walked out. This was the first she'd heard he hadn't left town.

"I hope everything's all right with him," Holly murmured, staring off at the mountain where the marshal was now residing.

"I think he needs this place for a while," Caleb said. "I know I did."

"And I have to leave." Logan's eyes cast down.

Holly stepped close. She hugged Logan gently. For all he'd said before, she could still see the young man he'd been. "If you need anything, you know where home is."

He nodded, his arms going around her. "I need to find me again. I need it so bad."

"You will. I'm behind you," she whispered. "Always."

"We all are." Caleb shook his hand. "Anything you need, you know where to find it."

Wolf and Logan went into Callie's cabin, and Holly was left alone with her men.

She looked at them, each so perfect in their own ways, each oddly incomplete without the other. No person was an island. She'd lived like that for far too long, forgetting what it was to find the pieces that were missing, to be whole and complete.

"I could use a beer. I'm not going to try anything else. Your screwdrivers suck," Caleb teased.

"My screwdriver is perfect. Holly say so." Alexei slapped at his partner's arm. The men stepped off the porch and started toward the truck.

"Holly lies because she wants to get some," Caleb joked.

"I am okay with this. And I will to be giving her some," Alexei said. "I think I will be giving her some on Zane's desk. We will see how he likes it. The sheriff gives us permission."

She laughed and hurried after them, pushing her way in between the men and grabbing their hands.

That was her place. Always between them.

* * * *

James, Hope, and a new arrival to Bliss will return in *Pure Bliss*, now available.

If you'd like to know what Wolf and Logan do in Texas, check out *Siren in Bloom*, now available.

Author's Note

I'm often asked by generous readers how they can help get the word out about a book they enjoyed. There are so many ways to help an author you like. Leave a review. If your e-reader allows you to lend a book to a friend, please share it. Go to Goodreads and connect with others. Recommend the books you love because stories are meant to be shared. Thank you so much for reading this book and for supporting all the authors you love!

Sign up for Lexi Blake's newsletter
and be entered to win a $25 gift certificate
to the bookseller of your choice.

Join us for news, fun, and exclusive content
including free short stories.

There's a new contest every month!

Go to www.LexiBlake.net/newsletter to subscribe.

Siren in Bloom
Texas Sirens Book 6
By Lexi Blake writing as Sophie Oak

Re-released in a second edition with new content.

For psychologist Leo Meyer, peace and comfort come through strict discipline and order. It's one of the reasons he was chosen by Julian Lodge to be the Dom in residence at his club. His time there has been a near-perfect existence filled with a daily routine free from the chaos of emotional attachment. With the exception of his brief relationship with Shelley McNamara, that is. She may have been the only woman he ever truly loved, but he was confident he had put her out of his mind until she walked into his club on the arm of another man.

Shelley McNamara is tired of waiting for her new life to begin. After finally finding freedom from an abusive marriage, she is eager to discover who she really is. After her encounter with Leo Meyer, she knows that the first thing she wants to explore is the lifestyle he exposed her to during their brief time together. She's been promised her new Dom will be an excellent fit, but she can't imagine anyone could fill the hole left by Leo. Until she sees Master Wolf.

After a devastating injury forced his retirement from the Navy SEALs, Wolf has been restless and lost. Hoping to reconnect with his estranged family in Dallas, Wolf accepted a new job working for Julian Lodge. His first assignment is training a beautiful woman named Shelley. Her fiery nature unlocks feelings he didn't know he was capable of after a life spent in combat. The closer they become, the more certain he is that she is his ideal mate. The only catch is that her relationship with Leo may not be as resolved as they both believed.

Just when Shelley believes the looming shadow of her deceased husband has finally cleared away, a dangerous killer arrives at her door seeking retribution. Leo and Wolf will have to put their grievances aside, leverage all their training, and work together to keep her safe and claim her heart.

* * * *

Shelley watched as Julian Lodge's perfectly formed body wielded the whip. There was a crack through the air and a snap back, and then a thin, red line welled on the white flesh of Finn's back.

Shelley took an unconscious step away from the stage and right into Wolf's chest.

"Shhh, it's all right, sweetheart," Wolf whispered against her ear. "Finn loves this. From what I understand, Finn has been Julian's submissive for years. They know what they're doing and what it takes for Finn to find his subspace."

She gasped as the whip cracked again, the sound violent, like a snake striking from nowhere. She kept her voice low. "I don't see how Finn isn't screaming."

"It sounds worse than it is."

She looked over and Leo was standing right beside them. She thought he'd walked away, felt more comfortable with him walking away. But he was standing right there beside his brother, dressed almost identically. Two amazingly gorgeous men.

Yeah, if she hadn't had ménage fantasies before, she sure as hell had them now. Why had she ever put that down on the questionnaire?

Because there was a part of her that wanted what Trev had found. Because there was a part of her that wanted the balance of two men just in case one of them turned out to be a criminally minded douchebag. Because she didn't trust herself anymore.

And because the whole month she'd spent talking to Wolf, she'd had fantasies about Leo suddenly turning around and both men wanting her. But that was all it was, a fantasy.

"Don't be afraid, sweetheart," Wolf said, his arms encircling her. He was so protective, but could she trust him?

"She isn't afraid. She's worried. That's her worried face. Her brows wrinkle, and she gets this deep line right in the middle of her forehead."

Trust Leo to have noticed that.

"Sweetheart, we don't have to play with the whip if you don't want to," Wolf assured her. "But you should know that what you hear, that cracking sound is something Julian controls with the flick of his wrist. Really look at Finn's back. Julian is in complete control. That whip can be horrible if he handles it wrong. Or it can whisper across Finn's skin.

277

It can bite on the right side of pain. It can be what Finn needs it to be. Do you see any blood?"

She didn't. There were several pink lines on Finn's flesh, and now she could see the way he'd relaxed, his shoulders slumping and head lolling back. Finn seemed to be getting what he needed.

"He feels like you did when I spanked you." Wolf's voice was a deep rumble over her skin.

"You spanked her?" Leo sounded like Wolf had said he'd beaten the crap out of her.

Julian turned and stared back because Leo's voice had carried through the dungeon.

"Sorry," Leo said, holding a hand up.

She felt Wolf move behind her as Julian turned back to his task. That crack split the air again, but she saw it differently now. The spanking Wolf had given her had been so different. It had changed her world.

Wolf leaned over behind her, speaking to Leo. "She ignored certain key parts of our contract. She was assaulted, and she didn't call me. I went to her place, and she was there with some fucking former SEAL mercenary shit."

"Holder?" Leo asked the one-word question with a sort of hushed awe.

"Yeah, how did you know?" Wolf asked. "Wait. He called you, right?"

"Yes," Leo replied. "Did you say she was assaulted? Get back here. We can't talk up here."

She was pulled back, two arms on either of hers. She almost stumbled, but Wolf held her up. He finally cursed and shoved a bulky arm under her knees, hauling her against his chest. He followed his brother as Leo made his way through to the back of the crowd. She could hear the whip crack again and again, Finn's soft moans filling the air, making her believe he was enjoying the experience.

What would it be like to trust someone the way Finn trusted Julian?

"Explain." One word, but Leo made it sound like a long Shakespearian speech.

"She had her laptop stolen on the train," Wolf replied before she could get the words out. She was rapidly figuring out her response was

278

not required.

"She was robbed?" Leo asked like he gave a damn. Logan had followed him, staying behind Leo like a properly trained lackey.

"Yes, I was," she managed, keeping her voice down because even she knew not to disrupt a scene. "Though the thief was an idiot because I bought that laptop bag at Target, and he had full access to a handmade Versace. I know which one I would have stolen."

Wolf turned her toward him. "Are you sure about that? He could see it? He had obvious access to something that was more valuable?"

She nodded. "Yes, he stared at it. There's no way he could mistake my bag as the more expensive one. That Versace was beautiful. Mine was beaten up. I shoved it on the floor. The leather is warped. It got wet. I was stupid and set it down in the rain when I was trying to unlock my car. I can't replace it so it looks like hell."

"So the only thing valuable was the laptop, and it was visible?" Leo asked.

"No," Shelley said quietly, well aware she was still in the middle of a scene. This couldn't wait until later? "My laptop bag was big enough that I could close it."

Wolf and Leo shared a long look.

"I'll check into it," Wolf said, his words sounding like a promise.

"Have you read her file?" Leo asked.

"I have a file?" She wasn't aware of it. Crap. She should have been. Julian Lodge looked like the kind of man who kept a lot of files.

"Of course," Wolf replied. He turned back to Leo. "You think this is about her ex? I can go talk to Tag right now."

Shelley's skin went cold. What about her ex?

"No idea," Leo answered. "But if someone is coming after her, I want to know what it's about."

"I'll look into it," Wolf promised.

Leo nodded. "I'll let Tag know, but he's the one who trained Ben and Chase. They're specifically here to handle things like this. We'll meet tomorrow at noon. Chase is one of the best hackers in the world. If someone has said anything about her on the net, Chase can find it. If some asshole wrote an e-mail about her, Chase can give it to you."

"We'll be there," Wolf promised.

"I will?" Shelley asked.

"You will." Wolf and Leo said the words at the same time, with the same deep inflection.

"Fine." She couldn't fight both of them.

There was a long pause. She stared at the scene in front of her. She thought they were being overly protective, but then she hadn't had anyone who was protective of her besides her brother in years. Maybe never since her father died. Bryce had married her for specific reasons, and when those dried up, he'd ignored her.

"Did he hurt you?" Leo asked, putting his hands on her shoulders and turning her around.

"No." She looked into his face, stark and lovely. God, he was a beautiful man. "He didn't touch me. He just took my bag."

The whip cracked again. She turned her face back, but now she was flustered. Her heart was racing. Why had that man taken her bag when there was something much more valuable in his grasp?

Had it been random? Why wouldn't it be random? What could she have that someone really wanted? She was living hand to mouth. She'd lost all of the property she'd owned with Bryce.

"Hey, calm down," Wolf ordered, his voice commanding her. "We're going to handle it."

Leo watched her for a moment. "She sometimes has anxiety attacks, nothing serious, but she can get herself worked up. If you don't talk her down, she'll be anxious for hours. Shelley, why don't we all go up to my office and we can talk about what's making you nervous?"

Now Leo was making her nervous. God, the last thing she wanted was to become one of Leo's patients.

"I think I can handle this, brother," Wolf said, taking her hands in his.

Leo's eyes narrowed. "And I think I'm the one with the degree in psychology. If she doesn't want to talk to me, I'll go get Janine. Honestly, I should have thought about putting her in Janine's group in the first place."

Wolf squared off with his brother. "She's my sub, Leo. I have zero problem with her getting into Janine's group, but for now let me handle her in the way I see fit."

She wasn't sure what group they were talking about, but it didn't seem like the time to argue. Leo stood, his arms across his chest, and she worried for a moment that he was going to argue with Wolf.

"I want to stay with Wolf." She looked up at Leo. This was the longest conversation they'd had in fifteen months, and instead of being her friend, he wanted to be her shrink. She didn't want that. She wanted what Wolf could give her.

Leo took a step back, his disengagement clear. "Of course. Come along, Logan. We still have work to do."

The two men walked away, losing themselves in the crowd.

"Come on." Wolf pulled her back toward a corner of the room. She could still see the stage, but it was slightly darker away from the lights. Wolf settled his big body on a chair that had been shoved into the corner. "Sit down. We're going to talk for a minute. What's your safe word?"

She needed a safe word to talk? "Gucci. I have to find a chair. Hold on."

His hand came out to tug her to him, settling her on his lap. She was surrounded by him, his arms encircling her waist, the warmth of his chest touching her skin. "Did you do as I asked?"

"What did you ask?" She had to put her arms around his neck for balance.

Wolf's hand was on her knee. "I gave you some specific grooming instructions."

Oh, god. She shivered. He was talking about her pussy. She'd thought about him the whole time she'd been in the shower. She hadn't been able to think about anything else. She'd carefully shaved her mound, pulling the lips of her pussy apart and gingerly running the razor over her flesh. Every stroke of the razor had sensitized her skin. "Yes, Sir."

"Let me feel. Spread your legs."

She swallowed, hesitating. "But there are people here."

The Dawson twins were close, Kitten at their side. And Ian and Charlotte Taggart were cuddled together, not far away. She could see the big, sarcastic dude whispering to his wife.

Wolf's voice came out in a hard grind. "I don't care. And neither will they. Now spread your legs and let me feel your pussy or use your safe word."

It didn't exactly seem fair, but she'd known it would be this way going in. She could choose to obey or this particular portion of her evening would be over. And she wasn't sure she wanted it to be over.

Shelley took a deep breath. She was either in and willing to explore or she should walk away. She'd been so passive when it came to Bryce because she hadn't been willing to fight. She wanted to be done with waiting for something to happen to her. Wolf was giving her a choice. This wasn't some passive activity. She had to make the decision.

She spread her knees. She looked around, trying to see if anyone was watching.

"Stop it," Wolf said, his hands tightening. "You're not to worry about them. You're going to focus on me. Now, I gave you instructions, and I intend to find out if you followed them or if you're going to get another spanking."

She wouldn't mind the spanking, but in this case, she'd been a good girl. And despite the fact that it had made her uncomfortable, she'd only put on the clothes Wolf had given her. And he hadn't given her a pair of underwear.

He kept one arm wrapped around her waist, and the other found her knee. He forced her to open further. She could feel the cool air on her flesh. A thrill went through her. She'd never done anything like this, but she'd dreamed of it. In her darker fantasies, she'd been placed on display and touched and admired. Bryce had told her she was a freak when she'd mentioned her desires to him.

But she didn't want to think about Bryce. She wanted to think about Wolf's hand on her thigh.

"Tell me something, sweetheart." Wolf's voice was thick and dark, his lips tickling her ear. "Are you thinking about what happened on the train now?"

So this was Wolf's version of therapy. She had to admit, she preferred Wolf's hands on her to sitting in Leo's office.

Pure Bliss
Nights in Bliss, Colorado Book 6
By Lexi Blake writing as Sophie Oak

Re-released in a second edition with new content.

Bliss, Colorado, gave Hope McLean a second chance at life, but she's hiding a dark secret.

Raised as brothers, James Glen and Noah Bennett always dreamed of finding a woman to share their lives on the Circle G Ranch. James would run the ranch, while Noah served the town of Bliss as the resident vet. But when a woman came between the brothers, Noah fled for New York City and James was left to struggle for the ranch's survival alone.

Now that Noah has returned, he will do anything to repay his debt to James. When he sees Hope, he knows she is the woman they both have been waiting for. But just as their love begins to bloom, a nightmare from Hope's past returns to claim her.

To save Hope, and themselves, they will have to reclaim the brotherhood that was shattered and fight for their future

The Governor Trilogy
by Lesli Richardson (also known as Tymber Dalton)

Governor – Book 1
Lieutenant – Book 2
Chief – Book 3
Now available on all major e-book retailers, and in print.

He kneels for only one man…
She never comes in second…
Behind every good man is a real bastard…

Governor (Governor Trilogy - Book 1) by Lesli Richardson

I kneel for only one man—Carter Wilson, my best friend, chief of staff, and bastard extraordinaire.

It's a price I willingly pay to be owned by *Her*.

His wife.

Who is also, as of when we were sworn in this morning, my lieutenant governor.

I am Owen Taylor, governor of the great state of Florida.

* * * *

Lieutenant (Governor Trilogy - Book 2) by Lesli Richardson

I never come in second—that's just how my daddy raised me.

Except now, I find myself willingly choosing exactly that—being second. Publicly, I might seem to serve at the governor's pleasure, but that's nothing close to the truth.

He serves *me* at *mine*. Especially the pleasure part.

We both serve my husband, Carter. Or, as Owen dubbed him long ago, the bastard extraordinaire.

I never knew what I was really getting into when I met Owen and Carter. Maybe it's better I didn't. Maybe I would've run away if I had.

Boy, how I love him. *Both* of them. Somehow, they make being second okay. And in eight years?

It'll be *my* turn.

I am Susannah Evans, lieutenant governor of the great state of Florida.

* * * *

Chief (Governor Trilogy – Book 3) by Lesli Richardson

Behind every good man is a good woman. That's what they say.

They're wrong. Even my wife would agree.

The truth is, behind every good man is a real bastard—that would be *me*.

I knew from the day I met Owen that the only way I'd ever get him was to make sure I took whatever it was he loved and wanted most and hold it so close to me that he couldn't help but come with it.

He did.

And now…now there are people who want to tear the three of us apart.

I'll die before I let that happen.

I am Carter Wilson, chief of staff to the governor of the great state of Florida.

And, according to him and my wife, a bastard extraordinaire.

* * * *

Excerpt (NSFW) from *Governor* (Governor Trilogy – Book 1) by Lesli Richardson:

Now

It's hard not to shiver when the AC kicks on as I kneel, naked, on the floor of my new office, the carpet doing little to cushion my knees. My hands remain clasped behind my head, back straight, elbows out.

This is how he's trained me, and what he expects of me.

My knees are spread as wide as I can manage and still keep my heels tucked under my ass.

He circles me, inspecting me as he smiles and tugs on his shirt cuffs, adjusting the lay of the cufflinks. I know he wants to strip off that suit he's wearing and fuck me right here, spread over my new desk, but he's holding himself back.

Waiting.

I keep my gaze fixed straight ahead, even though my hard cock has a will of its own and is probably dribbling a puddle all over the towel Carter thought to put down before ordering me to kneel.

He might be a bastard extraordinaire, but he's also very practical.

He looks pleased with himself, and he has every right to be. He's the only man I kneel for and he damn well knows it.

It's a price I willingly pay to be owned by *Her*.

His wife.

Who is also, as of when we were sworn in at one o'clock this very afternoon, my lieutenant governor for the great state of Florida.

* * * *

Carter Wilson, bastard extraordinaire, is eight years older than me, a decorated Army veteran, my best friend, college roommate, one of my two closest confidants, my chief of staff…

286

And he's the Master and husband of Susannah Evans.

Susa owns me—mind, heart, soul, and body—and has ever since I first met her in college.

Since she owns me, that means I belong to Carter by default. It was the deal I willingly accepted all those years ago.

Susa grew up the daughter of a lawyer, a progressive Republican who pretty much ran the state GOP for decades. Still does, unofficially now. Benchley Evans was a county administrator, then a county commissioner, followed by four terms as a state rep, and two more as a state senator. The only reason he didn't run for the big G or a national office was a massive heart attack that made his wife put her foot down and demand he choose his family over party and politics for once in his damn life.

He also hailed from a family that first made their fortune in citrus and cattle. As freezes and canker and greening took down the citrus industry, and the exploding housing market chipped away at cattle lands, he'd already moved on to land development, jumping in early when acreage was still cheap.

That meant he could easily afford to send his only daughter to any college she chose, for any degree she wanted.

It was my luck—good or bad, you decide—that we ended up in Tampa together, selecting majors and minors that would help us with law degrees.

But she's also smarter than me in many ways. Far more ruthless politically. That's why, when Carter decided we could change our home state in good ways, Susa insisted it should be me who ran for governor on a third-party ticket.

This time.

After eight years—if I win reelection, that is—she'll be perfectly positioned for her own gubernatorial bid.

I'll do my best to get her elected. Once I'm out of office, I'll return to the private sector while still championing a few key causes that are near and dear to my heart.

But what I'll be looking forward to most by then is time out of the public eye.

For at least the next four years, my official residence is the Florida Governor's Mansion in Tallahassee. I can't simply choose to *not* live there, because it'd be a logistics nightmare for my security detail, as well as an unnecessary expense for taxpayers.

Considering two of the key planks in the platform we ran on were better budgeting and smarter spending, I can't do something that would so blatantly fly in the face of those ideals.

I especially can't cite wanting to be with Susa and Carter whenever I choose as the reason.

I still own my house just outside Tampa, next door to Carter and Susa's house and sharing the same backyard fence. But for the most part, I won't be staying there during my term. Besides, there's already a calendar full of official state functions, and many of them will be held at the mansion that is now my home.

My only consolation is that Carter, as my chief of staff, is expected to either be with me or be on call for me twenty-four/seven. No one will suspect anything untoward if he's spotted coming and going at odd hours. Susa's presence, both as Carter's wife and my lieutenant governor, will not raise many eyebrows, unless she regularly shows up at the mansion at an unusually late hour without Carter or staff of her own. One of the trade-offs we'd already talked about and figured into our plans was that by embarking on this path we'd lose privacy.

Carter is more than ready and willing to give me what I need and crave when Susannah is unable to. He's also ready and willing to be a warm body in my bed so I won't feel so alone every night.

Because before the whirlwind that was my campaign to become governor, the three of us shared a bed nearly every night.

* * * *

Where I'm kneeling about three feet from the far end of my desk, I can't be seen when Carter answers the knock on my office door after unlocking it and cracking it open to see who it is. He moves aside just enough to allow someone else to step in, and my breath catches, my pulse races.

Her.

"I only have a few minutes," Susa says in her usual clipped, all-business tone.

Carter closes and locks the door behind her and, moving faster than it seems possible for a human to manage, grabs a handful of hair, tipping her head back.

"*What* was that, *pet?*" he softly growls.

She's never allowed to use that tone on Carter and she damn well knows it.

Her entire posture and voice change, needy and soft, even as my own body responds to Carter's tone. "I only have a few minutes, Sir."

I struggle not to smile, not to laugh. With today's craziness, she likely forgot herself.

I only wish I could be there later tonight to watch when Carter reminds her who she belongs to.

He marches her around behind my desk and I allow my gaze to follow them. He bends her forward over the desk, making her put her hands flat on it, and hikes up her skirt. Since she's also wearing three-inch heels, it means her gorgeous ass sticks out nicely.

"Who said you could wear panties today, pet?" I hear the fabric rip and a quiet *meep* from her.

"Sorry, Sir. I thought—"

"You thought *wrong.*"

Another violation.

She's going to have fun sitting tomorrow.

She's lucky we already did a sound check one evening last week, before I took office, and we discovered Carter can't spank us in here if someone's in the outer office.

Like Julia, my administrative assistant.

Who, right now, is sitting out there at her desk, along with a trooper from my security detail.

Holding out the offending material, Carter walks over to me with a playful smile on his face. "Do you believe this shit? Looks like a certain pet has forgotten her place."

"I see that, Sir."

He turns from me, stuffing her ruined panties into his left front slacks pocket. I have a feeling they'll probably end up in my mouth later.

Not the first time he's gagged me with her panties.

Not saying I mind it, either.

"Loyalty."

I immediately relax into the position, knees still wide, but my back now rounded, my left hand on my thigh, my right flat on the floor, my gaze focused down.

It's a Carter thing.

It works—that's all that matters. Countless times he's put me into this position during the day behind a locked office door, but with my clothes on. Especially if it's been a rough day and I need a quick reset.

I can think about *Him*, about what we have together.

It's not a one-way street. Carter is loyal to us, always putting us first no matter what. That might sound odd to someone who doesn't know the three of us. There's a lot of bullshit out there about what people "should" or "shouldn't" do.

Carter sets his own path, trims his sails, and we follow.

Loyalty.

When I first idly floated what at the time I thought was a ridiculous proposition—running for governor—it was Carter, and then Susannah, who had my back and were my most vocal and vicious supporters.

Loyalty.

She is my queen, my heart and soul, my sun and my moon, all rolled into one. My muse, my reason for living. I would kill or die for her if it came down to it. I would—and have—embarrassed the hell out of myself just to make her smile.

Loyalty.

All of these things I think of as I slow my breathing and my back muscles loosen, enjoying a break from the more formal *Primed* position.

Primed is always performed naked. Frequently for long stretches of time. The bastard extraordinaire takes great pride in sometimes torturing me while in that position, expecting me to maintain it.

Or expecting me to fail to maintain it, which brings punishment.

Win-win.

But that's life with Carter.

I didn't say I didn't enjoy it.

* * * *

In *Loyalty*, I can hear what's going on but, because of where I'm kneeling and with my head bowed, I can't see.

But I can imagine, based on the sounds.

Her low, pained grunts as she struggles to stay quiet probably means he's pinching or maybe even biting the insides of her thighs.

Which are now, most likely, covered with her own juices.

She enjoys life with Carter, too. We wouldn't be here if we didn't. While this is not a place I ever envisioned myself being, now that I'm here I cannot imagine being anywhere else.

I don't even mean this office.

I mean with these two people, and especially with Carter.

Carter at his best is a loving, kind, gentle, compassionate, funny, brilliant, gorgeous, sexy man.

Since I consider myself straight, those last two are pretty damn fine compliments.

Carter at his worst is evil, sadistic, mean, brilliant, gorgeous, and…

Yeah, sexy.

It pains me to admit that.

No, I'm usually *literally* in pain when I admit it.

Not that he would consider any of those descriptors an insult.

And, again, not that I'm complaining, because I'm not. I wouldn't be here if I didn't want to be.

I know I don't have to speak up and remind him of the time. It might not seem like he's watching the clock, but I'm sure he's calculating exactly how much he can cram into what little time the three of us have alone together right now.

Maybe perhaps *literally* cram.

That doesn't even bother me anymore.

After a few minutes of him torturing her, he speaks.

"Boy."

I'm on deck. I smoothly rise to my feet even as they sting, full of pins and needles and protesting they still need a moment to recover.

Carter smiles at me and my cock twitches. "Come here."

His fist is buried in her hair, her cheek is pressed against the desk, and her skirt is now rucked up around her waist. She's gorgeous and mussed, her blue eyes wild with that special kind of energy Carter has a particular way of building in both of us.

That *please fuck me* look.

Our times together have been few and far between lately, first with our grueling campaign schedule, and now with taking office. We went from sleeping together every night to sometimes barely seeing each other for days at a time.

That, above all, has been the most difficult part of all of this, losing that privacy, that time together. Not even sexy time. I mean being able to close our eyes, take a deep breath, and relax with our heads in Carter's lap.

We've all had adjustments to make. Susa and I trust Carter to take care of us, though.

Like right now.

I'm sure whatever Carter has in mind will carry us through until the next rare time the three of us can be alone together.

Because it will have to.

* * * *

Author Lesli Richardson, who is better-known by her more prolific wild-child Tymber Dalton pen name, lives in the Tampa Bay region of Florida with her husband (aka "The World's Best Husband™") and too many pets. She writes a wide variety of heat levels and genres, from mainstream sci-fi all the way to scorching ménage.

The two-time EPIC award winner and part-time Viking shield-maiden in training loves to shoot skeet and play D&D with her friends. She's also the bestselling author of over one hundred and fifty books and counting, including *The Reluctant Dom, The Great Turning, Cross Country Chaos*, the Bleacke Shifters series, The Great Turning series, the Suncoast Society series, the Love Slave for Two series, the Triple Trouble series, the Coffeeshop Coven series, the Good Will Ghost Hunting series, the Drunk Monkeys series, and many others.

She lives in her own little world, but it's okay—they all know her there.

She loves to hear from readers! Please feel free to drop by her website and sign up for her newsletter to keep abreast of the latest news, snarkage, and releases.

* * * *

Website: http://www.tymberdalton.com

About Lexi Blake

Lexi Blake is the author of contemporary and urban fantasy romance. She started publishing in 2011 and has gone on to sell over two million copies of her books. Her books have appeared twenty-six times on the *USA Today*, *New York Times*, and *Wall Street Journal* bestseller lists. She lives in North Texas with her husband, kids, and two rescue dogs.

Connect with Lexi online:

Facebook: Lexi Blake
Twitter: authorlexiblake
Website: www.LexiBlake.net

www.ingramcontent.com/pod-product-compliance
Lightning Source LLC
Chambersburg PA
CBHW032126040825
30617CB00014B/42